BLADE and BONE

Also by Jon Sprunk

Blood and Iron
Storm and Steel

Shadow's Son
Shadow's Lure
Shadow's Master

JON SPRUNK

BLADE and BONE

THE BOOK OF THE BLACK EARTH
—— PART THREE ——

an imprint of Prometheus Books
Amherst, NY

Published 2018 by Pyr®, an imprint of Prometheus Books

Cover illustration © Jason Chan
Cover design by Liz Mills
Cover design © Prometheus Books
Map by Rhys Davies

Inquiries should be addressed to
Pyr
59 John Glenn Drive
Amherst, New York 14228
VOICE: 716–691–0133
FAX: 716–691–0137
WWW.PYRSF.COM

22 21 20 19 18   5 4 3 2 1

Library of Congress Cataloging-in-Publication Data

Names: Sprunk, Jon, 1970- author.
Title: Blade and bone / by Jon Sprunk.
Description: Amherst, NY : Pyr, 2018. | Series: The book of the black earth ; part 3
Identifiers: LCCN 2017014365 (print) | LCCN 2017014523 (ebook) |
     ISBN 9781633882706 (ebook) | ISBN 9781633882690 (paperback)
Subjects: LCSH: Fantasy fiction. | Epic fiction. | BISAC: FICTION / Fantasy / Epic.
Classification: LCC PS3619.P78 (ebook) | LCC PS3619.P78 B54 2018 (print) |
     DDC 813/.6—dc23
LC record available at https://lccn.loc.gov/2017014365

Printed in the United States of America

This book is dedicated to Jenny, Elizabeth, Nick, Matt, and Chaudry.
For all the adventures we've shared together.
Also to my son, Logan.
May your life be filled with such love and friendship as I have known.

He who seeks knowledge in the darkness finds only himself.

—Akeshian proverb

AUTHOR'S NOTE

I've included a brief glossary at the back of the book. Thank you for reading—I hope you enjoy book three of the series!

CHAPTER ONE

Lhotar et'Murannor, the youngest son of Moloch, forty-ninth king of Nisus, strained one final time at the chains binding him between the stone pillars, and then he hung listless. Flies crawled in the gruesome wounds covering his body, as the blood pooled on the dusty tiles beneath his royal feet.

The king is dead. Long live the king.

"I accept your surrender, Prince Lhotar."

The voice echoed from the darkened archway leading into the royal palace. Lord Pumash squinted against the harsh light of the afternoon to see the face of the tall man standing there, their new liege. His eyes shone in the shadows like pieces of amber plucked from a fire. *Like the fires that are still devouring our city.*

The nobles of Nisus gathered at the foot of the portico. They had been collected by gray-faced servants and brought here for this demonstration. By the tears and bitter curses of those around him, Pumash could see it had worked. They were cowed. And how could they not be? Glancing back over his shoulder at the smoking city behind him, Pumash still could not fathom the ease with which this great city had fallen, laid low in a single night. A night of terrors, many of which had continued into the daylight, making it all the more surreal. He hadn't been able to sleep all night as he watched the reflections of flames dance in the windows of his manor home. Through the barred glass he had seen the inhuman invaders roaming the streets like packs of wild dogs, killing indiscriminately and—though it could barely be believed—devouring their kills.

Murmurs filtered through the crowd of aristocrats. Pumash tried again to look at the new king, but there was something terrible within that gaze. He called himself the *Manalish*, although Pumash had no idea what the title meant. Some in the crowd whispered another name—the Dark King, who had so recently taken control of Erugash and Chiresh. A great achievement by any measure, but how long would it last? The other kings were no doubt mobilizing to quash this growing threat on their western border. It was only a matter of time.

Sepulchral tones called down from the doorway. "Lord Pumash of House Luradessus, come forward."

Pumash jerked upright. With a quick glance at Lhotar's body, he stepped forward and made a low bow. "I am Pumash, my l—" He caught himself. "Great *Manalish*. How may I serve?"

He put every ounce of his charm into the question, knowing these might be the last words he ever spoke. It was not unheard of for new monarchs to eliminate the entire noble caste, to remove potential rivals and replace them with their own retainers. But who would this new ruler put in the nobility's place? All his soldiers were . . . dead.

The *Manalish* stepped forth from the palace entrance, and yet his visage remained in shadow. *As if the sunlight refuses to touch him.*

"Come," he said without inflection as he strode back inside the palace.

The assembled nobles whispered among themselves, clearly agitated. *No, they are terrified. And for good reason. By tomorrow we could all be food for this man's inhuman legions.*

Moving quickly without wanting to appear he was hurrying, Pumash followed in the new ruler's wake. The first thing that occurred to him as he trailed across the blood-smeared tiles was the lack of soldiers. He had been hosted by several monarchs in his lifetime, and all of them surrounded themselves with bodyguards. This one, however, walked alone. Was it hubris? Or a subtler form of intimidation?

Instead of going to the royal audience hall, the *Manalish* led him to the grand staircase. As they climbed, Pumash mentally composed a list of replies to questions he might be asked. Men of power wanted quick answers delivered with a combination of deference and confidence. It was a technique he had perfected during his career as a dealer in exotic slaves. Once he knew what this new king wanted, he would be able to maneuver himself into an advantageous position. Yes, he would survive this disaster, and he might even prosper. After all, there was opportunity to be found in such turbulent times.

They emerged onto the palace roof. A group of men in gray shrouds were assembling something made from silver-metal girders at the center. Pumash had no idea what it was supposed to be. Some kind of sculpture, perhaps. A monument to the new regime?

The *Manalish* went to the western edge of the roof. Pumash followed, and together they looked down at the city below. The destruction was worse than he had feared. A pall of smoke hung above several neighborhoods, cloaking dozens of fires. Entire buildings had been reduced to rubble. He tried to estimate how much of the population might have been killed, but the number eluded him.

The new king's voice intruded on his thoughts. "What do you see?"

Pumash cleared his throat. "A city at.your feet, Great Lord. A people eager to follow your law."

The *Manalish* waved as if swatting a midge. The backs of his hands were cracked and pitted like the bark of an old tree. "My new order has no need for laws or service. Seizing Nisus was necessary because Merthul occupies the Seventh Celestial House this cycle. As the ancients knew, possession of the heart cannot be accomplished without first securing the body."

Pumash's lips froze, the words he had intended to speak clinging to his tongue. What was all this nonsense? Astrology and old proverbs? "Sire, I don't—"

A loud sizzle made Pumash jump. It had come from the metallic sculpture. The construction was finished. The gray-cloaked henchmen stood back as arcs of green energy crackled and snapped inside the lattice of silver girders. A ball of purple smoke grew at its heart. It looked like a miniature storm cloud. Suddenly, Pumash felt very exposed.

He jumped a second time as thunder crashed directly above the palace. A blanket of steely black clouds had appeared over the city in what had been a blue sky only moments before. Dread knotted his insides as lightning etched the clouds above, in the same lurid hue as the electricity running through the sculpture. A barrage of destruction rained down, striking different spots around Nisus. From this vantage, three short steps behind his new liege, Pumash saw it all, and wished he couldn't. But neither could he close his eyes. For an instant he had an idea of pushing this usurper off the roof, but it skittered away almost as swiftly as it formed. Now he understood. The new king needed no guards. He was a force of the natural world.

Pumash exiled such thoughts from his mind as he watched the mayhem below. Everywhere the green lightning struck, a dark miasma rose from the ground. People poured out of their homes. Echoes of their screams merged into a vast, guttural growl, like the warning of a predator just before it pounces for the kill. His horror grew as the nobles below collapsed in the street, clawing at their faces and chests. Then, even more horrifying, they got back up. Something was wrong with their eyes, and their mouths masticated as if they were suddenly ravenous.

Pumash swallowed as he watched the transformation. Suddenly he had a vision. These undead soldiers would spread across the land, perhaps even the entire world. Nothing could stand before this dark onslaught.

The *Manalish* turned to him. "You see the future, Pumash."

"The *zoanii* will oppose you."

"Yes, they will. And they will die. I bring a message to the world. You have glimpsed it already. So what role would you play in my new empire?"

There was no decision to make.

Pumash fell to his knees with his head bowed. "I pledge to serve you, Great One, from this day forward. I am your faithful . . ." He almost said *servant*, but he knew this one would demand more. "I am your faithful slave."

A hand rested upon his scalp. "I accept your surrender."

Pumash's relief fled as something took hold of him. Not from the outside but from within. A seizure locked all of his joints in place. He thrashed, or tried to, as the terrible feeling rumbled inside him.

"It comforts me that you came willingly into my service," the *Manalish* said, still gripping his head. "It will make this process a little less painful."

Pumash's eyelids fluttered as the power exploded inside him, spreading through his veins like rivers of black fire. Green lightning filled his vision, and then there was only darkness.

Dust devils spun across the desert floor, riding over the sand dunes. The sky over the northern reaches of the Iron Desert was marred by scudding clouds, tinged with gray and black.

Lying prone on the flat top of a boulder, Three Moons took another swig from his canteen and grimaced as the warm water trickled down his throat. *I don't see the appeal in being sober. Especially at a time like this.*

The town of Omikur loomed like an eyesore against the barren sky, less than a league from their position. Its walls, pitted and charred, showed signs of a magical battle that dwarfed anything he had ever seen. And he'd seen a lot in his eighty-odd years in this world. From what Jirom had told them, a full legion of Akeshian elite with *zoanii* support had besieged this town for weeks. He could well believe it. He had been on the receiving end of Akeshian wizardry before. What he found difficult to understand was how this town had survived.

But the siege was long over now. The grounds outside the walls were vacant except for remnants of the battle—jutting spars of wood, earth embankments, and mounded mass graves.

Three Moons rolled over onto his side. "Tell me again why we're out here."

Paranas, the captain of the Bronze Blades, was sprawled beside him, holding a spyglass to his eye. "We're following orders."

Three Moons called to the spirits of the air to bless him with a cool breeze, but they were keeping their distance. They wanted nothing to do with this place. *Can't say that I blame them.*

"I know. But we haven't been paid since we left Erugash. Hasn't our contract run out yet?"

The captain squinted at him. "You bucking for some extra duties, warlock?" He went back to his study of the town. "Besides, it's your old friend who sent us out here to see if any of the western crusaders survived. If you had reservations, you should've taken them up with him."

"Jirom don't listen like he used to," Three Moons muttered. "He's too wrapped up in the cause."

Everything had changed at Erugash. Jirom had changed. Close brushes with mortality could do that to a man, but Three Moons sensed it was something different with his old friend. Jirom had taken the rebellion and made it personal, as close to his heart as his lover-lieutenant. They had escaped Erugash as it burned, an unwashed army of slaves and hired soldiers, and clawed their way through the desert to find solace. And no sooner had they found a spot to set down roots than Jirom sent the Blades on this fool mission. Finding allies in a dead city? Madness.

"Well, you had your chance," Paranas said. "The patrol's back."

With only a slight exaggeration of huffing and sighing, Three Moons dragged himself back down the rear slope of the boulder, keeping a low profile against the weathered stone. The mercenaries had made their camp on the leeward side, hidden from the city ramparts. There were only twenty-one of them left. *You can't even call us a company anymore. Just a band of misguided fools, too old and stupid to find another line of work.*

Three Moons snorted at the idea. *What else are we fit to do?*

The recon team slipped into camp.

"We did the whole circuit, Captain," Sergeant Niko reported as he shook the sand from his cloak. "The gates are all blocked with debris. We could try to excavate, but it would be slow work. Noisy, too. There are a couple of breaches in the curtain wall that might work."

Captain Paranas handed him a waterskin. "Any sign of inhabitants?"

"Not a soul. No movement on the walls. Not even birds. If there's anyone inside, they're keeping out of sight."

Three Moons couldn't shake the dread that had latched onto him ever since they arrived here. It sang on the wind and nestled in the ground beneath him. The spirits were uneasy.

Harunda spat in the sand. "It's fucking eerie, is what it is. Those runaway slaves sent us out here chasing ghosts."

Three Moons caught Paranas's gaze, but the captain shook his head. This was probably a busted mission, and nerves were worn raw. Their little band was degenerating into a collection of bad attitudes. *Who can blame us? After all the bad luck we've seen, all the brothers and sisters killed, we're broken.*

Niko looked up at the sky. "Would be nice if it rained. Even just a little."

Three Moons asked, "What do we do now? Hang out and watch the place fall to pieces?"

The captain picked up his pack and slung it over his shoulder. "We're going in. We've got a mission to do, and daylight is fading." He raised his voice. "Everyone, grab your gear. There's no telling how long before we get back."

The rest of the band emerged from the shade around the boulder's base. They wore minimal armor, but every soldier carried a crossbow in addition to a blade or axe.

Niko's scouts took the point, leading them across the wasted plain. They reached the town's outer wall without incident to a small breach in the southwest quadrant. Even though all of the town's gates appeared to be unguarded, Three Moons was glad they would make a covert entry anyway. No matter how calm things looked, they were out here all alone.

As always on these sorts of delicate missions, Three Moons felt even more like a misfit. He had never been much of a fighter, even in his youth, but here he was, surrounded by tough, capable men and women. In the past, he would have nipped into his private stock of liquor or narcotics to ease his anxiety, but he had given them up months ago. Right after the Erugash affair, to be exact. Something in the back of his mind had told him he would need every wit for the coming storm. And when the spirits whispered to him, he tended to heed their advice.

Niko and a wiry lady scout named Jauna crawled into the breach first. Sweat oozed from Three Moons's scalp and rolled in large drops down his face as he waited. A couple of minutes later, Jauna reappeared to give the all-clear signal. One by one, the mercs entered. •

They emerged inside the town through a cellar window under a demolished pottery shop. The street was empty except for pieces of rubble and the desiccated carcass of a dead ox. Signs of destruction were everywhere. Windows shattered, rooftops torn from buildings, walls pocked and seared, cracked pavement. The hairs on the back of Three Moons's neck started to rise. *Not one damned sign of life. Jirom, why in the twelve eyes of Nabu did you send us here?*

Following the scouts, they moved west to the next intersection where

BLADE AND BONE

a partially collapsed building had spilled into the street. Their first objective had been to enter the town without being seen. The second—the real mission—was to make contact with the foreign crusaders and deliver the rebellion's message. *Maybe they're all holed up in the governor's citadel.*

Niko glanced around the next corner and signaled back. The Blades set out, moving deeper into the town.

Like most Akeshian cities, Omikur clustered around a central hub of civic buildings. This was also where the upper castes lived, close to the seat of power. As such, Three Moons expected to encounter resistance sooner or later. The silence gathered around them like a stifling blanket as they moved from street to street. His nerves vibrated like a stretched cord every time a stone or piece of debris clattered underfoot, and one thought echoed in his head. *This is a trap. This is a trap. This is a—*

Niko stopped at the crossing and held up a closed fist. The mercs pressed against the buildings on either side of the street, weapons ready. Three Moons strained his senses, but everything was quiet. The spirits were silent, too. That made him even more nervous.

Standing next to the captain, he whispered, "Looks like no one's home."

Instead of commenting, Captain Paranas eased his way forward to join the scouts. Three Moons stuck with him. Thirty paces ahead, the street ended in a broad chasm cutting through the town. Shards of broken tiles crunched underfoot as the Blades approached, stopping at the edge of the impediment. The trench was at least fifteen feet across at its narrowest point and extended through the buildings on either side of the street. Strata of mud pavement and earth descended far down into the crevice before it was lost in darkness. A sickening odor rose from the trench, making his stomach curdle. Something lurked in those depths. He could feel it. Something that did not belong to the natural world.

Three Moons muttered, "Coming here was a mistake. We should leave."

Captain Paranas was studying their surroundings. "Not until we do what we came for."

All was quiet, but an atmosphere of malice radiated from the empty windows and stained walls around them. Even from the flat, gray sky above.

Three Moons didn't know how he'd missed it before. "You don't understand. I don't think there's anyone left alive here."

Captain Paranas grunted. "What? In the entire town? That's ridiculous. You're supposed to be our ace in the hole. So try to shine some positive light on the situation, eh?"

"Sorry, Cap. But there's some bad mojo here."

"Get hold of yourself, Moons. Where's Niko? Niko!"

Three Moons winced as the captain's words echoed down the street. Maybe he was overreacting.

Niko appeared beside them. Dust caked his face. "Here, Captain. I think I found a route around the divide."

"Good. Your people take point. Everyone else, form up on their asses."

The mercs said nothing as they filed past. Three Moons took his customary spot in the center of the formation, heading north along the edge of the trench and into a dark alley. Three Moons squinted at the thin slice of sky overhead. The sunlight was fading fast, and he didn't want to be inside these walls when night fell. Then he heard a sound, like a stone dropping on hard pavement and skittering away. He spun around, one hand dropping to the fetish bag tied to his belt. There was nothing behind them but buildings and broken street.

"What?" Pie-Eye asked, looking back too.

Three Moons shook his head. "Nothing. Just hearing things."

They had hardly gone another dozen yards before Three Moons stopped again. This time he was positive he had heard something. A different noise this time, almost like dry leather being dragged over stone. "What was that?"

Captain Paranas whistled, and the entire band came to a halt. Three Moons strained to listen. There it was again. Coming from one of the nearby buildings, though he couldn't say which one for sure.

The captain pointed at the nearest doors on either side of the alley. The Blades formed up without a word. While Niko and Jauna watched from the ends of the street, the rest of the band assaulted the entrances. Three Moons held back a moment as they rushed inside. Fear emanated from the doorways, so thick he could taste it. Still, he followed his brothers into the left-hand entry.

They charged into a long washroom dominated by two large copper tubs. Smashed potsherds were scattered about. Dharpa and Finum stood in the doorway at the far end. Three Moons and the captain joined them at the threshold of a larger room that occupied most of the building's lower level. It looked to be some sort of woodworking factory, with long tables cluttered with metal tools and raw timber. Two closed doors faced them from the opposite wall. Just as they started to enter, a crash sounded from back in the alley.

Captain Paranas ordered them to stay put as he ran back outside. Three Moons hesitated. There was something wrong in this building that tickled his otherworldly senses. But he followed the captain out anyway.

Outside, the alley was empty except for the scouts. Niko gave him a hard look, as if asking what was going on. Three Moons held up his hands in ignorance as he entered the door on the other side, into a dyer's shop. Wooden tubs and drying racks lined the walls. Ino's squad stood in the middle of the room, all of them staring at the deep shadows shrouding the far end of the chamber. Low sounds issued from the gloom, and it took Three Moons a moment to realize they were the sounds of a fight.

"What are you standing around for?" he shouted as he pushed past them.

As his eyes adjusted, Three Moons saw Harunda and the captain grappling with someone. It wasn't until he moved closer that he noticed it was a civilian. Short and thin and mostly bald with stringy gray hair hanging down to his collar. He had gaunt features as if he hadn't eaten in days, and his hands were black with filth. Harunda was holding the man around the waist while Captain Paranas slammed him repeatedly in the face with the pommel of his sword. Three Moons was about to demand they stop their attack on an unarmed civilian when the stench hit him. A sickening odor like maggot-filled meat that had been left out in the sun for days clogged his throat. He gagged and coughed at the same time.

The civilian grabbed Harunda by the arm and tried to bite him. Captain Paranas gave up trying to subdue the man and stabbed him through the stomach instead. The blood froze in Three Moons's veins as the civilian ignored the blade piercing his guts. The man's gaping jaws reached toward Harunda's exposed forearm. His teeth were stained brown, his tongue bright red. His eyes were black and empty.

Struggling against his revulsion, Three Moons wracked his brain for things to use against the possessed. Silver and fire topped the list. As he reached into his bag to find some silver coins, he heard a meaty thud. Captain Paranas had brought down his sword with both hands. The blade plunged into the side of the civilian's skull. The bone crumbled inward through the ruined flesh. Thick, black blood oozed from the wound, spilling a dark river down the civilian's shoulder. Finally, he fell to the floor.

Harunda slumped against the edge of a dyeing tub, with a hand pressed against his neck. "Fuck, Captain! What kind of shit show have we stumbled into here? That guy . . ."

"What happened?" Three Moons asked.

"He came out of nowhere," Pie-Eye answered. "He didn't say nothing. Just charged us with his bare hands. Before I knew it, he was all over me, scratching and biting."

Harunda pulled away his hand to reveal gouge marks on his neck, trickling blood.

"Get that cleaned out," Captain Paranas ordered. "Everyone, back outside."

The sound of creaking wood made Three Moons look over as three people—a man, a woman, and a teenaged boy with a disheveled ponytail—staggered out of a hallway at the back of the room. Their black eyes stared out from the gloom.

Captain Paranas backed away with his sword held before him. "Everyone, out! Now!"

"Captain!" a brother yelled from outside.

Spitting curses, Three Moons shoved Harunda out the door and into the alley ahead of him. They waited until the captain and the rest of their brothers were out, and then slammed the door shut behind them.

Dharpa and Finum were in the alley. Three Moons didn't have to ask why as they held their shoulders to the door across the way. Heavy blows pounded from the other side.

"We were attacked by crazy women!" Finum said.

"A whole mess of them," Dharpa added. "They came out of nowhere and swarmed us. We barely got out."

BLADE AND BONE

Three Moons looked down the alley in both directions. Citizens attacking armed soldiers? What was going on? Had everyone in this town gone insane? It was more than that. He couldn't get those black eyes out of his mind. He whispered to the spirits, but there was still no answer.

Captain Paranas spared no time. "You did the right thing. Secure those doors. Niko! Find us a way—"

A loud thud echoed from the door behind him as one of the wooden panels snapped outward. A grubby arm reached through the gap. While Dharpa and Finum leaned on the door, Ino chopped at the thrashing arm with his falchion. It took three cuts before the arm came off. Only a few spurts of black blood spilled from the severed stump, but a repulsive stench billowed forth. Choking against the foul odor, Three Moons turned away.

"We need to get out of here, Cap," he said. "Now."

"I'm starting to see it that way, too. We'll regroup outside town and rethink this whole situation. Niko?"

Dharpa and Finum wedged the factory doorway shut with loose pieces of wood. Ino and Mesane did the same for the door to the dyer's shop. The pounding continued from inside, but it looked as if the doors would hold for a while. Three Moons glanced at all the windows facing the alley and wondered how many more crazy people were hiding inside.

Niko jogged down the alley. "We can get back, but I suggest we hurry. There's movement all around us. I don't think we want to stick around to find out if they're friendly."

Captain Paranas nodded. "Lead the way. The rest of you, fall in and stay tight."

Niko started back toward the trench at a quick hustle. The Blades moved with purpose, crossbows out. Three Moons stayed by the captain. He was relieved their commander had seen the wisdom of a tactical retreat, but what they had witnessed disturbed him. What could have changed these people? A plague? Some infection that decimated the town and left only these horrific wretches? No, he sensed it was worse than that. The dearth of spirits nagged at him. *I fucking hate running. Let me die standing still. Preferably in the shade with a cool drink in my hand.*

The scouts abruptly changed direction, turning down a side alley between a pair of houses. After a few zigzags, they came to a broad street. The backs of tall buildings faced them on either side. Three Moons recognized them as temples by their stylized construction. Some were merely shrines with a stone pagoda and a couple of statues, but others were as big as palaces, decked out with gilt and glitter.

The mercenaries hurried down the street. Three Moons heard sounds in the distance but couldn't pinpoint them. The echoes were all wrong. A groan sounded behind him. He glanced back, but nothing was there.

A shout made him spin back around. For a second it looked as if a mound of garbage was attacking Finum. Then he saw the long, spindly arms reaching from the refuse, its fingers crooked into gnarled claws. It was a woman with dirt-streaked hair and the broken shaft of an arrow protruding from her rib cage just below the right breast. Her mouth hung open as she lurched forward.

The Blades reacted like an angry beast, surrounding the woman and pinning her to the street. By the time Three Moons arrived, she had been hacked apart, both arms and one leg separated from her trunk, with dozens of punctures all across her body, but still she kept moving until Ino planted a dagger in her forehead. Then her black eyes rolled back in her head and she spat out a mouthful of dark bile.

"Holy shit!" Dharpa shouted. "What's wrong with these people?"

"They're fucking insane!" Harunda shook the gore from his sword. It oozed like black tar.

Three Moons knelt beside the body. It was still now, with no sign of the terrible power it had possessed only moments ago. Black spittle dripped from the mouth. The teeth were sharp, like a dog's, but she had definitely been human, once.

"Wights," he whispered.

"What did you say?" Captain Paranas asked.

Three Moons cleared his throat. "Some call them ghuls. My grandfather called them wights. The dead possessed by evil spirits and brought back to an unholy semblance of life."

"Damn me! Who would do such a thing?"

BLADE AND BONE

Three Moons shrugged. "People willing to mess with the darkest arts without caring what it does to their souls."

"So how do we fight them?"

"It's not easy. Burning them's best, or so I've heard. Never seen one before today."

Captain Paranas shook his head. "Fuck it. We're getting out of here. Niko, find us an exit! Cut down anything that gets in our way!"

Three Moons looked around for a clear avenue of escape, but there was none to be had. Yet, the Bronze Blades were all business. This was what they knew, what they were trained to do. They were killers. Lovable and crazy, perhaps, but killers at heart. As long as they held to that, they had a chance.

"Captain!"

Three Moons followed Captain Paranas to join the scouts at the end of the block, and felt his heart drop into his stomach. A pack of twenty or so people, or what had once been people—shopkeeps, washerwomen, slaves, soldiers, scribes—were coming toward them from the east in a wild, seething mob. Their gait was more like a shambling gallop than a true sprint, as if they had lost all sense of humanity and returned to their animalistic roots.

There were alleys to the north and south, but they were narrow and dark. Anything could be hiding in those shadows.

Paranas pointed to the approaching mob. "Ino! Form up your squad in front. Everyone else, stack behind them. One volley with crossbows, and then we charge."

Niko frowned. "Cap—"

"Your scouts have rearguard, Sergeant," Paranas snapped back at him.

As the Blades readied their weapons, Three Moons watched the advancing pack of locals. He reached into his fetish bag and sorted through his paraphernalia. "Captain, I'm not sure what use I'll be. The spirits aren't talking to me here."

"Do what you can, Moons. We either push through or we die here."

"I picked a shitty time to stop drinking," Three Moons muttered.

Strings twanged as crossbow quarrels were launched into the mob, and then Ino's squad led the advance. They met the enemy between the high walls of two abutting temples. Three Moons wished they had heavy infantry up front clad in mail and tall shields. As it was, the fighting was bloody and vicious. The wights fought like beasts, clawing and biting. Even when stabbed through the vitals, they kept coming. And their eyes . . .

Three Moons couldn't help himself from staring into those hungry, black orbs. They promised an unholy appetite that even death could not satiate. Teba and Finum went down under the first wave of clawing, gouging assailants. The captain tried to rally the company, but the best they could do was form a tight cluster in the midst of the insanity.

A door in one of the temple walls banged open, and three ragged wights shambled out. Akeshian lancers, judging by their conical helms and tattered uniforms. The flesh of their faces was wasted away. They had lost their weapons, but that didn't make them any less intimidating as they leapt into the fray.

Captain Paranas met them with a broad swing of his sword that cut into the neck of one wight, tore clean through, and smashed into the cheek of the creature beside it. Dark blood and broken teeth exploded across the clay pavement.

Three Moons picked up a broken brick from the ground. Without the spirits' help, he didn't have many tricks in his bag, and there wasn't much time to consider alternatives. So, fighting his distaste for this kind of magic, he gathered a portion of his own life force and infused it into the brick. Cold pain cut through him as the stone shot from his hand, as if it had been launched by a trebuchet, and nearly took off the head of an incoming wight. The creature dropped to the ground, and Three Moons almost collapsed, too, as a wave of vertigo crashed down on him.

Captain Paranas thrust his sword through the temple of the undead lancer he had almost decapitated, and the blade stuck for a moment. Before he could pull it free, the last wight was on him. Just like the woman in the garbage, the creature was immensely strong. It tore open the captain's studded jacket with its bare hands. Paranas tried to retreat, dragging his trapped weapon, but the wight had latched onto him and held on fast. Three Moons came around behind the creature and stabbed the point of his knife up through its jaw, pinning tongue to palate. Black drool ran down from the wound, but the wight continued clawing at the captain.

BLADE AND BONE

Doors banged open down the street, and more undead appeared from nearby alleyways and temple yards, perhaps drawn by the fracas. Hunched figures loomed on the rooftops above. Undead. Scores of them.

Pain exploded in Three Moons's right shoulder as the wight with the pierced palate twisted his arm halfway out of joint. He kicked at its knee, but he might as well have been kicking a tree stump for all the good it did. The undead soldier kept wrenching on his arm as if it meant to tear it off. As Three Moons struggled to free himself, a steel point exploded from the wight's left eye socket. The thing thrashed for a moment, and then collapsed to the ground. Three Moons staggered back as his arm was released. Niko knelt behind the dead wight, yanking his dagger free.

"Try not to die, old man," Niko said with a wink. Then he dashed off to rejoin the melee.

The rest of the scouts were firing at the undead approaching from the west. Shots to the head dropped them in their tracks, but all other wounds were ignored.

Three Moons knelt down to retrieve his knife, holding his injured arm close to his body. His right shoulder burned with pain, reminding him for the thousandth time that he was a fool to still be caught up in these types of adventures. *I should be sitting in a comfortable inn with my feet up and a jug of whiskey at my elbow.*

As he stood back up, an old woman broke through the line. He tried to stab her through the eye, but the point of his knife slid past her temple, and they went down together. He landed on his injured shoulder, and the knife fell from his numbed fingers. As he held her at bay with his good arm, reaching for his weapon with the other—for just one more attack, one more spit in the eye of death—his calm shattered, and the awful realization of what was about to happen smashed down on him. Grimy fingernails tore at his clothing. A tall man fell beside him, and Three Moons found himself looking into Harunda's soft brown eyes, now staring blankly. *I'm sorry, son. I couldn't save us this time.*

Suddenly, the clawing was gone, and the old woman's corpse was flung away. Then Ino knelt down. "Moons, you all right?"

Three Moons shivered as the big Isurani hauled him to his feet. The old woman lay a few paces away, with the back of her head split open. Her final expression was almost ecstatic, as if she had glimpsed something sublime before she died. It scared the shit out of him. The daylight cast long shadows across Omikur's brick faces. Above them, the sky darkened into swirls of purple and black. More creatures emerged from the surrounding buildings. Three Moons couldn't count them all. Some wore the once bright robes of temple priests.

Three Moons tried to talk, but his chest felt as if he had inhaled a cloud of smoke.

"What's he saying?" Mesane asked.

Ino shook his head. "I can't make it—damn!"

Ino reached down. Harunda was holding onto his leg with both hands and tearing into his calf with his bare teeth. Three Moons shuddered as the black eyes rolled in Harunda's head, turning toward him.

Ino brought his falchion down with savage chops, not stopping until their brother lay still once again, his dark eyes staring up in accusation. Somehow Ino stayed on his feet. Shaking off his horror, Three Moons pulled off his scarf and wrapped it around the wound.

The rest of the company had formed a cordon to hold back the enemy. Yet, despite their efforts, the Blades were slowly being chewed up. The undead never stopped. Dharpa went down with a rotting Sun priest on his back. Mesane was pulled away and disappeared under a group of ravenous acolytes. Manchun's squad got cut off from the unit.

Captain Paranas took a step as if about to go after them, but then stopped. Three Moons saw him hesitate and understood. *If we go in there, we don't come out again. You have to let them go, Cap.*

"Fall back!" Captain Paranas shouted.

Ino grasped their commander by the arm. "Captain, we can't just leave them!"

Paranas shoved the big man's hand away. "Move out, soldier. Or stay and die. Your fucking choice."

Captain Paranas called to Niko. "We need a new way out of this hell. Avoid the most populated areas."

BLADE AND BONE

"But—"

The captain cut him off. "The parts of town that *used* to be populated. There's bound to be more of these things around, so think smart."

The scouts sprinted ahead. The rest of the company hurried along behind them. Everyone was battered and bloody. Ino limped on his own, defying anyone to help him. Three Moons smiled in spite of himself. His brothers' and sisters' faces may have been set in stony expressions, but he could read them as clear as sheep entrails. They were scared. *So am I. But we've still got some fight left in us.*

The captain grabbed Three Moons by the shoulder as they retreated down the street. "We need to buy some time. What have you got left?"

Three Moons searched his fetish bag until he came up with a large, bulging pouch. It was filled with dusty resin obtained from the sap of a torchwood tree. He closed his eyes to narrow slits as he concentrated. This was going to hurt. He hissed as he sliced away another portion of his life energy and fed it into the pouch. The leather grew warm in his hand. With every step, he pulled more power from inside him, gathering it slowly, cutting it away, and adding it to his creation. Numbness crept into him. With every siphoning, the world felt farther away. But he kept working as scenarios raced in his mind. He saw them all dying here, pulled down by packs of possessed corpses.

Three Moons stopped. The resin-filled pouch was smoking. He had packed as much of his life into it as he could manage. Holding tight to the invisible tether of power connecting him to the small bag, he handed it over to Paranas. "Throw it. As far behind us as you can."

The captain tossed the pouch high. It landed in the midst of the oncoming wights. Three Moons grabbed the captain's sleeve and turned him away as a fiery explosion detonated behind them. Three Moons fell, and his vision went dark. Then he felt people hovering over him. He heard voices, but had trouble placing them. He was falling away from the world, down into the cold arms of—

A hard slap rocked his head. Three Moons blinked as the world returned in sharp focus. Pie-Eye stood over him, his hand ready for another strike. "Should I hit him again?"

Captain Paranas put a hand on the mercenary's arm. "Ease up. You all right, Moons?"

Three Moons sat up. The cold had receded, though he still felt its effects lingering in his bones. The street behind them was engulfed in an inferno of bright red flames. Blackened body parts and half-exploded wights were strewn across the clay pavement, but the fires were too high to see anything on the other side.

Pie-Eye propped him up and put a bottle to his lips. Three Moons drank, and then almost spat it out. "Bleh. Water. You trying to kill me?"

"How long will that fire burn?" Paranas asked.

"Hours, maybe. There was enough powder in that pouch to take down a stone keep. But they'll find a way around it." *They won't ever stop. Not until they've killed every last one of us.*

Paranas clapped him on the arm. "Don't die on us yet, old man. Just relax. You did good."

Three Moons was too weary to complain when Pie-Eye hoisted him onto his shoulder and started to run. As he was carried away, he had a view of the scene behind. The tongues of flame reached toward the sky, writhing like living things. The street was blocked for the time being, but more creatures were climbing out of windows and leaping down from the nearby roofs. More than he could count.

With a tight grip on his fetish bag, Three Moons prayed for Pie-Eye to run faster.

CHAPTER TWO

Horace walked the streets of Erugash once more in his dream. The clay pavement was warm under his bare soles as he strolled along familiar boulevards. Off to the north, the queen's palace rose into the sky. Sunlight gleamed from its golden summit.

There were no people here. He had the city all to himself. Not even a bird's call marred the perfect quiet. Feeling nostalgic, he headed toward his old home. Yet, before he had found the right street, he heard them. Voices whispering in the distance, too soft to make out the words. Where were they? Horace stopped as one voice rose above the others.

"He is coming, Horace."

He knew that voice. "Mulcibar?"

"He is coming, Horace. You must learn to control your chaos before it consumes you."

"What does that mean? Mulcibar! What am I supposed to do?"

Panic rose inside him as he looked down the streets, trying to find his friend. But the voice was fainter now, as if Mulcibar were moving away from him. "Follow the call."

"Mulcibar? Mulcibar! What call? I don't know what to do!"

Then another voice spoke behind him. It was Ubar. "You must stand fast, Horace. A great storm is coming. A storm of the ages."

Horace spun around, but there was no one there. Just the dusty avenue. The sunlight faltered as a bank of black storm clouds rolled across the sky. A cold wind blew down, whipping his thin robe about his legs and making him shiver. Horace looked for shelter, but all the doors along the avenue were closed. He knew without checking they would be locked and barred. He was alone.

A sound like grinding rocks roared across the sky. He looked up as a great wave of water crashed over the city walls. Dark waters swirled with jetsam and green foam. Cracks appeared in the walls, and then they toppled, allowing the flood to wash into the city.

BLADE AND BONE

Horace turned to run, but the rising water caught him and picked him up in its frigid embrace. He kicked, trying to stay afloat, but a merciless current dragged him down, deep into the dark and icy waters. High above, he saw a point of bright light shining. He fought to reach the surface, but the current pulled him deeper and deeper. . . .

A hand shook him awake. Horace gasped as he opened his eyes. He was out in the desert. The dream was gone.

Jirom knelt beside him, holding a clay cup. "It's time," he said. His voice was low and toneless, as if he were the one who had just woken up.

Horace sat up and accepted the cup. A sip of the spiced wine awakened his senses. He had been having a lot of dreams lately. Nightmares, actually. Almost every night. Most of them were about the things he had seen and done in Erugash. But some were like this one. Visions of apocalyptic disaster. "Are we ready to move?"

The first indigo fingers of dawn painted the eastern sky. Sixty rebel fighters were breaking camp and preparing their gear. The air was cool, but it would warm soon once the sun came over the horizon.

Jirom nodded, but Horace could see something was bothering him by the firm set of his jaw. "Worried?" he asked.

"Always," Jirom responded with his customary shrug.

Jirom had taken over the leadership of the rebellion, with Emanon now serving as his second. Horace didn't know the details, but he knew his friend was the right man for the job. Jirom took his responsibility for the lives of the men and women under his command very seriously. He often couldn't sleep the night before a battle, and judging by the hollows under Jirom's eyes, last night had been no different.

"Don't worry. Your plans always work."

Jirom grunted. "There are no plans once steel is drawn. But come on. I let you sleep a little later than the rest."

With the cobwebs of the dream still lingering in his mind, Horace almost said he wished Jirom hadn't. But sleep was a luxury to an army in the field, so he kept quiet.

As Jirom went to join his fighters, Horace checked his boots for unwanted guests before pulling them on. The rawhide laces ran across the scars on his palms and the undersides of his fingers. He made a silent prayer to the spirits of his departed wife and son, and then put them out of his mind as he stood up. He needed a clear head for what he had to do today.

For the past three months, the rebels had been hiding out in the desert. And every week to ten days, they ventured forth to attack a different Akeshian outpost. They struck fast and slipped away before reinforcements could arrive. Horace had agreed to help with these attacks, mostly because he felt he owed something to these brave men and women who were risking their lives to make the empire a better place, something he had failed to do during his brief time as Byleth's First Sword. But he didn't like it. Killing and destroying. With every battle he felt more and more tarnished by the bloodshed. Yet, he couldn't back out now. Too many lives depended on him.

The rebels set off as the first rays of the new day arrived, across the rough tracts. The Iron Desert was as harsh an environment as Horace had ever seen, yet it had its variations. This far to the north, at the edge of the territory claimed by the Akeshian Empire, the dunes gave way to a flat plain of hard-baked earth and red clay. Worn boulders, sometimes in clusters but often standing alone, broke up the monotony. The only trees were the occasional scrub, clinging to life on the arid wastes. The sun, when it rose, would scorch the earth and anything else it could find.

A brisk hike of two miles brought them to this day's target. A dusty road cut through the desert to meet with a stone fort situated atop a low mesa. The stronghold was a crude affair of rough walls and two small towers protecting a cluster of inner buildings. It was a backwater post on the border of the empire, standing guard over a seldom-used trade route with Nemedia.

The rebels spread out in teams amid the field of rocks and boulders strewn alongside the road, hunkering down into the natural contours of the land. Weapons were drawn and readied. Bows strung and arrows laid out. Swords and axes covered to keep the advancing sunlight from reflecting off their blades.

Two men came over to hunker beside him behind a low boulder. Gurita and Jin—the last surviving members of his personal bodyguard from Erugash. They wore a mishmash of armor they had picked up from various battlefields and pieced together. Their weapons were simple and well-worn with use. Despite his protestations, these two had insisted on remaining with him, still performing the duties they had accepted back in the queen's city. Finally, he had admitted defeat and just let them be. As Mezim once told him, everyone needed a purpose.

"They're coming," Gurita said.

A distant pounding of hooves rumbled up the road from the south. Four large, horse-drawn wagons approached at a swift pace, sending up plumes of dust behind them. A score of lancers in imperial uniforms rode escort.

Horace studied them while keeping his head down. He tensed as two squads of rebel archers stood and released the first volley of arrows. Several lancers fell out of their saddles. The driver of the first wagon pitched sideways with three shafts puncturing his chest. The other teamster somehow escaped injury and grabbed for the reins, but a javelin caught him in the ribs before he could take control. The horses ran wild, pulling away from the wagons behind. The second flight of arrows raked the next wagon in line.

Rebel fighters emerged from hiding on both sides of the road to converge on the caravan. The cavalrymen wheeled and made a countercharge with impressive poise. Sharp screams echoed above the battle as blades cut deep and hooves stamped down on flesh and bone.

As the squad of rebel infantry in front of him charged into the melee, Horace waited. This was just the preamble. In quick order, the rest of the Akeshian cavalry were dragged down from their steeds and put to death. The rest of the wagon convoy tried to break through, but sharpshooters among the rocks took out their drivers. The heavy vehicles slowed to a stop, the last one swerving off the road to halt just a few yards from where Horace knelt. Its drivers slumped dead in their seat.

Horns called out from the fortress. The outer portcullis lifted, and a column of war chariots rode out. The rebels formed a square on the road. Jirom stood at the forefront, sword raised above his head as he shouted orders. The enemy raced toward them. The thunder of the horses' long strides and the rattle of iron-shod wheels shook the ground.

Horace waved at his bodyguards. "Go. Join them."

Gurita chewed his bottom lip as he surveyed the impending battle. "Perhaps we should stick with you, sir."

"I'm perfectly safe here."

Gurita shrugged. "A couple more swords isn't going to decide today's outcome. We'll stay with you."

Stifling a sigh, Horace watched the drama unfolding on the road. The chariots were fast approaching the rebel formation. When they got within two hundred paces, he stood up. It was his turn.

He sent a questing probe down into the pit of his stomach to his *qa*. He found the doorway to his power pulsing as if about to explode, so strained he was afraid to reach for it. But he did, bracing himself as he pulled open the mystic aperture. The sweet flow of magic filled him in an instant, rushing through him like the embrace of a long-lost love. Seconds passed as he stood beside the boulder, eyes closed, until he realized he had been holding his breath. He let it out with a sigh.

He delved down into the earth. The ground here was a deep layer of hard clay over a plate of underlying bedrock. He extended his sorcerous reach toward the road, and then sent a burst of intense *zoana* along that line. A heartbeat later, the ground in front of the enemy exploded in a shower of dust and gravel. Outcroppings of red stone thrust out of the ground under the Akeshians like massive fingers. Horses screamed as they were flung backward. Chariots swerved and flipped over, crushing their crews underneath. At the same time, the rebels launched a hail of arrows, arbalest bolts, and atlatl-flung javelins that carved up the enemy with brutal efficiency.

Horace searched the battlefield until he spotted Jirom, passing out orders on the far side of the road. His fighters began their advance for the final assault. Up the road, sentries watched from the fortress walls. They had to know what was coming next.

BLADE AND BONE

As he faced the fort, Horace could not help but think back to the night he had demolished the Chapter House of the Crimson Flame in Erugash. He still recalled the terrible rage that had fomented inside him and that pushed all rational thought from his mind until only the thirst for vengeance remained. This time he wasn't driven by revenge. In fact, he held no particular animus for the Akeshians inside the fortress. But this was war. The sides had been drawn, and just like those soldiers, he had his part to play.

Taking hold of his power, Horace formed two separate flows. One—a combination of fire and earth—reached for the main gate. Within seconds, the rusty iron was torn off its melting hinges. The second flow of pure Imuvar smashed into the southwest tower like a giant fist. Pieces of mason and mortar rained down until the entire tower collapsed. The second tower came down just as quickly.

Horace's heart beat harder as he flexed his power. When a flight of arrows came winging toward the advancing rebels, he flung them away with fierce gusts of wind and brought down the fort's side walls with a shrug of the earth. The magic surged within him, more intoxicating than the finest liquor, burning away all his doubts and insecurities. With a deep sigh, he released it.

The power went slowly, as if reluctant to leave him, and left a hollow absence in the center of his chest. That had been happening more often of late, the feeling that he wasn't completely whole unless he was wielding the *zoana*. Sometimes he woke up in the middle of the night, bathed in sweat and heart thumping, from a dream where he had lost the power forever, and it took him a long while to get back to sleep. The magic was a part of him now, as familiar as his face in the mirror. More sometimes, actually.

He turned when Gurita fell to the ground without warning, as stiff as a walloped cod. Jin collapsed as well, both men shaking in the dirt as if they had been struck by palsy. Then Horace spotted three men in long robes standing behind him, and he grabbed for his *zoana*.

Invisible cudgels of solid air struck him from all sides, and Horace almost blacked out in the instant before he could put up a shield around himself. Heavy thuds rocked the barrier from the outside, but it gave him time to clear his head. All three of the Akeshians were obviously *zoanii*, and powerful ones at that. He cursed under his breath. It had been only a matter of time before the empire laid a trap for them.

Bright flames erupted outside his shield. The air inside warmed up quickly, becoming too hot to breathe within seconds, and his boots began to smoke. Through the inferno, Horace glimpsed a boulder rising from the field a few yards away. It sailed toward him in a lazy arc.

Horace located the *zoanii* causing the fire and used a blade of pure Shinar to sever his connection to the magic. The flames sputtered out and died instantly. Next he shattered the boulder with a blast of Kishargal. As the shards of stone rained down, Horace's vision suddenly dimmed. Dark clouds roiled above, spitting gusts of bitter-cold wind and crackling green sparks. His stomach dropped as a vast wall of water rose from the desert wastes, high enough to engulf an entire city. Then a figure rose from the earth as if pushed upward from below by invisible hands. A tall man, very thin. His flesh was burnt black as if from a terrible fire, and his eyes glowed bright yellow. Horace felt his power dwindling as fear took control of him. A name hovered on the back of his tongue, but he was too frightened to voice it.

Astaptah. He's alive.

Horace stepped back and blinked.

The vision of advancing water and the terrifying figure vanished as the light of dawn returned. Sounds of scattered fighting echoed from the fort. Horace felt the energy of his shield draining away. Just as he started to reinforce it, a spear of ice pierced through the barrier, aiming for his throat. Horace raised his arm as he ducked his head away. The spear sliced across his forearm, drawing blood. At the same time, a powerful buffet of air struck him in the lower back. Horace picked up a handful of stones from the ground with his power and sent them hurling toward the nearest enemy. They exploded harmlessly before they reached the target. As a lance of fire jetted toward him, Horace tried another tactic.

He had first stumbled across the idea months ago when he still had access to the royal library in Erugash. It had been mentioned in a magical treatise as a theory, and he hadn't thought much about it until his exile from the city. Marching across the desert again had given him time to ponder that treatise, and so he began experimenting, far away from the rebel camp where he wouldn't hurt anyone else if something went wrong, but he hadn't had time to try a real test.

Now or never.

Horace twisted the *zoana* into a complicated weaving of all five dominions. Void magic surged within him. A moment later, he was standing twenty paces behind the sorcerers. As they looked around in confusion, he launched his counterattack. A sharp pillar of stone jutted from the ground to transfix one *zoanii*. The other two whirled to face Horace, but he was already sending lassos of fire to seize them. One of the sorcerers—a bald man with a black-and-gray beard—dispelled the fiery lariat heading for him, but the other man screamed as he was trussed up. Horace didn't make him suffer. The fire cinched around his neck and pulled tight.

The last *zoanii* waved his arms in a strange pattern as he sent a swarm of fiery orbs streaking through the air. Horace deflected them with a touch of Girru and conjured a globe of water around the man's head in response. The bearded sorcerer gasped and tried to bat away the liquid, but it remained in place until, at last, he was forced to breathe it in. As the sorcerer dropped to his knees, Horace put a pebble through his heart to finish it.

Breathing hard, Horace released the *zoana* and went to check on Gurita and Jin. They were groggy from the attack, but neither appeared seriously injured. As he helped them up, something tugged at his mind, like a silent call. He glanced at the fort. The sensation seemed to be coming from there, or maybe beyond. It was difficult to tell.

A dull ache throbbed behind his temples. He had overexerted himself, especially with that magical shift in position. He was stunned it had worked so well, but the memory of the vision he had experienced during the battle—so similar to his nightmares—tainted any sense of accomplishment. He was nursing a full-blown headache by the time Jirom emerged from the fort's gate and started over toward him.

Horace accepted a waterskin from Gurita and waited, watching Jirom approach. His friend's arms were covered in blood up to the elbow. Gore also coated part of his face and neck, drying in large swathes across his hide armor.

Reminded of the metaphorical blood staining his own hands, Horace tried not to look at it. "How many did we lose?" he asked.

"Eleven," Jirom replied as he came over to where Horace was leaning against a small boulder, sipping from a skin. "Not bad, considering."

"Yes. Considering."

Horace's voice sounded hollow, as if he were thinking about something else. Then Jirom noticed the dead Akeshians in burnt and torn robes lying on the ground.

"Trouble?"

"Not so much."

There it was again. The tone of preoccupation. Jirom lifted a hand to scratch his chin, then looked at his bloody fingers and decided against it. "We're just about finished inside. There wasn't much resistance once the walls came down."

That got Horace's attention. "Did you find what you were looking for?"

"Enough supplies to last us for a few weeks. Food, timber, horses, and about a dozen new recruits. And, of course, the most important thing."

"Water."

"There's a well inside and an entire storeroom of casks. We're loading them now. How are you holding up?"

Horace eyed him over the lip of the waterskin. "I'm fine."

Jirom turned toward the half-demolished fortress. Halil's squad prowled the battlefield, collecting their dead and finishing off the mortally wounded. "I've never seen you so destructive before. It seems like you were spoiling for a fight."

"Actually, it's just the opposite. I wish I was back at the base instead of here."

There it was. Just what Jirom had been fearing might come. He braced himself. "You don't have to do it, Horace. You don't owe us anything."

BLADE AND BONE

"Is that so? Do you have a few spare wizards hanging around that I don't know about?"

"You aren't a soldier, Horace. Don't get me wrong. You're tough. Maybe the toughest bastard I've ever known. You took down an entire city."

"I had a little help," Horace murmured.

Jirom faced his friend. "But you're no soldier. You think too damned much, for one thing. And killing doesn't come natural for you."

Horace met his eyes. "Does it come natural for anyone?"

"More so for some."

Horace looked away first. "No, this is important. Maybe the most important thing I've ever done. I'm just not sure that I'm ready yet."

"The rebellion existed before you joined us. It will continue on if you leave. It won't ever stop until everyone is free. The world is changing."

Jirom studied his friend, but Horace kept his eyes on the far horizon, as if searching for something. Answers, maybe.

"Yes, it's changing," Horace said. "But not always for the better."

Jirom tried to find the right words to ease Horace's mind. "We'll make it better. That's what we're doing."

Emanon approached. A fresh bandage was tied off around his upper arm. He carried his *zoahadin*-tipped spear in his good hand. "What are we doing? Besides sweating our balls off out here, I mean."

Jirom forced a smile, silently wishing his lover and second-in-command had left them alone for a little while longer. Horace bristled around Emanon. Jirom saw it now again, as Horace's expression changed from intent to practiced indifference.

"Making a better world," Jirom answered.

"Damn straight." Emanon cocked a smile at them both. "It's like trying to eat an elephant. Sure, it's a big fucker, but you just take it one bite at a time."

Horace didn't respond or smile back.

Ready to change the subject, Jirom asked, "How goes the packing?"

"We'll be ready to go within half an hour," Emanon answered.

"Good," Horace said. "We need to be on our way."

"Something wrong?" Jirom asked, feeling as if he was repeating himself and getting nowhere.

"The wind feels . . . wrong. It's not easy to explain."

Emanon gave Jirom a look that said, *Not this again.*

Ever since Erugash, Horace had been acting more and more strangely. He was often lost in his thoughts, sometimes saying things that made no sense. Jirom tried not to worry too much, since Horace was still reliable during their assault operations. But when the fighting stopped, he lost focus. Like this.

"Speaking of explanations, where the fuck were you?" Emanon asked.

The words seemed to take Horace by surprise. "I was right here."

"We needed you out there. An entire platoon of archers was waiting inside the fort when we made the final push."

Horace stared back. The absentness was gone from his voice, replaced by a serious tone that got Jirom's attention. "I got distracted."

Emanon stepped up to him. "You're always distracted, and it's getting people killed. Not to mention all the horses we could have captured today, if they weren't all cut to shit."

Jirom eyed the two bodyguards standing behind Horace. They had their hands close to their weapons, ready to draw.

"In case you forgot," Horace retorted, "I'm new to all this. But I'm doing my best."

"Your best better get a whole lot fucking better, boy. Or we're all going to suffer the first time we run into a cadre of real sorcerers."

Horace tilted his head toward the dead men lying around them. "Like these? While you were playing soldier, I was keeping these three from roasting you alive."

Emanon spat at his feet. "We were winning battles and killing wizards long before you decided to join the party."

"Maybe back when you were beneath their notice, but not anymore. Now you've got the entire empire hunting for you. They know this outfit had something to do with the fall of Erugash."

"Is that it? You miss your royal bitch of a girlfriend? After all the times Jirom risked his neck for you, you should be kissing his feet!"

BLADE AND BONE

"Em . . ." Jirom started to interject.

"No, its fine, Jirom," Horace said through gritted teeth. "First he drags us out into the middle of this miserable wasteland, and now he wants to cause trouble with the empire instead of laying low like anyone with an ounce of sense would do."

Emanon snorted, his eyes squeezed down into hard slits. "What would you know about sense? From what I heard, you've been playing with fire since you got to this land. Speaking of which, why didn't you go back home when you had the chance? Running from something?"

"I could ask the same of you. Why keep pushing these men so hard? What's the point in training them if you're just going to grind them into dust?"

The grin that split Emanon's face was humorless as he lowered the point of his spear a few inches. "Son, I don't need your permission to take a piss. But if you're looking for another scrap, I'd be happy to shove this pig-sticker—"

"Em!" Jirom thrust himself between them, shoving Emanon back a step.

Horace didn't let him finish. Without another word, he turned and walked away, heading toward the wagons with his guards.

Emanon started to go after him, but Jirom pushed him back. "Em, don't."

"Don't what? Chew him out when he fucks up? He's lucky that's all I'm doing. We lost some good people today, Jirom. Maybe they would still be alive if he had been doing his fucking job."

"You didn't help matters, Em."

"And you don't always have to take his side."

"I'm the captain. You know how it works. I'm not on anyone's side."

"You sure had me fooled."

"Em . . ."

Emanon sighed. "Dammit, I know. But Horace is a problem, Jirom. You can't control him, and that makes him dangerous. We're clasping a viper to our chests and hoping it only bites our enemies. Sooner or later, he's going to turn."

Jirom shook his head. Horace had changed since the first time they'd met at the end of a slave coffle. He was more guarded and certainly more powerful. But he was still a man of honor. Yet, to Emanon, everyone and everything was either an asset to his cause or an obstacle. "Horace would never do that, Em. He's dependable."

"Remember you said that when we're facing an army and your pet warlock is nowhere to be found."

Jirom winced as the words echoed his own misgivings. Without Horace, the rebellion's chances against the empire dropped from slim to nonexistent. Their stock of *zoahadin* was down to a score of arrowheads and the spear Emanon carried. Not for the first time, Jirom wished he still had the *assurana* sword. "I don't want to talk about it."

"Of course not. Maybe you can't control him, but you need to stop making excuses for him. The other men see it, and they wonder why you don't hold everyone to the same standard."

"I said we're not talking about it."

"Fine." Emanon held up a slip of papyrus. "Here's the final tally of the goods we seized today. It's a nice haul. You should be proud. But you also know we could be doing more."

Jirom suppressed the urge to sigh out loud. *I know, my love. You tell me that every day.* "Any word from the mercs?"

Two weeks ago Jirom had sent the surviving Bronze Blades out to Omikur on the off chance the western crusaders still held the town. He figured that since the westerners and the rebellion had the same enemy, perhaps they could work together. Emanon had been against the idea, of course, and now it was another source of tension between them.

"Nothing yet."

His tone said it all. *I told you it was a waste of time and manpower, but you wouldn't listen.*

Before Jirom could respond, Emanon shoved the slip into his hand and walked away. Jirom almost called out to him, but left the apology unsaid. *Why does he get to say whatever he wants, but I'm always the one apologizing?*

Seng found him. The small leader of the rebel's scouts moved with deceptive ease. He seemed mild-mannered, but Jirom had seen him become a whirlwind of murder in battle.

"Captain," Seng said. "We have four prisoners. A sweep of the area has revealed no hidden survivors. Fires are being set inside the fort, as instructed."

Jirom nodded, only half-listening. His men were loading the bodies of their fallen comrades onto the last wagon. Eleven dead. *Not bad, considering we were outnumbered. So why do I feel so guilty? Horace, don't you turn on us.* "We're heading back to base. Send out your scouts, but keep a team back to cover our tracks. I don't want anyone following us."

"Yes, sir. What about the prisoners?"

Jirom tucked the slip of papyrus into his belt. "Kill them. Let the new recruits do it if they want, but don't force them."

As Seng hurried off to follow his orders, Jirom surveyed the site. Smoke was rising from the interior of the fort, or what was left of it. *We need you, Horace. Don't turn on us.*

Satisfied with the day's results, Jirom went to make sure the booty was packed and everyone was accounted for. They had a long way to go to get back home.

CHAPTER THREE

The journey from Nisus to Hirak took nine days by river barge. Pumash spent the time trying to concoct a means to accomplish the impossible mission given to him by the master: to bring a city to its knees all by himself.

Pumash remembered kneeling at the *Manalish*'s feet in the palace at Nisus, with the master's strong hand gripping his head. Every time he closed his eyes, he felt the gelid darkness pouring into him once again, spreading throughout his body. What had been done to him? Each morning he awoke fearing he had become one of the master's undead creatures, and each morning he breathed a sigh of relief that quickly turned into a groan. Perhaps he was still alive, but at what cost? He had no choice but to obey or die.

"Shall I bring your baggage ashore, my lord?"

Pumash looked down at the small, spindly man hunched over beside him. Along with a crew of slaves to row the barge, the *Manalish* had included a small retinue of servants to accompany him. But not a single soldier.

"Not as yet, Deemu. Fetch me a car. With curtains," he added as the manservant skittered off through the dockside crowd. Pumash tried not to sigh, but his frustration was mounting now that he had finally arrived.

Hirak was built on a broad flood plain beside the Typhon River. Colossal bulwarks surrounded the city, their ancient bricks stained by decades of rising and falling waters. Above the wall, close-packed towers and tiered palaces reached high into the sky.

Deemu returned with a palanquin car carried by four brawny slaves.

"Take me to the royal palace."

Pumash stepped inside, leaving his servant to work out the monetary details. A few moments later, the litter rose and began its ascent up the sloped road to the city proper. They passed through the gates without being stopped. Beyond the outer walls, people clustered in the streets and gathered in doorways. Children and their parents gazed down from windows at the world below. The closeness of the buildings was confining, and Pumash found himself holding his breath for long intervals, not wanting to inhale too deeply of the oily miasma that clung to this city. Then his car entered the circular plaza at the foot of the royal palace, and he breathed more freely.

Ochre pavestones marched to the gated entrance. The massive white-stone structure was a circle of five round towers surrounding an inner alcazar, which rose almost as high as the royal palace at Erugash. All in all, it was a tribute to the engineers and architects of Hirak. And he had been sent to conquer it. By himself. Without an army.

His ride rocked to a halt outside the entrance. Guardsmen in bright scale armor stood at the gate, but none advanced to assist him. Pumash stepped out of the car, feigning a confidence he didn't necessarily feel. Yet, he had dealt with all manner of people in his years of slave trading. He put on his business mien as he approached.

"I am Lord Pumash et'Luradessus, envoy of the *Manalish* of Nisus, Erugash, and Chiresh. I have come to demand audience with King Baalberith."

He presented the scroll he had been given. It was a long tube of fine vellum stamped with a blob of black wax. The guard commander reached out for it, but Pumash pulled it away. "This is for the king's vizier. It is not to be opened by any other."

The commander stared at him for several seconds. Then he signaled for the gates to open. Metal screeched as the broad portal yawned wide, revealing a long path of white stones running through a green expanse. Two guards accompanied him, while Deemu and the rest of his retinue remained outside.

The outer courtyard was peaceful. A small army of gardeners tended the lawn and ornamental trees. Footmen in brown livery stood on the broad marble portico of the palace entrance. They bowed as they opened the carved oak doors for him. Inside, the gate guards passed him off to a pair of household guards, who wore the same livery as the door wardens.

Pumash was a little surprised to have been admitted without a prior appointment. He had been the guest of several kings of Akeshia, and all of them protected their privacy with a bureaucracy of ministers, chamberlains, and other ranking servants. His suspicion proved correct when he was steered into a large office off the main hallway. A man in a long brown-and-white robe stood beside an ornate writing desk. His head was shaved. He appeared to be a few years older than Pumash.

"I am the king's officiant," the man said, reaching out with his hand. "Any correspondence for His Royal Majesty can be left with—"

Pumash stopped at the threshold, standing with his hands crossed before him. "You are not Lord Haileth. I will see the Grand Vizier."

"His Lordship is otherwise detained," the officiant replied. Frown lines creased his forehead. "Now if you will just leave your—"

Pumash walked out and headed down the hall, deeper into the palace. He had been to Hirak twice before but never inside the royal residence. Still, he had a general idea of the layout.

Calls of "My lord! You must wait!" rang after him as his two escorts hurried to keep up. They shot glances at each other, and Pumash knew they were considering whether or not to lay hands on him. However, his nobility protected him long enough to reach the lofty rotunda at the center of the alcazar. The round walls of the chamber extended upward more than a hundred feet in an impressive marble tower. A broad staircase climbed the interior.

Pumash was about to start up the stairs when a raspy voice called to him. An older man stood in the doorway across from the entry hall. His silken robes were trimmed in cloth of gold. "Lord Pumash."

"Lord Haileth?"

"Yes. Please accompany me, my lord."

Pumash followed the Grand Vizier down another wide hallway. Four guards—soldiers in full armor this time, not mere footmen—appeared and walked with them. Pumash remained calm. Although he did not expect King Baalberith to appreciate the message he delivered, there was a certain protocol involved in matters of state, and so he did not fear bodily harm so long as he acted in the capacity as envoy.

Lord Haileth and the soldiers escorted him to what appeared to be a waiting room. It was small but well-appointed with soft divans and chairs. A painting of the Typhon River hung over a water sculpture.

Without explanation, Lord Haileth excused himself and left Pumash with the four guards. The sentries took up positions at the corners of the room but otherwise ignored him. So he sat on the stiffest chair he could find and waited. Outwardly, he was perfectly composed. But inside, his nerves were pulled taut. This entire venture had been doomed to failure from the start. Why send one man to demand the surrender of an entire city-state? He could not pretend to know the *Manalish*'s game, and now he began to wonder if this wasn't just an elaborate way to get rid of him. *No, he could have slain me in Nisus with a touch. For all his menace and mystery, the* Manalish *does not seem the type to waste a valuable resource.*

Yet, despite his self-assurances, Pumash struggled to sit still as time passed. Finally, after more than an hour of waiting, Lord Haileth returned.

Pumash stood up on stiff legs. "Grand Vizier, I have been authorized to present to you—"

"You may present your message to the king himself," Lord Haileth interrupted. "His Majesty is expecting you. Please follow me."

Pumash followed the older lord down another corridor. Two guards stood at attention flanking a large door bearing ornate trim. One guard opened the door with a slight bow, and Lord Haileth walked through. Pumash stopped at the threshold of what was obviously the grand audience hall. The entire court appeared to be assembled on and around the raised dais at the far end, and at the pinnacle of that tiered platform sat a tall, handsome man on an ivory throne. Pumash swallowed, his mouth suddenly dry as all the eyes in the chamber focused on him.

"Come forward, my lord," Lord Haileth said.

Pumash followed to the foot of the dais. Lord Haileth stopped there and bowed low. Pumash considered his response carefully. The degree to which he bowed would say much about how he perceived his status at this official event. He opted for a bow that was slightly lower than the obeisance given to a senior family member but not quite so deep as that reserved for a person of a higher caste.

King Baalberith returned a nod. "Lord Pumash, you come with a message from the upstart who seized Erugash. I hope you are not wasting our time with some notion of an alliance. We intend to see this usurper executed for his crimes against the empire."

Pumash steeled himself as he produced the scroll. "No, Your Majesty. It is an invitation for your city to surrender."

He held his breath as the words echoed through the hall. Lord Haileth froze with one hand extended to take the scroll as if recoiling from a serpent. The guards who had escorted Pumash into the hall grasped him by the arms and forced him down to his knees.

"Silence your filthy tongue!" The king was on his feet, his eyes bulging as he screamed from the dais. "How dare you utter such a thing in these halls?"

A nimbus of fire surrounded King Baalberith. Twin flames lashed out like whips to wrap around Pumash, and he cried out at the touch of the searing tendrils. The smell of his scorching robes filled the chamber, and he expected at any moment to feel the sorcerous fires burning into his flesh. Yet, there was no pain. The fiery nooses licked at his skin but did him no harm. However, something else was happening inside him. An unpleasant stirring in the center of his chest. It started slowly but grew stronger with each passing heartbeat. Pumash tried to lift a hand to his breast as the discomfort blossomed into pain, but the guards held him fast.

With a scathing stare, King Baalberith conjured more flaming ropes and launched them at Pumash, but they were no more effective than the first.

Pumash might have been tempted to laugh at the look of impotency on the monarch's face, but the pain growing in his chest demanded all his attention. Then, suddenly, the pain exploded, tearing itself in all directions like a river of tiny razors inside him. He tried to scream, unable to hold the pain inside, but his lungs were paralyzed. However, cries erupted from the guards holding his arms.

Pumash looked down to see the hands of his captors turning black. The guards tried to pull free, but they were stuck to him as the black tide advanced up their wrists and arms. The pain continued inside him, but it was a strange sensation as the agony flowed out of him. Or through him, as if he were a conduit through which this horrible energy was passing. But where did it come from?

Then he recalled kneeling atop the palace at Nisus, and the power that had flowed into him from the hand of the *Manalish*. This was the same power;

he was sure of it. For a moment, he reveled in the darkness that was consuming these men who had dared lay hands on him. Then he started to choke as the pain crawled up his throat. A terrible burning erupted behind his eyes. His ears buzzed. Then a rush of liquid surged into his mouth. Pumash bent over, retched, and looked in shock as a stream of vile blackness hurled from his lips. It spattered the lower-standing members of the court, and their shrieks of horror were added to the cacophony.

On the dais, King Baalberith gave up his attacks and retreated behind his throne. More soldiers hurried to form a wall before their liege. Pumash wanted to cry now as the black bile slowed to a trickle from his mouth. This was how he was going to die, vomiting before the court of Hirak. His legs gave out, and he dropped to his stomach with hardly enough strength left to keep his face from hitting the marble tiles. The entire court was falling down, too, thrashing and screaming as the blackness spread among them. Step by step, the dark virus climbed the dais, until it took the royal bodyguards and all that was left was the king, standing alone amid an island of death.

Die, great king. Die with me. Not the most noble of deaths, but I think we might both be glad to miss the horrors that await this land. The Manalish *will not be stopped. No, not until the entire world is swallowed in darkness.*

Pumash laid his head on the cool stone and gave in to the pain. His last breath was a long, rattling wheeze.

The hum of an insect played in his ear. A brush of a tiny wing tickled his nose. Eyes closed, he reached up to swat at it. And then he realized he was alive.

My lungs are breathing. I feel the hard floor beneath me. My head is pounding. Great Gods above! I am alive!

Pumash breathed deeply. Then an image came to his mind, of the last thing he had seen before losing consciousness. A woman of the court—middle-aged, long black hair, probably dyed to keep it that way—lying on the floor only a few steps from him. Her eyes had turned completely black as if they had been dipped in squid ink. Her rose-painted lips, which had been slightly alluring only a few minutes before, gaped open in a silent scream, bloated tongue lolling between her teeth like a dead eel.

He slowly opened his eyes. The woman was gone, as was the entire court. His dark vomitus and a few objects—spears, shields, a blue shawl—littered the dais, but all the people were gone save for one. King Baalberith remained, sprawled across one arm of his throne like a drunk. His face was purple and swollen. His eyes stared wide at the ceiling. They were completely black.

Pumash started to get up. His limbs were slow to respond. He had lifted himself up onto one knee when a cloth rustled on the dais. He froze as the king's corpse began to move. Its head rotated from side to side. The mouth yawned wide open and closed with a quick snap. Then the thing looked down at him, and Pumash remembered the black pestilence that had flowed out of him during the audience. How it infected the people in the room, slaying them even as it devoured him from the inside.

So that was what had happened to the court. They had died and come back to un-life, just as Baalberith was doing now. *It's the* Manalish. *He did all this . . . through me. He put that infection inside me and sent me here, knowing the plague would spread. A plague that kills its victims and then reanimates them as monstrous creatures. He doesn't need an army. Only a living host to carry his message of undeath.*

Pumash glanced at the weapons on the dais steps, but they were too far away to reach without taking several steps, and he was reasonably sure this thing—this creature that had once been human but now was something else entirely—could reach him before he got to one. So he remained perfectly still and held his breath, hoping against hope that the thing would leave him alone.

He clamped his teeth tight together as the king came down the steps. Those black eyes, like holes of pure evil, were focused on him. Then they shifted to the door behind him. Faster than Pumash could scramble away, Baalberith shambled past him and out of the chamber. Somewhere in the distance, Pumash heard noises, a faint susurrus of shouts and crashes that made him think of battle, followed by a deep rumble that vibrated through the stones of the palace.

BLADE AND BONE

Not knowing where to go or what to do, he made his way down the broad corridor through the center of the alcazar, sometimes stumbling as he suddenly lost his balance for no reason. With one hand on the wall for support, he returned to the rotunda. Dark gore was smeared on the once-pristine floors, and a big, bloody handprint was stamped on a painting of the goddess Ishara. But again, there were no bodies to be seen. The sounds of violence had grown louder.

He started up the circular stairs, wanting to get away from whatever was happening outside. Every twenty or so steps he would pass a tall window and look down on a different part of the city. Dark clouds ruled the sky, spitting thunder and dark green arcs of lightning. Fires had sprung up in several neighborhoods. He thought the streets would be packed with mobs by now, but they were empty. Perhaps everyone had fled?

The stairs ended in a large chamber at the tower's summit. Fierce winds blew through the broad windows. Down in the city, the fires were spreading, but from this vantage everything seemed remote, as if these events were happening in another place and time. This was no conquest. It was wholesale slaughter.

He was leaning over the window casement for a better view of the River Quarter, wondering how he was going to escape this death trap, when a brutal pain pierced his skull. Then a voice boomed in his head. The force of it drove him to his knees where he huddled on the tiled floor, tears running freely from his eyes.

Report what you have seen in Hirak, servant.

Pumash trembled as he replied. "Great Lord, I have been to see King Baalberith. While in audience with him . . ." He gasped as the pain continued to wrack his brain. ". . . a terrible sickness came out of me and infected the entire court. They are all dead. And the plague spreads throughout the city. Fires are burning—"

Pumash gasped as he was suddenly struck blind. He reached out with both hands as his vision went dark. A low moan passed his lips. Then he felt his legs flexing, lifting him up without his control. There was a sense of vertigo as he almost toppled over, but he remained upright. His legs carried him around the chamber as if going from window to window.

"Great Lord! What is happening to me?"

Be silent. All is going as I planned.

Pumash's vision abruptly returned, as did control of his limbs. He was standing by the eastern window, gazing down at the military district. There was some fighting in the streets, but it appeared to be sporadic and undisciplined.

Secure the city and remain in place. More orders will be forthcoming.

Pumash felt light-headed as a renewed panic set in. How was he supposed to secure a city all by himself? "My king, how—?"

He cried out as the pain returned, so intense he wanted to bash his head against the wall to free himself from the torment.

Assistance will arrive. Obey, servant. Or you will know suffering as you have never experienced.

The voice left him, and with it went the pain. But the memory of it haunted Pumash as he leaned against the wall. He didn't know if he could bear this existence anymore. Just a quick jump over this sill and it would all be over. . . .

Unless he brought me back as well. And perhaps he might. Who knows the limits of his power? No, death is no escape. If anything, I must fight to live for as long as possible.

The sounds of footsteps came from below. Pumash pressed his back harder against the wall until Deemu appeared. The familiar slump of his rounded shoulders made Pumash sigh with relief.

"Master?" Deemu called to him over the howl of the wind.

Pumash took in a deep breath and stepped away from the wall. "I am here. What is the status of the city?"

"It's . . . it's horrible, Master." Deemu stayed by the stairs, as if he were afraid to venture too close to the windows. "People are dying everywhere. Some *things* came out of the palace and killed the guards. And your bearers, too. I . . . I hid in the litter. Then the monsters—I don't even know what to call them—they ran off into the city, and that's when the screaming began. Now everything is chaos outside. Can we stay up here?"

"For the time being. But we'll soon need to get to work. I've been placed in command of Hirak. We must get it ready to receive the *Manalish*."

BLADE AND BONE

Pumash turned to look down at the city once more. He understood his role in the great lord's plan. He was to be the bringer of death to the empire. He was the tip of the infected spear.

"We must make the most of all opportunities," he whispered.

"Did you say something, my lord?" Deemu asked.

Pumash turned to his servant. "Come. We shall tour our new city."

Deemu hunched lower until his chin almost touched his chest. "But what about the monsters and the storm?"

Pumash held out his arm to wrap around the poor man's trembling shoulders. "No harm will come to us. Trust in the *Manalish*. These monsters you talk of, they are his creations. We have nothing to fear from them. And the storm is merely a soothing rain sent to wash away this city's sins."

Deemu's head bobbed up and down. "As you say, my lord."

Pumash held tight to his servant's arm as they started down the steps together.

Horace blinked in the dark. He had been dreaming again, about walking the streets of the ancient city. This time when he stopped at the foot of the great pyramid at the center, a door had opened and bright light poured out. A man stood in the doorway, peering out at him with glowing yellow eyes. Horace awoke at that point with his heart pounding and one thought repeating in his mind.

What if Astaptah is still alive?

As he rubbed the sleep from his eyes, he felt a pull in the back of his mind. A nagging sensation calling him. Pushing the feeling away, he reached across the bed of piled blankets, but the other side was empty. Sitting up, he looked around. She was gone. That wasn't unusual. Alyra tended to wake up before him most days. She was always busy with some project. She was even restless in her sleep.

They had been sharing a bed since Erugash. At first, it had been awkward, trying to reestablish intimacy after being separated for so long. But the things they had gone through together, in the catacombs under the queen's palace and during their escape, had forged a new bond between them. Horace didn't know if it was love, but it was better than sleeping alone.

Especially with his dreams getting worse. More nights than not, he thrashed awake from some nightmarish scenario. Sometimes he was back in the catacombs under Erugash, being tortured by Astaptah. Or he was running from an army of mud-covered *kurgarru*. Or battling invisible demons in the dark. The terrors were endless. But, despite the horror, something told him there was a point to these nightmares. A lesson they were trying to teach, if he could only decipher it.

Horace got up and went to the clothes hanging from spikes in the wall. After pulling on a homespun shirt and pants, and a pair of sandals that were on the verge of falling apart, he headed toward the curtain that served as the chamber's doorway. He passed the stack of the three large tomes he had taken from the royal library. Alyra had actually brought them from his manor, much to his astonishment, and they had carried them across the desert. All this way, but now they just sat, gathering dust in a corner of the room between piles of clothes and a battered trunk. Maybe they held the answers he needed to make sense of recent events, but he didn't even know the right questions to ask. Did it have something to do with his dreams? He promised himself he would crack open the tomes tonight.

After escaping Erugash, the rebels had fled into the Iron Desert, running for days until they found a chain of hills riddled with caves. Emanon had apparently discovered it years before and planned to use it as a refuge of last resort. It was large enough to handle all the refugees, but it was also stuck in the middle of nowhere, cut off from the rest of the world.

Outside his room, a narrow tunnel wound through the stone foundations of the cave. A short vertical shaft led to the surface. Pushing aside the heavy canvas sheet at the top, Horace blinked against the bright light.

The desert was an ocean of white-gold dunes broken only by the occasional twisted trunk of a scrub tree. This deep into the wastes there were hardly any animals beyond snakes, scorpions, and carrion birds. The Akeshians never patrolled this far out, and the only people who made their home here were scattered tribes of nomads. It was the perfect place to hole up and wait out the storm that was engulfing the empire. Yet, almost as soon as they had arrived, Emanon pushed for raids against the Akeshians. More often than not, Jirom agreed, and so began the campaign of hit-and-run attacks that had spanned the last couple of months. Horace didn't like it, but he felt outvoted.

This is the most insane way of fighting a war. But I have to give credit to Emanon and Jirom. They have already accomplished more than anyone—including I—thought they could, and still they keep fighting. Their path is clear. How I envy that.

Gurita and Jin waited at the entrance. Seeing Horace, they stood up straight.

"Good morning, sir," Gurita said.

"Morning. Have you seen Alyra today?"

"No, sir. Maybe she's gone to the command center?"

With a nod, Horace set off, with the two bodyguards following behind him. He headed around the steep bluff that made up the southern edge of the hill chain. The rebel camp was part village, part military compound. People prepared food and wove new clothing beside training yards where the fighters led volunteers in drills with wooden swords and spears. Some of the escaped slaves had chosen to join the rebel army, but not all. Most of them just wanted to find a peaceful life, far from those who had enslaved them.

Leaving the grunts and clacking weapons of the training yard behind, Horace made his way around the side of a tall hill. Coming around the bluff, he spotted two women sitting among some rocks. One of them was Alyra.

Motioning for his guards to stay back, Horace approached. He didn't know the other woman, though he had seen her around the camp. She was using a stone to crush a pile of blue leaves into paste. Then Alyra took the paste and spread it out over flat rocks.

"Alyra," he said, nodding to them both. "Good morning."

Alyra replied without looking up. "Morning, Horace. How did you sleep?"

"I came out to find you. Maybe we can talk and get something to eat?"

Alyra looked up at him, shading her eyes with a blue-stained hand. "I've already eaten. But I'm ready for a break. Excuse me, Ulma."

Alyra wiped her hands with a stained rag as she stood. "Shall we walk?"

Horace fell in beside her. Thankfully, his escort gave them some space. He was nervous about broaching a topic he had kept to himself for a while now.

"What do you want to talk about?" she asked as they passed a row of hides pinned to drying racks.

"I've been having the dreams again."

"The one where you're back in the catacombs?"

"No. This time I was in a strange city in the desert. No place I've ever seen before, but it felt familiar." He shook his head. "Maybe I'm going crazy out here. Soon I'll be a desert hermit living under a pile of rocks."

"Maybe." She nudged him in the side. "So what's really bothering you?"

You first, my dear. Lately she had been distracted, as if wrestling over a thorny problem. All of his attempts to get her to open up had been rebuffed. "I'm not sure what I'm doing out here. I don't seem to fit with what they're trying to do."

"Everyone wants you here, Horace. You're a hero to so many."

"I don't feel like one."

"And that's normally a very endearing trait," Alyra replied, nudging him again. "But maybe you don't feel accepted because you haven't taken the time to get to know these people. I'm not the only one who's noticed. People sense it. Like you don't want to be here. Like you're regretting your decision to join us."

"I just don't know what to do."

"About what?"

"I'm not sure if fighting the empire is the answer."

"No one wants to fight, Horace. Most of these people were servants or farmers before they joined up. I wish there was a way to win our freedom without the war, but there isn't. What you're doing is important. I know you aren't a soldier, but you've seen what the empire is capable of. They won't ever negotiate with this rebellion. We're no more than property in their eyes."

He didn't need a reminder. He saw Ubar's face all the time. So young and full of life, now just another casualty. Because of his reluctance to understand the stakes of this conflict.

Alyra stopped him with a touch on his elbow. "Horace, you can do things no one else can do. Miraculous things. But I think you're still figuring out how you want to use them. While the queen was alive, your choices were simpler. You just accepted her authority and abdicated your responsibility, but now you're free. Maybe for the first time in your life."

She was right. He wasn't used to being his own man. And maybe the burgeoning of his powers was the reason behind these dreams. Still, he couldn't shake the belief that they were more than just nightmares. He took a deep breath and let it out. He had to tell her. "What if Astaptah is still alive?"

Her eyes narrowed as if she suspected he was teasing her. "That's not possible. We saw him die."

"I know. I know. But I've been seeing him in my dreams. Seeing him rise back out of that molten rock, all blistered and burnt. And there's this feeling that comes over me in the dreams. Alyra, I know it sounds insane, but I'm starting to believe it."

She was silent for a few seconds. Long enough for him to begin to worry. Then she said, "Horace, I—"

"Master! Mistress Alyra! There you are!"

They both turned as Mezim hurried over. The man who had once been Horace's secretary when he was First Sword of Erugash had stayed with him in the months since. He had taken to growing out his hair, and he kept it oiled and tied back in a tight queue. He also sported a fine goatee. But despite these outward changes in his appearance, Mezim remained the same inside. Fastidious, professional, and eminently punctual. He also insisted on acting as Horace's secretary, even though it felt ridiculous now that they were living in caves in the desert.

"Good morning, Mezim," Alyra greeted him.

Mezim gave her a short bow. "I have been sent to find you. The war council is beginning."

Horace glanced up at the sun. It wasn't even halfway to its zenith yet. "Already? I thought it was supposed to be at noon."

"Commander Jirom moved it up, sir."

"The *beysid*?"

Mezim nodded. "It's been heard that he will force the issue today."

Beysid was an old title that meant "wise one." Following the exodus from Erugash, the rescued slaves had organized themselves by divvying up such duties as providing the basic necessities of life. Perhaps because they were accustomed to labor, they took up these responsibilities without complaint or hesitation. However, then they had gone a step further and elected a representative to treat with the rebel leadership, a move that had riled up some of the rebels. So far, Jirom had done his best to smooth things over, even meeting with this delegate, *Beysid* Giliam, on matters concerning the civilians, but he and Emanon had steadfastly refused to allow the *beysid* to attend military conversations.

So it appears he invited himself. Should be interesting.

Horace looked to Alyra. He wanted to finish their conversation, but she was already heading toward the command center. Shooting Mezim a grimace, he followed after her.

They arrived at a crease between the two largest hills. Gurita and Jin took up positions outside, and Mezim waited with them, as Horace and Alyra passed through a cordon of sentries. The guards stood aside, eyes level, as they walked through.

The crevice dipped down into a large cave with a bowl-shaped floor. Lamps hanging from ceiling chains illuminated the rebel command center. The leadership stood around a crude table. Emanon was talking to the gathered squad leaders as Horace and Alyra entered. "We still don't know much about what's happening there. We haven't been able to get an agent inside. Everyone we send fails to report back."

Horace whispered into Alyra's ear. "Is he talking about Erugash?"

She nodded as they took their places at the end of the table. The sergeants made room for them with respectful nods. Horace tried to appear friendly, but he was still unaccustomed to this group. They were hard men and women who had elected to go against the most powerful empire in the world with little more than second-hand weapons and sheer guts.

"Does the storm still rage over the city?" Sergeant Halil asked. The wide, shaved-headed sergeant always wore a scowl whenever Horace saw him, making him look like an angry, stubbly dog.

"It does," Emanon answered. "For going on three months now."

Concerned glances were passed about the table between the squad leaders. *I don't blame them. This all seems like a nightmare from which we can't awaken. Three months? Chaos storms have never lasted so long before.*

Sergeant Pulla spoke up. "What about Chiresh? Or Nisus?"

This time Jirom answered. "Those cities have fallen, too."

"How is that possible?" asked Ralla, one of the two female squad leaders in the group. She was tall and lanky and as hard-bitten as any of her brothers-in-arms. A mass of gray scar tissue was all that remained of her left ear, lost in the escape from Erugash.

Emanon answered. "There have been rumors that a new king rules in Erugash. No one knows his name, but they call him the *Manalish*. Don't ask me what that means, because we have no idea. But all reports from those cities have ceased in the past few weeks."

Horace caught Alyra's gaze. *It could be Astaptah.*

She looked away, too fast to be casual. And Horace realized it. *She already knew. Or at least suspected.*

Guilt washed over him as he considered the ramifications. This was all his fault. *If I hadn't pushed Byleth to engage with the rebels. If I had seen Astaptah for what he was before he launched his plot. Hell, if I had just made sure he was dead before we ran out of that dungeon, this wouldn't be happening.*

Pulla whistled low. "That's a lot of territory."

"We don't know how it happened," Emanon replied. "Only that the cities were attacked within days of each other."

"That's impossible," Ralla said. "No army could cover that much ground in less than a week, at best. And it would take a dozen legions to hit two cities at the same time."

Alyra placed both hands down on the table's surface. "The other cities won't stand for it. The delicate balance of the empire cannot hold if one monarch controls such a large fiefdom. The rest will band together to pull the upstart down. But that strife could be good for us, if we play it right."

Horace studied her profile. *This is what she lives for. This push and pull between crowns and nations.*

Jirom spread out a map of the region on the table. "We've sent a team to investigate. But until they report back, we have to assume the western empire is closed to us. And with the central lands heating up, we have to start looking to the east."

Horace bent closer for a better look. The eastern half of the empire was a mystery to him. Along the winding line of the Typhon River he saw cities with exotic names like Yuldir, Semira, and Ceasa.

A large circle had been drawn around the city of Epur near the fork where the Typhon branched off from the Akesh River. Jirom stamped it with his forefinger. "The Akeshians are massing here. We've gotten word that all seven of the remaining cities are gathering their forces. And they're doing it under the imperial banner."

Alyra glanced up with a frown. "That hasn't happened in years."

Not since they banded together to defeat Byleth's father.

"They'll roll right over the western cities," Sergeant Ralla said.

"Perhaps," Alyra said, but she looked uncertain.

Horace studied the map. A nagging feeling itched at the back of his mind. Something wasn't adding up here.

"In any case," Jirom said, taking back the conversation. "We're staying out of their war. While the enemy is focused on the west, we'll be striking here."

He tapped several spots along the northern edge of the empire. "These are the locations of remote imperial outposts. We'll continue our hit-and-run operations, capturing as many supplies as we can. Our goal is to provision ourselves sufficient to last until next year."

"Next *year?*" Sergeant Pulla repeated.

Horace noticed that Emanon was frowning but not offering much to the discussion.

"That's right," Jirom said. "We need time to train and outfit ourselves. By staying beneath the empire's notice, we will—"

"Die out here in the desert wastes," said a voice at the cave entrance.

A heavyset man in a long robe stood behind the cordon of guards. Most of his head was bald except for a halo of black-and-gray stubble around the back of his skull. "Commander Jirom," he said, "do you intend to keep the lawful representative of the people barred from your council, or will you let me pass?"

Jirom waved for the guards to let him enter.

"*Beysid* Giliam," Emanon said. "So nice of you to insist on joining us."

"Yes, well." The man's smile opened briefly, flashing rows of yellowed teeth, and then closed again. "It is only right and proper that the people know what you have planned, since it impacts their lives as much as your own. Don't you agree?"

Emanon growled, but Jirom answered with a civil tone. "Of course. As long as you understand the need for secrecy."

With a tight-lipped smile, and shoulders hunched as if by habit, the *beysid* leaned over the map. "Of course, Commander. All sensitive information will remain in my close confidence, have no fear. But I have reservations about this ill-conceived plan of yours. The first of which is the safety and security of the people while your soldiers are spread across the empire."

"Your safety," Emanon said, not bothering to hide his disdain, "might be better served if you allowed more of the refugees to join our ranks. We need more fighters, and you're sitting on hundreds of able bodies."

"I cannot force them to volunteer. Most of my people want to avoid the war. I'm talking about our long-term survival. We have no steady sources of food or water—"

"Doesn't look like you've missed many meals," Emanon said.

The *beysid* looked taken aback for a moment, but he recovered quickly. "Your soldiers have provided quite adequately for the past three months, but what will happen to us if the empire discovers this location while you are off securing more?"

"We leave fighters behind," Jirom answered. "But secrecy is our best defense. As long as the Akeshians don't know where we are—"

"How long can that last, Commander?"

The sergeants muttered at the *beysid*'s words. Horace wished Jirom would just shut the man up and continue explaining his plan, which had sounded reasonable.

"You seem to have a suggestion in mind," Jirom said. "So spit it out."

"Thank you, Commander. As we all know, we cannot remain here forever. We have no crops and no herds. Our first concern must be finding permanent settlement."

Jirom straightened up, his mouth a grim line. "*Beysid*, there is no place in the empire where we could safely settle. Perhaps if the Akeshians fall into civil war, the situation might change."

Horace shivered as a sudden chill enveloped him. His eyesight dimmed, and he had to hold onto the edge of the table to keep from losing his balance. He saw the massive stone pyramid from his dreams. Blinding light spilled from the doorway at its base. The invisible pulling returned, urging him to follow. Then the vision was gone, leaving him shaking and nauseous. With a mumbled, "excuse me," he left the chamber.

Alyra caught up to him at the top of the tunnel. "Are you all right? You're trembling."

"I just needed some air."

She peered into his eyes for a moment, and then nodded. "It's just as well. There's something I need to tell you."

The tone in her voice made his stomach tighten.

She took a deep breath and then let it out in a rush. "I've been given another mission."

"What does that mean?"

"It means I'm leaving."

He stared at her, not sure how to respond. His first reaction was anger, that she could do such a thing without talking to him first. Fear leaked into his heart, that what they built was all a sham and now she was abandoning him. Finally he was deluged with cool detachment as he considered how this might help him make his decision. "All right."

"Is that all you have to say?"

"I support your decision." He sighed, letting his anxiety drain away. "Alyra, you've been right all along. You're a spy, and a damned good one. So whatever you decide to do, I support it all the way."

She didn't say anything for a few seconds. When Horace reached out, he felt her shoulders shaking. "What's wrong?"

"I was afraid to tell you. I didn't think you would understand."

"This is what you were born to do, Alyra. You'll fight until every slave in this empire is free. I respect that. We all have our roles to play."

She grabbed him in a tight embrace. He hugged her back.

"What about you?" she asked. "What are you going to do?"

She didn't add *after I leave*, but it hung between them anyway. He thought back to his dream, or vision, whatever it had been. He could still feel it calling in the back of his mind. "I don't know."

He bit down on his tongue as the lie slipped out. *It's just a small lie. I don't know exactly what I'll do, although I have an inkling. . . .*

"I have to get back to the meeting," Alyra said, her voice clear again. "Can we have dinner together?"

A shiver passed through Horace, stronger this time. He ignored it and focused on Alyra. "That sounds good. See you then."

He listened as he started back up the tunnel to the outside, thinking she would say something else, but there were no sounds except for the soft tread of her feet as she went back to the table. Relieved, he went out.

As the council broke up, Jirom caught up with Emanon at the top of the tunnel ramp. "Hold on."

Emanon turned halfway around and waited. "I've got to check on the watch stations."

"I need to talk to you. We have to finish this."

"What's to finish? Everything is settled. We're lying low, just like you wanted."

"Just for now, Em. We don't have the strength to undertake a major attack. At least until the Blades return."

"There was no 'we' in that decision either, Jirom. You sent those mercs off without consulting me."

Jirom's teeth ground together as he counted backward from ten. "I didn't think I needed your permission, Em. I thought I was free to run the combat units on my own. That's what you said when you offered me command."

"I didn't think you were going to scatter our forces from here to the sea."

Jirom glanced around to see if anyone was overhearing their conversation. Seng and Ralla were talking at the table, but everyone else had left. "We need allies. Even counting the new recruits, we can field less than five hundred fighters. That's not enough to win this war, and you know it."

Emanon shook his head. "But a cause like ours loses momentum with every day we sit here. People set down roots. They get comfortable. They start thinking that mere survival is enough. When that happens, the idea of risking their lives for a notion like freedom becomes almost unthinkable."

"I'm not going to let that happen. These men need time to develop. It doesn't do us any good to toss them into battle half-trained. I'm trying to build an army."

"Time is a luxury, Jirom. Giliam was right about that. We can't last long out here. If the empire is distracted, then now is the best time for a big attack. We throw everything we have at the softest target."

Jirom clenched his hands into fists but kept them by his sides. This was why he had never sought a command position. He didn't have the patience. "Risk everything on one roll of the bones?"

"Damn right."

"Em, we're not ready yet. We have to wait. At least until the Blades return."

"You never should have let that old wizard go with them," Emanon grumbled. "You're too attached, and it's affecting your judgment."

Maybe, my love. But you're the one pushing us to run before we can even walk.

Jirom held out a hand as Emanon started to leave again. "Wait. What are we going to do about the civilians? Giliam may be annoying, but he represents a lot of people."

"This is *our* rebellion, Jirom. Those people are only alive thanks to us. If they can't fight, or won't, then we drop them off at the next stop."

"We can't just abandon them."

"Then leave them here or cut them loose." Emanon shrugged. "It's all the same. This is what comes with the big chair, Jirom. You make the tough calls, and you don't look back."

"So when my lover questions my decision to send scouts to Omikur, I should . . . what?"

"Tell him to shut his gorgeous mouth and get to work."

"So shut your mouth and get to work, soldier."

Emanon threw him a half-hearted salute and started up the tunnel again. Jirom called after him, "I'll go walk the perimeter with you."

"I'll be fine. Go check on the recruits. They need a strong hand."

As Jirom watched his partner leave the tunnel and walk out alone into the bright light of day, a memory flashed through his mind, of the night long ago when his sister had discovered him and Tabir fumbling with each other in youthful passion by the riverbank. He had chased after her, begging her not to say anything, but she told their father anyway. He and Tabir were exiled from the village. Jirom recalled walking away from his life with nothing but the clothes he wore, his hunting spears, and a package of food his mother had tearfully packed for him wrapped in an old blanket. His sister had stood by their father and the rest of the village elders, stone-eyed and not deigning to even wave good-bye.

Tabir had been a mess. He cried during the exiling ritual and cried harder as they trudged away into the brush. Tabir went out into the world empty-handed. His mother had packed him nothing, and he hadn't yet earned his spears. Jirom recalled how he'd felt bad for his young lover at that moment, how he had wanted to protect him, take care of him. Then how his heart had broken as Tabir turned and ran back, heedless of his cries to stop, back to the village. Jirom never knew if the tribe had killed him, or driven him off, or let him stay in shame. He just kept walking, off to start a new life.

Tabir of the kind eyes and gentle heart. He hadn't thought of him in years.

Jirom waited a couple of minutes, and then headed to the training fields.

CHAPTER FOUR

"**G**o get something to eat," Horace said as they approached the southern side of the chain's largest hill. A series of shelves and niches formed a crude ladder up the sheer slope. "Or grab some sleep."

Gurita leaned on his spear, and Jin stood beside him, striking a similar pose. "We're fine, sir," Gurita said. "You go on with your pondering. We'll be here when you come down."

Horace started up the hillside. The exertion felt good with the sun at his back and the open air. His anxiety lessened as he reached the summit. The hilltop was weathered and bare. Two guards stood watch.

Heat penetrated the soles of his boots as he walked over to the only spot with any shade, a small patch of stone under a thin overhang on the north side of the hilltop. He sat down and crossed his legs. The stone had a natural indentation like a saddle that made for a comfortable seat. He had found this spot a couple of weeks ago and had taken to coming up here whenever he needed some time alone. It was peaceful with an excellent view of the desert. Best of all, no one bothered him.

His last words with Alyra lingered in his thoughts. Sometimes talking with her made him more confused, but she wasn't the problem. He couldn't believe these powers at his disposal had been designed only to kill and destroy. There must be more to it than that. And these visions that plagued him day and night. What did they mean? They felt as if they contained messages, but he couldn't understand them. If doom was truly coming, what was he supposed to do?

The desert view—the dunes rolling under a flawless azure sky, the scattered lumps of rock thrusting up from the sand like nuggets of red gold—brought him some measure of peace. Certainly more than the close underground confines of the camp. Down in those tunnels, time seemed to stand still with the hours feeling like days and the days passing with frustrating sluggishness as the stone walls closed in tighter around him every moment until he couldn't breathe. . . .

BLADE AND BONE

Horace inhaled the dry desert air and let it out. It was time to begin.

Closing his eyes to narrow slits, he listened to the wind blowing across the hilltop. With each breath he focused on feeling it fill his lungs, and then a long exhalation that left him empty. Inhale and exhale, slow and steady. With each breath he slipped deeper into a calm state. As the outside world faded from his consciousness, he heard a slow rhythmic beat. Heavy and solid, it sounded like the beat of a giant heart.

As his power had grown, he'd begun to see the world differently. The elements of the *zoana* were vibrant and alive all around him, every moment of the day. Sitting here, he felt it rising up through the rock beneath him and floating in iridescent ribbons in the air around him, dancing at the edges of his vision as if inviting him to pick them up, and the temptation to be constantly embracing their power could sometimes become almost too much to resist. Meditation helped to sharpen his attention, and it also provided a relief from the stresses of his new life.

He was following a strand of Imuvar through the breeze, just playing with it to practice his control, when he felt the beckoning call tug again. It pulled him out toward the desert, far to the north. He shifted his mind's eye toward that direction, but all he saw were sand and sky. An endless ocean of nothingness.

A distant voice whispered on the wind, too low to make out, but it reminded him of the dream where he had walked the streets of the old city. Then, suddenly, he was there again. He stood on the ancient stones of a street with squat, angular buildings on either side. Horace held out his arm, feeling the sun beaming on his skin, just like in the real world. Ahead of him, the avenue opened into the now-familiar open plaza at the heart of the city. The massive pyramid towered above the skyline, drawing his gaze. What was it about this place that drew him back again and again? Was this his imagination of a perfect Akeshia?

A chill ran down the back of his neck as thunder boomed overhead. Black clouds rolled across the sky, blocking out the sun. Horace shivered as a cold wind swept around him. He gagged as he breathed in a foul odor. It reeked like moldering decay.

The sound of crashing water made him look beyond the pyramid. Huge black waves battered the city walls, cracking the stone and washing over the battlements. Horace took a step in that direction, wanting to help but not sure how. He reached for his *zoana*, but he couldn't find it. His *qa* was gone. The impotence yawned inside him like a bottomless pit.

Give me my power back!

He awoke with a start, opening his eyes. Dark clouds had gathered on the northern horizon while he was lost in the trance. A stiff breeze beat against him. As Horace started to get up, a flash of movement caught his eye from out on the desert floor. Shading his eyes, he looked closer. Shapes ran across the dunes. Hundreds of them, racing toward the hills. They ran low to the ground, sometimes dropping to all four limbs like animals, but they appeared to be people, with long, lean torsos and wisps of hair wriggling in the wind.

One looked up, and the blood slowed in Horace's veins as he saw the black orbs in their sockets. A sinewy jaw stretched opened in a silent shout as the invaders leaped forward in a ragged mass.

He reached for his power and sighed with relief as the *zoana* filled him like a river of molten iron. He had no idea what these approaching things were, but he could feel the malice radiating from them even at this distance. The itch told him that sorcery was involved, and that was all he needed to know. He wove an interlacing matrix of Imuvar and cast it between the invaders and the chain of hills. A small twister touched down amid the dunes, gathering speed as its tightly funneled winds spun faster and faster. The gusts tugged at Horace's clothes as he watched his magic work. He expected the creatures to scatter as it approached them, or perhaps even fall back in a haphazard retreat, but they charged right into the sandstorm as if it didn't exist. Horace held his breath, waiting to see them thrown back by the violent winds. The air left his lungs in a rattling gasp as the creatures appeared on the near side, scurrying faster. More were coming behind them.

The rebel sentries had spread the alarm. Fighters were emerging from the network of caves. Horace worked another sorcery as fast as he could, forcing the threads of *zoana* into the pattern he wanted. He thrust out his hand, and a blazing red sphere arched down from the hilltop. It detonated in the midst of a cluster of invaders, unleashing a torrent of fire that reached as high as the hill where he stood. Horace didn't hear any screams. Then a cold finger scraped down his spine as the creatures emerged from the fire, running forward even as their flesh burned off in flakes of black ash.

Horace swallowed the coppery taste that flooded the back of his mouth. He couldn't believe what he was seeing. No living thing could have survived those flames. The chill returned, much stronger this time, as he recalled the rumors about the *Manalish*'s invincible army.

Out on the desert plain, more of the enemy were closing in, racing past the dwindling inferno. They moved faster as they came nearer. Horace was contemplating another large-scale attack when the first peals of thunder shook the skies. The thunderclouds had rolled in with startling swiftness.

Horace sent multiple threads of the Kishar dominion down into the sand at the base of the hill. The material was denser than he expected, a few dozen feet beneath the surface, but he was able to shift it around. When he was ready, he searched for his first targets. A group of a dozen or so creatures was coming in fast from the northwest. Horace picked a spot in front of them and waited. A drop of sweat rolled down his nose to hang from the tip. When the invaders crossed the spot, he struck. The sand opened up beneath them, forming a hole more than twenty feet across and a hundred paces deep. Their fingers clawed for purchase as they slipped down the funnel he'd made. A moment later, he closed the chasm, and the sands covered the spot as if nothing had happened, leaving no sign of the creatures.

He was choosing his next targets when a crack of thunder echoed directly overhead, startling him. All of a sudden, the *zoana* poured out of him, leaving him empty as the tide of black clouds rolled over his position.

Down below, the first invaders reached the camp. The rebels had set up a line of defense among the rocks. A flight of arrows and spears rained down. A few creatures dropped, but the rest came on, leaping over the barricades. Behind them, many of the fallen creatures climbed back to their feet and rejoined the fight. Horace clenched his hands into tight fists, trying to find a solution.

He turned to the nearest sentry, who was staring at the scene below. "Go find Jirom! Tell him we need to pull back."

As the soldier hurried away, Horace considered his options. The rebels were grappling with the first wave of invaders in close quarters. They leapt onto the rebels like beasts, tearing with claws and even using their teeth. Another group was climbing the north face of the hill, bounding from hand-hold to handhold. Horror infested him at the sight, but he couldn't do any-thing more from up here.

Before he left the hilltop, Horace summoned more *zoana* and sent it tum-bling down the slope beneath him. Stones and heaps of newly formed gravel descended the hillside, sweeping away a dozen creatures. He sent another landslide of broken rock sliding on top of them for good measure and then turned away.

He half-climbed, half-slid down the ladder of handholds of the southern exposure. He had to find a way to stop these things before the camp was overrun. He just hoped it wasn't already too late.

Jirom ran up the sloped embankment along the western sweep of hills. The alarm bell echoed throughout the camp, accompanied by the shouts of fighters hustling to their stations. He and Emanon had planned for an attack on the base, but part of him marveled that it was actually happening. *Out here with nothing but sand and scorpions for days in every direction. How in the Seven Hells did they find us?*

As he reached the top of the bank, he looked across the dunes for tell-tale flashes of metal armor, but there was nothing to indicate an army was approaching. He frowned at the dark clouds hovering in the north. A storm was the last thing they needed. Then he spotted movement to the northwest. Several dark shapes moved across the sands. His initial instinct was to take them for hyenas, but they were too big. The way they moved was almost rep-tilian, fast and jerky.

"What are they?"

Emanon had appeared beside him. His lover appeared ready for a fight, almost eager.

BLADE AND BONE

"I have no idea. But they're coming this way. Fast."

More shapes moved in the distance, scores of them. The lump in Jirom's stomach threatened to rise. These were no animals, and not men either. At least, not any longer.

"I've already initiated the defense plan." Emanon hefted his spear. "Let's see how well they bleed."

They joined the western command post. A chest-high bulwark had been built out from the hillside. Fighters were arrayed along the barrier with weapons ready.

Sergeant Mamum came over with a salute. "We're all set here, Captain. Ralla's squad is on the southern flank in case they try sweeping around us, but we'll hold them here."

Jirom scaled the bulwark for a better view and cursed when the first wave of attackers leapt over the crest of the nearest dune. He drew his blade and hesitated. His first instinct was to jump out and be the first to meet them, but he had new priorities as commander of the rebel forces. Gritting his teeth, he dropped back behind the protection of the earthen shield.

"I almost thought you were going to charge straight into them," Emanon said.

"I thought about it."

Flashing his wolfish grin, Emanon moved down to the left anchor of the line. Jirom stayed put. He didn't have to wait long. In less than a minute, the first attackers reached the bulwark. Up close, they were even more unsettling. They had once been people, though they were now rank and filthy, some wearing hardly any clothes at all. Their skins were various shades of mottled gray. Some were so gaunt that their tendons stood out like cables under their leathery skin. However, what disturbed him the most was their faces. Black eyes glared from the bestial expressions racing toward him. It was as if their humanity had been ripped away and replaced with something demonic. Several of his fighters gasped or swore.

"Stand tall," Jirom commanded. "Fight together as one."

He was there to meet the first group of attackers to reach the bulwark. They leapt over it like a pack of wild dogs, and his tulwar cleaved into the chest of the frontrunner. When it dropped to the ground, he started to turn away, but the feral creature grabbed his leg with sharp claws and tried to pull him down. Jirom swung hard, shearing into its face, but the thing wouldn't relent. Its flesh was like thick hide. Black spittle dripped from its mouth as it tried to bite into his calf. Finally, Jirom pinned the thing's head to the ground with his foot and chopped with his tulwar until the blade severed his enemy's neck. As its head rolled free, the thing finally twitched and lay still.

The wind was picking up when the next wave came over the wall. Jirom chose his target and brought his tulwar down in a two-handed chop straight through the thing's forehead. The skull exploded in chunks of brown-and-black matter as the creature crumbled to the sand.

Jirom drew a breath and almost choked on the stench. None of the attackers bore weapons, but they didn't need any. Their clawed fingers ripped through leather and flesh as easily as if tearing papyrus. They seemed to feel no pain and no fear, and they fought on after receiving vicious wounds that would have dropped a normal man in his footsteps.

They all came from the northwest so far, but he didn't place much stock in that. If the enemy was smart, there would be another force coming from a different direction. Maybe more than one. And he had no idea how, or even if, they could counter such thrusts. His men were pushed back step-by-step by the tide of savage attackers. The only thing preventing a full-scale rout was their superior armor and the discipline he and Emanon had instilled. Still, it was only a matter of time before they broke.

Jirom was running to assist a squad of skirmishers trying to hold position against a half dozen things when one of his men dropped. One of the enemies grabbed the fallen fighter by an arm and dragged him behind the line. Jirom leapt after his fighter. There was no logic to his reaction, only a visceral response to the idea that a fallen brother would suffer further indignity after he had made the final sacrifice.

He cut into the hunched back of a thing as it tried to crawl over a skirmisher's shield. The blade of his sword bit into the creature's spine with a loud thwack like chopping into deadwood. Bits of bones came loose as he wrenched his blade free, but the thing didn't react. Mouth gaping, it continued its attack on the rebel fighter. Jirom aimed higher and swung with both hands. The vertebrae at the back of the creature's neck shattered as the steel blade cut through. Its severed head rolled down its shoulder to thump on the ground amid the churning feet.

The skirmisher nodded his thanks and turned to aid a comrade, even as Jirom plunged after his downed man. He had to cut through two more things before he reached the place where the corpse had gone missing. Three creatures were crouched over the body, their heads bobbing, jaws moving in chewing motions. Revulsion surged through Jirom at the sight. He speared one thing through the back and flung it away. He was raising his blade to strike at another when a sudden motion caught his attention. The fallen fighter's body convulsed as if it had been kicked from underneath.

Dread uncurled in Jirom's gut as the rebel thrashed on the ground. Surely he had been dead. His throat had been torn out. Viscera hung from his torn-open stomach, but the rebel was moving of his own volition. Jirom's gaze focused for a moment on the young man's shaved head. The flesh of his scalp writhed as if thick, ropey worms were squirming underneath the skin. Then the rebel opened his eyes, and black orbs stared out of those bruised sockets.

Jirom's entire body locked in place as the thing that had been his fighter stood up with jerky movements like a newborn foal taking its first steps. The other creatures had backed away from it, with its blood still wet on their lips. Jirom couldn't tear his gaze away from the horrifying scene.

Suddenly, the things all turned, including his former fighter. Jirom staggered back a step as his muscles unknotted from the paralysis that had gripped him. Part of him wanted to retreat, to get away from these monsters. With a growl, he shoved those thoughts aside and strode forward to meet the things with his sword raised.

They leapt at him, filthy hands reaching, bloodstained teeth gnashing. He severed a lower jaw and chopped into a bony pelvis. As he twisted away from their claws, yanking his blade free in a spray of brown gristle and stringy flesh, Jirom searched for the old familiar rage in his heart, his boon companion through so many battles. His savior and his curse. He yearned for its wild freedom, its blissful release from all cares and responsibilities. The primal focus of life and death. Yet it would not come. He slashed and cut his way through the knot of creatures, dismembering them one by one, and although he was at turns horrified and disgusted by what he saw, the rage remained beyond his grasp, walled off to him by an intangible barricade.

He almost swung out of instinct when a hand grabbed his arm. Pivoting with his sword upraised, Jirom stopped in mid-swing as Emanon stood behind him. His lover pointed to the west. Jirom followed the finger with his gaze, and his grip on his tulwar tightened. More of the things were coming. A lot more. They were still a long way off, but he knew right away his fighters couldn't withstand such an onslaught. Not after what he had just seen. Jirom knew what he had to do, even though he was loath to admit it. *Emanon's going to skin me alive.*

Jirom grabbed Red Ox by his arm. "I'm ordering a full retreat. Go spread the word to the squad leaders. We'll hold here until the civilians are loaded. Go!"

Ox nodded vigorously before he dashed away. Jirom shouted after him, "And someone find Horace!"

Alyra jumped out of the way of a pair of horses led by a young girl as she exited the command cave. The alarm bell bonged overhead. An attack? Out here? She couldn't believe the Akeshians had found them. *Unless we have spies among us. I expected that. It's exactly what I would do if I were on the other side.*

People filled the training yards. Families huddled together, looking around for guidance. A few fighters darted through the yard, possibly carrying messages for their commanders, but most of the people she saw were civilians.

She looked for *Beysid* Giliam. He was supposed to be in charge of these people. Yet after several minutes of failing to find him, she took the matter into her own hands. She had little idea of what Jirom and Emanon had planned, but if this was a real attack, then the only sound tactic was retreat. If the rebel leaders had other ideas, they could countermand her when they showed up. Until then, these people needed a sense of purpose before panic set in.

"Everyone!" she shouted. "Head to the eastern cavern!"

Blank faces turned to her, so she shouted her command again and waved. "Get moving!"

Slowly, a few people started in the right direction. The eastern cavern was where the rebels stored their food and water, and it was also where the evacuation would be staged. She only hoped the soldiers there were prepared to receive hundreds of frightened people.

"Mistress Alyra!" Dharma rushed over. The young woman carried her two-year-old son, Zak, in one arm and dragged five-year-old Lea with the other. A large bag was slung over her shoulder.

"It's all right," Alyra said. "Take a breath. Help me get everyone to—"

"It's Arbu, Mistress Alyra," Dharma sobbed. A young widow, she had met her new husband, Arbu, during the flight from Erugash, and they had married just a month ago. "He's been training with the fighters, but I'm afraid I won't see him again. He's not ready."

Alyra took the younger woman by the shoulders with a firm grasp. "No one is ready for this, but we all have to be strong for each other. Arbu is fighting for you, so you have to be strong for him. All right?"

Dharma nodded, wiping her eyes on Zak's sleeve. "Yes."

"Now go and find a sled."

After sending the young woman on her way, Alyra spent a few minutes herding others in the same direction. Everyone wanted to know what was happening, but she could only tell them what they already knew. The camp was under attack. She longed to go find Horace, but she knew he would be in the thick of the fighting. Besides, she had something else she needed to do.

Alyra pushed her way through the crowd and ducked into the narrow cave leading down to the living quarters. Her travel bag was already packed. As she grabbed it from the corner of the small chamber she had shared with Horace for the last couple of months, her gaze touched on the pile of clothes on his side of the room, and the feather-stuffed pillows he had pilfered for them on a raid. Their cohabitation had been a brief bright spot in her adult life, both simple and poignant in its intimacy. Horace didn't demand much from her but warm company, and that liberty had allowed her to relax for the first time in a very long time. Now, it felt as if she were waking up from a pleasant dream. Time to get back to reality. *Leaving never gets easier.*

She slung the bag's strap over her shoulder, checked the knife at her belt and the second blade tucked into her right boot, and picked up her all-weather cloak. She was ready to go. As she stepped out the curtained doorway, Alyra almost ran into Mezim hustling down the tunnel.

"Pardon me, Mistress Alyra! Is the master within?"

"No, I thought he was outside," she answered.

"Perhaps he is. I went to find him, but things were so chaotic." He puffed as if fighting for breath. "Well, I suppose I shall wait here for him."

Alyra took his elbow. "Definitely not. We're abandoning the camp."

"Abandoning? Then it really is that bad."

"Yes. Come along. I'll go with you."

Alyra tried to steer him up the tunnel, but he twisted out of her grasp. "I must get some things from my room," he said.

She looked into his eyes. "Mezim . . ."

He met her gaze without flinching. "I will wait for the master. However long that takes."

She knew she wasn't going to budge him without getting someone to carry him away. "All right. Be well, Mezim."

"And you as well, mistress."

She patted him on the shoulder before she hurried up the tunnel. The south yard was all but empty when she emerged from the cave. The sky had turned dark, with ominous storm clouds racing in from the north.

The easternmost cavern was the largest underground space in the hill chain, stretching almost a hundred paces from end to end. Teams of horses were being tethered to wooden sleds down the length of the cave, two animals to each sled. The sleds themselves were piled with supplies and people. This was the escape plan, a mad dash across the desert while the fighters held the enemy at bay.

Dharma spotted her from the back of a sled and waved, welcoming her to join them. Alyra waved back but kept walking. Part of her yearned to stay and help these people, but she already had her mission. *We all have to be strong for each other.*

BLADE AND BONE

When she got to the horse corral, Alyra slipped under the rope barrier. She found one already saddled, a tall white mare with a brown mane. Without hesitating, or giving herself time to reconsider, she swung up into the saddle. Drawing her knife, she sliced through the cordon rope, and then put heels to the animal's flanks. The mare leapt forward as if she had been waiting for this moment.

Shouts echoed behind her, but Alyra bent lower over her stolen steed's neck and kept riding. A fierce wind wrapped around them as they raced out of the cavern. Leaning down against the mare's powerful neck, Alyra turned her to the south and let her run.

Gurita caught Horace by the arm as he slid down the hillside. "Whoa, boss. What's going on?"

"We're under attack." Horace paused a moment to catch his breath. "Have you seen Alyra?"

"Saw her this morning at chow. Why?"

Horace had expected to see a crowd of people in the practice yards, but they were mostly empty. One thing he had to credit Jirom and Emanon; they were good at organizing people. The alarm bell continued to ring as he looked around. Where would Alyra have gone? Down to their room?

He started in that direction when he heard shouting coming from the western edge of the hills. Picking up his pace, Horace came around the skirt of the last hill in the chain when he saw the battle. The invaders had already reached the western bulwark. The rebels still held the wall, but they were being pushed back even as he arrived.

High above the battlefield, black clouds extended across the sky, broken only occasionally by shafts of dwindling gray light. He spotted Jirom in the thick of the fighting. Dread gripped Horace's insides as he noticed movement among the dead, piled behind the enemy lines. Corpses—some of them horribly mutilated—twitched or rolled back and forth as if possessed by spirits.

Then, one by one, they lumbered back to their feet. Ice slid through his veins as the recently revived dead joined the enemy ranks, clawing and gnashing their teeth like rabid animals.

Fighting back his fear, Horace turned to his guards. "Gurita, you have to find Alyra. Make sure she gets out safely."

"Jin will go," Gurita said. "I'll stay with you."

"No. You both go. We're leaving."

The guards glanced at each other, and Horace clapped them on the shoulders. "Go! We'll meet up later."

Gurita clearly wanted to argue, but he and Jin obeyed. As they ran back across the yards, Horace went to the rebels' defense.

He arrived at the bulwark using gusts of Imuvar to shove back the nearest invaders climbing over the wall, but the things were everywhere. He could see it was only a matter of minutes before they overwhelmed this position. Looking again to Jirom, Horace had an idea. If his conjurings didn't have much effect on these creatures, he had to take a more direct approach. He knelt and placed his fists on the ground. Calling upon the Kishargal dominion, he encased both hands in sand and then solidified them until they were rock-hard. His body hummed with the *zoana*, making him feel invulnerable. With a grunt, he jumped up and rushed into the melee.

As a rebel staggered back from the line, his face bleeding from rows of deep scratches, Horace leapt into the breach. His first punch connected with the forehead of a creature coming over the barricade. The thing's head whipped back as if it had run into a stone wall. Another enemy appeared in its place. Horace blocked its claws with his left gauntlet, the talons scrabbling uselessly against the hardened sand, and lashed out with the right with all his strength. His punch crushed the creature's chest to the sound of snapping ribs and sternum. It collapsed to the ground where it was trampled by its ghoulish comrades.

He still didn't understand what these things were. They were obviously human, but something had changed them. Twisted them into perversions of their former nature. He suspected dark sorcery, and that line of reasoning offered just one suspect. Astaptah. Only the queen's former vizier had the power and inclination to do such a thing. *He's created a monstrous army for himself. And if I don't find a way to stop them, they'll swarm over the rebels like locusts.*

After several minutes of fighting, he and the rebels cleared the western bulwark of the last invaders. Breathing heavily, Horace watched as Jirom's fighters moved among the dead, severing the heads from every corpse to make sure they stayed down for good. Horace could feel the residual sorcery emanating from the fallen corpses, could almost see it leeching into the ground with the thick, dark blood that spurted from their wounds.

Jirom stood a dozen yards away, leaning against the bulwark. Horace released his hold on the *zoana*. "We have to abandon the camp. More are coming."

Jirom straightened up, wincing a little. "I already gave the order, but we need more time."

Horace looked out over the desert. An approaching horde dotted the dunes. How could he stop so many? "Get going," he told Jirom. "Take everyone with you. I'll buy you the time you need."

"Horace, no offense, but you'll need help. I'll stay with a platoon."

"No." Horace turned back to him. "I'll do it alone. It won't be safe for anyone else to be near me when it happens."

"When what happens?"

"Just trust me, all right? Get your people to safety. And do me a favor. Look after Alyra, all right?"

Jirom hesitated for a few heartbeats, but then he nodded with a grim smile and strode away. The rebels left Horace alone at the bulwark, which was completely silent now except for the low whisper of the wind across the sands.

He hopped over the earthworks and headed into the desert, straight toward the enemy. He climbed the slope of the nearest dune, contemplating what he was going to do. He glanced up at the sky and roiling clouds. Thunder rumbled ominously. Did he dare call upon the storm's power? Did he have any other choice? Chaos storms were unpredictable, but it was the only thing he could think of that might stop these things.

When he reached the summit, his courage almost failed him. The invaders were closer than he had realized. Putting them out of his mind, Horace looked back over his shoulder. A line of horse-drawn sleds raced away to the east. Though the distance was too far to see, he imagined Alyra was on one of those sleds, being carried to safety.

Bolstered by that thought, he threw open his *qa* and grasped power within. Spurred by desperation, he folded the *zoana* over and over into an intricate pattern of Imuvar and Shinar. The magic soared high into the stormy sky. A heartbeat later, titanic peals of thunder shook the hilltop. The sky split open as the storm clouds began to swirl. The winds whipped about faster and faster until a hazy funnel began to form. Horace grabbed tight onto the tether of *zoana* still attached to him and braced himself, but nothing could have prepared him for the monumental force that seized him as the tornado touched down west of the hills. It felt as if the power was trying to tear him apart from the inside. He didn't dare try to close his *qa* now. There was no telling what the *zoana* would do if he cut it off, so he held on and tried to ride the tempest of energy.

Out on the desert plain, the tornado whipped up a cloud of sand and loose stone. Horace gritted his teeth and fought to hold the funnel in place. He could not allow wanton destruction here. He was aiming to slow down the enemy's reinforcements, hoping to give the rebels time to get away. But already the windstorm was threatening to break free of his control. Its foot dragged across the dunes, leaving a tortured trough behind it. But his plan seemed to be working. The invaders had been shoved back.

Horace was just starting to feel confident when a powerful jolt ran through him from crown to heels. His vision dimmed as his thoughts became muddled. The sand dunes vanished before his eyes, replaced by a long street of dusty stones. The great pyramid rose at the end of the road, highlighted in eerie green fire against a backdrop of ink-black sky. Strange stars wheeled overhead. Horace shook his head. This was only a dream. He had to wake up. The power surged within him, threatening to break free of his control. Desperate, he bit down hard on his tongue.

The fire-etched pyramid wavered before his eyes. A bright light shone from its base, like sunlight streaming into a dark room, and then Horace was flung away as the magic left him. He blinked as the desert returned. Thunder boomed overhead as he tried to remember where he was and what he had been doing. The powerful winds he had generated were dying down. Horace looked out to the northwest. His connection to the *zoana* had been severed as neatly as a knife slicing a string. He hadn't felt such power since . . . Erugash.

A woman stood facing him from atop a high dune about a quarter mile from his position. A black shroud clung to her slender frame, her face obscured under a deep hood. Horace squinted against the sand-laden winds swirling around him. Even from this distance, she drew his attention like a flame. There was something familiar about her.

The woman raised her arms, and a sudden wind blasted Horace, nearly knocking him off his feet. Shielding his eyes from the flying grit, he reached for his power. The *zoana* balked, but he forced it to his will. Feeling the magic sizzle in his veins, Horace formed a crude defense of hardened air around himself. A powerful gale buffeted his shield. He tried to form a counterattack, but the woman—whomever she was—sliced through his connection to the *zoana* again, and suddenly he was choking on sand as his barrier disintegrated. The wind battered him to his knees. He couldn't hear above its droning wail.

He looked to the east and couldn't see the rebel sleds. They were away. Relieved, Horace clawed for his magic. His *qa* resisted for a moment, but he coaxed a trickle of power from it. He used it to do the only thing he could think of. He wrapped the magic around himself and vanished inside it.

His sense of balance faltered as the world disappeared. Then he was falling upside down. Horace reached out for something to grab, but there was only air as he dropped. A moment later, he landed on his back on a hard, carpeted surface. Biting back a groan, he summoned a small ball of light.

The illuminance showed he was back in his underground room. His stomach felt unsteady, but Horace fought down the nausea as he scrambled to his feet. He had little time before the enemy arrived, and he sure as hell didn't want to face them down here in the tunnels. Just the thought of it triggered flashbacks to the catacombs under Erugash.

He looked for a bag but couldn't find one, so he grabbed the bedspread. He threw in a spare tunic and breeches and an extra pair of sandals. He considered the three tomes from the royal archives, but they were far too heavy. As much as it pained him, they would have to remain behind.

Then he spotted a bulging waterskin and a small sack beside the doorway. Going over, he found the sack held half a dozen hard rolls, some strips of jerked meat, and a handful of prickly berries. Had Alyra left them for him? Not willing to besmirch good fortune, Horace stuffed them in his makeshift bag as well. Then he took one last look around. He didn't think he'd be back here again, but it had been home for a short while. Just one in a long series of temporary homes.

A small trinket hung from a hook beside the bed. It was the sea turtle carving he had given to Alyra, now hung on a leather thong. He tucked it inside his belt. *I'll return this to you when I get back.*

Now that the rebels were safely away from camp, it was time to leave. But he wasn't going to join them. Not yet. His dreams and the strange yearning they induced had convinced him it was time to track down their source. And he had an idea where to start.

He was still looking around the room for anything he might have forgotten when a dull thud shook the caves and the ground shifted under his feet. Another thud echoed farther away, also making the caves shudder.

Horace was about to summon his power and form another transportation weave when someone entered the chamber behind him. Horace whirled around and saw Mezim standing there. "Mezim! What are you doing here? You're supposed to be with the civilians."

His former secretary bowed his head, as if in shame. "I wish to go with you."

"Mezim, I'm not . . ."

"Not what?"

Horace glowered at the man. This was exactly what he didn't need, but the rebels were long gone by now and he had already made up his mind. "I'm not going after the others. I'm striking out on my own."

Mezim nodded as if this was perfectly normal. "Of course, sir. I will assist you, as always."

A third thud struck the hills, this time closer. The ceiling groaned as if about to buckle.

Horace motioned for Mezim to stop talking. "Fine. We don't have time to discuss it. This entire place is going to fall down around our ears. You can come along if you want, but don't blame me if things get hairy."

Mezim hefted his own packed bag. "I'm ready to go. You won't regret this."

I hope not. Or we'll both be unhappy.

Mezim turned toward the exit shaft, but Horace stopped him. "We're not going that way."

Mezim frowned but stood quietly as Horace closed his eyes. He wasn't sure how to do this with two people.

"I hope I don't kill us both," he said under his breath as he fashioned the magical weave.

"What?" Mezim asked.

Without answering, Horace unleashed the power. Mezim's fingers dug into his arm as the darkness surrounded them.

Alyra shielded her eyes as she turned around in the saddle. The rebel camp was miles behind her, lost from view behind the sea of dunes, but the dark stain of the storm clouds remained etched above the horizon. A fierce wind blew at her back, seeming to urge her onward, but she didn't need its coaxing. She wasn't worried so much about what lay ahead of her as what followed behind.

They were still there. Two specks on her trail. She had noticed them shortly after fleeing the camp. Though she had pushed her stolen steed as hard as she dared for the last hour, the specks remained in view. Were they bigger now? The idea that they were rebels coming to capture her for taking a horse was ludicrous, but who were they? Her worst fear was that they were more of those shambling dead things. She imagined them riding on skeletal steeds, then pushed the thought out of her mind. Whomever they were, it was evident she couldn't outrun them unless she was willing to kill her horse, and she needed the mare too much to risk that. So that left her only one option.

She scanned the plain ahead for a suitable place. A pile of low boulders with some protruding scrub brush broke the plain to the south of her. She headed in that direction, urging her steed to pick up the pace.

When she got there, Alyra slid off the mare and led her behind the rocks. She quickly tied the reins to one of the forelegs and allowed the horse to roam, hoping she would stay in place. Alyra had little in the way of weaponry. She had her knives and whatever she could find or make. She cut off a long strip of cloth from the edge of her riding cloak. With the makeshift sling and a few egg-sized stones in hand, she climbed the boulders. Settling on her stomach, she squinted against the wind and waited.

The waiting seemed to last forever as the two shapes slowly approached. She could make out for sure they were men, both wearing light armor. One had a spear slung over his back; she could see the shaft bobbing above his shoulder. Both wore long cloaks with the hoods pulled down, and scarves wrapped around their faces. Neither appeared to be one of those living dead things, which made her feel a little better. Still, she kept tight hold of the sling just in case.

Then she rose up for a better look. *No, it couldn't be.*

But it was. The riders were Gurita and Jin, Horace's bodyguards. She recognized the distinctive red cord wrapped around the shaft of Gurita's spear and the fringe on the chest of Jin's leather vest. Alyra slid down from her perch.

She was waiting with her horse when the two guards rode up. "He sent you, didn't he?" she asked.

"Aye," Gurita said, pulling down his scarf. "He ordered us to make sure you got away safely. Hell of a mess back there."

She looked behind them. "Where is he?"

"Honestly, milady, we don't know. He was heading off to the fight when we saw him last."

"Well, as you can see, I'm fine. So you can go back and tell him—"

"Pardon me," Gurita interrupted. "But that storm behind us don't show no signs of letting up, and there's the matter that we're out here in the middle of the most gods-forsaken part of the empire. I'd say none of us is safe right now."

BLADE AND BONE

Jin pulled down his scarf, too. "It's true. All the rebs were running for their lives when we left. Ain't nothing to go back to."

"Unless you know where they're heading," Gurita added. "Then the three of us could meet up with them."

"Not a chance," Alyra replied. "I've got someplace else to be. And if you try to force me—"

Gurita shook his head in the slow, thoughtful way he had. "No, ma'am. Those aren't my orders, and I wouldn't follow them if they were. We're just here to keep you safe. So if you aren't going back, well then I guess that means we're coming with you. Are we riding on some more, or do you want to hunker down here for a spell?"

Alyra sighed. Damn Horace anyway. She put her foot in the stirrup and swung back onto her horse. "No, we keep riding."

"Jin's a good scout, milady, if you tell us which direction we're heading."

"Southeast."

Gurita nodded, and Jin rode out ahead.

Alyra turned her steed around to follow. "I hope you gentlemen brought enough food and water."

Gurita patted the bulging saddlebag hanging from his saddle. "Aye. We've got enough to get us to Thuum, and then some." When Alyra shot him a sharp glance, he shrugged. "We might not talk much, but our ears work just fine."

Alyra nodded, hiding her smile. "I'll remember that."

CHAPTER FIVE

Pumash stared at the dregs of wine at the bottom of his cup. From his seat upon the royal throne, he lifted his bleary eyes. "Deemu!"

He waited for what felt like an eternity before shuffling feet sounded in the outer hallway. The tall doors of the throne room opened, and his servant appeared.

"Deemu, I'm out of wine."

"Yes, Master. I shall fetch more from the cellars. But I have news from the city."

The city? Oh yes, Hirak. The city I helped destroy. It's all dead now, infested with walking corpses. Welcome to the glorious future of the empire.

"What news?"

"The, ah, army grows restless, Master."

Pumash sat up. "They aren't inside the palace, are they?"

"No, Master. I spied them from a window. They have finished their conquest of the city, and now they linger."

"Linger?"

"Yes, Master. They roam about aimlessly, almost as if they are walking while asleep."

Pumash resumed his slouch on the throne. "Well, what can you expect, Deemu? They must be tired after their exertions, no? Perhaps they would like some wine."

"I don't believe so, Master. They appear to be waiting for something. A sign, perhaps. Or a command."

Pumash stood, suddenly wanting to see the city. He swayed on his feet as the alcohol played havoc with his balance. "Attend me, Deemu."

Gathering up the hem of his new silk robe, borrowed from the late king's personal wardrobe, Pumash stumbled down the dais. Deemu was by his side at once, supporting him with a rounded shoulder. "Where are we going, Master?"

BLADE AND BONE

Pumash considered the palace's central tower, but then thought better of attempting that long climb. "To the north balcony."

Their journey seemed to take an inordinately long time, but they finally reached the terrace jutting from the palace's northern face, which enjoyed a fine view of the lower city and the broad sweep of the Typhon River. However, it was nighttime, and so the only view Pumash could enjoy were a few scattered stars in the sky overhead. Beneath him, the city was dark and silent. *It is a necropolis, home to only the dead. The very restless dead.*

When he concentrated, he could feel them. Like cold spots moving along his skin. He was connected to these living corpses. Possibly because he had created them. *No, the* Manalish *created them. I was only the vessel. I am not to blame.*

Suddenly, he didn't care about the dead things roaming the city. Or anything else for that matter. He just wanted to wrap himself around a jar of wine and drink this nightmare away.

"Master, what shall become of us?" Deemu asked.

"I wish I knew. Perhaps we shall survive this war, but I fear no one else will. Perhaps it will be you and I at the end, the last living souls presiding over a dead world."

"Master, I do not think I wish to see that world."

"Eh? But what can we do, Deemu? We are merely flotsam caught up in a great whirlwind. We must go where it takes us, or be smashed to pieces."

Deemu clutched at his sleeve. "But you are a great man, Master. Born to a noble family. There must be something you can do."

Pumash shook his head. The wine's effects were wearing off. "Such things no longer matter in this new world we're creating. Great or small, rich or destitute, we are all slaves now." He patted his servant's shoulder with affection. "Don't worry, Deemu. The *Manalish* will watch over us."

As long as we serve his purpose. Is this how my property felt, back when I was the powerful man Deemu remembers? Did they live in perpetual fear of my whims? How vexing to be on the other side of the leash. And yet, so fitting, eh?

Pumash shivered as a frigid chill enveloped him. Feeling the arrival of a new presence, he turned to see a figure stepping out of the shadows behind them.

"He sent *you*?" Pumash asked. Even in his befuddled state, he heard the plaintive whine in his voice and was ashamed. He struggled to control it. "This is my city."

Her sepulchral voice battered his ears. "This city, like all of the empire, belongs to the great lord, Pumash. You should be mindful of your place."

"And you should be mindful of yours, witch."

He tried not to stare as Byleth approached with slow steps. Her long shroud trailed on the floor behind her like a decayed wedding veil. Pumash braced himself, but she merely came over to stand at the balcony beside him. A strange odor followed her. Not horrible like he expected, but a mélange of old earth and ancient dust. The smells, he realized, of a tomb.

"I have been sent with a new mission for you, Lord of Hirak."

It took him a moment to realize she was being coquettish. Shocked, he tried his best to recover with grace. "From *him*?"

"Who else? None other can command such as you or I. Not anymore. When the great lord rules this world, we shall stand at his side, viceroys of a new empire. An eternal empire."

A dead empire, you mean.

"What is his command?" he asked, impatient to be away from her.

"Gather your forces and move east. You have been given a new target."

Of course. Epur is next, and then Yuldir. He will move upriver until he reaches the capital.

"What forces?" he asked. "I have a city filled with feral corpses. How can I move them?"

"They will follow you. You are bonded to them, and they to you. Can't you feel it?"

He kept his face impassive. "I feel nothing."

"That is too bad." She placed a withered hand on his chest. "So warm. I can feel the blood rushing through your veins."

Pumash tried to pull away, but something held him in place. Her sorcery. It forced him to stand rigid as she caressed him. He hissed between gritted teeth. "Why doesn't he send you to do his work? You were a queen once. I would think leading an army would fall under your purview. Or is your arrival here an effort to mitigate some failure elsewhere?"

BLADE AND BONE

The invisible force turned into a vise that closed around him with an iron-hard grip. Pumash gasped as the breath was squeezed from his lungs. His vision went blurry.

Byleth leaned closer until she was near enough to kiss him. She smiled, and he shuddered at the sight of her rotting gums framing bone-white teeth. "Try not to think too much, Pumash. Your role is to serve, but you are not irreplaceable."

"As you command," he managed to utter.

Suddenly he was free. He grabbed the balcony railing to keep from falling to his knees.

"There," she said. "That's better. We all play our parts in this grand scheme. I have my own mission." Her eyes blazed brighter, like flaring embers within their dark sockets. "He was promised to me, and I shall have him before all is finished. Alive or . . . otherwise."

Then the blaze died down, and her smile returned. "Now off with you, General. You have another city to conquer."

As she sauntered back inside the palace, Pumash sagged against the railing. His heart was pounding, and his lungs heaved like a pair of bellows. Yet he was alive. He should have known better than to push her. *She had a reputation for being dramatic when she lived, and apparently death has not cooled her temper.*

But who was this person who filled her with such rage? A former rival? Some *zoanii*, perhaps. Pumash was just glad it wasn't him. The undead queen would make a fearsome enemy.

Deemu shuffled over. "Are you all right, Master?"

Pumash stood up to his full height, ignoring the twinges in his chest. "Quite. Pack up my things, Deemu. It appears that we'll be heading east."

"Yes, Master. But may I ask, how will you convince *them* to follow?" The old man gave a significant gaze down at the dark city below.

Pumash had been considering that as well. He thought about going down to the creatures in the streets and making a grand pronouncement to rally them, but of course that was ludicrous. Byleth had said they were bonded to him. He would test that theory.

"Let me worry about that, Deemu. You worry about packing the wine."

He allowed Deemu to support him as they walked. His legs were still a little wobbly after tangling with that damned witch queen. He didn't relish the idea of being under her control. Having one diabolical master was enough. But everyone had a weakness. He just needed to unearth hers. "And find out where all the other living servants have gotten to. I hope the army hasn't devoured them."

"That would be a shame, Master."

Something shook him from the sweet escape of oblivion. Three Moons opened his eyes. He was lying in a nest of ratty blankets, half-buried in sand. Jauna stood over him, nudging him with her foot.

"The captain says it's time to get up, old man," she said. She had a weird way of talking out of the side of her mouth. Three Moons usually found it sensual, but right now he wanted to punch her in the face.

"How long till dawn?"

The sky was black. A few stars twinkled through the canopy of clouds. He smelled a storm coming but no rain.

"An hour. No more. Get up or get left behind."

As she turned away, Three Moons was tempted to send a noxious little spirit squirming into her breeches and leave her itching for a few days, but he didn't feel like expending the energy. Groaning, he threw off the blankets.

They'd escaped Omikur four days ago and hadn't stopped running since. West into the deep wastes, that was where Captain Paranas had led them. Three Moons hadn't complained. Anyplace was better than the mausoleum that Omikur had become. Two days ago, thinking themselves safe, they had stopped for an extended rest and paid the price. Screams awoke them in the twilight hours to the horror of another attack. The wights from town had followed them, appearing from the wastes like the fiends of hell.

The rest of that night and the next day were a painful blur as the

BLADE AND BONE

company ran. They froze at night and roasted during the day. But last night the captain had been forced to call for another rest. Even the Bronze Blades had limits.

He'd awoken half-expecting to be fighting for his life again. War was like that. It beat you down, made you feel all used up inside. And those were the good times.

Something nagged at him. A feeling of expectation. He tried listening to the spirits, but they remained silent. Maybe smelling the death surrounding the Blades. Maybe smelling worse to come. He had an inkling, and he didn't like it one bit.

Three Moons walked over to where a cluster of brothers were passing around dried jerky and water bottles. Food and water were going to become a problem soon. They'd only brought enough for the journey to Omikur plus a few days' extra, intending to resupply at the town. He took a couple bites and washed it down with tepid water, wanting to vomit the entire time. But the food revitalized him enough to seek out the captain.

Paranas stood on a long ridge east of the encampment with Niko. Three Moons joined them with a curse. "You should be ashamed, Cap. Making a man of my advanced age trudge all the way up here just to have a word."

Niko nodded to him, but Captain Paranas continued his survey of the desert to the west. It all looked the same to Three Moons. "What do you want, Moons? You should be resting. It'll be a long march today."

"You trying to kill me?" Three Moons thought about spitting on the ground but decided to save the moisture. "Don't answer that. But tell me this. What's your plan?"

"We're working on that, Moons."

By the grim line of Niko's smile, Three Moons guessed their plan was more of the same. "More running and hiding? Sure, that might work. But it seems these fiends following us don't want to let us go."

The captain turned his head, and Three Moons could see the exhaustion and worry etched into his hard-bitten features. He looked twice his actual age. "I would love some suggestions from our company wizard."

"We find a place to make a stand."

Captain Paranas glanced at Niko, who said nothing. "And where do you suggest we do that, Moons? You see any defensible positions around here? No, just sand and scrub for a hundred leagues in every direction. Except back in Omikur. You aren't suggesting—"

Three Moons shook his head. "No use going back there. But I feel something coming, Cap. There's a new scent on the wind."

"Dammit, Moons. Sometimes I just want to toss you and your spirit buddies into—"

A high-pitched whistle turned every head. Three Moons squinted. The western sentries were sprinting back from their positions.

Captain Paranas swore in three languages. "Get out ahead of us," he commanded Niko, who whistled to his scouts and darted off.

Three Moons followed after the captain back toward the camp. "We can't run much farther, Cap."

"Don't I know it? But what other choice do we have?" Captain Paranas stopped and pulled Three Moons close by the arm. "You keep close to me, hear? We're going to need you if we hope to see tomorrow."

The Blades left at once, following the scouts east across the sands. Three Moons started cursing under his breath after the first hour, and it developed into a continual litany of complaints and epithets from then on. The sun came up, painting the desert sky in a riot of gorgeous colors. Three Moons cursed each and every one of them. Every few steps he turned to steal a glance over his shoulder. Dark specks dotted the dunes behind them, pursuing fast.

"How do we stop these things?" Ino asked, hobbling beside him.

Three Moons shook his head. "They won't ever stop. They're infected with sorcery of the darkest stripe. Wights don't get tired. They don't feel pain. They'll run us down to the ends of the world."

"Thanks, Moons," Ino snapped. "You made me feel so much better."

Three Moons looked ahead. They needed a safe place to hole up, but the captain was right. There was no safety to be found out here. Then he spotted a small red blotch against the sand, about three points southeast of their course. Willing to grasp at any shred of hope, he hurried up the next dune ridge. As he crested the hill, he found it again. A tired sigh spilled from his lips. A mound of stone stood a couple of miles away. It looked big enough to provide some defensibility. He ran ahead to find the captain.

Paranas saw him coming. "Yes, we saw it, too. I already sent Niko's squad ahead to check it out." He opened his canteen and took a sip. "So what do we do when we get there? Dig in like ticks and wait for the end?"

"What else can we do? We fight to the last man."

"You know, Moons, you're a fucking riot."

They ran for their lives. The creatures were closer now. Close enough for Three Moons to make out their ravaged features whenever he looked back, which he tried to avoid doing, but he couldn't stop himself. He breathed another sigh when they finally reached the stone mound. It was higher than he'd dare to hope, the peak about fifty yards above the desert floor. The scouts were already scaling the steep sides.

Please, hallowed spirits. Let us find a ledge we can defend. Give us that much of a chance to survive this day. We'll worry about tomorrow when it comes.

Ignoring the burning in his lungs, Three Moons was attempting to climb the foot of the hill, and finding little purchase, when Niko shouted down from above.

"There's a cave!"

Captain Paranas didn't waste any time. "Find perches for defensive fire! Niko, post a lookout on the summit."

As the Blades climbed, Three Moons struggled. *You spirits love to fuck with this old man, don't you?*

Then Pie-Eye was there, taking his arm and hauling him up the rock. It was his bad arm that the wight had half-pulled out of the socket back in Omikur, but Three Moons kept quiet as the younger mercenary hoisted him up the side of the hill. After several minutes of grunting and swearing, they reached the cave opening. The entrance was cramped between two large boulders, but Three Moons guessed it had once been much wider. A massive lintel stone over the entry had been pushed back as the outer stones shifted. Based on the sand and soil packed into the cracks between the rocks, it must have happened a long time ago.

Captain Paranas was standing by the opening. "Niko and Jauna went inside. We'll wait for them before we set up a defense."

"Cap, I think this place was built by people." Three Moons pointed out the carved lintel. "But fuck me if I can tell you how long ago. Centuries, at least."

"Maybe it was a refuge for nomads. Whatever it was, it's lucky we found it. We can defend this narrow opening for one hell of a long time."

A chill ran through Three Moons. He reached out for the spirits and found nothing at all. Not even echoes of their presence remained. *Because of the creatures coming behind us? Or is it this place?*

"Cap, better let me have a look first."

He didn't want to go inside, but this was his job.

Niko reappeared before the captain could reply. "It looks all clear. There's a pretty big cave just inside the opening, and then a long tunnel down to another chamber below. It's damned weird."

"Weird how?" Captain Paranas and Three Moons both asked at the same time.

"The upper room is normal enough, but that lower one is full of jewels."

That got several heads turning.

"Jewels?" the captain asked.

But Three Moons didn't wait to hear any more. Bracing himself, he went inside. Behind him, he heard both the captain ask if there were any other entrances to the cave and Niko's negative response, but his mind was focused ahead. Visually, the interior cave appeared normal enough, but Three Moons's otherworldly senses were buzzing. He couldn't say precisely why. The spirits he was familiar with—the imps of the earth and sky—were gone, but something else dwelled here. He was certain of it. Whatever it was, it was as alien to him as a fire sylph would be to any of his nonmystical brothers and sisters. Everything was so still and quiet in here it almost felt like a temple.

Soft footsteps announced Jauna before she arrived, coming through the tunnel on the far side. She held a closed fist in front of her.

"Is that the way down to the jewel cave?" he asked.

"They aren't jewels," Jauna replied. "They're crystals. Biggest ones I ever saw, though."

She held out her hand and opened her fingers. Nestled in her palm was a handful of white sand. It shimmered like diamonds in the dim light of the cave. "The floor is covered with this. I was going to show the captain."

As Jauna left the cave, Three Moons approached the tunnel. His eyes had adjusted to the gloom, and now he detected a bluish glow from the passage mouth. It descended from the cave at a sharp but steady decline. At least, he thought it did. His vision had become watery since glimpsing the white sand Jauna had shown him. Reaching out to the walls of the tunnel for balance, he continued forward.

The footing was smooth but not slick. The same with the walls as he made his way down the tunnel, which opened after about fifteen paces into another cave much larger than the one above. As Jauna had said, it was filled with crystals. Massive crystals, some as big across as tree trunks, lined the walls and ceiling. The light came from across the chamber, where a section of the wall shimmered between two great crystal plinths. Walking across the white sand floor, he felt a strange buzzing all over his body, and a faint tone played in the air just at the edge of his hearing.

He stopped in front of the glowing wall. The section was wide enough for two men to walk abreast. He could see shapes moving within the glow. Was this some sort of window? And if so, where was he looking into? He had the feeling of powerful forces at play.

"No way out, Moons?"

Captain Paranas entered the cave, his boots crunching on the sand. The flame light of the candle in his hand danced in every faceted surface in the chamber. "It's a shame. But I guess this is a lovely place to die."

Three Moons had to force his gaze away from the shimmering window. "Bad outside?"

"They're gathering at the bottom of the hill. It's like they're waiting for something. Maybe nightfall."

"They didn't seem that smart before," Three Moons replied. "More like wild animals. Maybe it's this place. Maybe it wards them off somehow."

"I came down to find out if you had any ideas. Can you make another way out of these caves? Make like a secret tunnel or something?"

"Not here, Cap. The spirits are quiet. Maybe they're affected by whatever is keeping the wights at bay."

"So we stay trapped in here until the water runs out?"

Three Moons indicated the shimmering window. "This might be something we can use."

"A blank wall? I asked if you could dig us a way out, Moons."

"Blank?" Three Moons studied the shimmering section of wall again. Yes, he saw it now. The glow was coming from the spirit realm. He was the only one here able to see it. "There's a portal here, Cap. I might be able to get us through."

Captain Paranas came over to stand beside him. "A portal to where?"

"I have no idea. And I don't think there's any way to find out except by going through it. So we have a decision to make. Stay here in the cauldron . . ."

"Or leap into the fire." Captain Paranas pulled his sword an inch out of its scabbard and slammed it back home. "We'll stay put to see what happens outside. If things look bad, we can always—"

"Captain!" Pollo came running down the tunnel, slipping in the sand as he reached the cave. "They're coming!"

"Shit." Captain Paranas headed toward the exit. "Moons, you get started on that escape plan. Double time."

Three Moons turned back to the glow, patting his fetish bag for inspiration. He'd heard tales—legends, really—of enchanted doorways. According to the stories, they could lead to faraway places or even other worlds. That was the danger. You never knew where you would come out. What if this doorway led to the bottom of the sea? He might drown his brethren with one fateful step. *Still better than getting torn up and eaten by those things outside.*

When the first Blades came down the tunnel—Raste and Ivikson carrying Ino between them—Three Moons reached out to the glowing doorway with his inner spirit. It was a strange sensation as he made contact, like dipping his hand into a bucket of slime. But he felt the link establish between this world and the realm beyond the portal.

"Go on," he told the others. "Step through."

Raste, Ivikson, and Ino just looked at him. Three Moons waved his hand and growled. "There's a door here between the big stones. Trust me. Just walk through. And be ready."

BLADE AND BONE

"For what?" Ino asked.

"I've got no fucking idea," Three Moons replied. "Now get in there before I give up and leave you all here to die."

With wary glances, the three approached the wall, poking the air in front of them. When the points of their weapons passed right through the wall, Three Moons breathed a little easier. It had worked. The Blades seemed encouraged, too. All together, they took the last step. And vanished.

Three Moons concentrated on maintaining the connection as more Blades rushed down into the cave. Most were bleeding from scratches and gouges. Three Moons ushered them through the portal just like the others. Finally, Niko and Jauna came down, their knives coated in dark blood.

"Where's the captain?" Three Moons asked. The strain of keeping the portal open was starting to drag on him.

Niko went to the doorway and stopped, studying it. "He said to go through."

"Fuck that," Three Moons said. "No one gets left behind. Go get him."

"I'm not disobeying—"

They all looked back as footsteps pounded down the tunnel. The captain emerged, his free hand wrapped in a bloody cloth. "Get your asses through that doorway!" he shouted as he crossed the cave.

Niko and Jauna dove in.

Captain Paranas stopped where they had stood. "Those things won't be able to follow us, will they?"

Three Moons shook his head. "Not when I stop feeding the connection."

With a nod, Captain Paranas grabbed him by the arm and took a long step into the wall. Three Moons gasped as an icy cold sensation enveloped him. He was ripped from the captain's grasp and tossed back and forth like a child's doll. Every nerve in his body burned. It wasn't exactly agony, but it didn't tickle either. Then a great black wall rushed toward him. He flailed, unable to stop his forward momentum as he plunged into a space of utter nothing.

CHAPTER SIX

Horace's tongue lolled inside the chalky cavern of his mouth, unable to produce the tiniest iota of moisture. His lips were cracked and painful, and when he moved them, thin flakes of skin tore free and dropped into his mouth.

Blinking against the ruddy sunlight, he shaded his eyes as he took in the landscape in a long, slow turn. There was nothing but sand and sky in every direction.

"Here, sir. You need to drink."

Mezim leaned over him holding a stoppered gourd. As always, the former secretary was prepared.

Horace sipped the warm water. "Well, it looks like we landed in the middle of nowhere."

Mezim took the gourd back and re-stoppered it. "I would rather not experience that mode of travel again anytime soon, sir."

Horace had to agree. He didn't remember much from the journey. Just bits and pieces of memories. A vast darkness with no sense of up or down. A spinning sensation. They awoke in the middle of the night, stretched out on the cool sand like a pair of clubbed fish. He drifted in and out of consciousness during the night until the sun came up again. That had never happened before. Now he felt used up, and his head throbbed as if he'd been up drinking all night. *So where in hell are we? And where do we go from here?*

He reached for his bag, but Mezim grabbed it first, slinging it over his shoulder. "So where are we going?"

"I'm not sure. Someplace I saw . . ." He felt foolish saying it out loud, but Mezim had a right to know. "Someplace I saw in a dream."

He expected Mezim to scoff, but he merely nodded as he picked up their meager belongings. "Dreams can carry powerful messages. Especially the dreams of a *zoanii*."

Let's hope so, or this is going to be a really bad decision.

BLADE AND BONE

There were no landmarks to guide him. The sun was near its apex, pounding down with merciless heat. As he turned, the pulling sensation returned. It came very clearly from a certain direction, what he thought might be north, or roughly north. It was as good a direction as any. Forcing his legs to move, he started walking.

Mezim followed quietly, and Horace enjoyed the silence. It gave him time to think about their predicament. With every step, he felt more and more foolish for embarking on this journey. He had no idea where he was going, or why. Nothing except vague hints from a dream. *But a dream that felt as real as anything I've ever known.*

After some time, Mezim spoke. "Sir, I believe we should travel for as long as we can tonight—if we haven't reached our destination, that is—and then sleep during the day to avoid the worst of the heat."

Horace nodded, hardly listening. "That sounds good."

"Not that I'm complaining, of course, but we will need fresh water after tomorrow, too. Our food can last for three days if we ration it."

As Mezim continued to drone on about the logistics of their journey, Horace did his best to ignore the man, part of him wishing he had left him behind. Then he felt guilty because Mezim would probably be dead if he had. *Or even worse, one of those living dead things.*

Those creatures, he felt, were the key. He'd never heard of such things. He stopped walking. *No, wait.*

That had been a line in one of his tomes. *The Gahahag Codex*, if he recalled correctly. It said something about the day when "Death shall die" and the departed would return to the world of the living. At the time, he had just passed it off as more Akeshian superstition. Disturbing perhaps, but ultimately useless. But in light of what he'd just witnessed, he saw those words in a different cast.

Was this all part of some ancient prophecy? Was it the end of the world? The True Faith he had been brought up to believe had many references to the world's final fate, when the blessed would be lifted into the bosom of the Almighty while the damned would be left behind to wander a barren earth forever. If that was truly happening, how could he—or anyone—possibly stop it?

Pausing atop a low dune, he took a drink and dribbled some water over his face. This reminded him of his first trek across a desert, not long after he had washed up on the shores of Akeshia.

He was thinking about his friends, especially Alyra, when he saw something far out ahead of him. A faint shimmer lying against the horizon. A mirage? Perhaps, but it was the first interesting thing he had seen since landing in this wasteland. And it was in his path.

"What is that ahead, sir?" Mezim asked, coming to stand beside him.

"I don't know, Mez. But we're going to find out."

They quickened their pace.

Distances were tricky in the desert. Landmarks that appeared close could actually be many leagues away. Mountains on the horizon could take days to reach. So Horace was surprised when he climbed the next dune only to find the distant shimmer had solidified into a cluster of buildings behind a low wall. He marched straight toward them, leading Mezim.

As they got closer, Horace began to make out individual structures. The buildings were made of light-brown stone. The wall surrounding the settlement was broken in many places, and the city itself was much larger than he had first guessed, possibly rivaling Erugash in sheer land mass. He saw no people or animals, no sign of farms around it. Just sand dunes piled against the bits of wall and filling in the tumbled-down places.

The closer they got, the more certain Horace became that this was the source of the pulling sensation he'd been feeling. But who or what wanted him here? These ruins would be an ideal place for an ambush. Suspicious, he eyed everything as a potential threat. The sooner he figured out what was calling him, and why, the sooner he could get back to the rebels.

"Mezim, do you have any idea where we are?"

"No, sir."

"Stop calling me that. Just call me Horace."

"As you wish. Do you intend to enter this place, s—Horace?"

"I don't know yet."

Horace spotted a gate and angled his path toward it. Rather than a fortified barbican, this gate was just an open stone archway, broad enough for four or five large wagons to pass through at the same time. Tall pedestals on either side of the arch were topped with lumps of pale yellow stone that might once have been statues.

He stopped at the threshold. A wide avenue stretched before them, cutting through the city. Rectangular foundations and the rounded pediments of towers were scattered through the ruins, none of them higher than a single story, their jagged remains poking up like broken fangs.

Mezim stood beside him. His face and half-shaved scalp were slick with sweat. "Sir, I have a bad feeling about this place."

Horace felt it, too. His senses were especially alert, taking in every detail with a sharpness that almost made him dizzy. He could see the grains within the stonework around them. He smelled the sharp tang of the wind and tasted the aridness like tiny bubbles popping on his tongue.

"There are stories among the nomads," Mezim went on. "About ruined cities rising out of the desert. They are said to be home to unspeakable horrors that lay in wait for unsuspecting travelers."

Horace was only half-listening. Looking down the dusty avenue with the shattered buildings on either side, he realized this was the city from his dreams. A pile of stone rose above the low skyline at the center of the ruins. Worn and weathered by the ages and half-covered in sand, yet he could still make out the edges of the great pyramid. In his imagination, the city appeared as it once had been, as he had seen it in his visions.

Steeling himself, he stepped through the archway. As his foot landed on the ancient fired bricks of the street on the inside without incident, he continued onward, and Mezim followed.

They passed by a variety of buildings, from small domiciles to expansive structures with many sections that could have been anything from palaces to schools. Another difference from Akeshian style he noticed was a lack of exterior decoration. The remaining walls were plain brick and stone without flourishes.

Studying the architecture of the remains, Horace recalled something he had heard, perhaps from Mulcibar. "Weren't there more than ten city-states, once?" he asked.

Mezim nodded as he gazed into the ruins. "So I learned at the civic academy. Long ago, when the Kuldeans ruled this land, there were many cities. If this place is one of them, it could be hundreds of years old."

It certainly looked old enough to qualify. The stones still standing were eroded by time, their hard edges smoothed and pitted. Knowing what a desert storm could do, Horace had no trouble imagining these structures had withstood the onslaught for centuries. Yet, something else about them nagged at him. Some of the ruins leaned askew as if they had been knocked off their original foundations. He wondered if some cataclysmic event, such as an earthquake, had destroyed this city and doomed it to the sands.

He was gazing through the open doorway at the foot of a collapsed tower when a flicker of movement farther down the avenue caught his attention. Too quick for him to make out, it had moved in and out of his sight, darting behind a corner. Horace squinted. Was this the ambush he'd feared? He looked around for hidden attackers, but there was nothing.

"Sir, perhaps we should—"

Horace shushed him. "Follow me, but not too closely. Just in case."

He headed in the direction of the movement. Every block or two Horace caught a glimpse of fluttering dark cloth ahead like the train of a cloak or a loose dress. At first he thought the color was red, but then it was deep purple when he saw it again a few seconds later. The person, or persons, stayed one step ahead.

Horace was considering how to end this game of chase when he and Mezim came to a huge plaza at the center of the city, dominated by the titanic mound he had seen from afar. It was even more impressive up close. Its size rivaled the royal palace in Erugash in sheer area.

A woman in a long robe stood before the pyramid with her back to them. Her hair hung down in a long curtain of tight braids. Before Horace could think to approach, her voice called out, breaking the stillness of the ruined plaza.

"I've been waiting for you, Horace Delrosa."

She turned, and Horace was struck by her austere elegance. Not a classic beauty like Alyra, or a ravishing goddess like Byleth had been, she reminded him of a figure from an old portrait. Her robe was secured at the neck with a silver pin.

BLADE AND BONE

Horace stepped forward, still leery. "And who are you?"

"I was the last master of the Shinar. Until now."

Powerful gales laden with sand scourged them, lacerating flesh and reducing visibility to mere feet. The sky was hidden behind a blanket of gray, a gloom that Jirom suspected would last until morning and perhaps beyond. He stopped his push against the battering gusts and turned around.

Though he couldn't see it in this sandstorm, he knew the column of horse-drawn sleds stretched out behind him in a ragged line. They struggled past him at a steady limp, the people onboard wrapped in their heaviest clothing against the flying sand. His fighters were positioned in a wide cordon around the civilians to protect against more attacks. They had been hit twice since escaping the camp. The first had been a brief probe with only a handful of those dead things, but the second attack had been a concerted effort. The creatures had almost broken through his perimeter before they were put down. Less than an hour later, the storm struck, obscuring everything in an impenetrable haze.

Now he didn't know if the enemy was right behind them or leagues away. Anxiety ate at his gut, along with the fear that he was leading these people to their deaths. Either slowly wasting away in this desert or swift destruction at the hands of the living dead, there appeared to be no safe paths anymore.

To make matters worse, there was no sign of Horace. Jirom had hoped he would catch up to them in the hours after they fled the camp. After all, the convoy of sleds was moving at a snail's pace in this storm. At this point, he had to consider the possibility that Horace was dead. Guilt pierced his gut. They should have been better prepared. *How could anyone prepare to be attacked by the dead?*

Emanon appeared out of the storm. He removed the portion of his headscarf covering his mouth as he approached. "The man I was looking for."

Jirom grunted. "I figure we've come about two leagues. Maybe a little more. But we should be able to cross another two before full night falls."

"About that." Emanon spat to clear his mouth. "I'm thinking we should send the women and children ahead. Regroup the men here."

"Regroup for what? We don't know which direction they'll attack from next. Last time it came from our flank. These things don't seem to be slowed by this windstorm the same as us."

"Not a defensive measure. A counterattack."

Jirom's stomach almost heaved at the idea. Before he could reply, *Beysid* Giliam found them. The representative was draped in a heavy cloak. "I continue to voice my disagreement, Commander!" he shouted over the wind. "We must stop and make shelter until the storm blows over! My people—"

"Are under our command," Jirom said. "But if you want to wander off alone without our protection, then I can't stop you."

The *beysid*'s eyes tightened into narrow slits. "You would abandon us in this wilderness? That is not what we expected when we agreed to join this expedition. I'll remind you that assurances were made."

Jirom knew exactly what assurances Giliam was talking about. Not long after arriving at the hill camp, the *beysid* had engineered what amounted to a mass petition, calling for the rebels to vow to protect them until they could find a permanent settlement. To forestall a potentially disastrous fight, Jirom had agreed to take the vow, against Emanon's objections. He should have known it would come back to bite him in the ass.

"To hell with your assurances," Emanon grumbled. "We're marching on, and that's that."

Jirom was too tired to play diplomat. "It has to be done, Giliam. These creatures will run us down eventually. We need shelter, yes, but we also need to slow down the pursuit. We'll split our force into smaller units."

"Smaller units?" the *beysid* asked. "Wouldn't that make us more vulnerable to the enemy hounding us?"

"Yes, but smaller groups are more mobile," Emanon said. "If we split up and take different tracks, the creatures will be forced to either divide their force, too, or let most of us slip away."

The *beysid* turned around to look behind them. "Most of us. But some will be caught." He turned back to face Jirom. "And killed."

BLADE AND BONE

He almost sounds like he really cares about these people. Almost.

Jirom reached for his canteen. He took a small swallow, feeling the warm liquid slide down his parched throat. Too soon, he lowered the flask. "It's our only choice if we want to shake them for good."

Giliam stalked off into the sandstorm with the rest of the civilian elders.

Emanon eyed Jirom. "I thought you would fight me on that."

"I was about to, but I can't stand being on the same side as that pompous bastard."

Emanon chuckled, which expanded into a genuine laugh until it was interrupted by a rasping cough. "Damned sand. What are these things that attacked us, Jirom? You've been to more places than me. Ever see anything like them?"

"No, never. They're like monsters out of an old tale. Em, I think I saw . . . when some of our men fell at the camp, they rose back up alive again. Or not dead, in any case. They'd turned into those things. How is that possible?"

"Fucking black magic. Damn all wizards to the lowest hell!" His face softened. "Well, except your friend. Any sign of him?"

Jirom shook his head. "Not since we left. He said he'd hold them off until we got away, but that was the last time I saw him."

Emanon put a hand on his shoulder, massaging his muscles. "He's a big boy. Got an attitude like a royal princess, but he's tough. He'll turn up."

"In the meantime, we have to keep these people safe. We'll set up a tiered system of defense. Outriders, patrols . . . the whole thing."

"That won't be easy in this storm. Our men can barely see two paces in front of them."

"It's a good thing I have the best second-in-command in the world. You'll get it done."

Jirom had something else on his mind, but he hesitated to bring it up. They'd already had one fight about it, and now wasn't a good time. . . .

"What?" Emanon asked.

"The mercenaries."

His lover shook his head, looking down at the ground and the mounds of sand that had piled around their ankles as they stood here. "Jirom . . ."

"When they return, they could be walking into a deathtrap back at the hills, Emanon."

"At this point, we have to assume they're dead. And even if they aren't, we're in no shape to help them. Maybe after we regroup at the rallying point we can start putting out feelers for signs of them."

That was a sound plan, but it just didn't sit right. Still, Jirom nodded. "You set up the rearguard. I'll check the convoy."

They parted. While Emanon jogged back to the rear of the column, Jirom went toward the front. He found Sergeant Halil's platoon at the middle of the pack, spread out to cover both sides.

"Sergeant!" Jirom called out over the storm. "I'll need some of your men to run messages. We're switching tactics."

"What about this fucking storm?"

"We're pushing through, and pray to the gods it covers our tracks."

While Halil called in his fighters, Jirom glanced back to the rear. Emanon had already disappeared amid the flying sand. It felt as if they were separated by a thousand miles.

He was starting to hand out orders when the first cries reached them, coming from the rear of the convoy. He drew his sword. "Sergeant! Send half your unit to keep these people moving! The rest, with me!"

His feet sunk into the sand as he ran. A cold sweat sprung up across his chest and down his back. Even though he knew what he'd find, a shock ran through him when he arrived. The creatures had returned again. A dozen of them were tearing into the straggling sleds. There weren't enough horses to fit two to every sled, so some were only pulled by a single animal, and as a result they fell behind. One sled was tipped over, its horse lying still in the sand. Two small children with their throats torn out lay facedown beside it. An old man was screaming nearby as a corpse thing chewed on his chest. How did these things keep finding them?

Jirom cut down the creature gnawing on the old man. It took several whacks to finally put it down for good, the final cut shearing most of the way through its neck. The victim looked up with vacant eyes. His bare chest was covered with black-rimmed bites.

BLADE AND BONE

"Get to another sled!" Jirom yelled as he helped the man to his feet.

"Jirom!"

He turned to see Emanon, waving his spear from atop one of the disabled sleds. He pointed to a wave of creatures ravaging a group of rebels. They both sprinted to the melee together.

Jirom lost himself in the ebb and flow of the fighting. As he hacked through limbs and slashed open throats, he blocked out everything else. This was what he understood. Then he spotted a familiar face in the crowd. A young man named Finnu, whom they had rescued from the slave pits of Erugash. He'd been one of the first newly freed slaves to volunteer for the fighters. Jirom remembered how proud the youth had been to begin combat training. Now that proud face was pale and crusted in dried blood. His eyes were vacant dark orbs, his mouth an open pit filled with yellowed teeth. Without a moment's hesitation, Jirom separated the youth's head from his shoulders.

He cut down two more of the undead before he found Emanon. His lover was killing a once living woman with long, tangled hair. Exhaustion and futility were written large on his face. "About time you showed up. How are we?"

"Not good." Jirom kicked a blood-spattered corpse out of his way. "I sent the people ahead. Now we run."

"Oh joy." Emanon squinted through the flying sand and grit. "I think this was the last of them."

"You better hope so, or those civilians could be riding into a death trap."

"Isn't it fun being in charge?"

"Fuck you."

They turned and started to jog eastward, following the trail of sleds and picking up straggling rebel fighters as they went. Every few steps Jirom looked back over his shoulder, expecting to see more creatures on their heels. He had to figure out some way to get ahead of them for good, but they just kept coming.

One thing at a time. Let's get past this storm in one piece, and then worry about how I'm going to keep a thousand people alive in the middle of a desert while we're being tracked by an unstoppable enemy. Em's right. Damn wizards to the lowest level of hell.

CHAPTER SEVEN

They sat on sections of a fallen wall, facing each other inside a half-standing dwelling on the edge of the plaza. Between them, Mezim was setting out food from his bag beside a low fire. Horace found himself staring at the woman across from him. He had so many questions, but he didn't want to be the first one to talk. It seemed important to treat her carefully, whether or not her claim was true.

The last of the master of the Shinar. Until now.

Did she mean him? Mulcibar had told him, a long time ago, that he handled the void better than anyone in the empire, but he didn't feel like a master. If anything, the Shinar usually seemed to control him. And he couldn't shake the feeling it was responsible for bringing him here. The dreams and visions, the pulling in the back of his mind, the feeling that he was missing some vital knowledge—they all added up to bring him to this place, at this moment.

After several minutes, Horace finally broke the silence. "What is your name?"

She regarded him with cool, dark eyes. "Names have power. What would you give me in return for such knowledge?"

She had a strange way of speaking. It was Akeshian, though possibly a dialect Horace hadn't been exposed to before. "I have little to offer. I have no country, no wealth, and I left the only people I care about to come here."

The ends of her mouth turned up in a slight smile that reminded him too much of Byleth for his comfort. "Humble and cautious. Yes, you might have a chance."

"A chance at what? Forgive me, but I've had a long day. I'm not in the mood for games."

"I have been sleeping for a long time," she said. "But something woke me. A feeling I hadn't felt in a long, long time. The touch of the emptiness." She paused for a moment. "I dreamt of a battle on the sea. Ensorcelled lightning rained from the sky."

BLADE AND BONE

Her words reminded Horace of the night the *Bantu Ray* went down. The battle with the Akeshian warship. The green lightning. And the sensation of being more alive than he had ever felt before, until he almost drowned. "Are you the one who summoned me here?"

"We have both been summoned, it seems."

"By whom? For what?"

"I think you already know."

Horace couldn't help himself from looking around. The shadows from the cook fire danced on the walls, making him feel as if he were surrounded. "I really don't."

"You are here because this is where it began."

"Where what began?"

"The war, of course."

Horace frowned. "The war against the empire started in the slave camps where the Akeshians train their dog soldiers. No one knows anything about these ruins."

"I speak not of mundane power struggles, but of the eternal war between the forces that create and those that destroy."

"How can something eternal have a beginning?"

"It has had many beginnings, and many endings, down through the ages."

Mezim placed a biscuit and a bowl of porridge beside each of them. Horace picked his up out of habit even though he wasn't hungry. The woman didn't touch hers.

"I don't know anything about that," he said. "I'm not fighting in some grand war between . . ." He waved a hand over his head. "Whatever you said. I just want to learn how to control my powers so I can help my friends."

The woman shook her head as if she felt sorry for him. "You've been fighting this war since the day you were born, Horace. But only now do you begin to see it. At the edges. In your secret dreams."

He sat up. "What about my dreams?"

"They are a bridge between worlds. In dreams you can leave your mortal form and gain new insight, but they are also a portal through which outside forces can affect you. Guard your dreams, Horace, as you would guard your *qa*."

Her answers weren't helping, so Horace tried a different tack. After taking a bite of biscuit and washing it down with tepid water from a canteen gourd, he asked, "What happened to this city?"

"Nagath was one of the thirteen great cities of Kuldea. We called ourselves an empire, but we were more of a coalition of states than a true nation. We traded, we warred, and we elevated the art of sorcery to heights never seen before by man."

"What happened?"

"The gods took notice."

Horace blinked, not sure he'd heard correctly. "What?"

The woman stretched out her legs, crossed at the ankles. "The gods, Horace. They are quite real, I assure you. When we pierced the veil to the Outside, the entities on the other side became aware of us. They came through the gateways we had created, and the results were catastrophic."

"The Annunciation," Mezim whispered.

The woman glanced at Mezim for the first time and gave him a small smile. He turned away to huddle with his bowl of gruel.

Horace shook his head. "What is the Outside?"

The woman's attention returned to him. "It is the source of the *zoana*, which leeches through the veil into our world like water through a leaky dike. However, when we went too far in our explorations, larger gaps were ripped in the cosmic fabric. Sorcery ran rampant, beyond any magi's control. Any but a true master of the Shinar. And when the need was greatest, one such master arose."

Horace tried to control his disbelief, but he knew it showed on his face. "You say that was you?"

"Indeed."

"That would make you . . . what? A thousand years old?"

"It would, if I were still alive."

Mezim moaned into his bowl.

A year ago Horace would have scoffed at her declaration, but he had seen too much since then. He had seen the dead literally get up and walk again. "How is that possible?"

BLADE AND BONE

"I've pondered that myself over these long centuries. Was this a blessing, or a punishment? I've decided that it's equal parts of both, a sacred duty to await the coming of the next master."

"Me?" It sounded odd, coming from his own mouth. He didn't want to believe any of this, but her story answered a lot of questions that had been nagging at him.

"Time will tell." She tilted her head to the side, watching him closely. "You do not trust me."

"Should I?"

Her smile returned. "Of course not. But you would be a fool not to take advantage of what I offer."

Horace wasn't sure he wanted to know the answer, but he asked anyway. "And what's that?"

"The wisdom of my experience."

"So, can you teach me how to control the *zoana*?"

"No."

Horace waited for her to elaborate, but she just looked at him with her dark, mysterious eyes. "Why not?"

"Mastery is about Seeing what lies beneath the surface of things. You must gaze inward, into the core of your spirit."

"You mean my *qa*?"

"That is the doorway."

He considered that while he finished his meal. "I had a *ganzir* mat, given to me by a friend. But I lost it."

"Toys for children. All you need to know is already inside you."

"That's not very helpful," he muttered under his breath.

"Your problem," the woman said, "is a product of your birth culture. You have been conditioned to believe that man and the divine are separate entities. And that man must earn the grace to be reunited with his godhead. However, we are all spiritual beings. The divine dwells within us, guiding our decisions."

"How can that be true? I'm sorry, but it sounds like the god-made-flesh claptrap that these Akeshians believe about their rulers."

"They are right, to a certain point," the woman continued. "But everyone possesses this connection to the spirit realm. Those with the power to control the *zoana* simply have a more direct channel."

Horace tried to understand what she was saying, but he'd never been particularly pious. "So what am I supposed to do?"

The woman stood up. "Your feet are on the path, Horace. You must follow it to the end. You have a gift of exceeding rarity, Horace of Arnos. In time, we shall see if you control it, or if it controls you."

She turned and walked out. When she was gone, Horace felt as if he were just waking up from another dream. Had she been real at all or just a figment of his imagination?

Then he looked down at Mezim, shivering under his cloak. *No, she was real. As real as any of this.*

After checking to make sure Mezim was all right, Horace found a clear space on the floor and bedded down with a blanket. He was exhausted, but his mind was spinning. As he got ready for sleep, he realized the woman hadn't answered any of his questions. Not even her name. That thought stayed with him as he closed his eyes.

Alyra swayed to the rhythm of the cart as she watched the road behind them. Every now and then she reached up to check that her hair was still tucked up into the brimmed hat she wore. Gurita and Jin rode alongside, dressed in old robes over their armor. Between that and their desert scarves, they looked like a pair of shabby nomads. They weren't great disguises, but it was the best she could do on short notice.

Their trek across the desert had been faster than she anticipated. They reached the Akesh River and traveled along its banks until they reached the outlying villages. Finding a wool-seller on his way to the Thuum market had been a stroke of good fortune. She had traded her horse for "new" clothes for herself and her self-appointed guardians, and a ride into the city. She had wanted to sell Gurita's and Jin's horses, too, but the men wouldn't hear of it, with Gurita muttering about the need for a fast escape if plans failed.

Now, after two hours of slow riding, the walls of Thuum rose before them. She understood why Jirom and Emanon had selected this for her target. Though not quite as grand or imposing as Erugash, Thuum was nonetheless a major trading hub between the empire and the northern lands. Timber, silver, and exotic textiles flowed through its gates. King Ugurnazir was said to be a strong, vital man who reigned with a gentle hand.

To her relief, they passed through the city gate without being stopped. Once past the cordon of sentries, Alyra hopped off the back of the wagon and waved her thanks to the trader. He tipped his hat and kept driving along the wide boulevard that served as the city's main thoroughfare.

Gurita and Jin both looked to her as they dismounted. Forcing a smile, Alyra led them into a side street branching off the boulevard.

"So what's the plan, milady?" Gurita asked.

Alyra bit her lip as she looked around. This was a quiet neighborhood with tall, narrow homes packed shoulder to shoulder. Children played among the lampposts and cement stoops. An elderly woman wearing an iron collar walked past carrying two large buckets. "Please, don't call me that," Alyra said in a low voice. "We have to be very careful not to attract attention."

Gurita nodded. "As you say. Jin and I could pose as your brothers."

Alyra eyed their travel-worn garb. "Maybe. But for now just stay quiet. I have to find someone."

"Who's that?" Jin asked.

"A friend."

She started down the street. Before joining the rebellion, she had been a spy for the nation of Nemedia. She may have left that life behind, but she still had a few contacts from those days. People she hoped she could count on. Following half-remembered directions, Alyra wandered the backstreets of several self-contained neighborhoods.

Thuum was laid out a little differently than most other Akeshian cities. The royal district with the palace and official buildings lay on the eastern side, along with most of the temples. The northern skyline was dominated by the Stone

Gardens, a huge cemetery nestled on a long ridge where all the dead of Thuum, from kings and queens to the lowliest slave, were buried. Thuum's patron deity was Apsis, the lord of the underworld, and so its people had constructed this vast monument inside the city walls to honor the deceased. The rest of the city was a maze of streets connecting the various wards of dwellings and businesses.

Alyra noticed signs of storm damage in several places. Cracked walls. Blackened rooftops. Signs of recent repairs. It appeared the stories of increased storm activity were true, at least here. She thought of the rebels and their civilian convoy, and hoped they were safe.

After passing through a lane of coppersmiths, they found a cross street that curved around a row of small houses. Her contact lived nearby, unless she had moved. The last time Alyra had seen Natefi was more than five years ago. She had been placed by the network as a chambermaid in Queen Byleth's palace, but she hadn't been able to cope with the queen's nocturnal activities, so Alyra saw to it that she was reassigned. Now she was hoping Natefi would return the favor, or otherwise her mission was going to be much more difficult.

After circling the neighborhood twice, Alyra finally found the place, a small house at the end of a lane. She knew it by the bright red fence surrounding the front yard.

"Wait for me here," she told the men.

Gurita and Jin exchanged a glance and shrugged. Gurita kept watch on the street while Jin took out a brush and started working on his animal's coat. Thankful they hadn't argued, Alyra entered the gate and followed a path of sunken stones. She raised her hand to knock on the front door but hesitated. Five years was a long time. What if Natefi didn't remember her? Or, worse, wanted nothing to do with her? It was too late now to reconsider. Alyra didn't know anyone else in Thuum. She knocked gently.

A minute passed, and Alyra was just about to knock again—this time with more force—when the door opened. "Natefi?"

The woman inside looked different than the one she remembered. Her hair had been long and gorgeous, often decorated with pretty beads. But now it was tied up under a plain gray head cloth. Though she was a young woman, no older than Alyra, her face was etched with lines around her eyes, and her mouth was pulled down in a tepid frown. Her only garment was a shapeless dress of homespun wool.

The woman peered out. Then her eyes widened, transforming her face once more into the lovely young woman Alyra had known. "Alyra? What are you doing here?"

Then she glanced past Alyra to the bodyguards at her gate, and all traces of joy vanished from her expression. "Are you in trouble?" she whispered.

"They're with me. May I come inside?"

Natefi gave another glance to the guards, and then nodded. The inside of the house was small and mean. The scuffed wooden floor extended back to a doorway that Alyra assumed was the sleeping area. The front room served as kitchen, dining room, and parlor. A small round table sat to one side, and a narrow bench rested across from it. An older woman knelt at the table, rolling balls of dough while a small child, a boy of two or three, sat on the floor playing with clay blocks.

The sight of the boy made Alyra pause. "Perhaps this wasn't a good idea. I didn't know. . . ."

Natefi scooped the boy off the floor and held him close. The child squirmed a little, but his attention was on Alyra. "No, it's fine. Alyra, this is my son Davus. And my husband's mother Irina. Davus, this is my friend Alyra."

The mother-in-law watched with sharp eyes but said nothing as she continued to work the dough.

"Is there someplace we can talk?" Alyra asked.

Natefi put down her son and indicated the back doorway. Alyra followed her into a small sleeping room. Two beds barely fit in the room along with a narrow wardrobe with peeling white paint. The only window was covered with a shade, torn at the bottom.

"Alyra," Natefi said, "I never got the chance to thank you properly for getting me out of Erugash. I can't even remember much about those days, except that they were the most horrible of my life. Thank you so much."

"I was glad to help. How are you doing? You're married?"

"I met my husband not long after I arrived in Thuum. He worked on the docks, hauling cargo and doing odd jobs. He was very industrious."

Alyra detected the note of finality in the woman's voice. "Was?"

Natefi's eyes shimmered for a moment, but then she gave a smile. "Yes, he passed just after Davus was born. An accident while working on a barge."

Alyra placed a hand on her arm. "I'm very sorry. I had no idea."

"No, I'm all right. Having Davus is the greatest blessing of my life. But you're not here to talk about my family. The network sent you."

Alyra took a breath, considering a lie. But she owed Natefi the truth. "I'm not with the network anymore. I'm working with the rebel slaves."

"The uprising?" Natefi's face creased with genuine concern, making her look even older. "Alyra, is that wise? To go against the empire?"

"Probably not, but I'm doing it anyway."

The mother-in-law entered the room, carrying the child. "Natefi, you need to watch Davus. I am going to the market."

Natefi took her son and kissed him on the forehead. Or tried to. The boy leaned away with a coy grin, evading her lips. The mother-in-law glanced at Alyra and then left. The front door closed with a firm sound.

Alyra watched the mother and son, and debated asking what she needed to ask. "Natefi, I need your help."

"Anything, Alyra. Anything you need, I'll do it."

Alyra felt some of her tension evaporate. "Thank you. That means a great deal to me. First, I need a place to stay. Obviously, we won't inconvenience you here at home, but—"

"Don't say another word. Of course, you're staying with us. It's safe, and no one would think to look for you here in the Rows."

"Thank you, but there isn't enough room here for all of us and my guards."

"Where did you pick up those two? They look like trouble."

Alyra lifted her eyebrows. "Oh, they are. But not in the way you mean. Is there someplace nearby they could stay?"

"There's a bunkhouse about a block from here. Day laborers and dockmen use it, mostly. It's cheap and inconspicuous."

"Thank you. This is all a big help."

"It's the least I can do. Listen, I know you can't tell me about your mission, but what happened in Erugash? All we hear are rumors about a new king in the west. Is it true he's conquered Nisus and Chiresh and Hirak, too?"

Alyra kept her face from registering surprise. She hadn't heard about Hirak. "We think so, but there isn't much information coming out of the western empire. This new king has everything locked up tight. That's why I'm here, to find out if his eye is turning toward Thuum."

"As far as Erugash, that's a story for another time. Right now I need to get out of these clothes before they stick to me."

"Of course!" Natefi exclaimed. "Forgive me. You must be tired and famished. I'll get water from the well. It will just take a few minutes."

"I can get it."

"No, I insist. Plus, you shouldn't go out unless you absolutely have to." She touched Alyra's blond hair. "You kind of stick out. Anyway, I can show your men where they'll be staying on the way."

Alyra felt a little guilty letting this woman take care of her, but she was too tired to fight it. What she didn't expect was for Natefi to shove Davus into her arms. "Here. I'll be right back. Davus, be good for Alyra."

With that, the woman hurried out the door, leaving Alyra holding her son.

"Hello, Davus," Alyra said. "I'm your mother's friend."

He regarded her with big brown eyes.

"Well, let's sit down and get acquainted, shall we?"

While the boy picked up a pair of blocks and began banging them together, grinning at her, Alyra considered the next steps of her plan. Her best bet was to infiltrate the circles of power in this city. That meant the nobles and possibly the royal palace. That meant dealing with *zoanii*, which always filled her with apprehension. But Jirom had selected her because she was willing to take those kinds of risks. She considered repeating the palace slave routine but discarded the idea. She didn't have the time for that scenario to play out. No, this time she would have to be more direct.

Smiling at Davus, she fine-tuned her scheme.

Jirom shivered as the cool desert wind swept over him. The moon had not yet risen, but the stars were out in full force, like an army of lights twinkling above them.

He stood between two tall dunes, observing the convoy as it passed. They hadn't stopped for longer than a few minutes at a time since the evening before yesterday. Fear could do that to people, driving them far beyond their normal limits. But everyone had a breaking point, and he could see that many were reaching theirs.

At least they had outrun the sandstorm. And their enemies, for now. They'd been attacked once more this morning, but only by a small group of the living corpses. As much as Jirom hoped that was the last of them, he suspected it wasn't. Their enemy seemed to have an endless army, and the undead could track them through anything, as the sandstorm attacks had proven. He didn't have any idea how the convoy was going to elude them for good. So he kept his people moving. They traveled at night with lit torches, both for light to see and because fire was supposed to be a good weapon against unnatural things, and so the people had made torches from anything they could find or spare from the sleds. It made everyone feel a little safer. Everyone except Jirom. He saw those brands as sign posts leading the enemy right to their position.

"Commander Jirom!"

Jirom winced as *Beysid* Giliam's voice found him. He turned slightly toward the approaching official. "Giliam."

"Commander, I need to speak with you about these conditions. My people are literally falling down from exhaustion. We need to—"

Jirom couldn't resist cutting the man off, just so he'd shut up. "I know. We'll be stopping soon for an extended rest."

Giliam looked as if he was going to object out of habit. Instead, he nodded vigorously. "Excellent. And perhaps now you'll tell me how you plan to deliver us to a safe haven."

"I wish I knew how to get rid of you," Jirom grumbled under his breath. When the *beysid* frowned, he said aloud, "We're still working on a plan. Right now we're focused on keeping you alive."

BLADE AND BONE

"Of course. The needs of the moment are imperative, but planning for the future is always—"

"Commander!"

Jirom held up a hand to the *beysid*'s face as he turned to the rebel fighter jogging toward them. "Report."

The fighter's name was Ilum. "Sir, the forward units have discovered something ahead. They say it looks like one of those flying ships crashed in the sand."

That got Jirom's attention. He had seen what those flying vessels had done during the siege of Erugash. "Show me where."

Leaving Giliam behind, Jirom and Ilum ran up the convoy line. He spotted Emanon on the way, talking to a couple of sergeants, and waved for him to follow.

Emanon came running. "Another attack?"

"No. The scouts found something."

They caught up with the advanced units about half a mile ahead of the convoy, both squads clustered together atop a low dune. When he reached them, Jirom started to ask where this airship was, but then he saw it in the gully below. It was bigger than he imagined, lying half-submerged in the side of another dune. It had the familiar lines of a galley, but without the rigging or banks of oars. The ship had landed on its side. Many of the wooden boards along its upward side had buckled and split apart.

"Damn," Emanon said with a low whistle. "Let's take a closer look."

Jirom detailed one squad to form a perimeter around the ship and the other to stop the convoy for a short rest. Then he and Emanon went down to the fallen ship. They went around the stern to the other side of the vessel, stepping over the long furrow that it had plowed when it landed, and climbed up onto the railing. Emanon headed for the cabin at the rear of the tilted deck, but Jirom went to the large hatch he assumed led down into the hold. He had been on a troop transport, a long time ago. If there was anything worth scavenging—weapons or supplies—it would probably be below.

It proved difficult to undo the hatch with one hand while holding himself up with the other, but Jirom managed to wrench it partway open. Of course, it was completely dark inside. He shouted for someone to bring him a torch. After one of the fighters climbed up with a lit brand, Jirom held it over the hatchway. The cargo hold ran the full length of the ship, except for a bulkhead with a hatch at the rear. The floor was mostly clear, but heaps of things were piled on the lower side of the ship. Then the smell hit him. The reek of death. He could make out the forms of bodies amid the mountain of boxes and barrels. Several dozen at least, all tangled in a mass of twisted limbs and broken torsos. By their plain clothing, he took them for servants. Then he spotted a couple of iron collars. Slaves, then.

The cargo itself seemed more or less intact. He prayed there would be food and water. Just as he was standing up, a call from Emanon drew his attention. With the torch, Jirom made his way across the deck. The cabin was cramped. A man in a blue robe lay slumped over a desk that was fixed to the floorboards. The silver slashes on his collar and long queue of hair tied at the back of his skull proclaimed him as a high-ranking member of the *kunukatum* scribe caste. Jirom judged he had been dead for a few weeks, at least.

Emanon stood up from behind the desk. "Look at what I found." He held an *assurana* sword in a lacquered black scabbard. "Just like the one you lost when your old pal defeated us at Sekhatun."

Ignoring the jab at Horace, Jirom took the sword. He pulled the blade out a few inches and found only plain steel instead of the red alloy of a true *assurana*. "This is just a replica."

"Damn. I knew it was too good to be true."

"Anything else worthwhile in here?"

"Just the locker." Emanon pointed to a box bolted against the left-hand wall. It was secured with two brass locks. Strange designs covered the locker's top and sides.

"Em, maybe we shouldn't fool with this one."

Before Jirom could stop him, Emanon jabbed the point of his spear into the keyhole of one of the locks. A spark flickered inside the hole. Emanon jumped back, cradling his hand. The spear's tip was scorched. As Jirom reached for him, the locker's lid sprung open, and a cloud of black smoke billowed out. Coughing as the acrid vapor filled the cabin, Jirom hauled Emanon away. In doing so, he caught a glimpse of papyrus documents burning inside the locker. Sitting amid the papers was a broad black shield. Its surface was dark and glossy like enamel. On a whim, Jirom reached into the inferno and grabbed the rim of the shield. The flames singed his fingers, but the metal was still cool. With the shield and ersatz *assurana* in hand, Jirom followed Emanon out of the compartment. They dropped to the deck, coughing and spitting out flecks of ash.

"Someday you're going to get yourself killed," Jirom muttered.

"Probably. What did you find there?"

Jirom examined the shield. It was lighter than it looked. A black metal handle and a band of aged leather were mounted on the inside. "Ever seen anything like it?"

"It's probably just a showpiece, although why anyone would want a black shield for a trophy is beyond me." Emanon rapped on the shield's face with the head of his spear. A deep tone rang out. "Huh. It's more solid than it looks."

Jirom ran his hand over the outer surface and discovered tiny raised lines and curves. He tilted it to look at the surface from the side but couldn't make out the pattern.

"Did you grab anything else?"

Jirom shook his head, still studying the shield. There was something strange about it. For some reason he had the impression it was old despite its pristine appearance. Very, very old. "There are supplies below, along with a mess of bodies. Have a squad start pulling out what we can use, especially water. How about you?"

"Just these." Emanon reached inside his leather breastplate and pulled out the end of a rolled document. "The captain's log and charts. I figure we can use them to keep our bearings out here."

"Good thinking. Maybe we should stop here for a spell—"

They both turned their heads at the same time. Shouts were coming from the convoy. Up on the nearby dune, the advanced fighters were waving furiously at them.

"Fuck," Emanon said.

Jirom slid down the deck and started running when his feet hit the ground. A bad feeling roiled in his stomach, bolstered by the screams echoing in the night.

Emanon beat him to the top of the dune. Torches were waving and bobbing at the rear of the convoy. The civilians hurried to get away from the fracas, terror written across their faces. Battered by the constant fear and exhaustion, they were on the verge of total panic.

Jirom and Emanon arrived at the back of the formation to find the rebels holding off a wave of undead. His fighters battled with the discipline he had worked hard to instill in them, their lines forming a living bulwark around the rest of the convoy. Emanon had charged into the thick of the fighting. Jirom was about to join him when someone shouted a warning behind him. He turned and cursed as he saw the shapes emerging from the dunes to the south.

"Em!" Jirom called out.

He had slung the shield onto his arm and drawn the new sword without realizing it. Both were exceptionally well-balanced. Praying they weren't made of cheap steel that would snap at the first clash of combat, he sprinted toward a supply sled that had veered out of the main convoy and was now getting dangerously close to the approaching enemy. The driver hauled hard on the reins to steer it back into line, but there was something wrong with the assemblage. Jirom reached the errant sled at the same time as the undead horde.

As two walking corpses lunged for the cowering driver, Jirom kicked one in the stomach and sent it hurtling back while he impaled the other through the neck. The creature was a petite woman with half a face. She came right for Jirom, sliding up the blade of his sword until she was stopped by the cross guard. Her rotten jaws snapped at his face. Jirom bashed her in the forehead with his new shield. Bone crunched as he freed his sword. He cut through her slender neck as she fell.

The sled had overturned, spilling most of its cargo. Jirom sliced through the traces, freeing the lathered horse, and shoved the stunned driver toward the animal. "Get out of here!"

Another cluster of undead leapt at him from the darkness. Jirom stood his ground as the driver climbed onto the horse and sped away. He cut into anything that got close, lashing the fake *assurana* like a thresher's flail. There seemed no end to the undead. As soon as he cut one down, two more shambled up to take its place. Jirom retreated while keeping them at bay.

The shield held up under the onslaught, fending off clawing hands and gnashing teeth. The attacks thudded uselessly against its glossy surface. Jirom used its narrow rim to break jaws and shatter noses. Shoving back a pair of lanky male corpses that could have been brothers in life, Jirom cut them down with chops to the knees, followed by stabs to the backs of the head to keep them down.

Something caught his eye. A light flickered on the sands beyond the undead. Slowly, it resolved into a ghostly image in the shape of a man. Alert for new horrors, Jirom squinted at the apparition. *Horace?*

The ghost-Horace pointed behind him as it opened its mouth as if to speak. Then, as quickly as it had appeared, it vanished.

Jirom wheeled around and spitted the undead woman leaping at his back. What had just happened? There was no time to ponder the strange vision. He was surrounded now. Spurred by instincts honed in the fighting pits, he leapt to his right, swinging his sword in a broad arc. He cut down three undead and created an opening. Keeping up his shield, Jirom darted through and kept running. He didn't head back to the convoy. Instead, he ran south, leading the enemy away from his people.

A quick look back showed him that his fighters were dealing with the rest of the attack. He couldn't see Emanon but knew his lover would lead the people to safety. Jirom concentrated on staying ahead of his pursuers. For dead things, they were astonishingly quick. They stayed on his heels as he cut between a pair of low dunes, now angling to the west.

The sound of pounding hoofbeats almost made him stumble. Jirom peeked back to see a man on a horse racing up behind the undead. A few of the creatures turned toward the new arrival, but the rider skillfully steered his mount around them. Jirom grinned as Emanon came up beside him. Jirom switched his sword to his off hand, and then grasped the extended arm, hopping up behind him in the saddle. Together they raced ahead of the creatures.

Jirom took a moment to bury his face in the back of Emanon's neck and grasp him tight with his free arm. For a short moment he stopped caring about the rebellion or his responsibilities. He just wanted to be with this man he loved, imagining they could keep riding forever, away from this dreadful situation.

All too soon, Emanon steered back toward the convoy. Jirom looked over his man's shoulder. Several sleds were swarming with undead; some of them had even caught fire. The creatures huddled around the immobile vehicles, hunched over the fallen. Dark spittle dripped from their mouths as they feasted.

About a third of the convoy had been lost. The rest were fleeing to the east as fast as they could manage. The sheer number of bodies lying in the sand made Jirom want to scream. Then he saw movement among the dead. The twitching of limbs. The slow rise of heads, their eyes pitch-black in the firelight.

"Easy there, big guy," Emanon said. "You're squeezing the breath out of me."

Jirom loosened his grip, but it didn't help the frustration brewing in his chest. He was failing these people, and they were paying for it with their lives. "What are we going to do?"

Emanon turned his head to look back. "We keep going. That's all we can do. We keep going, and we stay alive until we can make the bastards who did this pay."

The ones who did this. Who was that? The *zoanii*? The *Manalish*? Jirom didn't know whom to blame, and that made it even more maddening. But Emanon was right. They had to focus on the task before them. Staying alive. He would worry about vengeance for the slain another day.

Trying to forget the crashed airship and the supplies his people desperately needed, Jirom told Emanon to take him to the head of the convoy. They had a long night ahead of them before they could rest. He prayed that the gods would let them live that long.

CHAPTER EIGHT

Horace swallowed the last bite of hard biscuit and washed it down with a mouthful of tepid water. The last cool breezes of the morning fled as the sun rose above the rooftops of the ruins.

Last night he had dreamt again. They were getting stronger. Dreams of death and destruction, of a great black sea swallowing the world. It had ended with him plunging under those dark, icy waters, gasping for breath, and that was how he had awoken. Gasping and terrified in the darkness before dawn. He had lain awake in his blanket afterward, waiting for the light.

Mezim sat on the opposite side of their meager campfire, licking the crumbs from his fingers. "Sir, I did an inventory of our supplies. We have two full skins of water, a dozen biscuits, and six strips of dried meat. If we're careful, it should last us three days."

Horace nodded. He was thinking of Alyra, trying to remember what her hair smelled like. The wood carving of the sea turtle lay in his hand. The grains and grooves pressed against the smooth plain of his palm.

"Excuse me, sir." Mezim pursed his lips as if considering something unpleasant. "I do hate to be a bother, but I feel it's my duty to speak up when I see trouble."

Horace tucked the carving back into his belt. "Out with it, Mezim."

"I was just wondering how long we'll be staying here."

That's a good question. I was wondering the same thing myself.

"It's not just the food supply," Mezim continued in a lowered voice. "It's this place. And . . . forgive me, but I do not trust *her.*"

There was no need for Mezim to spell out whom he meant. Horace had been thinking all morning about the woman they had met last night, who she was and why she was here waiting for them. If he didn't know better, he would have sworn he was still dreaming. "It's going to be fine, Mezim. We're not staying long. But I need some answers, and I think she's the only one who can help me."

BLADE AND BONE

"Be wary, sir. She is . . ."

Mezim's eyes grew wide as he looked past Horace. Then he dropped his gaze and busied himself with cleaning up the campsite.

Horace looked over his shoulder and saw the woman standing behind him. She looked exactly as she had the night before, with the same dress and her hair arranged in precisely the same manner.

"Come with me," she said. "I have much to show you."

Standing up, Horace said to Mezim, "Stay here. I'll be back soon."

Mezim only nodded as he kept his eyes averted.

Horace followed the woman out of the half-standing shell of the building and onto the street. Curling wisps of sand blew before them, creating tiny dust devils on the pavestones.

Quickening his step to catch up to the woman, Horace started to ask, "Where are we——?"

He lost his train of thought as the ruins transformed around him. The broken walls with their hollow windows vanished, replaced by elaborate, intact buildings, their façades and roofs bright with colors of green, blue, and pink. Fallen towers rose to their full height, gleaming in the early light of day. Most shocking of all, Horace suddenly found himself surrounded by people. They looked Akeshian with their copper-hued skins and dark hair, but their attire was very different. Most of them, male and female, wore simple white tunics that exposed their left breasts, and their curly hair gleamed with oil. Their accessories were mostly beaten copper and gold.

Horace caught up to the woman as she continued to stroll amid the crowd. The people didn't seem to notice them. They talked, but he couldn't understand what they were saying, their language being nothing at all like Akeshian. "Is this another dream?" he asked.

"Not quite," the woman answered. "We walk the border of the dream world, but our minds remain conscious. In this state, we have the ability to create whatever we choose, and even project those constructions into the minds of others."

"Why have you brought me here?"

They came to the edge of a great, circular court. A huge pyramid rose before him, blocking out most of the sky. It was constructed much differently than the queen's pyramid in Erugash. It had three tiers, with the lowest rising fully half the way up its total height. The top tiers were much smaller and sloped more sharply inward, and capped with four narrow prongs that extended up, one on each face of the pointed summit, like stone daggers aimed at the sky. Horace felt tremendous power radiating from within the structure. It called to him, and he recognized it as the sensation that had drawn him to the ruins.

"Is this the home of the king?" Horace asked.

"It was a place of learning," the woman answered. "For half a millennium, magi from every corner of the empire gathered here to study, contemplate, and debate. It was a place of peace, a refuge from politics and strife. It is where I first came to learn of my talents."

Horace found himself wanting to approach closer, but he resisted. He tried to imagine what it must have been like to study here, at a place where people weren't constantly trying to kill you. "So what happened?"

He ducked his head as thunder crackled above the city. In the blink of an eye, the sky had turned from clear to darkest night. A bolt of vivid green lightning sliced down from the heavens to strike the pyramid's top. Stone exploded and rained down. A crowd of people standing around the periphery of the court scattered. Their screams rang off the tall buildings. The devastation continued as sprays of chromatic light shot across the sky, accompanied by deep rumbles that shook the ground.

Horace turned to face the woman, but she was gone. He spun around, but there was no sign of her anywhere. People were running away in panic. Thinking perhaps she had been lost in the crowd, Horace dashed away from the falling debris. As he ran, he tried to remember this was all just a dream.

A high-pitched whine was the only warning he received before a blazing ball of light fell from the sky. He lifted his arms over his head as the flaming missile landed right in front of him. The sound of a violent detonation rocked the city.

When Horace lowered his arms, a smoking crater stretched across the street. Several people lay sprawled out around it. He knelt beside a young woman who was caked in a layer of fine gray dust. He reached down to see if she was still alive, but his hand passed right through her. It was all just an illusion.

Horace made his way through the street, observing everything as it happened. More lights fell across the city, vaporizing the buildings and knocking down walls. Bodies lay all around him like broken toys.

He came to a huge stone arch in the city ramparts. A beaten track ran out from the gateway to the desert beyond. More flaming missiles rose from the south. This time he had the chance to see them begin their journey, and he sensed the presence of sorcery out on those wasted plains. This was a coordinated attack by scores of *zoanii*. Maybe hundreds.

A group of defenders, men and women in long robes, stood atop the city's outer wall. Their hands were raised to ward off the attacks, and Horace could see the magic forming between them like an ethereal shield. Some of the approaching meteors exploded against the shield with muffled thuds, but many more attacks got through. Explosions lit up the city with incandescent fire.

The devastation was complete. A city incinerated in minutes, erased from the face of the earth. Out on the desert plains came a great, dark wave, rushing toward him with gathering speed. Horace took a step backward. *This is not real.*

Suddenly he was hurtling up into the darkened sky. Arms and legs waving as he fought to find his balance, he passed into an ocean of stars. Finally, he realized he had no control over what was happening and stopped fighting it. Still he kept climbing higher into the cosmic soup. Something was approaching. A cloudy barrier, glistening like a curtain of dewy gossamer. He struck it and went through as if it were nothing more substantial than cobwebs. On the other side there was only darkness. No more stars. No sun, no moon. Nothing at all.

Then he felt a vast and powerful presence, like a leviathan swimming beneath him in a languid sea. Horror punched a hole through the center of his chest at the sight of its gargantuan form, the contours conforming to nothing he had ever seen before. There were others, too, barely perceptible to his Sight. All equally huge, swimming through this nether space beyond the veil. He could feel their hunger awakening. Long, gangly limbs unraveled, questing in his direction. Out of instinct, he drew on his *zoana*, and the power filled him instantly. He lashed out with a bolt of searing fire as hot as he could make it. The white flames jetted out toward the titan closing in on him. The mammoth beast rolled over onto its side to avoid the fire. As its tentacles drew nearer, Horace wrapped himself in a cocoon of pure Shinar and braced for the impact. He blinked, and a rush of movement seized him.

He was standing once more in the ruins. The dream was over, though his heart beat madly. Legs shaking, he stood in the broken stone archway looking out across the desert. A cold wind washed over him, ruffling his clothes. The only light came from the half-moon, hanging low over the drifting dunes. An entire day had passed?

"We thought ourselves civilized."

Horace tensed as the woman appeared beside him. She, too, was looking out over the plains. "An empire steeped in sorcery, as close to the gods as mortals could become. But we were ruled by pride. We battled for dominance over each other with armies and trade, and finally with all the arcane powers at our disposal."

She gestured at the derelict city. "This is a testament to our zeal. And our folly. In the end, it did not matter who was more powerful. All that mattered was that we destroyed ourselves. All that we had created turned to dust. Once, I thought the pain would fade with time. Now I know better. Time only makes the loss more unbearable."

"You were really here," Horace said, finally believing her.

"Shall I tell you a tale?" she asked, her voice turning slightly wistful. "Of a girl who discovered she had tremendous power at her fingertips. She had a dream that her power could unite the warring cities and bring about a new age of peace. But, unbeknownst to her, the very power that fueled her campaign of conquest was simultaneously fraying the fabric between the worlds. When the Great Ones entered our world, it was at her invitation."

Horace recalled a passage from the Maganu *Book of the Dead*.

> *Seven are the Lords of the Abyss,*
> *Seven the evil fiends who tear at the souls of men.*
> *Seven are the steps on the ladder down to the underworld,*
> *Seven the watchers at the Gates of Death.*

BLADE AND BONE

Mulcibar had been studying that tome right before he was abducted by Lord Astaptah. "Seven are the Lords of the Abyss . . ." he whispered.

"Indeed," the woman said. "Seven great lords presiding over countless hordes of evil servants. They have ever sought to return to this world and reestablish their ancient dominion."

"But you pushed them back?"

She nodded, her gaze cast far off into the distance. "Yes. Eventually and at great cost. When the last invader had been banished back to the Outside, we repaired the tear in the veil as best we could, but what was left was no longer worth calling an empire. Our people were easy prey for the Akeshians, who swept in and seized these lands."

Horace could still feel the resonance of the illusionary battle, like a dark blot on the edge of his vision. "That seems to be a common tale in this land. Someone rises up to conquer, and they cause untold misery to everyone around them."

"Power always brings the risk of corruption, Horace. Since the beginning of time, mankind has worshipped two primordial forces." She held up her hands. "The light that creates, and the darkness that destroys."

The woman brought her hands together, palm to palm. "They are forever joined, and forever in conflict. Order against chaos. The sun and the serpent. The Great Ones come from a realm of pure destruction, and they seek to return the cosmos to that nothingness. I suspect you have felt their influence in the back of your mind. Watching you."

He remembered the presence that had haunted him in Erugash, the feeling that someone or something was monitoring him.

"You made a choice," she continued. "Not to embrace their chaos. In doing so, you broke free of their influence and set yourself against them."

Horace shook his head. "I was just protecting myself. I'm not part of this war."

The woman's face was perfectly smooth like the finest porcelain. "You are, whether you wish it or not. A master of destruction has arisen, and so the universe requires a master of creation to balance the scales."

The chill Horace had been feeling pierced straight through his chest. He knew right away whom she meant. "Astaptah. So he *is* alive."

"He has worn many names over the ages. You need to beware of him, Horace, for he is your match and more in every way."

He thought back to everything he'd learned about the former queen's vizier. The storm machine, the way he'd hidden behind Byleth, building his power over the years. "So how can I stop him?"

"I have already told you. The knowledge resides inside you. You must face it, or fail."

"And what if I fail?" he asked in a whisper.

"Darkness returns to the world and extinguishes the light. All that you cherish will be eradicated."

Those words rested heavily on his mind. He could admit to himself he was afraid. Not just of facing Astaptah again but of the darkness that lay inside him, nestled against his heart like a blood-bloated tick. It had been lodged there ever since the day he lost his family. Every time he used his magic to fight or kill, that old pain flared up again, suffused with rage. How could he fight Astaptah and his own heart at the same time? But if he didn't, he knew what would happen. As much as he wanted to pass it off as a delusion, he had felt the presence of those vast entities beyond the veil. It may have been a dream, but he couldn't get those images out of his head.

"All right," he said. "How do I start?"

"As with everything," she said with a smile. "At the beginning."

The landscape changed again, and Horace's stomach dropped as a circle of tall stone walls rose around them, topped by tiers of empty seats. It was a perfect replica of the grand arena at Erugash. He half-expected to hear the roar of the crowd. The woman stood behind the retaining wall above him, just a few steps beneath the vacant royal box.

"What is this?" he called up to her.

"Clear your mind." Her voice filled the arena. "Find your center and let it guide you."

He tried to do as she suggested, but it was difficult to concentrate after all he had seen and heard today, not to mention their new surroundings. He took a deep breath and held it. His *qa* opened naturally, and the *zoana* surged into him, filling him with its sweet power.

BLADE AND BONE

The sand swirled around him, forming several sinkholes. Horace backed away as four man-shaped figures of craggy earth crawled out of the ground. They came toward him with lumbering strides. Calling forth the Imuvar domination, Horace split it into four streams of hardened air and struck the rock men, all at the same time, with a blow to their chests. Two of them collapsed into piles of grown rubble at once. The other two required additional smashing to render them inoperable.

Horace looked up at the woman. She showed not the slightest recognition of his success. Wearing a neutral expression, she lifted a hand. "The adversary's resources are inexhaustible. If you defeat one army, another rises to takes its place."

Horace wondered if the woman was referring to the horde of undead that had attacked the rebel camp. The ground rumbled, and a dozen more rock men crawled from the depths. Not sure what the woman wanted from him, Horace drew forth more power and demolished them one by one. As a wave of new arrivals climbed out of the ground on the far side of the arena, Horace changed his tactics. He used a combination of fire and water to superheat the moisture inside the rock creatures. They exploded in clusters of two and three. Yet, as fast as he destroyed the earthen constructs, more rose to take their place.

"You must look with more than your eyes, Horace," the woman said. "The *zoana* is the weft of the cosmos's fabric. Visualize it and see what lies within."

Horace tried to do as she said while he continued to detonate the advancing creatures. He extended his Sight to his opponents and saw the power coursing through them. Pure *zoana* made up the framework of their stony bones and sinew.

"Look at the vertices of their construction," the woman instructed.

Horace used a gust of air to shove back a nearby rock man as he focused. There, at the joints of the magical framework of each creature, he saw tiny motes of Shinar.

"All things, great and small, are bound together in the void," the woman said. "Use the positive aspect of your power to unravel them."

Another creature lunged for Horace. He was so wrapped up in what he was seeing he almost didn't notice the rock man grabbing for him with its huge, amorphous paws. Horace stepped back to escape, tripped, and fell on his ass. His vision of the rock men's inner workings wavered for a moment. Then he saw what to do. He untied the Shinar bindings holding his assailant together. As easy as snapping his fingers, the creature fell apart in a shower of fine grit. With a quick glance, Horace did the same with the rest of the rock men, destroying them in an instant.

Horace stood up and brushed the sand from his clothes. "How was th—?"

A sheet of yellow flame appeared off to his left. Almost as wide as the entire arena floor and taller than him, it rushed toward Horace. With no time to prepare, Horace wrapped himself in a bubble of hardened air. He winced as the wall of fire washed over his position. Some heat bled through the shield, making the air inside painful to breathe, but after a couple of seconds the wall moved past him.

Horace was just about to drop the shield when two more walls of flame, burning higher and more intensely, appeared in front of and behind him. Like the first one, they advanced toward him, their wavering tongues licking at the sky. Horace poured more of his magic into the bubble.

"There is no barrier," the woman said, "which cannot be battered down."

As the walls converged on him, the temperature inside the bubble soared as if he were trapped in an oven. Sweat poured down Horace's face as he looked for a way out. Yet, wherever he went, the flames would catch him. His shield buckled as the first wall enveloped him, and it completely collapsed as the second wall hit. Pain exploded all around him as he summoned a strand of Mordab. He envisioned his flesh turning black and peeling away while he worked. A moment later, he was encased inside a shield of cool water. He maintained a trickle of Imuvar so he could breathe.

The water shield sizzled and roiled as the flames passed over, but it held long enough for Horace to survive. He glanced at his hands and arms. The skin was red and painful, and his clothes were singed, but the fire hadn't burned him too badly. Then he looked up and swallowed hard. Three walls of bright flame had appeared and were rushing toward him. He was wracking his brain for a way to defeat this threat when he thought back to his battle with the rock creatures. He squinted and studied the fires. Points of void energy pulsed within them, anchoring their structure. Once he had identified the bindings, they were just as simple to untie as those holding the rock men together. In the span of a couple of seconds, the flames vanished.

Horace started to breathe a deep sigh. Yet, his throat constricted, cutting off his breath. A liquid heaviness filled his lungs. He was drowning. Memories from the night the *Bantu Ray* went down off the coast of Akeshia battered his thoughts. Once again he felt the chill of the water and the crushing pressure on his lungs. Falling to his knees, Horace tried to call upon the Mordab dominion to banish the water inside him, but his *qa* was fluctuating wildly out of his control as fear set in.

"What will you do," the woman said, "when there is no foe to grapple with? No barrier to break down? What will you do when your own body has become your enemy?"

Horace could barely hear from the intense pressure in his ears, but her words echoed inside his skull. What was he supposed to do? He focused his mind's eye on the liquid in his lungs. What kept him from coughing it out? He was trying to break the chokehold around his throat when he noticed the points of Shinar floating in the water. Of course. It was created by magic, so it operated by the same rules as any other conjuration. He unbound the void energy, and instantly the water vanished.

The woman gazed down at him, still without expression. Gritting his teeth, Horace stood up. "I've had enough—"

Deafening thunder drowned out his words. The sky turned black in the blink of an eye, churning with ominous storm clouds. A brilliant nimbus of ghastly light coalesced amid the clouds as a crackling lightning bolt stabbed down from the heavens. It struck just outside the arena's stands, accompanied by booming peals.

Horace conjured a shield of Shinar around himself and the woman, but she rebuked him. "Do not fight the storm, Horace. Search out its core and infuse it with your will."

Not sure what she meant, Horace sent a probe of *zoana* up into the sky. Through it, he felt the temperature of the air above the arena drop sharply. The winds buffeted his ethereal senses, and a vivid smell of ozone filled his head as his questing acuity reached the clouds. The power of the storm surrounded him, pulsing in different directions from moment to moment. Horace quested in circles for a couple of minutes. It was a strange sensation, with half his perception roaming high above the ground while the rest of his consciousness remained trapped in his body below. And then he found it. Passing through a bank of clouds, he almost ran into a dazzling sphere of yellow-green light. Tendrils of energy radiated from the core, undulating as they floated through the storm like a thousand independent tentacles.

As he was considering how to approach this phenomenon, a tendril brushed against him. A shock ran through him, so intense he felt his mortal body below shiver from the contact. For a moment he saw himself as part of the storm. The clouds were his shell, and the winds were his breath. He was vast and omnipotent, ruling above the stolid earth—

Horace blinked. He was himself again, but the memory of the storm's vast power remained lodged in his head. How could he fight this? Then he heard the woman's voice, speaking as clearly as if she were standing right beside him.

"Beware, Horace. These storms of chaos are fueled by both sides of the Shinar. Harness your creative impulses."

Horace reached out with his ethereal senses, probing the brilliant sphere. There were no vertices of void that he could see, but the chaotic nature of the storm made it difficult to observe. Everything was in flux. Yet, if he could just latch onto it somehow, perhaps he could—

A powerful jolt ran through him as a titanic force thrust him away. He sailed backward through the angry clouds. Focusing his will, he stopped his momentum and reversed course. He had an idea. Calling upon the Shinar, he sharpened the power into a lance and extended it toward the center of the storm. A swarm of tendrils tried to block his path, but he batted them away. When he was close enough, Horace stabbed. A flash of green light filled his vision. Suddenly, he wasn't in the storm. He was standing in the desert at night. Fires burned around him. He caught a glimpse of a hulking man. With steel and shadow in his hands, he battled a mob of bestial creatures. It was Jirom, and he was surrounded by undead like the ones that attacked the rebel camp. Their filthy claws reached for him, seeking to pull him down. An undead crouched behind him, unseen, gathering its long legs to leap. Horace pointed and started to shout a warning—

Another electric spark jolted him, and then he was back inside the storm. The tendrils lashed at him from every direction. He tried to hold on, but the backlash was too great. He felt his grip on the power slip away. He blinked.

He was lying on the sand, looking up at a clear sky. The arena was gone, replaced once again by the ruins of the broken city. The woman stood next to him.

"I couldn't . . ." he said. His voice was raw. It hurt to speak. "I couldn't stop it. It was too powerful."

"Because you failed to harness the positive side of the Shinar," the woman said.

Horace stood up slowly, feeling a host of aches and pains all through his body. He was bathed in sweat. "I saw things in the storm. A friend in danger."

"The Sight sees many things. Shadows of the past and ghosts of possible futures."

"Was it real?" he asked.

The woman spread her hands and smiled. Horace left her and walked away.

He traveled through the sand-caked streets of the ruins without any clear destination in mind. Through occasional gaps in the outer wall he glimpsed the desert beyond. The dunes marched toward the far horizon, seemingly without end. He hadn't merely imagined Jirom battling those walking corpses. He felt as if he had actually been there. And if it was real, then Jirom and the rebels needed him. He had to go back.

Resolved, he headed back into the heart of the ruins.

Mezim hummed as he packed their belongings. Horace sat on the low wall dividing their borrowed home, his chin propped on his hand. Leaving was the right decision, but he was still debating where they should go.

They could go to Erugash, where it all began. Astaptah might be there. Horace could confront the danger directly, ending this conflict once and for all. Yet, he thought he should find the rebels first. In his vision, Jirom had clearly been fighting for his life. However, he had no idea how to find the rebels. Going back to the camp and trying to follow their days-old flight through the open desert seemed impossible, and he had no idea where they may have gone. But he knew who might.

Taking a deep breath, Horace stood up. "Ready?"

"Most certainly, sir." Mezim hopped to his feet and hefted the bags. "I shall be quite happy to leave this place."

They left the building and found the woman standing in the street outside. Her appearance never changed. Hair exquisitely coiffed and lustrous. Attired in the same robe with not a speck of dirt to mar its perfection. She regarded him with large, dark eyes.

Horace stood opposite her, meeting her gaze. Mezim cleared his throat and headed toward the city's southern gate, his sandals kicking up tiny clouds of dust as he hurried away.

"I know who you are now," he said. "In the *Book of the Dead*, you are called Eridu. The Mother of Chaos."

Her smile was bleak. "A damning title, if ever there was one. I cannot say it wasn't deserved."

"You were an agent of the Great Ones. What made you change your mind?"

"I saw the future. Saw what my actions, and their hungers, would do to the world. I wanted to rule, to conquer, to live forever in the memories of men. Not to destroy everything."

"Instead they tried to forget you ever existed."

"Life is not without its cruelties. But I cannot protest. I was given a second chance."

"I have to go. My friends need me."

She turned her head slightly to the side as if looking past him. "You have traveled beyond the Gate of Death, Horace. You know the danger that awaits mankind. You must do as you feel is right."

BLADE AND BONE

"I have to know before I go. Why did you choose me?"

"Sometimes choice is an illusion. We are born, we exist, and then we pass back into the void. In that time, we swim amid unseen currents, pulling us ever onward. For the great and small alike, this remains a truism."

"I think I understand, but I don't like it."

"We accept that."

With a small nod, he turned to follow Mezim.

"Horace," she called behind him. "Beware the enemy. He will know you are coming."

He kept walking. Dust devils twirled around his feet, spinning off into the dark corners of the ruins.

He met Mezim outside the crumbling stone gate. Horace inhaled deeply, savoring the clean air of the desert. The sunlight felt good on his face. It was hot already and going to get much hotter.

"Let's walk," he said.

Mezim nodded, and together they hiked out onto the dunes. Horace picked the tallest mound and headed that way. It took some effort to get to the top, scaling the slope of loose sand. When they did, Horace paused. For the first time, he glanced back over his shoulder. The ruins were gone. Nothing lay behind them but empty desert.

"Where were we?" Horace whispered.

"Do you know where we're going, sir?" Mezim asked.

Horace pulled out the wooden turtle carving. He didn't know where the rebels were right now, but Alyra might be able to point him in the right direction. Then maybe he could avert the impending doom he felt hovering over all their heads.

"Not exactly," Horace replied. "But I have an inkling. Hold on tight."

Summoning his power, Horace focused on the carving and opened a hole in the air. They stepped through.

CHAPTER NINE

Pumash winced as another bolt of lightning stabbed down from the storm-riddled sky. A sharp pain pierced him just beneath the heart while the thunder shook the ground. It left him quickly, but a faint echo remained.

Different town, same aftermath.

Niruk lay between Hirak and Epur. Renowned for its fine pottery, which was made with a distinctive blue color, the town hosted only a small garrison and few defenses. It had been widely said by the town's noted fathers that commerce was Niruk's armor.

Looking down from the roof of the governor's palace, Pumash thought they must be wishing today they had invested in better walls and more soldiers. Not that those would have helped them.

Smoke rose from many parts of the town. Bodies filled the streets. The undead crawled over them, ripping off flesh and gouging out the organs to eat. He drank deep from the silver cup, which Deemu had found for him, to keep from thinking about the gruesome repast going on below.

Pumash turned away from the edge and walked back inside. The upper floors of the palace were reserved for the governor and his family, and they were appropriately luxurious. The furnishings were fine hardwood and silk, the décor tasteful.

When he had entered the palace with his phalanx of corpse soldiers, they found a dozen servants locked in a subcellar. Deemu had actually been the one to coax them out, assuring them that the carnage was over and they would be unharmed. Pumash had immediately ordered the palace closed to the non-living, keeping himself and his new servants safe. For the past two days he had feasted and drank in a fashion that almost allowed him to forget the horrors waiting outside the doors. Almost. It was difficult to enjoy himself when he knew that everyone else in the town had been slaughtered. *What is the point of all this? This town posed no threat to the master's campaign. Most of the people living*

BLADE AND BONE

here were tradesmen and farmers. There was hardly any garrison at all, and only a handful of lesser zoanii.

With a sigh, he held out his cup for an old servant woman to refill. There was no point in trying to figure out his Master's plan. His role was merely to execute the commands of the *Manalish*.

Deemu hustled into the reception hall, his slippers flapping on the marble tiles. "Master, a guest has arrived. It is the—!"

The tall double doors of the chamber slammed open to the crackle of shattering plaster. Pumash's cup hit the floor with a hollow ding. *She* stood in the doorway. Her power rolled into the chamber ahead of her, cold and dark like the embrace of a tomb. His tongue stuck to his palate for a moment before he could speak. "Welcome, Byleth. Care for some wine?"

A veil hid her features except for the eyes, and they were subdued at the moment. Merely two dark pits peering out from the folds, but he had seen when they blazed like smelting furnaces, and the sight was enough to put the fear of hell in him.

"It is time for the next attack," she announced, again with that tone that made him want to shove a spike through her skull. "We shall take Epur."

Pumash held out his hand for another cup and snapped his fingers when it wasn't presented quickly enough. The old woman jumped to obey. "We just took this town. Why not pause to enjoy the fruits of our . . . er, *my* . . . labors?"

"Your attempts at humor are a waste of effort."

"Clearly," he whispered under his breath.

He wished the *Manalish* would send her away, but she was his favorite. That much was apparent, talking to him as if he were no more than a servant. He considered putting his hands on her and allowing the master's power to take over, but he didn't dare. *You cannot kill what is already dead.*

"The master has commanded, and we must obey."

"But what's the point of all this? We conquer a town, and then our army kills and eats everyone. There's no one left to reap the fields or squeeze the grapes. So I ask you, what is the point? Mere destruction for its own sake is meaningless."

"It is not wise to question the—"

"Question the master. Yes, yes. I commend you for your zeal, my dear. By all means, conquer away. Just send one of our undead soldiers to Epur with a note tied around its neck, saying, 'Surrender or you all die.'"

He went to take a drink when the cup flew from his hand to smash against the wall behind him. A moment later, an invisible force clamped around his throat, cutting off his breath. Pumash tried to grab at the power choking him, but his fingers found only a band of iron-hard air. It drove him to his knees as it squeezed tighter.

"It is not wise to mock his commands, Pumash. You have been given a unique honor. If you are unwilling to perform your duties, another can be found to take your place, and you shall be tossed outside to contend with our hungry army. I trust I am making myself clear?"

Pumash nodded vigorously, and the band of air vanished from around his throat.

"Now, shall I inform the master that you are prepared to do his bidding?"

Pumash struggled back to his feet as he gasped for air. "Yes. I am."

"Excellent. I'll be away for a short time, but I shall see you in Epur."

He managed a shaky bow as she left the chamber. "Yes, my lady," he said to her departing back.

Once she was gone, Pumash straightened up. His throat was raw and painful. He needed a drink.

Deemu rushed over. "Master! Are you hurt?"

"It seems I will live, Deemu. For now. But I need a new cup."

"Master, are we going to Epur now?"

Pumash started to answer yes, but then an idea came to him. It was bold, even reckless, and it might get him killed. But it was obvious his days were already numbered, and if this idea paid off, he might be able to supplant Byleth in the *Manalish*'s eyes. If he had to be involved in this malignant operation, he wanted to be at the top. Or as close as he could get.

Pumash pulled Deemu aside from the other servants, who were busily cleaning up the spilled wine. "No, Deemu. We'll get the undead started in that direction, but then you and I are heading elsewhere."

He thought of the empire's central lands. Yuldir was too close to Epur, and Semira was too far. But Thuum might work. If he could get the city to surrender peacefully, without a single death, it would hasten the *Manalish's* plan. And other cities might well follow. He knew the people of the empire far better than the *Manalish* or even Byleth. They would welcome a benevolent ruler, and the *Manalish's* campaign for imperial domination would proceed much more smoothly this way. *And leave behind enough people to actually rule, instead of just a swarm of half-living beasts.*

"We're going to Thuum, but it must remain a secret. Understand?"

"Yes, Master. But what will we find there?"

"Salvation, Deemu. Now, where's my wine?"

The sun beat down, turning the wastes into an oven. They had found a valley of black stone and stopped there for the afternoon, weathering the worst part of the day.

Perched atop the valley's southern lip, Jirom held the shield he had found in the crashed airship. He ran his fingertips across the indecipherable raised patterns on its outer face. The jet-black surface reflected nothing. The metal was cool to the touch and showed no signs of chipping or denting despite all the use it had seen recently.

After putting the shield aside, Jirom reached for his canteen. But it was empty, so he clipped it back on his belt. They were running out of water. The last attack by the walking corpses cost them several supply sleds, and the heat was taking its toll on the rest. The convoy was on its last legs. Slowed by too many wounded and sheer exhaustion, he had been forced to call for this rest, but it ate at him. In their weakened state, another attack could finish them off. He eyed the carrion birds soaring overhead. *You might get your wish soon enough. I hope you fucking choke on my carcass.*

His fighters were stationed around the steep walls of the canyon, keeping watch over the desert. Sergeant Ralla's platoon was nearest to him. They were a mix of old and new rebels from all across the empire and beyond. The sergeant herself was from Chiresh. Her corporal, Suh, hailed from a village outside Semira. The brothers, Kulag and Naven, were from Etonia, far to the northwest along the Midland Sea. Ulm came from the Great Desert, fire-haired Yella from Scavia, and Horvik came from some town between Hirak and Epur.

Men and women from so many places, all coming together in this crusade against the empire. All of them looking to him for salvation. Jirom found himself missing Three Moons. The old witch doctor would have had some advice about their situation. Or at least a barbed remark. *I hope you're still alive, old friend. Even though we might never meet again.*

He imagined Three Moons sitting beside him now, clutching a jug of some potent spirit.

"*Ah, don't go getting all maudlin on me, Sergeant.*"

I don't think we're going to get out of this one alive, Moons.

"*So what? We've had a good run. Certainly lived longer than we expected to. Remember that skirmish outside the gates of Getae?*"

Yes. It was right after I'd joined the Company. I was barely seventeen.

"*That was a hell of a scrap. Those Scavian freebooters had us dead to rights, but we got through it. Just like you'll get through this mess. Maybe.*"

I miss Longar. Hell, I miss all the old-timers. Captain Galbrein, Hillup, Furuk, even that evil bastard Skawl.

The imaginary Three Moons took a long pull from his ghostly jar. "*They're at peace now, Sarge. We're the ones who have to keep on suffering. We never understand that until the end. Stop fighting it.*"

Fuck you, Three Moons. I'm not giving up until they put me in the ground.

"*That's the spirit! Fight them to the bitter end!*"

You're not making any sense.

"*When did I ever?*"

I could use some advice.

Imaginary Three Moons nodded, suddenly sober. "*Yes, you could.*"

"Jirom!"

He looked down the crude path leading up the canyon wall. Emanon was climbing toward him, followed by a couple of sergeants and the last person he wanted to see. The eminent *beysid*, protector of the people. *Maybe he'll slip and break his neck in the fall.*

Jirom stood as the small party reached his perch. Emanon handed him a full canteen, and Jirom gave him a grateful smile before taking a drink.

Beysid Giliam didn't wait to catch his breath but launched right into a complaint. "Commander! Are you trying to kill us?"

Jirom eyed the sweaty politician, debating whether or not to push him off the ledge. "We've stopped for a rest. Isn't that what you wanted?"

"Yes, of course. But now I hear we're going to start marching again in an hour."

Jirom didn't realize he had slipped the shield onto his arm until he noticed Giliam stealing glances at it. Still, the *beysid* continued his tirade. "My people are exhausted. They need a real respite. They need sleep."

Emanon rolled his eyes, clearly thinking the same thing Jirom was. "I suppose they also need water, *Beysid*. And we're in short supply. Not to mention that those creatures are still out there, probably closing in on us as we speak. Now, I haven't seen you pick up a spear yet, but if any more of my fighters are hurt, it might just come to that."

Jirom's voice rose with every word. "And I'm getting very tired of your constant whining. We're at the end of our rope. I'm not sure any of us are going to survive this journey."

The *beysid* switched mannerisms so quickly that Jirom thought he must have missed something. "Commander, you misunderstand me. We are extremely grateful for all the efforts of your courageous fighters." Giliam beamed at Emanon and the sergeants. "But we are simple people. Just servants and farm hands. We are not accustomed to such rigors."

"*Beysid*, with all due respect, you're going to fucking get accustomed to it. Because it's not going to get any easier. In fact, the days to come are going to be more brutal than anything you've ever seen. So I suggest you grab what rest you can because we're moving on. Anyone who wants to stay here is welcome to do so. I'll even leave you some shovels so you can start digging your own graves. Now get the fuck out of my sight before I forget my manners."

Giliam stared at him, his mouth agape. Then, after another quick glance at Jirom, he turned and left, retreating down the cliff path.

Emanon waved the sergeants to move away, and then he faced Jirom. "Have I told you how much I love you today?"

"Yes, but I could stand to hear it again."

Jirom looked down the cliff face, past Giliam's sweaty head to the people huddled below. He felt worse for the children. They were succumbing to heat in droves. They wouldn't make it much farther. *I have to do something to save them. But what? I can't conjure water and safety out of thin air. Horace, where are you?*

"No sign of pursuit," Emanon offered.

"We've heard that one before."

"Just saying." Emanon looked around to make sure no one was near enough to overhear. "Jirom, I don't think these people can make it to the rendezvous."

"How far is it?"

"At this rate? Too far. We're crawling across this desert like ants." Emanon glanced back to the west, the same direction Jirom couldn't stop watching. "Not that it matters. Those dead things seem to be able to track us anywhere."

"So we can't outrun them, and we can't fight." Jirom took another sip of water. "What about turning south?"

"Into Akeshian territory? Jirom, I hate to break this to you, but we're too weak to fight off even a small company of legionnaires. And once we leave the deep desert, there wouldn't be any place to hide. Unless you're talking about leaving the civilians behind. . . ."

Jirom shook his head firmly. "No. We won't abandon them. But what if we could avoid the Akeshian patrols? We have enough fighters to screen the convoy in every direction. Seng's scouts could handle the extra duty."

"Maybe." Emanon rubbed his chin. "What's the point? Those ghouls are eerie, but dead is dead either way. At least if we keep running, there's a chance some of us will reach the refuge."

"I'm not fighting so only some of us survive, Em. We're all in this together. We all live or we all die."

"So what's the plan? Where are we going?"

"Thuum."

Emanon stared at him. "You want us to take Thuum?"

BLADE AND BONE

"It was our next target anyway. And it's the closest city by at least fifty leagues."

"It was our next target when we were at full strength, which we're not, and properly prepared, which we aren't. And we don't have any recent intel on it."

"Alyra's there right now."

"You assume she's there. We haven't had any word back yet."

"We'll get word when we arrive."

Emanon laughed while shaking his head. "When we arrive, eh? We're just going to stroll up and knock on the gates?"

"I've got a plan."

"Shit. I know that look."

"What? Don't you trust me?"

"With my life. But that look always gets us in trouble. So tell me."

Before Jirom could respond, a shout rang out from the northern clifftop. They both looked in that direction to see a rebel fighter waving both arms above her head. Jirom cursed. *Not now. We're not ready.*

"Maybe it's just a small attack," Emanon said.

Jirom hoped he was right as they rushed around to the western side of the valley, which was faster than going down into the canyon and scaling the northern slope. They arrived at the north guard post, and Jirom's stomach sank as he saw a massive horde of living dead loping toward their position. *It's not fair. Dear gods, it isn't fair!*

He had the sudden urge to throw himself at these foes in a suicidal charge, exhausting his rage until they were beaten into the bloody sands or until they killed him. Another shout came from the east. A signal of more enemy sighted.

"Double fuck," Emanon growled. "We can't hold both positions. Not with this many."

Jirom knew that. The suicidal urge was subsiding as he considered their options. They could make this their final stand, or they could flee. But which direction? He figured they had about five minutes before the first enemies reached them.

"South," he said. "We go south now. The civilians run as fast as they can while a detachment remains behind to slow down pursuit. It's our only hope."

Jirom looked to Emanon and said, "I'll stay behind."

At the same precise moment Emanon said, "I'll stay with the rearguard."

Jirom pointed to the sentry who had alerted them. "Tell all the sergeants we're leaving now. They have to get everyone moving or we're dead. Understand?"

The young woman's eyes were wide with fear, but she kept her composure. "Yes, sir. Which way are we going?"

The valley had a great crack that ran from its floor to the south and exited into the desert. The slope was steep, but Jirom thought the sleds could manage it. "Take the southern defile and keep going. And don't stop until the horses start dying."

As the sentry scooted down the canyon wall with her orders, Jirom surveyed the northern plain. "We can't stay up here. They'll push us off the edge with sheer numbers."

"We'll set up at the opening of the defile," Emanon said. "The dead will have to climb down the cliff and go through us, or go around the entire valley. Either way, it will give our people time to get away."

"Sounds good."

Emanon slid down the cliff face, kicking up scree and clouds of dust. Jirom stayed up top, surveying the enemy. He wished he had some grand strategy that could defeat them, but all he could do was hold them off for a few minutes. He would give his left arm for another five hundred fresh fighters, or even a company of lancers. Armored horsemen would cut right through these undead. He revised that theory at once. The creatures had no fear of pain or death, obviously. They might withstand a cavalry charge better than living infantry. So how could they be stopped? He didn't know, and that terrified him.

As the first enemies came over the nearest dunes, Jirom made his way down the cliff, hopping from ledge to ledge. He made it to the bottom without breaking his neck, although the bottoms of his sandals were sliced to shreds.

The last of the sleds was leaving as he arrived. Emanon had a score of fighters positioned at the mouth of the southern pass, closing in behind the departing people. Every man and woman was armed with a long spear. Many had shields as well. *If only we'd had time to properly train and outfit these warriors, they would have been a force to make the world tremble.*

Jirom forced himself to smile as he walked among them, clapping their shoulders and sharing looks of respect.

"We're going to stand here," Emanon said, "and we're not going to break. I don't care how many of those rotting bastards come at us. We hold fast. Right?"

Twenty voices raised a cheer that echoed down the black rock valley. Jirom smiled at Emanon as they took their place in the center of the line. Jirom drew his sword. So far the faux *assurana* had performed almost as well as the real thing. He silently thanked its maker. Then he focused on the fight to come. If the undead showed signs of skirting around the valley, they would have to adjust the plan, but he had no illusions that they would last long in the open.

As it turned out, he needn't have worried. The enemy came right for them.

Mutters rose from the line of rebels as the first undead appeared at the top of the north cliff. Jirom was the first to curse as the walking corpses jumped, throwing themselves over the edge. They tumbled down the rocky slope, breaking bones and leaving wet trails smeared down the side. Hope flickered inside Jirom as the undead piled on the valley floor, but it vanished when they climbed to their feet.

"Harutuk's bloody cock!" a fighter cursed.

Jirom flinched as familiar faces appeared among the enemy shambling toward him. Men who had been under his command, now dead but still alive.

"Form up tight!" he shouted, pushing his feelings aside. "No one breaks. We hold them here."

As the enemy came nearer, Jirom's frustration and hopelessness turned to anger. Someone or something had changed these people into monsters. Whether it was imperial *zoanii* or the gods themselves, they had created a race of abominations, and he couldn't abide it. He held back the tide of his emotions as he cut down a former recruit. The young man's jaws, dripping black saliva, snapped as if he were ravenous for his life back. When a woman he and

Emanon had rescued from the slave pits of Erugash shambled toward him, Jirom hacked through her slender neck and kicked the headless body to the ground. Dark ichor soaked into the ground under their feet.

By some miracle, the line held.

The undead crashed against it like an avalanche, but the rebel fighters stood their ground. They chopped the enemy down until a wall of bodies started to form at their feet. The stench of rotting flesh became intolerable, but they fought on. With each passing heartbeat, Jirom became more convinced this was to be their last stand. Having evaded death for so long, the prospect did not concern him as much as he might have supposed. Emanon, battling beside him, looked almost peaceful as he slashed and sliced against the unending horde. At least they would die together, united to the end.

Jirom was shoving a corpse back with his shield when an idea struck him. His gaze flicked to the top of the defile mouth. Thirty yards above them, the black stone of the valley transitioned into the red limestone that was found throughout the rest of the desert. Boulders and large stones covered this transitional area on both sides of the defile. A couple of the sergeants had suggested using these stones to create some defenses, but there hadn't been time. Looking at them now, Jirom had another idea.

"Hold the line!" he shouted to Emanon as he backed away from the fighting.

The undead surged into the gap his absence left, but Emanon and Red Ox moved to fill the breach, hacking violently to keep the enemy at bay. Jirom hurried down the defile. With every step, he almost turned back to rejoin his men, knowing they were fighting and dying because of him. But this idea might save them, and he had to take that chance.

He quickly found a place he had seen before during his survey of the valley, a natural chimney formation in the defile wall. It led most of the way up to the top. Putting away his sword and slinging the shield over his shoulder, Jirom started climbing. The chimney was pocked with small holes and ledges that made for reliable handholds, and he scaled it quickly. The top was capped by a solid roof. Jirom was forced to make a dizzying climb out and over the knob of stone, hanging just by his fingers. He kept moving without considering what would happen if a hold slipped. A minute later, panting and sweating, he reached the top. He spared a glance over the side. The undead filled the black stone valley, their numbers unfathomable. They crawled and ripped at each other in their attempts to reach the line of humans holding back their inevitable advance. Jirom turned away from the scene. He had no time to lose.

He found the largest boulder on this side of the defile. Situated right at the edge of the cliff, it was taller than him and wider than his arm span. He got behind it and pushed. The stone didn't move. Jirom dug in his heels and exerted every ounce of his strength. The muscles bunched in his thighs and shoulders, threatening to tear themselves to shreds, but it was no use. The rock was too massive.

Giving up, Jirom leaned against the boulder. He needed a lever, but there was nothing around he could see that might work. Then he spotted a crack running across the top of the cliff. It extended outward about twenty feet from the precipice, widening as it got closer to the edge.

Jirom went over to peer down into the crack. It was deeper than it looked from the outside, with smaller cracks radiating out on each side. Stepping back, he got a better view of the situation. The entire eastern spur of the cliff was shearing off and hanging only by a few narrow fingers of stone. Jirom drew his sword. He felt bad about damaging such a fine weapon, but nevertheless he got down into the crack and started hacking. The weapon's point held up for a few blows, but slowly started to fold up as Jirom plunged the tip into the tenuous stone over and over. Chips of rock flew up into his face as he worked. He cut away the stone anchors that he could see. Then he climbed out far enough to peer over the side of the cliff.

There were only a handful of rebels still standing with Emanon, and they were being forced back foot by foot by the tide of undead. Hoping this was going to work, Jirom dropped back into the crack and set his back against the western face. He wedged his feet against the other side and began to push. As he applied pressure slowly, an ache developed in his lower back. He ignored the old injury and kept pushing. For several long seconds, nothing happened. It felt like trying to lift a mountain. Then he heard a cracking sound, like stone splitting apart. A second later, the eastern face of the cliff fell away from him with a thunderous roar. It collapsed so fast that he started to fall after it.

Jirom scrambled for something to grab as his legs dangled over open air. His right hand closed around a tiny spur of stone.

With many grunts and curses, he climbed back to the top of the cliff. As he lay on his side, panting, Jirom gazed down on what he'd done. The entire top half of the defile's west face had sheared off, falling down to clog the ravine below. Scores of undead had been buried by the falling rock, but—thankfully—none of the landslide had touched the rebels. Emanon and the survivors dispatched the handful of enemies who remained on their side of the blockage. On the far side, the horde of undead seethed and clawed at the mountain of stone in their way. But already some of them were turning away, heading east or west along the main valley floor. Presumably to find a route around. They weren't stopped, but he had bought his people some time.

Forcing his shaking limbs to obey, he began the slow descent down the rock chimney. When he hit the defile floor, Emanon was there. His lover grabbed him in a tight embrace and kissed him with such fervor that Jirom almost forgot where they were.

When Emanon pulled back for breath, he snarled, "If you ever do something that crazy and stupid again, I swear I'm going to . . ."

"What? Stop loving me?"

"Never, you beautiful bastard. How in the seven holy fucks did you come up with *that*?"

Jirom paused to admire his handiwork. The southern route was completely blocked by broken stone. It was also serving as a tomb for several of his fighters. Only five, besides Emanon, had survived. *We keep paying in blood. How long until we all succumb?*

Pushing away the macabre thoughts, Jirom disentangled himself from Emanon's embrace and gestured to his fighters. "Let's get moving. Can everyone march?"

Red Ox had a gash on his left shin that was bleeding profusely, but a makeshift field bandage slowed the flow enough that he could travel. The others had scratches and bruises, but nothing that would slow them down. Jirom hoped they had reserved some of their energy because they had a long trek to make, chasing after the sleds on foot.

BLADE AND BONE

Emanon led them out, and Jirom fell in at the rear. Every few steps he looked back to the rockfall. There was no sign of pursuit yet, but he knew the undead were still coming for them. They would never stop.

Three Moons opened his eyes and groaned. Holding a hand to his pain-wracked forehead, he sat up. *I hope to hell I'm dreaming this.*

The cave was gone. The desert, too. Instead, he sat inside a ring of huge stone megaliths. Like towering sentries, the stones formed a perfect circle around a clearing. Beyond them rose a forest of huge trees. Three Moons couldn't identify their deep black wood or the broad teal leaves. Up through the dense canopy was an expanse of orange that didn't look like any sky he'd ever seen before. Even the grass underneath him was strange, its turquoise shafts topped with spaded points. His thirteen comrades lay around him in the clearing. Some were coming to.

Three Moons stood up slowly, nursing his injured shoulder. The forest went on in all directions for as far as he could see, limited as that was by the lush foliage. Fear had settled in the pit of his gut. He jumped when a hand tapped him on the back.

"Easy, Moons," Captain Paranas said as he spun around. "I suspect I already know the answer, but I'll ask anyway. You have any clue where we are?"

Three Moons shook his head. "Not a one."

That wasn't entirely true. He had his suspicions, but they were too dire to say aloud. As the rest of the Blades woke up, they joined him in looking around. Their expressions ranged from professional wariness to outright disbelief.

"Are we dead?" Ino asked.

"Can't be," Pie-Eye said. "I don't see no heavenly garden."

Raste snorted. "You think you're going to paradise, Pie?"

"Fuck right I am!" Pie-Eye checked his weapons. "I'm a fucking hero is what I am. Everyone knows heroes sit at the table of the gods with bunches of pretty girls to serve their every pleasure."

"This isn't paradise," Ino said. "It's downright eerie."

Captain Paranas spoke up. "All right. Stow the chatter. Niko? There you are. We need to know where we are. That magic doorway took us a long way from the desert, and I need to know which direction we take to get back."

"Get back?" Pie-Eye asked.

Three Moons said nothing. This had been his doing, and he didn't want to be the bearer of what would surely be some unwanted news. *I hope we haven't jumped out of the cauldron only to end up roasting in the fire.*

"That's right," Captain Paranas said. "We're going back to report what we found. We still got a war to win, soldiers."

Raste made a rude comment under his breath, but the mercenaries got busy. Wounds were cleaned and bound while the last remaining scouts—Niko, Jauna, and a younger man named Syanos—fanned out to search the area.

Three Moons went over to the nearest megalith. It stood almost three times his height. The sides were smooth and flat, giving no indication of its purpose. *Unless it's just a landing spot for that portal. But who built it and why?*

"Moons," Captain Paranas said in a low voice. "We need some answers here."

"I know, Cap. But I don't have anything to tell you. Wherever we are, it's no place I've ever seen before."

"So give me a guess. You're the wizard."

Three Moons shot him a hard look. The kind he used on green recruits who asked too many questions. "We're a long, long way from home. And maybe there's no way back."

Captain Paranas took off his helmet and ran a hand through his sweaty hair. "That's what I was afraid you'd say."

Three Moons squinted at the stone. Despite what he'd told the captain, the queer feeling in his stomach hadn't left. In fact, it was growing stronger. It was similar to the connection he'd felt with the portal, but not as localized. Like he was supposed to be here.

He was further inspecting the stone when a shout rang out. Raste was on his knees, yelling and writhing. His right hand was held tight by the mouth-like blossom of a tall plant.

BLADE AND BONE

"Get it off!" he yelled as blood ran down his wrist.

Before Three Moons could react, Ivikson pulled out his sword and chopped through the stalk of the plant. Raste rolled away, clutching his wrist. Three Moons hurried over and knelt beside him.

"Easy, boy. Let me see."

He rolled back Raste's sleeve to get a better look. The head of the plant was still attached. It held on with rows of tiny serrated teeth. They moved back and forth, even after it had been severed from the stalk, slowly sawing through the flesh. Three Moons drew his knife and placed the point against Raste's wrist.

"Wait!" Raste cried. "What are you going to do?"

Three Moons nodded to Ino and Pie-Eye. "Hold him."

Despite Raste's loud objections, they pinned him to the ground while Three Moons worked. He tried prying the teeth back from the wrist, but they were dug in deep. He didn't think he could get his knife underneath them without cutting an artery. Putting down the blade, he reached for his fetish bag. He had a couple of drying compounds that might kill the ravenous plant before it ate Raste's hand. He was searching for them when he came across a small bone pipe. *Yes, that would work. If we were back in our own world. But here, who knows?*

Three Moons placed the pipe to his lips and blew an experimental note. It carried, far louder than he intended and with perfect clarity. The high grasses on the fringe of the clearing parted, and a small creature appeared. It had the general shape and size of a mole rat but with a coat of bright blue fur.

The creature waddled straight into the midst of the Blades as if they weren't there. Ino saw it and almost tripped in his rush to backpedal away. "What is *that*?" he yelled.

"You can see it?" Three Moons asked.

"Of course I can fucking see it!" the northerner shouted.

Three Moons held out a hand to stay Ivikson's attack. "Just calm down."

The creature looked like a rock spirit, the kind he had summoned and dealt with all his life, but in the flesh. The spirit came over to Raste, who was still shuddering in agony.

Three Moons grasped Raste by the bloody wrist. "Can you help us?"

The spirit reached up with both paws and tugged on the plant mouth. The hungry flora pulled free with a faint rustle of its leaves. The spirit placed it reverently on the ground. Three Moons wanted to kick the carnivorous plant far away, but he held back out of the respect the spirit was showing. "Pie, give me some help."

Three Moons held up Raste's injured hand. Some of the flesh was mottled and oozing blood, but it looked like the damage was superficial. "Wrap him up and give him something to drink."

While Pie-Eye got to work, Three Moons bent down closer to the spirit. "Where are we?" he whispered. A voice replied, as clear as new-spun crystal, in his head.

You are strangers to the overworld. Why have you come?

The overworld? He'd never heard the term before, but it set off alarms in the back of his head. This place resembled too many old legends—stuff he'd learned at his grandfather's knee—for him to take it lightly. In the legends, people who got caught in the nether realms either never returned or they came back many years later with their minds and bodies horribly altered. At the time, he had understood those tales as lessons to not meddle with forces beyond his ken. *I should have paid better attention.*

"We got here by accident," he said to the little creature. "Through a doorway. Do you understand?"

"Moons." Captain Paranas was standing over him. "Are you talking to that thing?"

"I think it's a spirit of the earth, Cap. It's talking to me." He tapped his skull. "In my head."

"Ask it to conjure up some wine," Ino muttered. The big Isuranian was pale. Sweat ran down his face, though the temperature in this place was cool. Far cooler than the desert they had left behind.

You and your den mates came through the hole between worlds? The earth spirit wriggled its tiny nose. *You are* maya-*touched. You are the den leader?*

Maya-touched? What was that? When the spirit said it, Three Moons felt a brief tug on his personal energy, like a psychic handshake. "I don't understand what you mean. I talk to the spirits in my world. We need to get back there."

Yes. You flesh creatures should return to the underworld.

Three Moons was about to ask why they should leave when the little spirit suddenly turned with an intent expression. Then it vanished straight into the ground as if it had dropped into a hole, but there was no hole there.

"Moons," Captain Paranas said quietly. "What the fuck is happening?"

Three Moons stood up and turned in a slow circle, straining with all his senses—earthly and otherwise—to penetrate the woods around them. Something was out there, just beyond his perception. He could feel it watching them. "We need to move. Now."

Captain Paranas didn't argue. "Everyone, move out! Niko, pick a direction and blaze a trail. We're moving, people!"

Pie-Eye helped Raste up before they followed the rest of the Blades. Three Moons stayed behind for a moment. He wanted to see if the little creature would return. He had so many questions, the first of which was how he and the Blades could get back to their own world. Obviously the spirit creatures were able to travel back and forth. Or did they? Perhaps they merely—

"Moons!" Captain Paranas shouted. "Get your ass moving!"

With a growl of frustration, Three Moons hurried after his brethren. Branches with blue-green leaves whipped him as he hobbled along as fast as his old bones could manage. The captain was right in front of him, with the rest of the Blades strung out along a rough trail Niko had found. Three Moons hoped they were going in the right direction. Wherever that was.

Get a grip on yourself. You're the only one who can get them out of this mess. Now think! How do we get back to our world?

He thought back to everything he had learned about the spirit world. Stone circles were supposed to mark sites of great importance, usually places where the spirit lines intersected, but he didn't see how that helped their present circumstances. There was no portal on this side of the veil. And that was what they needed. Another portal.

After an hour, the captain called for a rest, and the Blades fell out along the trail. Three Moons had just enough energy left to walk over to where

Raste sat beside Pie-Eye. Raste's sleeve was soaked with blood from where it had leaked from the field dressing. "He'll need that rewrapped," Three Moons said.

He was just about to sit on the ground when Jauna appeared, tugging at his sleeve. "The captain wants you."

Swallowing a bitter curse, Three Moons followed her to the head of the company where Captain Paranas was wiping his sweaty face with a rag while he talked to Niko. Both men looked over as Three Moons joined them.

"Any ideas how to get out of here yet?" the captain asked.

"I'm still working on that, but I think we should keep moving."

"Well, come look at this."

Captain Paranas and Niko led him off the trail. The ground was softer here and covered in a layer of black loam. It reminded Three Moons of the swamp where he'd been born and raised, only strange and twisted. He kept expecting something bad to jump out of the bushes at any moment.

After pushing through a few yards of bluish shrubbery, and keeping a sharp eye out for more of those flesh-eating plants, they entered another clearing. A trickling creek of quicksilver entered from their right to flow into a broad pool. Sunlight danced across the mirror-bright silver water, making him blink.

"You think it's safe for us to drink?" the captain asked.

Three Moons knelt on the shore of the pool and dipped his finger into the liquid. It was cool to the touch. When he pulled his finger out, the silvery stuff dripped like normal water. It was completely odorless. "I guess there's only one way to find out."

Bracing himself, he cupped some of the water in his hands and took a sip. It was slightly sweet, refreshing the desert-shriveled tissues of his mouth and throat as he swallowed. He didn't detect any foul tastes. He took a bigger sip. "It should be fine. It's not like we have a lot of choice in the matter."

As Niko went back to fetch the rest of the company, Captain Paranas squatted down beside the pool. He took a sip and then splashed some on his face. The silvery water ran down his neck and clung to his beard. They both refilled their waterskins as the other mercenaries arrived. Ino sat down beside the pool and immediately plunged his injured leg into the water. Three Moons was about to urge caution, but it was too late.

The Isuranian sighed with gusto. "That feels fucking marvelous."

Raste sat down by the water and looked over. Three Moons shrugged. Raste slowly unwrapped the bandages from his injured hand. The skin had turned a little gray, but the sores were closed. He lowered it into the pool, and a smile spread across his face. The other Blades started to strip down for a dip.

"You think that's a good idea?" Three Moons asked the captain.

He let out a long breath. "Hell if I know, Moons. But we've been out on that desert for weeks. I think we need the chance to unwind. If you're concerned, then you can have the first watch."

With that, Captain Paranas kicked off his boots and waded into the shallows. The rest of the mercenaries were jumping into the pool. Three Moons hadn't seen them smile since forever, but now they were laughing and splashing each other, the silver water streaming down their naked bodies. Three Moons found himself smiling at their antics in spite of the dread he felt surrounding this place. The more he thought about it, the more he was convinced that coming here had been a mistake, although the portal's existence indicated that someone had wanted to come here long ago. He wished he knew more about that. He had the suspicion it was vitally important to their current situation.

Three Moons walked around to the creek that fed the pool. When he got to the tributary, he looked up its channel. The creek ran down a gentle slope. Farther up in that direction, maybe a mile or two, two tall hills formed a V. Higher elevation would give them a better view of the area. He was about to head back and suggest that to the captain when something caught his attention. Just a flash of movement in his peripheral vision. Pale and roughly man-sized, it slipped away with exceptional speed. Another pale shape dashed through the brush on the other side of the creek.

Three Moons rushed back to the others.

"Moons!" Captain Paranas drank from his canteen as he stood knee-deep in the pool. "I take back what I said. Screw the watch and get in here. It'll make you feel ten years younger. Maybe more in your case."

"We got trouble, Cap!"

Despite their horseplay antics, the Blades reacted to his warning with practiced professionalism. They dashed out of the water and grabbed their weapons. Crossbows were loaded, swords and axes bared, as the mercenaries formed into a loose line along the pool, keeping the water at their backs. As he glanced around, Three Moons noticed his brothers and sisters were looking pale. Their skin was blanched, especially on their legs and lower torsos. Was the silver water infected with something?

Before he could think to do anything about it, the edge of the clearing erupted in violence. Eight gray-skinned figures charged from the brush, hissing and growling like wild beasts. They stood on two legs but moved low to the ground, leaping high as they attacked the Blades. But what caused Three Moons to stop and stare were their faces. They had no eyes, just a smooth slab of skin where their eyes should have been.

Ino spitted one through the stomach with his sword, and the thing writhed even as it pushed itself up the blade to grab the Isuranian with its long talons. Crossbow bolts tore into the things, but they kept coming regardless. Meghan dropped one with a bolt to the forehead before drawing her sword and moving to help Raste.

"The heads!" Three Moons shouted as he pawed through his fetish bag. "Take off their heads to stop them!"

But the Blades didn't need the warning. They fought as a unit, pinning the creatures to the ground and splitting open their skulls. More eyeless fiends emerged near the mouth of the creek, but Niko and Jauna headed them off, cutting them down with their long knives. Captain Paranas waded into the brunt of the melee, warding off filthy claws with his shield as he chopped down foes one after another.

Three Moons watched as his comrades pushed the enemy back. His vantage allowed him to observe the creatures in better detail. They behaved much like the wights they had encountered in Omikur, even down to the way they moved and fought. He recalled what he'd seen when examining the bodies of the fallen fiends, and then he understood. *Just like that little mole rat was the fleshy equivalent to the earth spirits back home, these things are the spirit version of the wights we found in Omikur.*

BLADE AND BONE

Suddenly, a host of legends he had previously forgotten about took on a new meaning. Legends about the demons that inhabited the nether realm. They were said to be eaters of human flesh. Insatiable and unstoppable. *And blind. In the old stories, the demons were described as blind but able to hunt with their supernatural senses. But how did they get into the physical realm?*

More of the blind fiends appeared from the woods around the clearing. Even with their renewed zeal, Three Moons could see that the Blades would eventually be overrun if they stayed here. He shouted to be heard above the din. "We have to run! Follow the creek!"

Captain Paranas nodded. He grabbed Pollo and Pie-Eye, then sent them to join Niko and Jauna, and the four of them grabbed their clothes and armor before they charged along the water's bank. The rest followed in a semi-orderly manner. Three Moons kept to the middle of the pack. He marveled at his ability to keep up. It was as if he had shed twenty years. The rush of the blood through his veins was intoxicating. At the same time, all his senses were thrown wide open. He saw colors and details all around with amazing clarity. He heard his brothers and sisters breathing hard as they ran. He felt the tremors of their footfalls as they retreated from the pool. *What was happening?*

Ino ran beside him, his injured leg forgotten. The big man gave him a grim smile, revealing silver teeth.

It must be that strange water. It's changing us somehow. It might be killing us, for all I know. But it may also be what keeps us alive.

More pale-skinned fiends emerged from the brush but only in small numbers now. The Blades cut them down without breaking stride. The company moved almost at a full sprint.

Captain Paranas met his eye. Three Moons could see their commander wanted some good news, but he merely shrugged back, having none to offer. *Maybe we would have been better off back in the desert.*

With a grimace, the captain ran ahead to the front of the company, leaving Three Moons to wonder how long they could keep running.

CHAPTER TEN

Years ago, when the Nemedia intelligence service prepared her to infiltrate Akeshia and plunder its secrets, Alyra had been faced with an interesting challenge. Namely, how to blend in with a people of darker complexion so seamlessly that she could move among them unnoticed. Her blond hair and pale skin were hard to miss.

In Erugash, the network had gotten past the problem by inserting her into the queen's palace where her exotic features made her a favored pet. But that gambit wouldn't work here in Thuum. Or would it?

She and Natefi had spent all night discussing various possible ways to get her connected to the local power structure. Included in their ideas had been one to color her hair and skin with pigments. Beyond the difficulty in dyeing skin in a realistic way, Alyra had no way to color her blue eyes. She could try to pass herself off as a child of mixed parentage, but that would also raise suspicions. Blended-race children rarely rose above the lowest castes, and that would limit her chances to enter the homes of the elite.

In the end, Alyra decided against disguising herself. It was too problematic, and there were no easy excuses if her ruse was discovered. Instead, she would embrace her differences. She and Natefi spent the day grooming her for a grand performance. She oiled her hair until it shimmered and piled it high atop her head in a coiled braid. She applied kohl around her eyes and colored her lips bright red. Finally, she put on a dress Natefi's mother-in-law made from a beautiful sapphire-blue fabric they found in the neighborhood market. Gold-plated earrings and necklace completed the ensemble.

Looking into a small brass mirror while touching up her hair, Alyra had to admit she would definitely stand out.

"You look lovely," Natefi said as she returned to the back bedroom of the tiny home where Alyra was getting ready. "Is there anything else you need?"

"No, I don't think so." Alyra turned with practiced ease, enjoying the slim lines of the dress. "Except to thank you. And your mother-in-law. I couldn't have done this without you."

Natefi clucked her tongue. "We're happy to help. Anyway, you have the most difficult job. I honestly don't know how you do it. I would be petrified down to my toes."

Alyra gave a confident smile she didn't entirely feel. "I'll be all right. Now, don't panic if I'm not back until morning. These things have a tendency to last all night."

"Please be careful, Alyra."

"I will. Wish me well."

Natefi closed her eyes and whispered something. When she opened her eyes again, she said, "There. You'll be fine."

Natefi wrapped a long cloak around Alyra's shoulders and ushered her to the front door.

It was an hour past sunset, and the street was quiet. Gurita and Jin waited outside the yard gate. They had undergone a transformation, too. Instead of dingy, mismatched armor, the men wore chitons of the same blue cloth as Alyra's dress. Their sword belts and weapon sheaths were still a little battered despite a thorough polishing, but they would pass muster. The biggest change was with the men themselves. Alyra had never seen either of them freshly bathed and shaven. They were rather handsome. *Maybe we'll pull this off after all.*

Gurita gave her a solemn nod before he took the lead, striding down the street with one hand on the pommel of his sword. Jin followed behind her. As they marched through the dark avenues, Alyra reviewed her plan. It wasn't much of a scheme, she had to admit. Natefi had discovered a fete hosted by a member of the royal court. The king wouldn't be in attendance, but still it was a chance to insinuate herself into the upper layers of Thuum society. If she could get inside. There hadn't been any way for them to get an invitation, so Alyra was forced to rely on her natural talents. If she failed . . . *Don't think about that. Think of success. You can do this.*

Bolstering her confidence, Alyra remained lost in her own thoughts until they reached the gates of a large estate in the eastern quarter of the city. The manor house was huge, its tiered triple rooftop and many minarets jutting above the high walls. Cheery flames danced in the windows, making the mansion look as if it were burning on the inside. She wished she could have afforded a proper carriage for her arrival, but her funds were limited. In fact, after buying the fabric for the dress, costume jewelry, and makeup, she was almost broke. This plan needed to work.

A quartet of sentries in silvery mail and tall gleaming helms stood outside the gates. A footman in orange livery came forward as Alyra's party approached. She had prepared a lengthy excuse for why she didn't have an invitation. She started to deliver it until the footman gave a deep bow and said, "Welcome, my lady. May I announce your arrival?"

"Uh, yes, please."

She gave him her name as he walked her inside the gates. Her true name. She had decided that was her best ploy, to tell the truth . . . up to a point. Her story was that she had fled Erugash during the attack and come to Thuum seeking protection. She had prepared some harrowing tales of peril in case she was pressed for details.

They entered a large courtyard bordered by rows of tall shade trees on either side and the manor's façade straight ahead. A group of thirty or forty men in decorative armor stood about the court, talking and drinking from wooden cups.

"Pardon, my lady," the footman said. "But your escorts must remain here."

"Of course."

Alyra turned to her guards. "Keep your ears open," she whispered. "If you hear screams, get out of here fast."

"If there's screams," Gurita said with a frown, "we'll be coming to fetch you right quick."

Not wanting to get into an argument with her "servants," Alyra gave the men a tight-lipped smile and followed the footman. They passed through an arched arbor between the trees and followed a path of polished stones to a grand garden. Elegant beds of flowers of every type and color filled the grounds, divided by a network of tiny streams and stone bridges. The air was filled with the heady scent of a hundred thousand blossoms. Glowing lights floated above the garden on invisible tethers of sorcery, lending the entire scene a ghostly aura.

As amazing as the grounds were, they appeared almost plain compared to the finery of the guests. Noblemen and noblewomen dripping with wealth sauntered about. Most of the men wore long robes heavy with precious metal stitching. The women were more extravagant in their breezy dresses of silk and lace, festooned with gold and shining jewels. A trio of musicians played softly over the murmuring conversations.

Putting on her most alluring smile, Alyra strolled into the garden. The footman bellowed behind her, "Lady Alyra Delrosa of Erugash!"

Heads turned to view her entrance. Alyra's step didn't falter, although her insides stirred at the sudden attention. Her decision to mention Erugash in her introduction was tactical. The city's fall would surely be a topic of conversation here. She had chosen to use Horace's last name because . . . well, because it felt right. She was playing a part, after all. Why not play it to the hilt?

Her target was none other than the host of this lavish party. Lord Hunzuu et'Allamur was old nobility, able to trace his ancestry back to the early days of the empire. It made for romantic speculation, if you were Akeshian nobility, but Alyra was mainly interested in his close ties to the royal court here in Thuum. Lord Hunzuu was one of King Ugurnazir's oldest friends and closest advisers. If anyone had information she could use, it would be him. Also, he was said to have a penchant for younger ladies. Tugging down her neckline, she headed toward the largest grouping of nobles.

Slaves approached, offering all manner of delicacies on silver trays. Alyra declined them all except for some wine from Lord Hunzuu's private vineyard. Glass in hand, she searched for the venerable host among the array of gilded guests.

After walking past several groups, all of which watched her intently and then erupted into whispers as she passed by, Alyra found her target. Lord Hunzuu was even older than Natefi had described, looking at least seventy, though he carried it well. He was also quite short, with a bald pate and deep wrinkles. A cluster of elders surrounded him at a respectful distance, but it was the man talking to the old lord who made Alyra stop in her tracks.

From just a casual glance, he seemed to fit in with this crowd. He was in his middle years with patrician features. His robes were of the finest quality, his hair oiled and coiffed, but there was something about him that made Alyra suspicious. Maybe it was the way he stood, leaning too close to the old lord as if pressing him on an important matter. Lord Hunzuu nodded occasionally as if agreeing with his companion.

Alyra circled around the men, trying to overhear their conversation, but they were talking too low. She noticed another older man admiring her. By his dress, he was of the *hekatatum* military caste. Perhaps a retired general. She gave him a bright smile as she strolled closer, pulling him in with her eyes.

"My dear, you are simply radiant this evening," he said in a voice that was smoother than she had anticipated. "By your hair, you would seem to be a child of the sun. But I think you may be more suited to nocturnal pursuits, eh?"

Not the worst tactic a man had ever used on her. "Thank you, Lord . . . ?"

"Not a lord," he corrected with a slight wave of his right hand. "I am Mohar Dhaberi. *Kapikul* of His Majesty's First Heavy Lancers. Retired."

"I am Alyra."

"So I heard. You made quite the entrance. I admit I couldn't take my eyes off you since you arrived."

Alyra allowed him to kiss her hand and draw her closer. He raised his glass, and they clinked the rims together. "Tell me," she said, turning to face their host again. "Who is that man talking to Lord Hunzuu? I've never seen him before."

"Ahem. That, my dear, is the envoy."

She allowed her eyebrows to lift a fraction of an inch.

"He arrived yesterday," the *kapikul* confided. "Or was it the day before? In any case, he claims to have come to Thuum with a message from the new king of Erugash."

Alyra almost choked on the wine she'd been sipping. *Kapikul* Mohar patted her gently on the back and took the opportunity to run a hand down to the top of her posterior. "Now, now, dear. Don't take a fright. You are well protected here, believe me."

BLADE AND BONE

"Of course." Alyra recovered by pretending to look relieved. "Thank you, Mohar. What message does the stranger carry?"

"Who can say? They say he will only divulge it to our king, but the king will not see him. Perhaps that is why he hovers so close to Hunzuu, eh?"

Perhaps, indeed. It took Alyra a few minutes to extricate herself from the officer, and he only let her go after she promised to find him later in the evening. She gravitated toward Lord Hunzuu's entourage, pretending to admire the flowers as she wandered closer. She was surprised to see an envoy of the *Manalish* out in public, but she understood the nobles of Thuum would want to be cautious. This was like finding a serpent in your home. You wanted it gone, but you also needed to take care it didn't bite you before you cut off its head. She wondered how long King Ugurnazir could keep him at bay.

Alyra saw that Lord Hunzuu was finally alone. She started in his direction, but stopped abruptly when she almost ran into a tall man. She felt the blood leave her face as she recognized the mysterious envoy standing right in front of her. "Pardon me, my lord. I didn't see you."

She raised her gaze to his eyes and couldn't entirely suppress the shudder that ran through her. Though he had a kind face, there was a haunted look in his eyes. A chill ran through the warm night air.

"I have not had the pleasure of meeting you." The envoy extended his hand. "I am Pumash, lately of Nisus. If I heard correctly, you are from Erugash."

"Yes, I am. At least, I was."

Alyra kept her answer vague. This was a man she didn't want knowing too much about her. Suddenly, she regretted coming here tonight.

"Forgive my rudeness, but you are clearly not a native Akeshai."

"I was born on Thym. I was taken captive when the empire seized control of the island."

"Ah. And I sense the story of how you escaped bondage to rise to the cream of society must be quite epic. However it must wait for another time. Forgive me again, but I must take my leave. I sincerely hope we meet again so I can better make your acquaintance."

Alyra couldn't tell if he was flirting or toying with her, so she mumbled something about how nice it was to meet him. She didn't get back complete control of her nerves until he swept past, heading for the garden's exit where he met an older man—clearly a servant, judging by his mean garments. They left the party together.

Alyra watched them go. *Get hold of yourself! It's over, and you have work to do.*

She had only taken two steps, though, before she almost ran into her target. Lord Hunzuu was even shorter up close. Alyra was glad she hadn't worn taller heels. "My lord!"

"Aren't you just enchanting, Lady . . . ?"

"Alyra, my lord." She bowed her head.

"Well, Alyra. There are many lovely bouquets here tonight, but you out-shine them all."

"My lord is too kind."

She kept her eyes lowered as she spoke, playing the part of a flustered ingénue. He took her hand and led her on a slow walk through the garden. The musicians played a more festive tune. A group of ladies deep in their drinks started to do a temple dance, laughing as they stumbled into each other.

Lord Hunzuu summoned a slave who provided them with fresh drinks. Alyra pretended to take a sip. "You have a lovely home, my lord."

"Thank you. It was built by my grandfather, the fourteenth lord of House Allamur. Would you like a tour of the grounds?"

Alyra allowed her hip to brush against his side. "I'd rather have a look inside." She looked down at her feet and pretended to recover her shyness. "My lord."

With a predatory grin, Hunzuu led her around to one of the manor's side entrances. A pair of guards came with them. Once inside, Lord Hunzuu released her hand and stepped back. "Forgive this intrusion, Alyra. One learns precaution when reaching a certain age and station."

The guards came forward and searched her person. They were swift and professional, patting her down from torso to the edge of her skirt. Alyra kept her thighs pressed tightly together and pretended to be frightened. She even managed to make her eyes water slightly.

When it was over, the guards stepped back, and Lord Hunzuu hurried to take her hand once more. "Now, now. It's over, and we can continue our tour. That will make you happy, yes?"

She nodded and allowed him to lead her down the hallway. They climbed three flights of steps to the manor's top floor. Here the decorations became lavish with marble sculptures and gilded oil paintings. Lord Hunzuu talked incessantly as they walked, plying her with compliments and boasting of his family's status, but Alyra only listened well enough to respond with the occasional nod or murmur of agreement. She peered through each open doorway as they passed, creating a map of the house in her head.

Suddenly she realized the guards had stopped well behind them. She and Hunzuu were walking alone toward a grand doorway at the end of the hall. She had the awful feeling it would be his boudoir. *Where is his wife? Probably outside drinking herself into oblivion.*

Alyra searched for a distraction. She spotted another doorway off to their left. The room beyond it had a warm feel, with chestnut-brown walls and a rich burgundy carpet covering the floor. "What's in there?" she asked, pulling in that direction.

"That's just my study. But I think you'll like what's in here."

Lord Hunzuu tugged her arm back toward the grand doors. Or tried to. Alyra kept pulling him toward the study, until he had to either manhandle her or follow. With a doting smile, he gave up and allowed her to take the lead.

The study had a slightly musty smell of paper and leather. A large writing desk dominated the right-hand end of the room. Two deep chairs sat before it, facing each other. The wall opposite the door was filled from floor to ceiling with bookshelves and scroll racks. An oil lamp burned in the window behind the desk, casting flickering shadows across the ceiling.

"My lord, you have so many b—"

Alyra's statement was cut off as the nobleman grasped her tightly by both arms and spun her around. He pressed his body against her.

"My lord!" She shoved him back a step. "I . . . I . . ."

Despite her training, his aggression took her by surprise. In that moment he advanced again, clearly aroused. Alyra stepped back, or tried to. A hard surface had appeared behind her. It felt like a sheet of cool iron against her back, and she realized it was a plane of solid air. *Oh lords of light. He's* zoanii*!*

She raised her hands, but there was little else she could do while staying in character. He pressed against her again, more roughly this time. Her skin crawled as he kissed down the side of her face, nuzzling her neck. His breath smelled of wine and raw fish. Alyra closed her eyes and tried to focus on something else. If she let him wear himself out, perhaps she could put him to bed and have a little time to look around. But she shuddered with revulsion as his hands roamed over her body, triggering painful memories from her years in the palace at Erugash and all the humiliations she had suffered there. Her hand stole down to the side of her leg as he lifted the hem of her dress.

"So lovely," he murmured as he rubbed his hardness against her.

Alyra didn't think. She just reacted. Her fingers closed around the smooth hilt of the stiletto tied to the inside of her right thigh. She drew it and brought her arm up in a swift stab through his left eyeball. At the same time, she pulled his face against her neck to muffle his sudden cry. She felt the blade scrape against the bone socket as it plunged in all the way to the hilt. Lord Hunzuu stiffened against her, his body jerking for several seconds. Then he went limp and collapsed to the floor. Her knife stuck in his eye. She put a foot on Hunzuu's chest and yanked the blade free with a grunt.

For a moment, she stood still, listening. There was no sound of activity outside the room, no shouts of alarm. Quietly, Alyra went over and closed the door until the latch clicked shut.

Her hands shook as she went to the desk. Her breathing was erratic. *Stay calm. It's over. Just focus on the job.*

She hit the motherlode on her first try. A sheaf of scrolls sat in the center of the desk, held down by a pair of long silver paperweights shaped like daggers. Lord Hunzuu must have been reading them recently. Paging through them, Alyra found several letters between the nobleman and Lord Pumash. She wondered who this *Manalish* was. Which of the city's *zoanii* had seized control after the queen's demise? Alyra searched the letters but couldn't find an identity. Pumash spoke only of his master in the most reverent and frustratingly vague terms. But what she did uncover was chilling.

BLADE AND BONE

Lord Hunzuu had been brokering a treaty between Thuum and this *Manalish*. The late lord had promised to steer King Ugurnazir into accepting a treaty whereby the armies of the west could move freely through his land. Alyra understood the benefit to Hunzuu and Thuum; they were hoping this would save them from a brutal takeover as other Akeshian cities had suffered. Yet she couldn't see how this agreement benefitted the new king. Up to this point, he had taken cities with frightening ease, so why stop now? Not to mention that allowing Thuum to remain independent only placed a potential enemy at his flank. It didn't make strategic sense.

However, one thing came through loud and clear as she read the letters. The *Manalish* was even more of a threat than any of them had realized. Alyra thought back to all the planning sessions with Jirom and Emanon, with them so focused on how to defeat the Akeshians. Now those plans seemed naive. The true threat had been hidden right in front of them. She needed to get this information to the rebels.

Alyra rolled the letters up and thrust them down her dress. She went to the window. It looked down over the eastern side of the estate grounds. No magical lights shone on this side of the manor. She didn't see any sentries either, although she expected there to be some kind of regular patrol. Moving quickly, she ripped down the window curtains. They were soft linen, but she thought they would do. She tied them together at the ends and wound them into tight ropes. She tied one end around Lord Hunzuu's neck. A pool of blood had formed under his head. She searched her feelings for any regret but couldn't summon any. This was war.

Alyra took the free end of the makeshift rope and wound it around her left forearm before opening the window. She kicked off her shoes, climbed up on the sill, and swung her legs out into open space. Then, after making sure the stolen documents were secure, she jumped off. The line went taut as it caught against Hunzuu's corpse, and then smoothly lowered her to the ground. There was a faint thump from the window above as the body hit the wall, but Alyra was already disentangling herself from the makeshift rope. Then she was sprinting across the lawn. Her nerves were calm now, her thoughts clear.

She scaled the wall and dropped down on the other side, the loose dress allowing more freedom of movement than its appearance implied. She was making new plans even as she hit the street, padding down the hard clay on bare feet. First, she had to retrieve Gurita and Jin without drawing attention, and then find a way to get this information to the rebellion. She only hoped Jirom and Emanon would understand.

This changed everything.

Six days.

Six days ago, they were fighting for their lives against a horde of undead in the valley of black stone. Six days of tracking through the brutal high desert. Not everyone survived. The road south was littered with makeshift graves. The convoy that limped into Akeshian territory was much reduced from the one that had fled the hidden camp.

Jirom touched the leafy branch hanging over his head. It was green and healthy. No deeper contrast could be made. It felt weird to wear clean clothes. He still wore his sword, of course. Not the fake *assurana*. After the abuse it had suffered at the valley of black stone, that blade would never be usable again. Such a shame.

Emanon returned down the white gravel footpath. "No sign of her yet. Are you sure of the time?"

Jirom glanced back toward the cemetery gate. "Meet at the center of the Stone Gardens every night at midnight. That was the agreement."

Emanon stood beside him, gazing through the forest of trees and granite monuments. The Stone Gardens were a unique feature of Thuum. While the other cities of the empire buried their dead in caves outside their walls, the people of Thuum had created this vast wooded graveyard to honor the lord of death. Jirom couldn't decide if it was beautiful or macabre. Right now, he was just glad to be inside the city walls.

"I still can't believe we're actually here," Emanon said. "Glad I didn't lay odds against it."

"When did you become such a cynic?"

BLADE AND BONE

Emanon shrugged and resumed his watch.

Despite the showing of confidence, Jirom was just as amazed. Not just that they had survived the journey but that he had managed to get half a thousand people into the city without being arrested. Fortunately, Thuum was still far enough from the western problems that it allowed free passage through its gates during the sunlit hours. The rebels and civilians had entered in small groups, posing as what they were: refugees seeking safety. They were still struggling with finding them all places to stay. Some of the civilians had been taken in by people in the lower-caste sections of the city, but they needed to find permanent arrangements.

"You know," Emanon said, "it won't be long before the locals start asking questions about all these new faces. And when the government finds out there are escaped slaves living under its roof . . ."

"Stop reading my mind."

"Sorry. Sometimes I forget what it was like to be leading these missions. You know, I like things better now."

"I bet you do. You don't have to do anything except—"

A shadow dropped down from the tree, landing on bent legs with hardly a sound. Seng, their scout master, stood up. "Someone comes."

Jirom forced his fists to unclench. *I'm wound up like a coil, ready to strike at anyone. Will that feeling ever go away?*

"Stay out of sight."

As Seng disappeared into the trees, Jirom peered down the pathway. Someone was approaching from the east end. A woman, and she appeared to be alone. Jirom and Emanon watched until she got closer before they stepped out to meet her.

Alyra stopped with one hand reaching inside her long cloak. Then she spotted them and came forward. "I didn't expect to see you here for another few weeks. I'm guessing you had trouble."

"We never made it to the second camp," Jirom explained.

"The dead found us no matter where we went," Emanon said. "We had to come here to get beyond their grasp."

"So you brought the people here?" she asked. "What were you thinking?"

"We were thinking we wanted to keep on breathing," Emanon said.

Jirom shushed his second-in-command. "Can you help us find places to put them?"

"I'll try," Alyra replied. "But Thuum might not be a long-term solution."

"Why not?"

She opened her cloak and pulled out a bundle of papers. "The Dark King's emissary is in the city. Read these. They talk about a deal being forged between his master and Thuum's ruling class."

"Shit fuck." Emanon spat on the grassy ground, and then stamped the spittle into the soil with his heel. "Does the local king support it? What's his name?"

"King Ugurnazir," Alyra replied. "And, no. Not yet. But I'm not sure how long he can defy this peace offering. We've seen what those undead legions can do. Who could stand before such a force?"

Jirom rubbed the stubble on his chin. "That's a good question. Will any place be safe?" He looked to Emanon, not wanting to bring up the obvious but feeling he had to anyway. "What about leaving the empire altogether? Perhaps Nemedia would take us in."

Alyra looked between the two men. "They would, but that's a long trip north back across the desert."

Emanon swatted a low-hanging branch. "Hell no. We almost killed ourselves getting here, and now we're going back out into the wastes crawling with those things?"

"But if Thuum makes an alliance with this conqueror, it's only a matter of time before we're found out," Jirom said. "They'll hunt us down and put us to death as an example. The rebellion will die here."

"Then we make sure that never happens."

"And how's that?" Jirom asked. "Do you have access to the king's ear? Some secret form of persuasion you never told me about?"

"Nothing secret about it. We take over this city, just like we talked about."

Jirom couldn't help himself. He laughed out loud. "Take over? Are you insane? We have less than two hundred fighters left."

"So we fight smart. We hit the right places in a coordinated effort."

"Thuum is the smallest of the empire's cities," Alyra offered, although the doubt was clear in her voice. "And has never been considered a great military power."

BLADE AND BONE

"Even so," Jirom said, "we'd be facing at least a thousand soldiers, highly trained and defending their homeland. This won't be like fighting garrison troops on the border."

Emanon grinned his wolfish grin. "They'll be too busy to worry about us, with all those slaves running around."

"Gods in heaven," Jirom muttered. "Don't you remember what happened in Erugash?"

Alyra was nodding. "This time we won't have an army besieging the walls while a power struggle between *zoanii* is going on behind the scenes."

"Exactly," Emanon said. "It's completely different this time."

"What about the emissary?" Alyra asked. "He will report whatever happens here."

Emanon looked to Jirom. "We could have Seng's squad take him out before the attack."

Alyra shook her head. "I'll handle it."

"Do you want us to send a couple of swords with you?" Emanon asked. "In case things get messy."

"I'll handle it," she repeated.

Emanon flashed a smile at her. "Just making sure."

"Anything else?" Jirom asked Alyra.

"Can I talk to you for a moment? Alone."

Jirom gave Emanon a look, and his lover made an exaggerated courtly bow before leaving.

"Have you heard anything from Horace?" Alyra asked. He heard the worry in her voice.

"Nothing." When Jirom saw the hope leaving her eyes, he added, "But he can take care of himself. He'll show up when we need him."

Like he showed up when our convoy was being torn to shreds?

Fighting his own angst, Jirom put on a brave smile. Alyra nodded, though she didn't look convinced. "I know," she said. "But I have a terrible feeling."

"Are you sure you can handle this emissary on your own? He could be more powerful than he appears."

"I'm taking precautions."

"All right. Should we plan to meet back here tomorrow night? Emanon is going to want to get started on this insanity right away."

She shook her head. "Better make it two nights from now."

"Be safe."

Jirom waited as Alyra slipped away. The path wound between palatial tombs that glowed in the moonlight. She knew what she was doing. He had faith she would execute her mission, whatever it took. He just wished he felt as confident about his side of the plan. How in the hell was his ragtag band going to take over an entire city?

Seng reappeared beside him. "The Gardens are quiet. Nothing unusual out there tonight, Commander."

Not for long. Soon enough the streets of this city will run with blood. And I'll be the one responsible. Is there a better alternative?

"Sir." Seng looked up. "I can make a toxin that will incapacitate the soldiers, if you wish."

"Fuck, yes." Emanon returned, ducking under an errant branch. "That's the kind of advantage we need. How much can you make?"

"I will need to find the ingredients, but it is a simple recipe. Provided with the time and materials, I could theoretically brew enough to douse the entire garrison." Seng looked back to Jirom. "If you wish it."

Jirom ground his teeth together. "Fine. Get started."

Seng trotted down the path ahead of them. As they followed, Emanon gave Jirom an appraising glance. "I didn't think you would go for it."

"Is that why you had Seng pitch it to me?"

Emanon shrugged. "He came to me with the idea. I thought he should be the one to make the case."

The moon was setting. A bird called out from the branches overhead. The shrill cry cut through the stillness of the night. "We can't afford to play nice anymore. We're at the ragged end of our rope here. We either win, or we die."

Emanon grasped his shoulder and squeezed. "It's never easy."

You're damned right. And I think it's going to get worse.

BLADE AND BONE

Horace brushed flakes of millet from his clothes, but they were everywhere so he eventually gave up.

The grain barge had turned the final bend. Thuum loomed before them, resting on the banks of the Akesh River branch. Far to the northwest, following this tributary, were the hills where the Akeshii tribes had originated. He wondered who lived in those distant crags now, and if they would someday descend to conquer the Akeshians and continue the chain of history. *All empires fall eventually.*

For once, his transportation sorcery had worked exactly as he planned, depositing him and Mezim on the shore of the river, where they hitched a ride on this barge in exchange for some menial labor. It had been some time since Horace had worked on a ship, even an ancient flat bottom like this. The past few days had passed in a predictable rhythm, giving him time alone with his thoughts. The memories of what he had seen in the ruins played in his head. The woman told him he had been summoned to stop the spread of chaos across this land, but his thoughts were dominated by the visions of the city drowned by the flood and his brief, horrifying journey into the Outside. Every night he awoke from a nightmare in which he was floating once again in that black nothingness as something vast and terrible approached.

Seven are the Lords of the Abyss. Seven the evil fiends who tear at the souls of men. . . .

The barge had to wait to dock until a skiff of Thuumian inspectors came out. Horace stayed out of their way as they climbed over the cargo. Finally, the barge was given permission to land. The piers were crowded with scores of river vessels. Most of them were barges like the one they had arrived on, but there were some small river galleys, too. Pleasure craft, judging by their size and pristine condition.

As soon as their ship touched the berth, Horace nodded his thanks to the boat master, and then he and Mezim hopped off.

"I'm glad to be back in civilization," Mezim said.

Horace started down the docks. They weren't as crowded as the ones in Avice or even Tines, nor as chaotic. Akeshians in general, he reflected, seemed to live more orderly lives, but something in him missed the hustle and bustle of his home.

Once they were inside Thuum, Horace's plans hit a roadblock. He had no idea how to find Alyra among the thousands of people. He didn't even know the basics of her mission. Was she living in the royal palace as a slave again? He couldn't see her going back to that existence, but then again she was the most driven person he had ever met. It made sense to start there, in any case. He just hoped she knew how to find the rebels. The feeling of doom hanging over his friends had only grown stronger over the past several days, leaving his stomach tied in knots.

With Mezim in tow, Horace entered the city proper. The buildings grew taller the farther inland they went. Humble homes and riverside storehouses gave way to towers and temples. Most of the grander buildings were made of pink marble, a detail that lent the city's interior a welcoming atmosphere. The distinctive stone was also used in the many statues and sculptures that lined the streets. Flowering vines hung from the rooftops and scaled tower walls. Every element of the architecture was ornate, from the hand-carved pillars to the scrollwork trim around the windows and doors. He'd never seen such a civic dedication to aesthetics.

When he commented to Mezim about it, the man replied, "Thuum is called the 'Rose of Akeshia.' The pink stone comes from a nearby quarry. It is highly prized, but they rarely export it."

A tree-covered ridge ran along the northern edge of the city. Its upper slopes were enclosed behind a long wall that looked more decorative than military. "What's up there?"

"I believe those are the famous Stone Gardens of Thuum. Some sort of veneration of their death cult, from what I recall."

"Death cult?"

"Aye. These Thuumians are in love with death. At least that's what is said. They even keep their dead with them inside the walls."

They turned onto a major artery that passed through the middle of the city. To the east, the wide road led to a series of rising pink tiers, capped with jagged battlements and fluted minarets. Uneasiness stirred in his stomach. Was this the wisest course? He felt as if he were walking into a lion's den. His *qa* quivered as if reminding him of the power waiting behind it.

Stopping in the middle of the street earned him some strange looks. Horace reached under his belt and palmed the wooden sea turtle. He thought of Alyra as he cast out his senses to find her trail. After a couple of minutes, he gave up. There was a general indication she was here in the city, but he couldn't discern any more than that. *Stay calm and think. What would Alyra do?*

"How do we find where the lower castes live?"

Mezim looked back the way they had come. "Many would dwell by the river. But there will be enclaves where the servants and lesser craftsmen gather."

"Let's find one of those. Someplace near the palaces but out of the way."

Mezim led Horace down several side streets. Away from the main avenue, the buildings were smaller and less decorated.

Horace spotted what appeared to be an inn house on the corner next to a lofty five-story building. "That one should work."

"Master, may I ask how you intend to find Mistress Alyra? Your explanation lacked certain details."

"I'm working on it. Do you have any money?"

Mezim unslung his shoulder bag and started rooting through it. "Some. But may I ask another question?"

Horace tried not to sigh but failed. "Of course."

"What if she doesn't know where to find the others?"

"I'm working on that, too."

The inn was a small affair run by an old woman wearing a long brown shawl around her shoulders over layers of clothing. Just looking at her made Horace sweat in sympathy. She rented them a room on the top floor. After taking their money, she went back to her perch on a stool by the front door and closed her eyes.

Horace handed Mezim his satchel. "Why don't you go upstairs and take a rest?"

"What about you, sir? You look exhausted."

"I'm going to take a look around. I'll be back before nightfall."

Mezim took their bags upstairs, and Horace left the inn. Back in the street, he considered his options. His entire scheme rested on the idea that Alyra would base her mission out of a home or apartment, probably in a poorer neighborhood. For one, she hadn't taken much money with her. Second, she would want to stay out of sight until she made her move, and it was easiest to remain hidden among the multitude. He started walking. He had no clear destination, but it felt better to be doing something.

On a whim, he turned a corner and found himself on a street lined with weavers. Stacks of baskets, bowls, rugs, and other woven goods crowded each line, leaving only a narrow path for people to walk. Horace picked his way along, enduring several calls for him to stop and inspect the wares. At the end of the avenue, he turned another corner. This lane was lined with drinking houses on one side and a row of homes on the other. A gaggle of half-naked children played in the street, chasing each other.

Horace chose a tavern at random. He was heading for the door when he spotted a glimpse of golden hair. It flashed among a small crowd of women walking away from him, but then was gone.

Horace hurried after the blond hair. He reached the women, who were carrying clay jars and baskets of laundry. They fell silent as he passed by, their gazes following him. He stopped at the next intersection and looked around. People walked along in each direction, but none of them were blond, and none were Alyra. He started a few steps down the left-hand street, heading east, when another glimpse of yellow hair made him turn. A young woman in her teen years came out of a potter's shop. She was obviously Akeshian judging by her copper skin and dark eyes, but she had dyed her hair gold.

Deflated, Horace slouched against a stone post. The enormity of the task he had set for himself was starting to dawn on him. He could spend weeks, even months, searching for Alyra in a city this size.

He was heading back to the inn when a squad of soldiers appeared at the end of the street. By their gleaming steel armor and bronze tabards, he knew they weren't mere militia. Royal troopers. He turned around and froze.

BLADE AND BONE

Another squad in the same livery was approaching from the opposite end of the street. This squad surrounded a tall man in bright red robes. Horace started to reach for his power but stopped himself. He didn't know how many *zoanii* were nearby, but if he used sorcery every one of them would know his precise location. *Keep your head and think.*

Pretending that he saw something interesting in a fruit-seller's stall, Horace ducked under the shabby awning. A middle-aged man with a long, oiled beard stood behind the table. Horace glanced around for an escape, but the street here had no alleys. He was trapped between the two squads. The soldiers advanced purposefully, but they didn't seem to be searching the crowd too hard.

Behind the stall was a doorway set in a deep alcove. Horace pulled out one of his few remaining coins and tossed it to the fruit-seller. Then he ducked into the alcove and pressed himself into a corner. He held his breath and waited. Minutes dragged by, until he considered poking his head out to take a peek. Then the fruit-seller greeted someone, and a trooper came into view. The soldier gave the produce a casual glance. Behind him, the two squads met in the middle of the street. The Crimson brother's gaze swept all around. The scarlet tattoos on his bare scalp glittered in the sunlight like the scales of a serpent.

Horace squeezed himself tighter into the corner. He was prepared to summon his power at the first sign of trouble. He might be able to take down the Crimson brother and soldiers without too much collateral damage. But then he would have to fetch Mezim and get away as fast as possible.

Flashes of steel caught his eye as the squads separated, each going their own way. The fruit-seller tried one last time to interest the soldiers with his wares before they moved on. The Crimson brother was the last to leave, still looking around as if searching for something. Or someone. After a score of rapid heartbeats, he moved on as well.

Horace released the breath that had been pent up in his lungs. This was going to be even more difficult than he had anticipated. He wished he had brought a cloak with a hood. *Sure. That wouldn't be suspicious at all in this heat.*

After a couple of minutes, the fruit-seller beckoned to him. "It is safe now, stranger."

Horace peeked out from the alcove. The soldiers were disappearing into the crowds far down the street in either direction. He eased out of his hiding spot. "Thank you."

Horace reached for another coin, but the fruit-seller held up a hand. "No need." He tossed Horace a lime. "Eat. You look unhealthy."

Horace caught the fruit, and then he slipped down the street. He took a roundabout route back to the inn, feeling paranoid about being followed. Once he got back inside its shaded confines, with the old woman snoring by the door, he just wanted to bury himself in a bed and stay there. His nerves were wound so tightly he almost blasted a hole in the wall when the innkeeper awoke with a start. He nodded to her and hurried up the narrow stairs.

When he got to the room, Mezim was asleep in a nest of blankets on the floor. Horace kicked off his shoes and lay down on the only bed, feeling slightly guilty. He made up for it by placing the lime beside Mezim's pillow. But he couldn't sleep. His thoughts jumped around, refusing to leave him in peace. So he stared at the ceiling watching the beams of sunlight crawl across the walls, and wondering where Alyra was.

CHAPTER ELEVEN

The Last Day was one of Thuum's most affluent gaming houses in the city's upper west side. Once a stately manor house, and then an elite brothel, it had been refurbished as a club for gamblers with deep purses. Horace looked around the main room from his seat at the bar, nursing his horribly overpriced glass of imported wine. Mezim sat beside him, both of them wearing new clothes that had cost them nearly every bit of silver they had, all in an effort to blend in with the highest tiers of Akeshian society. Instead, they both received their share of stares from the clientele.

Mezim could not stop fidgeting in his blue silk jacket, pulling at the collar or brushing barely perceptible specks of dust from his sleeves. He sipped from his glass sparingly as if it held holy ambrosia and managed to look guilty at every moment.

For Horace, it was clearly his appearance that drew the most attention. With his foreign features, he was unmistakable no matter what garb he wore. The looks he received came in two varieties—the curious and the overtly hostile. He did his best to ignore both as he continued to scan the crowd. On the theory that Alyra would be attempting to infiltrate Thuum's upper crust, he and Mezim had begun a systematic search of the most exclusive public venues. A very costly search. They had sold everything of value they owned, including Mulcibar's amulet, which pained Horace the most. But he didn't think twice about it. He had the overwhelming impression that time was running out, that something dire was about to happen. So he dragged Mezim from gaming house to whorehouse to wine bar throughout the city's finer neighborhoods.

He and Mezim spoke little during their expedition, instead listening hard to the conversations around them, hoping to pick up some mention of a western woman seen circulating among the nobility. So far without any luck. What they *did* hear was a lot about the troubles in the empire's western reaches. Every tongue wagged with rumors about the Dark King and the recent murder of a high-ranking court official here in Thuum. Supposedly, they were tied together. And now people were saying that Epur had fallen as well. These ill tidings rang throughout every high hall in the city, shading every conversation with hushed tones of fear. Everyone wondered if Thuum would be next and what that would mean. Horace knew well enough. It meant the tide of war and ruin would spread farther. More people were going to suffer.

"Can I freshen up those glasses, gentlemen?" the bartender asked. He was a smart-dressed young man whose face seemed frozen in a perpetual smile.

Horace waved him off, and Mezim put a hand over the rim of his glass. They needed to retain their senses. *And we can't afford it anyway. How many more taverns can we visit before we run out of money? Two? Three?*

Early this morning he had woken from the now-familiar dream of the world being swallowed by a rising sea of black waters. He had seen Alyra plunge into those waters, swept away like a piece of flotsam in a riptide, and he hadn't been able to get the image out of his mind. It goaded him to search harder. Now it was past midnight and they were no closer to finding her than when they had arrived in this city. It was enough to make him want to seize his power and start knocking down buildings until he found her.

"Sir, perhaps we should be leaving."

Mezim nudged Horace's arm and glanced toward the front door. Half a dozen royal militia officers had just entered. Their weapons were still scab-barded, but it looked as if they were searching for someone.

"Yep," Horace replied under his breath. "That's our cue to leave."

As the officers headed toward the bar, Horace and Mezim avoided them by weaving through a group of noisy gaming tables where gamblers threw dice and flipped over cards. Horace exhaled with a loud sigh once they had slipped out the door.

The balmy night air carried scents of smoke and flowers. The Stone Gardens were only a couple of blocks away. Horace was tempted to take a quiet stroll alone through those shaded bowers. He needed to clear his head. But he couldn't let go of his personal quest.

"Come on. Let's hit one more on the way back." Waving for Mezim to follow, Horace headed toward the next public house.

Mezim plodded beside him, looking as if he could fall asleep at any moment. Horace skipped past the next two taverns and a smoking den. Finding Alyra was going to be almost impossible, but what if he drew her to him? He was thinking of ways to get her attention without calling the authorities down on his head when he felt the itch between his shoulders. He looked back, but the street was mostly empty behind them. A handful of revelers stood outside the last wine shop they'd passed, laughing and singing. Tugging on Mezim's sleeve, Horace turned right at the next intersection and increased his pace, but the feeling they were being watched kept after him.

The spying could be magical. If that was the case, then running wouldn't do any good. Horace had learned techniques to keep hostile sorcerers from penetrating his mind but didn't know if they would work against scrying. Opening his *qa* just a tiny bit, Horace wove a defensive shield around his thoughts. The itch remained, but maybe that was his imagination.

Frustrated, Horace steered them back toward their lodgings. The night had borne no fruit, but they could start fresh in the morning. It took them several more blocks to leave the upper-class neighborhoods and return to their impoverished hideout.

They were turning the last corner onto the street where they were staying when torchlight brought both men to a halt. A crowd of soldiers filled the street halfway down the block, surrounding their inn. Cursing under his breath, Horace pulled Mezim back behind the corner. Careful to stay out of sight, he peeked around the edge.

"We should leave," Mezim whispered. "Find another place to stay and never return here."

Horace held up a hand for quiet. He wanted to see precisely what these soldiers were doing. A pair of guards stood outside the door of the inn, and lights moved inside, presumably more soldiers searching for them. Horace felt the purse on his belt. He had only a few coins left. Wherever they went, it would have to be cheap. Maybe down at the riverside quarter. He was making new plans when he glimpsed a flash of deep red among the soldiers. His blood chilled as a Crimson brother exited the house. *They must be tracking me with magic somehow.*

BLADE AND BONE

"All right," he whispered to Mezim. "I've seen enough. We can—"

His words were cut off as he was grabbed from behind. As Horace fought to stay on his feet, he was dragged backward and pushed against the wall. He spun around, ready to unleash his power, until he recognized the two men holding them. "Jirom? Emanon? What are you doing here?"

"This one's going to be one hell of a hard nut to crack," Emanon commented.

Jirom nodded as he studied the massive stone blockhouse. He and Emanon lay prone on the flat roof of a tenement across the street from one of their primary targets. Elsewhere in the city, groups of rebel fighters were casing other locations, scouting for what was going to be—in Jirom's mind—either the most epic battle in modern history or a swift, brutal massacre. *Or both.*

"But it makes sense," Jirom replied. "This is one of only three arsenals in the city?"

The target building was situated on the edge of the government quarter, abutting a residential neighborhood. Close enough to the palace to be a problem, but it also had several avenues of escape if things went wrong.

"Aye," Emanon replied. "They don't let the soldiers keep their weapons in the barracks ever since a mutiny about thirty years back. So they keep everything in these big storehouses. If we control them, we control the weapons."

Jirom pointed out the few windows in the arsenal, all of them buttoned up tight with iron shutters. "We could pack the place with oil-soaked straw and set it alight. The brick of the building might contain the fire, but that would ensure the Akeshian militia can't get to their arms."

"That's good. Setting them on fire would require less manpower. But we should leave one armory intact. We'll need weapons to arm the slaves."

Jirom backed away from the edge of the roof and turned over on his back, thinking through the plan. "That's a big risk, Em. If we lose control of that armory, the battle's over. We're outnumbered more than ten to one as it stands."

Emanon slid back to join him. "We won't be when the slaves are freed to join us. Then we'll outnumber the militia. That's the only way we take the city."

Jirom sighed into the cool night air. The stars were out in force, cast across the sky like a multitude of jewels. The moon was setting early, its half-full radiance limning the city in silver fire.

Emanon rested his chin on Jirom's shoulder. "You're worried. I understand. I remember how it was for me, being in charge."

"I just don't want to fail our people. They've already suffered so much. A defeat here could end us."

"I know. But you're doing everything anyone could do."

"What about the information we got from Alyra?"

"That drivel about the nobles making a deal with the *Manalish*?" Emanon grunted. "I believe they'd want to save their own skins, but I can't see the king going for it. He would be reduced to a mere regional governor. These Akeshian kings have egos bigger than their cities. They think they're entitled to rule."

"The divine right."

"What's that?"

Jirom shifted his sword to keep it from digging into his hip. "It means their authority is derived from the gods."

Emanon grunted again, this time with greater disdain. "What a bunch of horseshit. Kings hold power because they have a lot of spears to back them up. But we're going to turn those spears against this king. No one's going to stop our cause."

Jirom kissed his man, reveling in the feel of their bodies pressed together. He wished they could leave this city, this entire country, and find some quiet place to be alone for the rest of their lives. But he knew it couldn't happen. Not until every slave was free. Neither of them would be able to live with himself until that became reality. And so they would fight again.

Jirom broke the kiss first. "But what if the information is true? What if Thuum makes a deal with the *Manalish*? Isn't that the greater threat?"

Emanon leaned back and ran a hand through his long hair. "One step at a time. Once we take the city, we'll have a safe haven. We can reach out to see just how invincible this *Manalish* really is. Or we can stay out of it. He's really the empire's problem, eh? Maybe they'll destroy each other and save us the effort."

If only that was true.

Jirom had the sneaking suspicion that no matter which side prevailed, the empire or the new conqueror, it would spell more trouble for the rebellion. "Once we hold Thuum, we can send out messengers to the rest of the empire that runaways are safe here."

"Exactly." Emanon scratched at Jirom's stomach. "So what about that other idea?"

"Seng's plan? I don't know, Em."

"Yeah, there's more to that little guy than meets the eye. But it's minimal risk for us, and it could save a lot of bloodshed."

"It doesn't feel right."

"Not honorable enough for you?"

Jirom punched him lightly in the stomach. "Maybe."

Emanon kissed him on the forehead. "Listen. No one loves your high-minded ideals more than I do."

"Is that so?"

"It is. But we've got to be practical. Like you said, we're facing long odds. It will take time to free a significant number of slaves and get them armed."

"And even then, they'll only be marginally effective."

"Right," Emanon said. "So this tips the scales more in our favor."

"But poison?"

Jirom couldn't shake the feeling that poison was the coward's weapon. When he'd been a mercenary, such tactics were considered a last resort. The Company, his last and most successful outfit, had never used it. *Maybe if we had, we wouldn't have lost that final battle.*

"Tell him to brew his mixture," Jirom said, trying to keep the disappointment from his tone. "We attack tomorrow night."

"I'll take care of it." Emanon craned his neck upward. "Look. Something's happening over there."

Jirom glanced down the street. Men with torches crowded around a building a couple of blocks away. "Militia. Maybe we'd better move out. I've seen enough here."

"Wait a moment." Emanon crept back to the edge of the roof and looked down. "I don't believe it."

Jirom moved to join him. He started to ask what Emanon meant when he saw them for himself. Two men in fine tunics hiding around the corner from the milling soldiers. Torchlight illuminated their faces. It was Horace and Mezim. "Shit."

"You figure those soldiers are searching for them?"

"Who else?"

Emanon swung his legs over the side of the roof. "Let's go."

They descended silently in the dark, down to an alley between the tenement and a large building studded with narrow shops—all closed now—around the ground floor. Horace and his manservant stood at the mouth of the alley, talking while they watched the soldiers down the street. Emanon padded toward them, and Jirom followed. Emanon grabbed the servant and pulled him back, clamping a hand across his mouth before he could call out. Jirom yanked Horace away from the corner. The servant kicked and tried to punch Emanon, which earned him a clout to the forehead with a clenched fist. Horace glared with wide eyes. He was sweating, and his hands were raised, possibly readying a sorcerous attack. Jirom held up a finger.

"Jirom? Emanon?" Horace said. "What are you doing here?"

Jirom motioned for Horace to keep his voice down. "We were wondering the same thing. When did you arrive in the city?"

"Just yesterday. We've been looking for you. Well, for Alyra actually, hoping she could lead us to you."

"This isn't the place for a discussion." Jirom looked to Emanon. "Take them back to the safe house?"

"We don't want to draw attention," Emanon grumbled. "Let's go to the park. Plenty of quiet there."

"Good idea."

Jirom led the way to the high ridge running along the northern edge of the city, skirting the government ward. Emanon walked beside him, saying nothing, but Jirom could tell by his lover's body language that he was bothered. He decided to leave it alone.

The Stone Gardens were empty at this hour. Jirom picked a spot along a secondary path behind a row of hibiscus trees.

When they were finally secluded, Horace burst out loud. "What's the rebellion doing here? Is everyone here? Even the families?"

Emanon turned away as if he wanted to leave. Jirom frowned. "Yes, we're all here. There was trouble after you left."

A shadow of guilt crossed Horace's face. "I'm sorry. There was someplace I needed to go. It doesn't matter."

"Doesn't matter?" Emanon whirled around with murder in his eyes. "A lot of people died while we were being hounded across the desert. But it doesn't matter because you were safe and sound!"

Horace surprised Jirom by facing the hostility calmly. "That's not what I meant. Please forgive me for leaving without telling you first. I thought you would be safe once you got away from the camp."

Jirom interjected. "We managed to escape, but those undead found us no matter where we ran. Coming here was our last option."

Horace looked from Emanon to Jirom. "Have you seen Alyra?"

"Yes. We met with her last night."

Some of the tension left Horace's face. "That's good to hear. I need to see her as soon as possible."

"She's getting us information about the city's defenses," Emanon said, spitting out each word. "She's doing her part."

Horace nodded. "I understand. We're here to help."

Emanon grunted, and Jirom noticed his lover kept one hand on the hilt of his belt knife. "We're glad to have you back."

"As soon as we collect Alyra, we can leave," Horace said. "I suggest heading west—"

"We're not leaving," Emanon growled.

Jirom winced as the words carried over the trees. He reached out to put a hand on Emanon's arm, but his lover shook it off, half-drawing his knife with the motion.

"We're here to take over this city," Emanon continued. "We can't keep running forever."

Horace looked to Jirom with obvious concern. "I don't think that's wise."

"We've been doing the impossible since long before you joined up," Emanon said.

"Trust me, I know," Horace replied. "But it's not going to end the way you think it will."

Emanon started to mutter a sharp retort, but Jirom cut him off. "What do you mean, Horace?"

The younger man took a deep breath before he responded. "The rebellion is just a small part of a bigger problem."

"The fuck you say—"

"Em!" Jirom said, putting force behind it. "Shut up and let him talk."

Emanon glowered at them both, but he remained silent, while still clutching his knife.

"This is hard to explain," Horace said. "While I was away, I learned a lot about this conflict."

"Where?" Jirom asked.

Horace shook his head. "It wouldn't make any sense if I told you, but please trust me on this. The empire isn't the real threat. There are bigger forces at play."

"You're talking about the *Manalish*," Jirom guessed.

"It's Astaptah," Horace said.

Emanon shook his head. "Byleth's pet counselor? I thought you killed him."

"I thought we had, but he survived. And he's extremely dangerous."

Jirom put the pieces together. "Alyra passed along some information about a possible connection between the rulers here and the *Manalish*. If he's behind the undead attacks, why did he come after us?"

"He was aiming for me," Horace said. "It's . . . complicated, but the reasons aren't important right now. We need to get as far away from here as possible."

Emanon threw his hands toward the sky. "And where should we go? Back to the desert and into the arms of those dead things? Or maybe we should just drown ourselves in the river and be done with it, eh? Don't you understand? This is our last chance. If we take the city, we'll have some semblance of safety. We can recruit more fighters, make weapons—"

"No place is safe," Horace said.

"What do you mean?" Jirom asked. "No place is safe?"

"Just that. There's no place Astaptah can't reach. He'll sweep over this city like a black tide, gathering up more dead soldiers with every victory. We need to get our people and run."

"Wrong," Emanon said. "This city is exactly where we should stay. You left us to die in the desert, and we're not letting you take over the operation now that you decided to come back."

"I didn't . . ." Horace looked to Jirom.

Jirom pressed his lips into a firm line and said nothing. He trusted Horace, but it was obvious he wasn't telling them everything.

Horace dropped his gaze to the ground. "I understand. But I meant what I said. We're here to help. If you're convinced that trying to take over this city is the best option, then I'm with you."

Jirom tried not to sigh out loud as he clapped Horace on the shoulder. "That's what we wanted to hear. We'll do this together, and then afterward we can plan for what to do about the *Manalish*, eh?"

Emanon still looked as if he wanted to kill Horace where he stood, but he kept it together.

"So what's your plan?" Horace asked.

"We'll tell you about it, but right now we need to get under cover before the sun comes up."

"When can I see Alyra?"

Jirom looked to Emanon. "Tomorrow night."

Horace nodded, and they all started back down the shadowed pathway. They picked up Seng's squad and left the park by a different gate.

As they traveled down a footpath lined with white stones, Emanon pulled Jirom aside. His lover waited until Horace and Mezim were out of earshot before he spoke. "I don't like this, Jirom."

"Everything's going to be fine. With Horace back, we have a fighting chance against the local sorcerers."

"At what price, Jir? We can't depend on him. Look at what happened back at the camp. He left us to die. He's a fucking coward, and he'll cause more harm than good."

Jirom glanced down the pathway. Horace and the scouts were almost out of sight. "He's on a mission, the same as us. But we have the same goals."

"No, Jirom. He's working alone. And when we really need him, he'll vanish again."

"You're wrong. He's solid."

Emanon strode away, following the scout party. As Jirom watched him disappear down the trail, he couldn't help wondering how everything had gotten so turned around. But it didn't matter. He had a duty to fulfill. In two nights he and his fighters would be rolling the dice against long odds. That was his focus. Everything else, including love, had to come after that.

". . . and as Emanon is freeing the slaves at the warehousing district, my unit will hit the militia barracks," Jirom said, concluding his explanation of the battle plan. "Then all that's left is to wipe up the last remnants of organized resistance before we march on the palace."

Horace scratched the back of his head as he digested the information. Mezim said nothing, sitting beside him in the small cellar beneath the cheese merchant's shop where the rebels had set up their command base. Jirom's squad leaders stood around the room, reminding Horace of the war councils held back at the desert camp. Only now the situation was much more desperate. They weren't planning a rebellion anymore. This was a battle for survival.

The plan was bold, bordering on foolhardy, but there was a certain flair that Horace had come to associate with Jirom's style of warfare. "Didn't you guys already try this at Erugash?"

BLADE AND BONE

The rebel sergeants bristled. One tall woman with a scar running down her face looked as if she wanted to draw her sword and stab him where he sat.

"That was different," Emanon grumbled.

"Different circumstances entirely," Jirom echoed. "We won't be shepherding a thousand unarmed civilians through the chaos, for one thing."

"No," Horace said. "You've armed them, and now you expect them to stand against trained soldiers."

"What the fuck do you know——?" Emanon started to challenge before Jirom cut him off.

"Our information suggests the troops here at Thuum are unseasoned. They haven't had an armed conflict in generations. A swift, decisive attack should demoralize them right from the start. Once we take out their company officers, the rest should fold up."

"You hope so," Horace said.

"Yes."

Horace went over to the crude map of the city that was pinned to the wall, brushing aside a string of aging cheese in his way. "How many *zoanii* live in Thuum?"

Emanon shuffled through some papers. "There's a small chapter house of the Crimson brotherhood. We've only counted six brothers there."

Horace frowned at the mention of the brotherhood. He'd had enough contact with them to last a lifetime.

"And we can add another dozen *zoanii* to the population," Jirom added. "Including the king and his retinue. Thuum isn't known for its sorcerers. That's one reason why we chose it."

Horace tapped his chin as he tried to visualize how he could fight off eighteen magical opponents, six of them temple-trained members of the Crimson Flame. They would feel his presence and general location the first time he unleashed his magic. Unless the city was already well on its way to falling at that point, the *zoanii* would converge on him like a pack of wolves. He needed some kind of distraction. "What if we . . . ?"

He lost his train of thought as the wiry man who led the rebel scouts entered the cellar. Behind him followed a woman in a cloak with the hood pulled down. Horace's heart felt as if it had stopped as she reached up and pulled it back. He rushed forward as their gazes found each other. He was one long step from her when he stopped. They hadn't parted on the best terms. Then, suddenly, she was in his arms, squeezing him as if they hadn't seen each other in years.

"Alyra," he said. He inhaled the sweet scent of her hair.

"So you came all this way to see me?"

Horace smiled at Gurita and Jin, standing behind her. They nodded back. "Yeah, I kind of missed you."

She poked him in the ribs. "Kind of?"

He took a deep breath. "Alyra, there's something I want to—"

"I'm sorry," she said. "For leaving without saying good-bye. I saw my chance to get away, and I took it, but that's no excuse. I should have found you first."

"I did the same thing. I left after the attack on the camp."

"You were here in Thuum all this time?"

Horace shook his head. "No. I was . . . I'll tell you later."

Alyra nodded and gave him another fierce hug. She nuzzled his whiskered chin. "You need a shave."

"The first chance I get."

Horace held back a sigh as they parted. Now, more than ever, he wanted to get away from this place, as far as they could go. To someplace where there was no rebellion, no battles to be fought, no more dangers. He wanted to ask if it was too late for them to leave, but he could see the answer in her eyes. Determination like he had never witnessed resided in her clear blue gaze. *She has made her choice, and so have I. Though I feel this will not end well for any of us, it's what we have to do.*

He turned to Jirom and Emanon. "All right. Let's go over it again. What do you need us to do?"

"Well, your part is simple," Jirom replied.

"Yes," Emanon added. "You keep the Akeshian sorcerers from stomping on us like a pack of roaches."

A sharp retort came to mind, but Horace swallowed it. "Understood."

BLADE AND BONE

Emanon looked to Alyra. "We have something else in mind for you. Come on."

As the two of them left the cellar, the bodyguards and rebel sergeants filed out behind them. Alone, Jirom and Horace stood by the map.

"You really think this can work?" Horace asked.

Jirom gave him a lopsided smile that was eerily reminiscent of Emanon's grin. "What could go wrong?"

Horace looked to the exit. Alyra had gone, leaving him with the hollow feeling that he might never see her again.

Jirom touched his shoulder. "Look. Here is where we'll set the first fire."

Putting aside his misgivings, Horace focused on the plan.

CHAPTER TWELVE

Jirom sipped from his canteen to wash the bad taste out of his mouth. It was almost time. The waning moon rested a fingerbreadth above the city's western wall.

He stood in a dark alley across from the first target. His fighters were positioned. Elsewhere in the city, Emanon and Silfar commanded equal-sized companies. When the moon set, they would launch simultaneous attacks on the city's three main armories, followed with secondary targets ranging from barracks and water towers to key access points. The hope was that the concerted offensive would overwhelm any local resistance, but that wasn't what worried him.

Almost half of each unit was comprised of civilians. At first, Jirom had only intended to use the non-trained civilians as eyes and ears, but as their plan evolved, he and Emanon realized they didn't have the numbers to pull off a takeover of the city. Not unless they counted every able-bodied man and woman under their command. It had to be done, and so he had acquiesced to the inevitable. But it weighed on him. People he knew were going to die tonight. He could only hope the casualties would be light. Hope that the Akeshians would be taken by such surprise that they chose to surrender rather than fight to the death. He didn't put much faith in those hopes.

Jirom checked his gear. The black shield was strapped tight to his forearm. His sword was sheathed at his side, along with a long knife and a war-axe. He wore only his leather cuirass, breeches, and boots. He wanted to be unhindered when the fighting began. Despite the slight chill in the air, he would be sweating once the blood began to flow.

A voice called softly from behind him. Jirom gritted his teeth and turned. *Beysid* Giliam sidled up to him, looking slightly ridiculous in a tight-fitting leather harness over his normal clothing. A slender blade Jirom had never seen him draw was at his side. *Gods, what have I done to deserve this?*

"Commander," Giliam said in an exaggerated whisper. "A moment."

BLADE AND BONE

"What is it?" Jirom growled back.

During the planning the *beysid* had presented a constant stream of objections, most of them connected to concern for his own well-being. When Jirom and Emanon discussed including the civilians in the fighting units, they thought Giliam was going to die of apoplexy as he stuttered and gasped out his protestations. In the end, the other civilian leaders finally outvoted him, and there had been little for the *beysid* to do thereafter but to accept the decision. Still, Jirom didn't trust him at all. As a consequence, he had placed Giliam in his own strike team where he could keep an eye on him.

"I've been thinking . . . perhaps I should lead the people on this attack."

Jirom lifted an eyebrow as he stared at the *beysid*. "You?"

"Yes, yes. They respond better to someone they know. I know the plan. We wait outside the building, watching for trouble while you and the warriors do your business inside."

"No. You're coming with me."

Giliam stood his ground for a moment, but then wilted as soft footsteps came up behind Jirom. After a timid glance in that direction, the *beysid* slunk back to his assigned position.

Jirom turned his head. "You certainly have a way of scaring the shit out of him. Thank you."

Horace wore a dark gray cloak over his clothes, which helped him blend into the night. "I hardly know him."

Jirom resumed his study of the armory. Its stone walls rose three stories high, pierced only by narrow windows on the upper floors and two solid doorways at the ground level. "That's why. To many of these men and women, you're little more than a legend. The foreign wizard who destroyed the Sun Temple at Erugash and killed a queen."

"I didn't kill her," Horace whispered.

"That's the thing with legends. They take on a life of their own. But don't worry about Giliam. Before long he'll be pestering me again with some fool idea."

Horace laughed. It was just a low chuckle, quickly cut off, but it was the first time Jirom had heard him laugh since his return. "Do you always talk so much before a battle?"

Jirom smiled. "I suppose so. It never gets any easier."

"Fighting?"

"No, fighting is the easy part. It's the waiting that kills me."

There was a minute or two of silence between them. Then Horace said, "He's a good man. Emanon, I mean. He's strong like you."

That made Jirom want to laugh. "No, not like me. He's cold steel wrapped around the heart of a volcano. He means . . . everything to me."

Horace clasped him on the shoulder. "Everything is going to be okay."

Jirom winked at him, but the gesture was lost in the darkness. "Damn right it will. You understand your assignment?"

"I stay here and wait like a trapdoor spider to see if any *zoanii* show up to the party. My only question is what you plan to do about the city's soldiers. Won't they come in force when you start your attack?"

An uneasy feeling passed through Jirom's stomach. He had neglected to tell Horace about Seng's covert activities, partially because such sensitive information needed to be kept secret, but mainly because he still didn't feel right about it. "We've taken precautions to keep them out of the fight."

After a moment's hesitation, he explained. "We smuggled poison into the stewpots at the militia mess halls. It's not lethal, but it should disable them."

Horace didn't respond for a few seconds. Then he said, "What about the palace?"

"The royal phalanx has its own mess hall, and we couldn't get inside. But we think they will stay put to protect the king."

Horace scratched his clean-shaven chin. "So we just need to worry about the *zoanii* and their personal guards?"

"Yes," Jirom responded.

"All right then. Let's get started."

Jirom summoned his sergeants. As they huddled close, he said, "We're going to make this as quick and simple as possible. We get inside. We take out the sentries. The outside squads make sure no one escapes to spread the word. When we've secured as many arms as we can carry, we set the fires and get out. Any questions?"

Everyone shook their heads, and Jirom dismissed them. His insides were stirring, the way they always did before a fight. He knew the feeling would die down once the action started, but it reminded him of all the battles he had fought over the years. *How many more before I am through?*

Setting those thoughts aside, Jirom strode to the front of his war band. The men looked to him. In their faces he saw fear and hope intertwined. He felt as if he should say something to inspire them, but he had no more words. They would fight and win, or die. No grand speech would change that.

"Come," he said and drew his sword. "Let's get this over with."

A muffled crackle of thunder answered him. Jirom glanced up as new trepidation crawled up his spine. The sky had been clear at sunset, but now thick black clouds were scudding over the city, blocking out the stars. A storm could be a boon tonight, hiding them from the Akeshians. But heavy rain would make arson more difficult. *Another double-edged sword I am forced to grasp.*

At Jirom's signal, the first squad raced across the street to the stout iron door that served as the armory's side entrance. Armed with crowbars and mallets, the scouts quickly wrenched the door open. Sergeant Seng waved his shortsword before leading his soldiers inside.

Jirom turned to Horace. "If we're not back out in ten minutes . . ."

"I'll start making some noise," Horace answered.

With a nod, Jirom led the rest of his team across the street. He charged inside the armory to find a short hallway. The din of battle rang out from open doorways on either side. Taking the first door on the left, he ducked into a long, narrow room where a pair of militia soldiers dueled with Seng and another scout. Jirom barreled his way between them and added his weight to the attack. Spotting him, the militiamen tried to withdraw, but Jirom pressed his advantage. Within seconds, both enemies lay dead on the floor.

Without pausing, Jirom went to the door on the far side of the room and wrenched it open. Another hallway led deeper into the armory. With Seng's squad following behind him, he kept moving. They found two empty office rooms and what appeared to be a watch post, also vacant. Jirom was starting to wonder where all the guards might be when he burst through a door to find himself in a massive central chamber. Rows of racks were filled with weapons—swords, spears, maces, and polearms. Down a side branch he could see stacks of shields, helms, and body armor. Another wing was devoted to missile weapons.

Jirom signaled to a corporal. "Get everyone together and load up on gear. Where are the sentries?"

"I think I found them, sir," Seng called out.

Jirom went to the front of the chamber nearest the main entrance. There, in a short foyer, lay five watchmen. A sixth was slumped in a chair.

"What's wrong with them?" *Beysid* Giliam asked.

Jirom hadn't heard the man approach. "Poison." Then, to Seng, he asked, "Are they dead?"

Seng knelt by the fallen soldiers. He peeled back their eyelids and felt their throats. "No, sir. Not yet. It works slow at first. They probably reported to duty feeling fine, but then the toxin overcame their senses."

"Quite inventive, Commander," Giliam said, obviously meaning it as a compliment.

Jirom ignored him and went to the front door. He unbarred it and peered outside. The street was quiet. He left the door open. Back inside the main hall, the rest of his men had arrived and were loading weapons into burlap sacks. Even Giliam picked up a few. Meanwhile, the scouts unpacked heavy jars from their sacks, which they placed around the hall.

Seng found him again. "The floors are wood, but many of the supports are stone. The plan may not work as intended."

Jirom had seen that, too. But he didn't have any better ideas. "As long as this place gets too hot for anyone to enter after we've gone, that's enough."

The small man nodded and darted away to supervise his scouts. Jirom counted out one minute in his head, and then started moving his men back out the side door. Seng was the last one out as he lit the long taper fuse from a tinderbox. Then he and Jirom ran after the others.

Sheets of rain greeted them. The squads gathered across the street. The sergeants did a quick headcount to make sure no one was missing. Giliam stood with the civilians, pressed into the doorways and under awnings to keep dry. Most of them were flushed with excitement. They'd done well so far. Inside the armory, flickers of orange could be seen through the open doorway.

BLADE AND BONE

Jirom found Horace right where he had left him.

"There hasn't been any activity out here," Horace reported. "Not even a patrol."

Jirom called to his sergeants. "Send out units ahead and on both sides running parallel to the main group. Ralla, you take the rearguard. I don't want any surprises."

The point squad was just setting out when shouts erupted from down the street to the east. At first, Jirom thought these were a response to the armory fire, but a quick glance confirmed that the flames were still contained inside. And the noises were coming from a couple of blocks away. *What now?*

He wiped the rain from his face. They were the only rebel unit in this neighborhood. Still, Jirom decided to investigate. If it was a problem, he wanted to meet it head-on while his men were fresh. There was no telling what chaos would emerge in the hours to come.

"Move out!" he shouted, pushing his way to the front.

By the time he reached the end of the block, the rain was coming down harder, making it impossible to see more than a dozen yards in any direction. Shouts reverberated from the buildings on either side as water sluiced down the street. Jirom caught up with his point squad at the next intersection. They were huddled around the base of a statue of a tall woman in elegant robes. Seng was staring through the downpour in the direction of the cries, which had grown louder.

"Can you make out anything?" Jirom asked.

The scout leader shook his head. "Only shapes moving in the dark. Something in the street. Maybe corpses."

Spurred on by the cries coming from ahead, Jirom waved his men forward. The scouts took to the sides of the avenue, moving quickly from places of cover, but Jirom strode down the middle. If there was danger here, he wanted to draw it directly to him and let Seng's scouts do what they did best.

The screams came from a row of homes at the edge of the government ward. Bodies lay around the entrance, washed clean by the deluge but with deep scratches and gouges pocking their flesh. There were no weapons beside them. The corpse of one man was missing its face. Then a woman fell from an upper-floor window, striking the pavement with a wet thud and faint cracks of bones breaking. In the window above, a dark shape loomed. Just for a moment, and then it darted back inside, but it had been enough for Jirom to see.

The living dead had found them again.

"They're here," Horace said, coming up beside him. "Those dead things."

For a moment Jirom forgot about the rebellion, about his men and the battle plan. The dead had followed them to the city, and these citizens had no means to fight them. Thanks to him, even the local militia was too sickened now to protect them. Even though these people might be his enemy, he felt for the innocents among them. The people who were being dragged from their beds and devoured by walking corpses. His fingers tightened around the hilt of his sword, and he pulled the shield into guard position. "Come on."

"You're not going to—"

Jirom answered with a growling shout as he charged ahead.

He kicked open the front door and strode inside. Horace came in right behind him. The entry was a long hallway extending through the center of the first floor. They followed the sounds of carnage to an open door at the back and arrived to see two pale undead in ragged garments crouching over the remains of a mother and babe. The creatures lifted their heads as Jirom entered, their bloody jaws opening in silent yawns.

His sword clove through the skull of the first undead before it could get to its feet. The second creature reacted faster, launching itself at him. Jirom got his shield up in time to keep the thing's fangs at bay. Its claws reached around the barrier to scratch at his arms and chest. He kicked it back with a boot to the stomach, and when the undead hurled itself at him a second time, his sword's point was there to meet its open mouth. He shook the weapon free as the creature slid off, black ichor bubbling from the fresh hole in the back of its head.

Horace raced to Jirom's side, hands raised as if to unleash his magic, but there was nothing left here to fight. "Are you all right?"

Jirom jerked his head toward the door. "There will be more."

Out in the hallway, the rebels tramped through the building, kicking in doors and engaging the enemy within. Jirom was about to explore farther into the first floor when a body came crashing down the stairs from above.

BLADE AND BONE

"Watch out!" Horace shouted.

But Jirom had already recognized the man as one of his light infantry. "See if you can help him!" he yelled as he charged up the stairs.

He found another of his soldiers on the landing of the second floor, his head tilted back at a shocking angle and almost ripped from his neck. The hallway was clear, but hideous groans and hisses came from an open door near the back end.

Jirom shouldered his way inside to find three undead crouched around the body of another of his fighters. Both of the rebel's arms had been stripped of flesh down to the bone, and the third fiend was gnawing on her thigh. Shuddering with disgust, Jirom waded among them. He chopped down one creature as it rose to greet him, separating its head from its body with a savage blow. The others leapt on him. He met the first with a vicious bash from his shield, knocking the thing backward, but the last undead wrapped its bony arms around his legs and tried to drag him to the floor. Jirom repeatedly smashed the pommel of his sword down on the pate of the creature holding his legs as it tried to chew through his leather breeches. Each blow struck with the dull thunk of metal against hard bone. He had managed to pound a hole in the skull, from which more black blood oozed, when the first undead fell on him, clawing and biting.

Using his shield to keep the creature on top of him at bay, Jirom was trying to angle his sword for a killing blow when the undead lifted off him. Jirom sat up, ready to meet another lunge, when he saw the thing flung into the far wall with enough force to shatter its spine. Horace stood in the doorway, one hand extended toward the undead. His hand dropped, and the creature slumped to the floor.

Breathing hard, Jirom leaned back against a wall and took a moment to collect himself. The night was still young. And judging by the din of the battle raging through this building, there was still much fighting to do before he could move to the next objective.

Horace stepped over to inspect the fallen rebel, but she was dead. The bite marks on her legs and chest were already festering with dark pus. With a grimace, Horace drew his belt knife and stabbed her through the eye socket.

We can't risk that our dead will come back to fight us. Gods, what a mess.

Jirom nodded his thanks. "Ready?"

"It's going to get worse before this is all over," Horace said, still looking down at the dead woman. "Much worse."

Jirom let out a long breath, releasing with it all the worries about things he could not control. "Probably. But we'll keep fighting anyway, because that's all we can do. It's all we have left. We fight until they put us in the ground."

Horace pulled out his knife. It slid free with a wet sucking sound. "And then sometimes we get up to fight again." Then he looked Jirom in the eyes. His gaze was filled with suppressed anger. "I told you this war was bigger than the rebellion. We're not fighting for freedom anymore. This is about the survival of humanity. You need to remember that."

Jirom thought of Emanon, who was probably on his way to the slave quarters to free more people at this very moment. Was this all for nothing? "Help me secure this building, and then we'll decide what to do next."

They climbed to their feet. Jirom shook the gore from his blade while Horace wiped his knife clean and put it away. Then together they went out to find more enemies.

"Is everything to your liking, my lord? Do you desire something to eat? Perhaps some shaved ice?"

Standing on the balcony, Pumash shook his head. His gaze was focused on the palace. Its sloped tiers were awash in the radiance of a hundred lamps, torches, and burning braziers, tinting its marble façade in shades of gold and orange. Just a few bowshots away and yet seemingly beyond his grasp. He tore his eyes away. "No, thank you, Lord Nimuur. I am quite comfortable."

Pumash walked back inside the suite. He had been fortunate to find such a staunch ally upon his arrival in Thuum. The lord of House Lamipetra was eager to please. Perhaps too much so at times.

"I merely stopped by to make sure you had everything you needed, Lord Pumash. Eh, may I send a slave to clean up?"

BLADE AND BONE

Pumash glanced at the piles of gifts scattered about the chamber, tokens from Nimuur and his friends. "No need. My servant will take care of it."

"As you wish." Lord Nimuur turned as if to leave but hesitated before taking a step in such an obvious display of showmanship that Pumash felt sorry for the older man. "Since I am here, my lord, I wanted to convey how honored we are that you chose to stay with us."

Pumash ground his teeth together. "Yes, so you've said. It is very generous of you."

Lord Nimuur smiled and made an expansive gesture with one hand. He was a tall man in the latter half of his fifth decade. His silk robe was trimmed in accordance with his *ha'jun* rank. "It's nothing! We must all help each other in these troubling times, eh?"

Pumash wanted to smash the man's face into one of the frescoed walls. Instead, he went over to a sideboard table and refilled his glass. It was a robust vintage of northern wine that he found delectable. "Indeed, my lord. Neither I, nor my master, will forget your abundant generosity when Thuum joins the new empire."

Pumash grimaced as he said those words and hid his displeasure with a sip of wine. So far the king had refused to see him, and his entire scheme hinged on subverting the city before the *Manalish* found out what he was doing. Time was growing thin.

"Yes," Lord Nimuur said. "We have heard of the happenings in the west. We would greatly prefer to have a peaceful transition of power here in Thuum. There is no need for armies. Just pens and papyrus, eh?"

Pumash forced himself to smile back at this pandering fool. "Precisely, my lord. When we take control of Ceasa, we will need new governorship in all the empire's cities. Your House would make a fine . . ."

YOU ARE NOT IN EPUR.

Pumash dropped the wine glass and clutched his temples with both hands as the voice crashed inside his head. The excruciation made him cry out. His knees buckled.

Lord Nimuur's mouth fell open as he stepped back. "My lord, are you ill?"

Pumash squeezed his skull tighter to keep his brains from spilling out. "Get out!"

The nobleman stumbled in his haste to get to the door. "I shall send for a physi—"

"Get out and stay away!"

When the door closed, Pumash collapsed to the floor. The agony intensified with every passing second. "My lord! Please!"

YOU WERE INSTRUCTED TO CONQUER THE CITY OF EPUR. INSTEAD, YOU HAVE GONE TO THUUM. EXPLAIN YOURSELF.

"I sent your armies ahead, lord! With the queen! They will take Epur as you commanded. Oh, stop the pain! I beg you, lord! Please stop. . . ."

His voice died down to a whimper as the torment subsided. Sweat ran down his face. His hands were shaking.

You have a plan.

Pumash nodded, and then realized no one could see him. "Yes, Great King. I will deliver this city to you without the need for invasion."

They will come to me of their own will?

"Yes! An entire city. Intact and unblemished. You will need living servants when you take control of the empire."

I have you.

The thought of being the last living person in Akeshia chilled Pumash to the bone. "Great One! Please! Allow me to do this for you, and you will see the value in—"

You will go to the court. Command King Ugurnazir to surrender at once.

Pumash swallowed, fearing to reveal how he had been barred from the royal presence since his arrival. "I have tried, but the king will not see me. He refuses to even meet—"

YOU WILL DO AS I COMMAND!

The agony returned, sharper than before. It drove Pumash down until his face was pressed to the floor. After several seconds it departed, leaving him weak and panting. He managed a feeble reply. "Yes, lord. I shall obey."

Then the presence was gone from his mind, vanished as quickly and completely as it had arrived. Pumash lay back on the cool floor and took several deep breaths. If the king of Thuum wouldn't see him, he would have to try harder. He would put pressure on the nobles. He could stir up the commoners with fears of invasion. But he had to act quickly. Remnants of the pain still echoed inside his head.

Climbing to his feet, he called for Deemu. Then he went to the table for more wine to fortify him. His hands continued to shake as he sloshed the dark wine from the decanter into a tall-necked glass. They didn't settle until he'd taken a long gulp. As the alcohol warmed his throat, he took another deep breath and let it out.

He was fully in control of himself by the time his servant entered. "Deemu, get out my best garments. We're going to the palace."

The servant's eyebrows rose as if he wanted to ask about the lateness of the hour, but he merely bobbed his head in agreement. "Yes, lord. Shall I have a messenger sent to request a formal audience?"

"No. We'll surprise them."

Half an hour later, he arrived at the royal palace in one of Nimuur's palanquins. Pumash exited and climbed the semicircular white steps to the main entrance. Sentries on either side of the bronze valve bowed as they opened the door before him. With Deemu following a step behind, Pumash took a moment to straighten his robes and then entered.

As he had several times already, Pumash crossed the vast atrium. The floor was made from river stones, a style that lent itself to the chamber's earthy, welcoming atmosphere. The high walls were painted in majestic frescoes all the way up to a row of round skylights bordering the chamber's ceiling.

In Akeshian fashion, several chambers separated the royal presence from the outside world. This, the outermost foyer, was a place where petitioners and those hopeful for royal favor came to wait their turn. Beyond it was another sizable foyer for those with a better chance to see the king. There might be waiting rooms beyond that, but he hadn't made it that far yet.

His heart beat faster as they approached the large doors at the other end. A squad of royal guards stood before it. Pumash stopped a dozen paces away and signaled to Deemu. With a bob of his head, the servant rushed forward. He spoke to the sergeant of the guards for a few seconds, and then the sergeant went inside. Deemu returned to Pumash's side. "He will deliver the request, my lord. But he believes the king has already retired for the evening."

They waited for several minutes. Pumash straightened his stance as the king's majordomo finally came out with the guard sergeant. A heavyset man in fine robes, Hannumah always moved with purpose. Though his appearance was that of a soft court functionary, he could be as hard as iron when the situation required.

Deemu cleared his throat as he stepped forward once again. "Our pardon for calling at such a late hour. But my lord's need to speak with your king is very great."

"Need or not," the majordomo replied. "His Divine Majesty is retired. Come back tomorrow at the second hour with the rest of the petitioners."

Deemu sneaked a glance back at Pumash. "The matter cannot wait until morning. My master comes with an offer of peace and brotherhood between our lieges."

Pumash listened, but he could see the barely veiled contempt in Hannumah's eyes. This venture was doomed. He suspected it would be the same when they returned in the morning. More pleading on their part, and more denying on the majordomo's part. The man possibly wanted a larger bribe than what they had delivered to him so far. Pumash could have Lord Nimuur send another payment to the palace, but that wouldn't help them now, and now was when he needed the audience. He stepped forward, aware that he was breaking protocol but not caring as the memory of the *Manalish*'s voice echoed in his head.

"Excuse me, Lord Hannumah. I *must* see the king tonight. As my man has said, it is urgent."

The majordomo met him with a cool glance. "And as I have said, my liege is retired for the evening."

Hannumah gestured over his shoulder, and the guards advanced. They were being shown out. Desperation clawed up Pumash's throat.

"We must see the king!" Dread roiled in his gut, threatening to make him sick. "If the king won't see us . . ." Pumash hesitated, grasping for an answer. "Destruction will rain down on this city!"

The few people standing around the chamber looked over, but no one moved. Pumash held his breath, wishing for something to happen. For the

Manalish to use him as a conduit as he had before, for the power to spill out of him. But nothing happened. His heart thumped hard against the inside of his rib cage. *Master, why have you deserted me?*

As the guards edged closer, Deemu looked back nervously. "We can return tomorrow, Master."

Pumash didn't move. Yes, they could try again tomorrow, but somehow he didn't think the *Manalish* would care about contingency plans. His commandment had been clear. They had to see the king now. Or never.

The sergeant reached out to take him by the arm. Pumash looked him in the eyes, unable to fight the despair welling up inside him. He had failed. It was over. Pumash groaned as a sharp pain rippled through his stomach. The convulsion wracked his entire body.

Deemu rushed to his side. "Master! Are you unwell?"

"I . . ." Pumash tried to swallow but found it impossible to fight his rising gorge. He was going to be ill.

The pain ran up his spine, jerking him upright. His insides were burning. He couldn't breathe. He tried to clamp his jaws shut, but he couldn't hold it back.

A jet of pure darkness erupted from his mouth, striking the guard sergeant right in the face. The officer staggered backward, dripping with black bile. Then the screams began as the darkness exploded from the sergeant in many directions like the arms of a squid lashing out. Each tentacle struck a guard, and they fell to the floor writhing, one by one.

A peculiar sensation enveloped Pumash, as well. The pain had another edge, a tinge of pleasure that rippled through him like delicate fingers dancing along his nerves.

The majordomo had backed away toward the inner doors. Pumash faced him. He felt the power bubbling inside him, ready to be released again, and allowed himself to smile. It must have made for a horrific expression, for Hannumah turned with a yell and tried to get through the doors. Pumash reached out—not with his arms but with this new power—and gave the majordomo some assistance. The stream of blackness surrounded the functionary like a second skin and then spilled away as he fell, leaving behind a withered corpse.

Pumash stepped over the bodies on his way to the interior doors, which now stood open. Deemu huddled on the floor, quivering like a frightened child. Feeling generous, Pumash held out his hand. "Come. It is time to see the king."

Deemu took a long shuddering breath as he joined him. "Will they let us see him, Master?"

Pumash reached out, again with his newfound power, and shoved the doors open wider. *This is what it must feel like to be zoanii. To hold the power of life and death in your hands. No wonder they rule the empire.*

"Of course, Deemu. Nothing can stop us."

With his servant in tow, Pumash walked through the doorway as a new man.

Alyra leaned out of the alley's mouth for a peek, but there was nothing new to see. The plaza outside the royal palace was empty. In another few minutes, a patrol of soldiers would march past on their regular circuit, and then the area would be quiet for another half an hour. Gurita and Jin were positioned farther down the alleyway, almost invisible in their dark cloaks.

She had chosen this spot between the Royal Scriptorium and the House of Elders for her lookout post because of its clear view of the palace gate. The royal abode ascended in tiers of massive stone blocks into the midnight sky. Her assignment was to watch the palace during the attack. If there were any signs that the royal guard was mobilizing, she was to send word to Jirom. What he would do about that, she had no idea. The rebels' hands were already full. Not to mention that any raw recruit could have been tasked with this job. *They want to keep me out of the fighting.*

She tried to console herself with the knowledge that her worth to the cause was more significant, but it didn't help. She still felt isolated and shoved to the side. She was calculating how long she would have to stay in order to technically honor her obligation when a staccato of marching feet echoed down the plaza. Alyra peeked out from her hiding place and saw a palanquin borne by eight slaves crossing the plaza. It was heading toward the palace gate.

She frowned. It was awfully late for an official visit. Did this have something to do with the rebel attacks? She turned to gesture for her guardians to remain in place and almost jumped when Gurita appeared beside her.

"Pretty late for a social call," he whispered.

"Stay here," Alyra said as she started to leave her spot.

He clutched her elbow. Not hard but just enough to stop her from leaving. "Where are you going?"

"For a closer look." She twisted out of his grip. "I'll do my job, and you do yours by watching my back."

Gurita drifted back into the shadows. Thankful for the obedience, Alyra slipped out of the alley. There wasn't much cover in the plaza. Hoping that no one was paying attention, she sprinted across the pavestones. She didn't stop until she reached the statue of a Thuumian general. Heart thumping, she ducked behind the wide marble pedestal. After counting to ten, she peeked around the stone base. Now she had a much better view of the approaching palanquin. Thin curtains covered the car windows, blocking her view of the interior.

Alyra was considering her next move when the vehicle stopped at the gate. An older man in plain clothing stepped out from the other side of the palanquin to speak with the sentries, and Alyra realized she had seen him before. At Lord Hunzuu's garden party, speaking to Lord Pumash.

Alyra squinted at the palanquin window. The envoy of the *Manalish* must be inside. Why was he here? To finalize a deal with King Ugurnazir?

Alyra sat back on her heels. There were too many guards present to attack the envoy. Even if she got to him before they could react, she probably wouldn't survive the attempt. And if she had miscalculated and Lord Pumash was not inside the car, she would die for nothing. *But I can't just sit here.*

Alyra waited until the car was entering the gate. Then, while the guards were distracted, she bolted back across the plaza. The trip back seemed impossibly long. With each hurried step she waited for a call to halt or an arrow in her back. Relief washed over her as she returned to the safety of the alley.

"That was risky," Gurita said.

Alyra caught her breath. "Yes, but I found out what I needed to know. Where's Jin?"

"Here," the other bodyguard answered as he leaned out of the shadows shrouding the other wall.

Alyra fought to keep the rising excitement out of her voice. "I need you to go find Jirom. He'll either be at the central armory or on his way to the militia barracks."

"What did you see?" Gurita asked, now peering out into the plaza. "Who is that?"

Alyra kept talking to Jin. "Tell Jirom I left my post to investigate the envoy. He'll know what you mean."

"Now wait a minute," Gurita said. "We're supposed to be making sure none of the royals come out to play."

Alyra nodded. "You will be. If you see any signs the royal phalanx is preparing to leave the palace, find Jirom's group immediately."

Gurita's bushy eyebrows rose. "I don't like the sound of this. We have our orders, and Master Horace wants—"

"We don't have time for this," Alyra interrupted. "I'm leaving, Jin is informing command, and you are keeping an eye on the palace. Understand?"

The men exchanged a long glance, but they finally nodded. "Fine," Gurita said.

Jin took off, back down the alley.

Alyra took a moment to place a hand on Gurita's arm. "I'll be careful. Don't worry."

He shook his head. "I'm going with you, milady."

"No, you have to keep watch on the palace."

"With respect, ma'am, I don't have to do any such thing. My first duty is to protect you, and that's what I'm going to do. Now, do you want to stand here arguing all night, or shall we get started?"

Alyra held his gaze for a moment but finally nodded. "All right. Let's go."

"And hope the boss doesn't find out about this," Gurita mumbled under his breath.

BLADE AND BONE

He'll just have to get over it.

A measure of relief filled Alyra as she headed back down the alley. As much as she felt guilty about abandoning their post, this was the right decision.

She was concocting a fresh plan as she stepped out onto the next avenue. First, she needed to make a quick stop at Natefi's house, and then back to the noble district to execute her scheme. Lord Pumash was bound to have some kind of incriminating evidence about his mission. A missive with instructions from his master, perhaps. Or a journal that shed light on their plans. Something she could use against him.

Only one thing concerned her. If she found the proof, where could she take it? She glanced back over her shoulder at the spire of the royal palace. To the king? She scoffed at the idea, but then reconsidered. *Well, I'll cross that bridge when I come to it.*

Drawing her cloak tight around her, she hurried through the benighted city.

CHAPTER THIRTEEN

Horace stood in the middle of the intersection at the edge of the government district. He looked down each of the four streets in turn. They were all quiet, but that didn't shake the uneasy feeling in his gut.

Behind him, Jirom was meeting with his sergeants, planning their route to the next target. The battle with the undead had sidetracked them somewhat. Fortunately, their casualties had been few, and so Jirom had decided the attack would go on as planned. Horace held some misgivings about that, but he kept them to himself.

Jirom came over holding the map of the city. "I think we have it figured out. We're close to the north market. We'll head there and then turn—"

Hurried footsteps approached from the south as one of Seng's scouts came into view. Horace forgot his name. He was taller than Jirom but as thin as a blade. A jagged scar ran across his shaved scalp.

"Sir," the scout said. His voice was naturally hoarse, as if he had gargled with gravel as a child. "We've encountered a platoon of local militia. They occupy the market square. By the look of things, they don't intend to leave it anytime soon."

"What do you mean, Urlik?" Jirom asked.

"They look like hell, Commander," the scout answered. "They can hardly stand up straight."

"More of the undead?" Horace asked.

The tall scout shook his head. "No, sir. They're alive, but maybe not for long. I figure maybe they ate some of the sergeant's brew."

"Can we slip past without them noticing?" Jirom asked.

Again, Urlik shook his head. "I don't think so. They look ready to fall over, but they're alert. The sergeant says we can go around them, but it means adding a few more blocks to our route."

"How long will that take?"

"An extra half hour. Maybe longer if there's more militia in the area."

Jirom cursed. "We don't have time for this. Tell Seng to prepare for an attack. We'll clear the market and keep going."

Horace turned to Jirom as the scout hurried off. "What if we tried to talk to them?"

"You mean parley?"

"Why not? If they're ill, they might welcome the chance to avoid a fight."

Jirom frowned as he looked down the street. "It means giving away our advantage of surprise. And that could mean extra losses. Losses we can't afford."

Glancing at the sergeants gathered nearby, Horace lowered his voice. "Jirom, there are undead inside the city. The Akeshians aren't our primary concern anymore."

"I know, Horace. But the plan remains the same. We take the city, and then we worry about the undead."

"All right, but if we can get by without fighting these soldiers, we save some time."

Jirom called over to his squad leaders. "Assemble for a fight, but wait for my command." As the rebel fighters got into formation, he turned back to Horace. "Okay. Let's go see if these sons of bitches want to talk."

Hiding a smile, Horace went with him down the avenue. They passed the palatial homes of merchant lords and master tradesmen at the upper end of the artisans' quarter. Seng met them two blocks down the street. The short scout leader blended in so well with the shadows that Horace didn't spot him until he was almost next to them. Jirom didn't flinch.

"Any new activity?"

Seng shook his head. "Not so much. They are hunkered down at the center of the market. They are quite vigilant. It will not be possible to enter the square without them noticing."

"Keep your men hidden," Jirom instructed. "We're going to try parleying."

Seng's thin eyebrows rose slightly. "Sir?"

Jirom sighed. "Just keep out a sharp eye. The other squads are moving up."

"As you say, Commander."

Jirom waved for Horace to follow. "Come on. Let's get this over with."

The street ended in a broad courtyard at the end of the next block. The dark bulks of the surrounding buildings loomed in the darkness. The only light came from a bonfire at the center of the square. There, amid a jumble of empty stalls, was a posted group of militiamen. Most stood, leaning on their spears, but more than a few were sitting around the fire. Someone called out a warning as Horace and Jirom approached, and the alert members of the platoon stirred themselves to form a quick wall.

Jirom held up his hands, and Horace did likewise. But before they could say anything, a command rang out from the militia. "Fire!"

Bowstrings hummed as a swarm of arrows fired from the second rank of the spear wall. Jirom grabbed Horace's shoulder and pulled him down to the ground. Horace had enough presence of mind to erect a barrier of solid air around them. Arrow shafts snapped as they slammed into the shield.

With sword in hand, Jirom shouted, "Now!"

Rebel fighters rushed the militia position from several directions at once. The fighting was fierce and brief. The Thuumians hardly put up any resistance as they were overrun. Many of them fell where they stood, or sat.

As they got back on their feet, Horace said, "They didn't even give us a chance to speak."

"They were too afraid to take a chance," Jirom said. "Or too sick."

"Are we taking prisoners?"

Jirom shook his head. "Not tonight."

Horace turned away from the massacre, trying to keep his mind on the goal. Jirom was right. They couldn't afford sensibilities. They either took the city tonight or they died trying. There was no middle ground.

As the rebels were finishing the last of the butchery, a familiar face entered the plaza. Horace waved to get Jin's attention. The bodyguard came over, his eyes watching the scene of slaughter. "Sir," he said. "Lady Alyra sent me to find you and Commander Jirom."

"What's happened?" Horace asked.

At the same time, Jirom asked, "Trouble at the palace?"

Jin shook his head. "No, the palace is quiet. But Lady Alyra has changed her plans."

BLADE AND BONE

As Jin explained that Alyra had left to investigate the Dark King's envoy, Horace's stomach sank. What was she thinking? *She doesn't know about the undead in the city.*

Horace grabbed him by the arm. "Tell me where this manor is."

"In the noble district, about three blocks east of the palace."

"You'll take me there," Horace said. He looked to Jirom, expecting an argument, but the big man was busy overseeing his fighters. "Jirom, I have to go."

Jirom nodded. "I heard."

"I'm sorry, but if she's in danger . . ."

"I said I heard. Go, but be careful. This city is going to erupt before tonight is through. There's no telling what you'll run into out there. I would send some men with you, but—"

"No. You can't spare them. Finish the battle, Jirom. I'll find Alyra and return as soon as I can."

Mezim appeared beside them. He appeared unhurt, but some blood was splashed on his left wrist. "Sir, I would like to come with you."

"No, Mezim. Stay with Jirom."

Mezim looked downcast by the order, but Jirom winked. "Don't worry. I'll take care of your secretary."

With a parting nod, Horace followed Jin out of the plaza.

Hiding behind a hedge of bushes, Alyra studied every detail of the lofty mansion down the street. It was nestled among a neighborhood of grand estates, locked behind multiple gates and guard posts. Behind a high wall, the house itself consisted of several wings stacked about and on top of each other. Torches illuminated tall arches piercing the outer walls, throwing shadows across the elaborate bas relief carving bordering the windows and doorways.

Normally, she would spend days, perhaps even weeks, studying this kind of mission before she went in. But she didn't have weeks or days, or even hours. Lord Pumash could be back anytime.

This manor was where the envoy had been residing during his stay in Thuum. It was owned by House Lamipetra, a wealthy noble family that had several palaces in and around Thuum. Alyra presumed Pumash was currying favor with influential families, and the Lamipetras were his latest conquest.

As she watched the torches outside the gate flicker, Alyra wondered again if this was the right move. The rebel attack was underway, but she truly felt she could do more here. If the *Manalish* got control of Thuum, he would control the northern empire. From there it would only be a matter of time before he launched an attack on the capital. As much as she hated the empire, she didn't want to see its resources fall into the hands of a single tyrant. She had the feeling it wouldn't be long before his ambitions sought out new lands to conquer. If she could find some definitive proof of the *Manalish*'s intentions, maybe she could broker an agreement with the king.

"Well," Gurita said. "Are we going to do this or not?"

Alyra steeled herself. Time was getting short. Now was her opportunity. "Stay here. Once I'm inside, there won't be anything you can do to help me. So just watch. If something goes wrong, report back to Horace."

Gurita looked at her sideways, but he nodded.

Taking a deep breath to settle her nerves, Alyra left their hiding spot. During previous visits to this manor she had mapped out three possible points of entry. The first was the side entrance mainly used for deliveries and the manor's many servants. It was guarded by one sentry at all hours, but he often fell asleep at night. The difficulty there was that the gate was old and rusty. It would squeal when opened. The second route was to hop the wall. There were a couple of spots where that was possible, but it didn't get her inside the main house. Then a third option had revealed itself. She and Natefi had quickly fashioned an outfit that would fit the part. Checking to make sure her make-shift disguise was properly in place, including the transparent veil covering the lower half of her face, Alyra walked directly to the main gate.

The sentries on duty became alert as she appeared outside the lattice of bars. "Hello, lovely," one of them called out as he came over.

The guards were dressed in simple tunics girded with broad leather belts. Torchlight danced on the points of their tall pikes.

BLADE AND BONE

"Mistress Annuka sent me," Alyra replied, drawing on her years of experience as a handmaiden to play the part of a demure lady of the evening. She had decided on this tactic after discovering the lord of this manor had prostitutes delivered several times a week for his private use.

The guardsman opened the gate and greeted her with a smile. "Another delivery for his lordship, eh? He's a randy old goat, isn't he?"

While the other guards jested, Alyra pretended to be too shy to reply, using her eyes to draw them in. The guard who had admitted her reached out to touch her face, and she backed away. "I'm only for His Lordship," she said, putting fear into her voice.

While she spoke, her right hand stole down to her thigh where her knife was strapped.

"Yep. Better not, Urib," another guard said. "His Mightiness don't like the goods soiled before he has a chance to play with them."

The lead guard let his hand fall, but he continued to leer at her. "That's all right, lovely. I'm sure we'll have our fun before you leave us."

She cowered appropriately as they waved her through, but then one of their number—the guard who had warned Urib—fell in beside her on the walk to the manor proper. Alyra remained quiet. They reached the door, which the guard opened for her. She thought he might come inside, but he remained outside the threshold.

"Do you know where to go?" He pointed to the grand staircase at the end of the foyer. "Just up those steps and to the left."

Nodding her thanks, Alyra slipped inside. She looked around, taking in every detail as she ascended the marble stairs. The doorways in the foyer would branch off into common areas for eating, relaxing, and recreating, with the kitchens likely in the back of the house. What she needed would be upstairs.

Alyra followed the guard's directions, turning down a long hallway that ran through the western wing of the manor. She listened carefully, but the upper floor was quiet except for faint strains of music coming from the end of the hallway. Yellow light spilled out of an open doorway. Alyra itched to check the closed doors on either side, but she first had to play her part. Taking a deep breath, she stepped into the lit doorway.

It opened into a lavish bedchamber, with walls painted in vivid frescoes of erotic scenes. The bed sitting in the center of the room was more of a round divan piled with silk pillows and a fur coverlet, all of them in purest white that reminded Alyra of Queen Byleth's chambers back in Erugash. The music emanated from a silver orb that floated above the bed, playing a languid song with dual harps.

Nimuur, the lord of the manor, stood at a sideboard with a glass of brown liquor in hand. He was an older man and wore a somber suit of red and black. Alyra didn't expect to see his wife sitting on the divan in a low-cut gown. They both smiled as she entered.

"Oh, Nimuur," the lady of House Lamipetra purred. "This one is exceptional. Just look at those gorgeous blue eyes!"

The lord came over and held out a second glass to Alyra. "I had no idea she was coming tonight, Javinka. What a lovely surprise."

"We'll have to send Mistress Annuka something to show our appreciation."

Lord Nimuur smiled. "Indeed we shall. Dear, would you mind letting us see more of you?" He leaned closer. "My wife enjoys it more if you take it slow."

Alyra nodded shyly and reached for the clasps of her dress. She unfastened one and let the fabric fall to reveal her left breast. Lady Lamipetra leaned back into the pillows. "So lovely," she whispered.

While her husband sat in a chair by the sideboard, Lady Lamipetra beckoned to Alyra. "Come here, little dove."

Alyra made a show of taking off her slippers one at a time, never taking her gaze off the woman. Lady Lamipetra's smile grew as she writhed on the divan. As she walked closer, Alyra toyed with her right shoulder clasp, playing the tease. She bent down over the lady. Instead of a kiss, she blew a gentle stream of air while sprinkling fine dust from her right hand into the woman's open mouth. Lady Lamipetra gasped, her eyes opening wide for a moment. Alyra embraced her, pretending at lust as she placed one hand over her mouth to keep her from shouting. Lady Lamipetra struggled for a moment before she went limp, her eyes drooping halfway shut. Alyra stood back up.

"I must say, my dear." Lord Lamipetra looked over at his wife sprawled on the divan. He was clearly aroused by the sight. "You must have a magic touch. I've never seen her overcome so swiftly."

Alyra sauntered over to him. The rest of her dress fell away, drawing his eyes. "Mistress Annuka schooled me in the arts of love herself, my lord."

"Oh? She did?" His tongue darted out to wet his lips as he stared at her chest. "How interesting."

Alyra bent down until their faces were almost touching and lifted her right hand. She pursed her lips and blew, and the dust puffed into his face. Lord Nimuur jerked back with a gasp. "What was th—?"

He slouched back in his chair before he could finish his question. Alyra checked his eyes to be sure he was under, and then got to work. After fastening up her dress, she wiped the last of the dust from her hands. The blue lotus pollen worked fast. Lord and Lady Lamipetra would enjoy a long sleep filled with wondrous dreams, giving her time to accomplish what she'd come to do.

Taking an oil lamp, Alyra left the bedroom. The hallway outside was still clear. Moving quickly but quietly, she checked the other doors. The first two were locked, and she didn't want to take the time to pick them just yet. The third room was another bedroom with masculine décor. The fourth was a spa. Alyra finally found success on her fifth try.

The door opened into a combination library and study. Low tables of expensive hardwood stood on the purple-and-gold carpet. The spines of hundreds of books gleamed in the lamplight beside racks of scrolls. On a podium against the far wall sat a pair of old stone tablets inscribed with hieroglyphic lettering. She scanned the tables, but they were bare. There was no desk or strongbox to search.

Starting with the books nearest the door, Alyra moved around the room. She wasn't exactly sure what she was looking for, but she felt there must be something important here. The tomes were mostly mundane with a heavy slant toward romantic fictions and quite a few erotic folios. Definitely not what she was seeking. She needed some kind of proof linking this noble house to the *Manalish*. Incriminating letters would do nicely, but she felt her luck running out as she scanned title after title. Perhaps the lord had a hidden safe somewhere on this level? The problem was that she only had a finite amount of time. Sooner or later, someone would find the lord and lady of the house as she had left them.

Alyra swept past a row of books bound in dark red leather and then went back as the curious runes etched on the spines pricked her curiosity. She didn't recognize the lettering, but it was done in a fine hand in gold leaf. She took one down. The book was very old. The leather binding was supple and worn, the gilded edges of the pages darkened with age. She opened to a vivid drawing of a diabolical figure on the first page. It was a combination of a woman and a lioness. The look in her wide eyes was almost feral in its hunger. Large talons raked the body of a man tied down spread-eagle before the creature. Alyra found herself both horrified and fascinated as she paged through the book. There were more drawings, each more frightening than the last, and chapters of demonological text. The entire shelf was taken up by the red-leather books, and there were more on the next shelf, including a large cyclopedia of spells supposedly for the conjuring of demons.

She was studying the cyclopedia, and wondering why Lord Nimuur owned such books, when she heard voices in the hallway outside. It sounded like at least two men, maybe more. Alyra put the book back on the shelf and crossed the floor to the windows in the wall facing away from the door. She threw back the heavy drapes and pushed on the casement frame. The window didn't budge. Alyra looked for a latch or lock but didn't see any. Then she noticed the thin line of solid silver running around the edges of the window. It had been sealed. The bars of the lattice itself were also silver, shined to a mirror polish.

Who seals a window with actual silver? And why?

The questions were moot. She couldn't get out this way without a battering ram. She was just turning around to look for another way out when the library door latch lifted. She froze. It was too late to douse the light and hide. She reached for her dagger as the door opened. When two guards in house uniforms entered, Alyra threw her weapon with practiced precision. Its narrow point caught the first guard in the cheek, causing him to cry out and stumble, clutching his face. He dropped his sword in the process. Alyra lunged for the weapon. She almost got her fingers around the hilt before the other guard caught her by the hair and yanked hard. Biting her lower lip to keep from yelling, she pivoted and kicked out. Her heel connected with the thigh of the guard holding her hair, but found only hard muscle under the skirt of boiled leather. Pushing off with that foot, Alyra freed herself from his grasp. The guardsman stepped toward her with his sword raised just as her hands closed around the fallen weapon's hilt. She spun and thrust. His mouth opened wide as he looked down at the blade piercing his lower abdomen, right beneath his armored belt. He stumbled back and fell, holding his stomach.

Alyra jumped to her feet. The first guard had lost consciousness. Snatching up her stiletto, she ran back out into the hallway. She wouldn't allow herself to be captured. She knew what to expect. Execution, probably preceded by torture. But she had lived under the threat of imminent death for so long that she no longer feared the prospect. Her only regret was that she hadn't completed her mission. *That's a lie. More than anything, I wish Horace was here.*

She headed for the stairs, thinking she might be able to get out through a side door on the ground floor. She was almost there when she caught the sound of heavy footsteps coming up the staircase. More guards. Alyra's feet almost slipped out from under her as she reversed course.

Heading back down the hallway, she went to the spa door. It was locked now. Alyra shook the latch, but it wouldn't budge. Cursing, she went to the next door. It was locked, too. Keeping her rising fear at bay, she ran back to the pleasure chamber. Lord and Lady Lamipetra should still be asleep. If she could get out a window, she might be able to escape, depending on how many sentries were out on the grounds. She was planning a route through the gardens at the rear of the estate as she ran up to the pleasure chamber door. She was a step from the threshold when a man in a House uniform stepped out. They surprised each other. The guard lifted his hands. Alyra reacted out of instinct. She stabbed him through the throat with her dagger. The point entered without resistance until it struck something hard. Distantly, Alyra thought to herself, *That's his spine. Twist the blade before you pull it out.*

She did so, and the guard collapsed at her feet. A stream of blood soaked her front and pumped out on the floor.

The nobles were still sprawled where she had left them. Across the room, two tall windows looked out on the night sky. The curtains were tied back, allowing faint moonlight to stream through the clear panes. Alyra headed toward the windows. If they didn't open, she would have to break the glass. The noise might attract attention, but she hoped to be long gone before anyone arrived to investigate.

Alyra was almost to the windows when she noticed a figure standing in the shadows between them. It was a short woman in robes of gauzy black material. Alyra froze in place, lifting her bloodied weapons. The woman stood with her back to the door, but there was something about her that commanded attention. Fingers of ice clenched around her heart as the woman turned around. A long veil covered her face. Her eyes were pure black in deep-set cavities. Alyra couldn't hold in a gasp as a familiar voice spoke from inside the robe's deep hood.

"I should have expected to see you here, my dear."

Alyra shook her head. This couldn't be real. She was dead. Yet there was no mistaking that voice she had known for more than seven years. "Queen Byleth? How . . . ?"

"Not queen any longer, darling Alyra. If you're asking how I survived the attempt on my life . . ."

Byleth pulled down the top of the veil to reveal a ravaged face. The skin was dark like ancient leather and stretched tight over the skull. Her nose was mostly gone, leaving a gaping hole in the center of her face. Edges of yellow bone peeked through the ruined flesh. "I didn't."

Alyra swayed on her feet and would have fallen if not for the fear running through her veins. The walls of the room seemed to shrink around her as she struggled to take in enough air.

Two guards entered the room. They plucked the sword and dagger from her hands and grabbed her by the arms. Alyra felt her control of the situation collapsing. Then she remembered her duty here. She had two objectives. The first was to try to escape, but the second was to inflict as much damage to the enemy as she could. She dipped her knees, feigning weakness. "The sorcery. The same power that animates the legions of the *Manalish*, it has affected you as well."

Byleth walked over to the sleeping Lady Lamipetra and trailed a gloved finger down the noblewoman's chest, through the cleavage, and across her stomach. "You always had such a keen mind. That's one of the things I liked about you, Alyra. Well, that and your luscious body. Tell me, does Horace still enjoy your favors?" Those black eyes turned toward Alyra again. "Where is my former First Sword?"

"Far from here," Alyra answered before she could stop herself.

Byleth sauntered over, her gait halting every other step in a jarring limp as if her joints didn't work properly. "Is that so? In that case, we'll have to extend an invitation he cannot refuse, eh?"

Alyra held her breath as the late queen of Erugash drew nearer. She didn't need to pretend to evoke a look of terror. She knew precisely what Byleth was capable of, but her focus was clear. When Byleth came up close, leaning her ruined face nearer as if coming in for a kiss, Alyra slowly drew her last throwing dart from its thigh sheath. Holding her breath, she ripped her arm free and stabbed upward. A shock ran up her wrist as the *zoahadin* point plunged into the underside of that decrepit jaw.

Byleth fell back onto the floor, screaming as she writhed and clawed at her neck with gloved hands. When one guard rushed to the former queen's side, Alyra didn't waste the opportunity. She jammed her heel down on the instep of the man still holding her, evoking a sharp cry. As his grip slackened, she grabbed his wrist with both hands and twisted hard, driving him to the floor.

Suddenly free, Alyra ran. She sprinted for the large windows. She was on the second floor. A fall was risky but far less perilous than remaining here. She braced herself to hit the glass, throwing both arms across her face. She leapt and cried out as something grabbed her around the neck, yanking her back hard. The grasp around her neck didn't let up as Alyra hit the hardwood floor, but instead grew tighter until she couldn't breathe. She tried to pull it away, but the grip was as hard as a band of iron. She turned on her side and looked back. Byleth was sitting up, assisted by the guard now. Black pus dripped from under her chin as she stared at Alyra with those depthless pits.

"Oh, no," Byleth hissed. "You aren't leaving us yet, my dear."

Alyra's heels beat on the floor as she was dragged backward by the invisible lasso, back toward her former owner.

A litany of worries plagued Horace's mind as he followed Jin through the dark streets of the city. *I should have stayed with her. Damn both our prides. And damn Jirom, too. I should have convinced him to leave. Now we're fighting poisoned soldiers and the undead both, and if anything happens to Alyra . . .*

Lights glowed in some of the windows of the mansions in the noble quarter. Here lived the lowest tier of the upper class: successful merchants, military commanders, mid-level priests, and lesser functionaries of the court. As such, the streets were wide and clean. And quiet. Horace imagined there would normally have been militia patrols to dodge, but they hadn't seen a single soul since leaving the rebels. *The soldiers are probably too sick to report for duty. And everyone else is hiding inside.*

Still, he remained alert for trouble. Not just for patrols but *zoanii* as well. They knew he was in the city, or at least they suspected, and his use of magic back at the plaza would draw their attention like iron filings to a lodestone.

Jin paused at an intersection of wide boulevards, peering down the streets leading north and east in turn. Cypress trees lined the cement divider between the lanes.

"Which one is it?" Horace asked. After another minute of pondering, he hissed, "Hurry up!"

Jin went to the eastern street. "This way."

After another few blocks, they came to a street lined with palaces. It reminded Horace of the neighborhood where he had lived in Erugash. He almost expected to see his old manor around the next corner.

Jin took him to a walled estate, stopping twenty yards from the gate. "This is the place."

Horace studied the estate. No lights burned in any of the windows. No guards stood outside the entrance. "You're sure?"

Jin nodded. "We should go around to the back. Less obvious."

Horace followed him down an alley between the manor and its neighbor. A narrow street ran behind the estate, leading to a rear entrance. The gate was wrought iron but likewise unguarded as far as Horace could see. "Where is everyone?" he asked.

Jin shrugged as they reached the rear entrance. Peering through the bars, Horace saw a path leading into a small garden. Beyond the rows of flowers and fruit trees lay the manor house. Jin pushed the gate. It swung open on creaky hinges, causing a screeching clamor. Horace winced and froze in place. Jin drew his sword. However, after a minute no one had come to investigate the racket. They went inside.

Stealing through the garden, Horace focused his attention forward, toward the house. Everything was quiet. The back door was bronze set in a lavish frame. A quick check revealed it was locked. Horace reached out with his magic. He found the internal latch and sprung it open.

The bottom floor contained dining and cooking areas and several parlor rooms. Moving through them quickly, Horace and Jin discovered nothing. No people. Not even in the servants' quarters.

"This is damned strange," Horace whispered.

Jin pointed with his sword to the broad staircase climbing to the second floor. They took the steps as quietly as they could. Even though the place felt empty, Horace couldn't dispel the dread coiling in his stomach. A faint scent wafted in the still air. He couldn't place it, but it followed him, growing stronger as he climbed the stairs.

The hallway at the top was sheathed in rich hardwood, glowing from years of diligent polishing. Moonlight spilled in from windows at the far ends, to the left and right, but in between those lighted poles were only varying shades of darkness. The doors on either side were closed. Horace considered summoning a light but decided not to. He didn't want to alert anyone they were here.

He and Jin checked the doors as they passed, lifting the latches quietly. They were all locked. Horace had almost gone all the way to the end of the hall when Jin stopped him, pointing to the floor. There was a dark stain on the hardwood, in front of a door. Horace knelt down and touched it. It was tacky. A streak of red stained his fingers. Blood.

Jin took up a position beside the door with his sword raised. Horace steadied himself, and then blasted the door off its hinges with a powerful burst of wind. They both rushed inside.

The room was appointed like a bedroom, with several low divans and cushions. Two large windows were set in the far wall, their curtains open. After taking a couple of steps inside, Horace stopped as he was hit by a powerful stench of blood and shit. Long, dark shapes lay on the floor. He summoned his light.

The amber illuminance shone on fifteen bodies, all laid out side by side on the floor in two rows. They were all on their backs, their legs extended, arms folded over their chests. Their poses were peaceful, but one look was enough to see that their deaths had not been. Large, gaping holes dominated the chest of every corpse. It took only a brief glance to confirm that their hearts had been ripped out. Black crust rimmed the gruesome wounds. Horace grimaced. He knew that telltale residue. The destructive half of the Shinar had been used on these people.

Horace checked to see if Alyra was among them. He found seven women, but none were her. Rather than relieved, he felt more anxious. Where was she?

"What do you make of this?" Jin asked, kneeling beside one of the bodies.

Horace looked at what Jin was pointing out. The bodies of three men bore puncture and slashing wounds as well as having their hearts torn out. The injuries looked as if they had been made with a thin blade. All three men wore remnants of a uniform. They had been young and in good physical condition. "They were probably household guards," he said. "Someone took the time to kill them twice."

Jin pointed to a pair of corpses at the other side of the room. "I think those are the lord and lady of the house. Who did this?"

Horace brushed his hands on the front of his robe. He felt unclean just being here. "I don't know, but Alyra isn't here. Let's go—"

A strange feeling came over Horace. His sight grew dim, and a great pressure squeezed his chest. Then he heard something, like someone calling his name from far away, but not with a voice. With a thought. Singular and powerful, it vibrated in his mind like a struck harp string.

"Alyra," he breathed.

BLADE AND BONE

"Sir?" Jin asked.

Horace closed his eyes and turned in a slow circle. The strange sensation was coming from the north. It felt close by.

"Come on," he said.

They raced down the stairs and out the back of the manor. Once they hit the street, Horace slowed his pace. Like a hound on a scent, he followed the feeling through the avenues and alleyways of the noble quarter. He didn't have a plan except to find her.

"What was she looking for here?" he asked.

Jin walked beside him, his sword in hand. "She said she wanted to find something on that diplomat. She told Gurita that he was the key to everything."

"What does that mean?"

"Sorry, sir. I didn't ask."

They were crossing a wide boulevard into another neighborhood of large mansions and stately parks when Horace spotted a group of low, lean shadows ahead of them. "Behind me," he said to Jin.

The undead had noticed them. They leapt over fences and bulled through ornamental hedges with preternatural swiftness. Counting seven of them, Horace unleashed a bolt of fire and split it into seven beams. Each beam punched into the chest of an undead creature. Flames erupted from their mottled skin, but they kept coming. Horace started to sweat. Any of those fiery bolts would have dropped a man in plate armor, but the undead didn't even break stride. They leapt at him, talons extended and jaws open wide.

Horace grabbed Jin and dove to the side, scuffing his knees on the hard clay pavement. He sent a gust of wind behind him, and the nearest undead tumbled away down the street. But the rest of the creatures reached them two heartbeats later. Jin cut down one with a slash to its temple, splitting its skull open.

Horace tapped into the Kishargal dominion and peeled up a section of the street pavement. He wrapped it up and over to form a clay bubble around himself and Jin. He reinforced the material with sorcery, making it rock-hard. As they sat inside the stony cocoon, Horace could hear the scrabbling of sharp claws on the outside. *They shrug off magic like raindrops. How do you kill that which is already dead?*

His frustration mounted. The *zoana* surged inside him, wanting release. He placed both palms on the interior surface of his hardened bubble and channeled the power directly into it. With a sharp thump that shook the ground, the bubble exploded outward in a hail of slivers. The undead surrounding him were knocked off their feet. They writhed in silence on the street, with most of the flesh ripped from their bones. Horace watched in amazement as the things slowly got back up.

Then he remembered the ruins in the desert and the woman. Looking again at the undead as they started to approach, he Saw through their skin and bones, down to the very core of their being. There he spotted the motes of darkness forming the framework of their physical bodies. They were tiny spots of void energy.

Just as he had with the elemental creatures at the ruins, Horace reached out with his power and unbound those motes. For a moment, the undead appeared different—tall and lean with gray skin that glistened in the moonlight. And no eyes. Horace blinked, and the image was gone. One by one, the undead collapsed and lay still.

His hands were shaking, but Horace felt calm inside. Then he noticed the sudden chill in the night air. The black clouds were growing thicker, blanketing the sky. *A storm . . . here? Now?*

Motioning to Jin, Horace started to run. The shadowy ridge to the north rose before them like a great black wave against the night sky, reminding Horace of his dreams. He eyed the purple-black clouds overhead. He had long ago stopped believing in coincidences. The storm and the arrival of the undead, they were connected, and it all led back to Astaptah.

Horace quickened his pace along the empty avenue, occasionally glancing back over his shoulder. He had to find her.

BLADE AND BONE

As he opened his eyes, Pumash couldn't remember where he was at first. Then he took in the high painted walls, the stately pillars supporting the vaulted ceiling, the cool marble floor on which he lay, and he remembered. Bodies surrounded him. Guardsmen, courtiers, ladies in fine raiment—all dead, their blank eyes staring at him in frozen horror. At the end of the grand chamber sat the royal throne, encrusted with gilt.

He remembered entering this chamber, and then . . . nothing else.

He groaned as he sat up, his joints crying out in silent protest. His entire body hurt, especially his head. He was rubbing his temples when a sudden movement beside him made him start. The corpses began to twitch.

No matter how many times he saw it, he would never get accustomed to the hideous manner in which the inert dead came back to their eerie semblance of life. He pulled his hands and feet close to his body, as far from the reanimating things as possible. When the corpse of a guardsman flopped over, almost touching him, Pumash swallowed a shout of revulsion. Suddenly he remembered everything. He had entered this chamber without invitation, striding proudly into the royal presence. And when the king and his advisers refused to acknowledge him, a shudder had run through his body. Like before but much stronger. Then he was laughing, a most hideous laughter as the chamber doors slammed shut behind him. People started screaming as the black pus poured out of him. Out of his mouth and nose, even out of his eyes. He recalled the hopeless feeling as the dark power flowed through him. He remembered thinking this was how things were meant to be.

I am merely an instrument.

He must have fallen where he stood because he awoke in the same place, sore and aching. He would have killed—again—for a jug of wine. He didn't even care about the quality of the vintage, just anything that would numb his mind. The dead rose to their feet and shuffled toward the door. King Ugurnazir leaned close as he passed by, as if smelling him, the royal jaws opening and shutting with loud clattering of hungry teeth, but His Majesty left him unmolested. Pumash breathed a sigh when the chamber was finally empty except for him. Then he heard a whimper.

Deemu huddled in a corner like a frightened rodent, his face covered by his arms except for a small gap in the crook of his elbow through which he viewed the room.

"Deemu," Pumash said, standing and groaning as his knees ached. "Come here. It's over."

His servant unwrapped himself and stood up on shaky legs. With a dutiful nod, he came over, dodging the pools of congealing blood and bile. Judging by the dark windows lining the upper half of the chamber, it was still hours until dawn. Pumash wanted to find the pantry and drink himself into oblivion until morning. He was about to order Deemu to lead the way when the floor shook beneath their feet. What now? When would this nightmare end? *Never. Not until I lie down for my final sleep. But what if that's not the end? What if he brings me back? Will I shuffle on forever in a lifeless world, forever rotting, forever hungry?*

Pumash felt weak. Clutching his servant's shoulder, they left the chamber, him directing Deemu with terse commands. Up those stairs, turn left, now right. He didn't know where they were going, just someplace away from the horrors of the night.

They passed a row of open windows in a long hall. Outside, a blanket of clouds filled the sky. Dark and ominous, their inky folds were etched in green light as the rain began to fall. Out beyond the palace walls, a faint susurrus of screams was rising. The dead were loose in the city. Thunder crackled.

Pumash suddenly lost his grip on Deemu's shoulder. He fell hard to his knees and cried out. Clasping both hands over his ears, he curled up on the floor, tears running uncontrollably down his face.

Deemu was at his side, stroking the back of his neck. "It's all right, Master. It's all right. You'll see. We'll weather this storm. After all, what choice do we have?"

His words only made Pumash shudder harder as the anguish of what he'd done washed over him.

CHAPTER FOURTEEN

Alyra drifted in and out of consciousness as she was carried out of the Lamipetras' mansion. Bound, gagged, and blindfolded, she was lifted onto the hard bed of a cart or wagon, and then rolled away. Somewhere along the way she blacked out for a longer stretch of time.

When she came to, hands were lifting her up. Rain drenched her clothes. A sudden crackle of thunder made her cringe. Then the sounds faded, and the weather vanished as heavy footsteps echoed softly around her. They were inside an enclosed space. She noticed a downward slope to the floor as they propelled her along. There was also an odor of damp soil mixed with something else, like old mortar. Where were they taking her?

She kept anticipating that the journey would end, perhaps with a prison cell, but the trek took them deeper and deeper into the unknown, until Alyra began to wonder if she could find her way back out of this place—whatever it was—even if she managed to free herself. *Don't panic. Think and wait for an opportunity.*

On and on they traveled for what seemed like miles, until the echoes of their footsteps fell away and a cool breeze brushed her face. There was a moment when she thought she heard fighting. It was brief and far behind her. She strained to hear, daring to hope that a rescue was underway. Then the noise ended, and she was carried forward by her captors.

Finally, they set her down on her feet, and someone took off her blindfold. She half-expected to be outside again, perhaps with open sky above. Instead, light from a dozen torches illuminated a vast underground theater. Tiers of stone seats encircled half the space. She and her captors had entered through a tunnel in the center of the seats onto a concrete floor, broken and littered with debris. Instead of sky, the inverted bowl of a broad dome arched overhead. It had to be at least a hundred feet above the floor at its highest point. A stage stood on the far side of the theater, backed by thick pillars. The entire place looked as if it was centuries old.

BLADE AND BONE

Then Alyra noticed a figure standing in the shadows of the stage, and an image flashed through her mind. She was back in the royal palace at Erugash, dagger in hand, on a mission to murder the queen. *If I had killed her when I had the chance, perhaps she would still be dead.*

"Welcome to the undercity of Thuum," Byleth's voice called across the distance. "Can you imagine the people who once lived here? They attended plays in this very stadium. They loved, they had children, and they eventually died here, only to be buried over the course of the ages until a new city reigned above their graves."

Alyra found her voice as the guards escorted her toward the stage. "You serve the new overlord of Erugash? The one they call the *Manalish*."

Byleth looked down. The wrap had fallen away from her face, revealing a swathe of rotted flesh and exposed bone. The bare sinews of her cheek twisted upward in a ghoulish smile. "He brought me back from the other side, Alyra. Oh, you have no idea the sights I've seen."

Byleth leaned closer, and the twin points of her eyes blazed brighter. "There is so much more to the cosmos than we ever imagined. The struggles of your slave rebellion are paltry in comparison. Even the empire's history is nothing but a few drops in time's vast ocean. The *Manalish* is eternal. His power will bring a new age to this world."

Chains were attached to the center pair of columns. The guards untied Alyra's hands as they moved her between the pillars. There was a moment when she was free, when the guard holding her left wrist let go to grasp the chain on that side. Alyra's hand dropped to the dart sheath at her thigh, searching for a weapon. Hope fled as her fingers searched the leather harness. It was empty.

The bronze cuffs snapped around her wrists, reminding Alyra of the collar she'd worn for so long. She tensed, wanting to stop this, but there wasn't anything she could do. Even without the guards, Byleth could wrap her in streams of unbreakable air. She needed to think her way out of this. "Who is this *Manalish*?"

"You remember my former vizier," Byleth replied. She rubbed her hand along Alyra's ribs in an intimate gesture.

So Horace had been right. "Astaptah."

"*Manalish* is his true title. It's from his homeland in Abyssia. It means 'sacred king' or some such."

Alyra tried to focus on the conversation, even as the guards secured her ankles with chains, too. "What's his plan? What is he going to do?"

Byleth smiled as she came around Alyra's other side, still touching her body. "Darkness will cover the entire world. All life will be extinguished, leaving only the peaceful solitude of death."

Alyra froze at those words, feeling them sink into her soul. "That's not possible. No one could . . . no one *would* do that. Why?"

Byleth held up her hand and moved her fingers. "Death is not the end, sweet Alyra. In fact, it's just the beginning. Mankind is going to ascend to a higher state of being, and it will be glorious."

"Horace will stop you." Alyra tried to sound convincing, but fear had begun to leak into her voice.

Byleth dropped her hand and moved in front of her captive. The guards formed a silent line behind her. The former queen of Erugash tilted her head to the side. "I'm counting on it."

Before Alyra could answer, invisible bands wrapped around her torso and began to squeeze. Alyra gasped as the air rushed from her lungs. Inch by inch, the unseen force crushed her insides. She struggled to think of a way to stop this from happening, but her thoughts were obliterated by the blood rushing into her head. Her vision blurred as she slumped in the chains. The pressure vanished, replaced by burning pain all across her skin, jerking her back to consciousness. Alyra couldn't stop the groan that rattled past her clenched jaws.

Byleth leaned against her, pressing their bodies together. A foul stench rolled from her open mouth as her pale tongue reached out to lick Alyra's cheek. "Let me hear you scream, my lovely."

Alyra bared her teeth and lunged. A barrier of solid air brought her up short, just inches from her tormentor's throat. "Go . . . to . . . ."

The squeezing began again, this time tighter. Byleth's laughter echoed in her head as everything went dark. Yet the pain continued, twisting deeper and deeper into her, ripping out her insides before starting again. She screamed in silence until her throat was raw, but there was no cessation to the torment. Eventually she stopped struggling, and all became noise buzzing in the back of her mind as a great lassitude crept over her. A rolling dark tide carried her down into its lightless depths. Her last cogent thought was not of the mission or all the people she had failed to help, but of the man she'd left behind.

Driving rain scoured the streets, splattering the clay while intermittent cracks of thunder shook the sky. Horace kept his head down as he walked beside Jin. There hadn't been any lightning, yet, but he could feel the energy of the storm building, as if it were feeding upon itself. He feared what was to come. Between this and the undead, the city might not survive the night.

Yet, despite the danger, one thing overrode his other concerns. The certainty that Alyra was out there. He felt her presence like an echo in the back of his mind, pulling him north. To the vast graveyard called the Stone Gardens. Why would Alyra leave the mansion to go there? Jirom had told him the expansive graveyard was often used for clandestine meetings. Was she following someone?

He and Jin passed under a footbridge to enter an older part of the city. After another block, they found a footpath leading up the side of the ridge. The paved trail was flanked by large white boulders that gleamed eerily in the storm's green light. It took him and Jin a few minutes to scale the slope. At the top, a pair of massive wrought-iron gates pierced the high wall surrounding the Gardens. The gates were never locked. Horace remembered Mezim saying it had something to do with the city's veneration of the Akeshian funeral god. Stepping inside, he summoned a ball of muted amber light.

Rain pattered on the leaves of the trees and flower blossoms before him. From this gate, a stone walkway branched into three directions. Taking the centermost one, he hurried onward. His sandals splashed through small puddles that formed in the shallow dips of the path.

He was rounding a long bend around an ornamental pool when a sharp tingle etched down the back of his neck. Horace skidded to a stop. The sensation of sorcery in the air was unmistakable. He reached for his *qa* as he stole forward, straining to hear above the pounding rain.

Elaborate tombs clustered on either side of the path. His light played across their granite faces. He was glancing through the stone forest when he caught sight of fresh earth on the sod. Motioning for Jin to stay quiet, Horace went to investigate. They found a large hole in the ground. It looked as if a wild animal had dug itself out of a burrow. There were more cavities at the edge of his light, beside fallen marker stones. *Is this where the undead came from? But who animated them?*

Thunder crackled overhead as the rain continued to pour down. The calling tugged at Horace's attention. He and Jin found the path again and followed it around another bend. Horace slowed down to get his bearings. Alyra's presence was getting stronger. He looked west along an aisle of green sward that ran between a pair of white marble obelisks. Beyond the monuments was a large copse of trees, their low branches obstructing the rest of the grounds. Cautiously, he headed in that direction. Past the trees, they found a tall mausoleum set into the side of a grassy barrow. The door was open.

Horace approached the tomb with care. The hint of magic still hung in the air. The outer door of the tomb was dark bronze. The latch was shattered and the hinges slightly warped, as if it had been wrenched open by a giant. Peering inside, he saw a second door set in the back wall of the mausoleum between a pair of stone sarcophagi. It also gaped open. Beyond, a long dark passageway delved into the ground.

"Tracks," Jin said, pointing to the floor of the tomb.

Several sets of wet footprints marched down the center of the mausoleum and through the inner doorway. Horace listened, but there were no sounds forthcoming. "I'm going in. You stay here and guard the exit."

"No, sir," Jin replied. "I'm going with you."

"Jin—"

"Sir, Gurita would never forgive me if I let you face this alone. So let's stop wasting time, okay?"

Nodding, Horace entered the door at the back of the tomb and started down the dank passage. It went far deeper than he imagined. After at least a hundred paces heading downward at a steady slope, it narrowed from a partial blockage where the right-hand wall had bulged inward. He squeezed past, feeling claustrophobic, and waited for Jin on the other side. The bodyguard's face was pale, but he kept up.

Past the impediment, the tunnel showed no sign of ending, and Horace began to wonder if he should turn back. There was no telling where this would come out. Then his light showed something protruding from the floor ahead. It was a post. Wood originally but now petrified into stone. As Horace wondered what it once was and how long it had been down here, he noticed the walls of the tunnel had changed from fitted stone slabs to weathered brick. They reminded him of exterior building walls. The ceiling rose and dipped in several places. Horace tried not to think of all the tons of earth and rock suspended above his head.

The passage abruptly turned to the right and dropped down over a ledge about five feet high. The remains of an ancient street were laid out before him. The walls on either side were pocked with vacant windows. The street itself was a depression with high sidewalks.

"What is this?" Jin breathed, staring all around. "Another city under the ground?"

"It's Old Thuum," Horace replied as he surveyed the area. "The new city is built on top of its bones. I saw the same thing in Erugash."

As they walked down the street, Horace thought of how this undercity had come to be buried. This land was seeped in ancient history. Entire civilizations had risen and fallen here. *And we're just the latest incarnation.*

Lost in his thoughts, Horace missed the light shining ahead of them until Jin nudged him and pointed it out. A tiny spark, it could have been a candle or a small lamp. It grew smaller, as if it was moving away from him. Nodding to Jin, he jogged after it.

They were entering an intersection of streets when Horace heard a sound like hard nails scraping over rock. Something darted through the shadows down the avenue branching to their right. It was too fast for him to get a good look at it, but Horace received the impression it was big enough to be a person. He had stopped for a closer look when a high-pitched cry echoed from ahead. A woman's cry. Not waiting for Jin, he ran ahead.

Twice more on his sprint down the dark underground street he glimpsed forms darting in the shadows. They moved low to the ground but very fast, making no sound except for the scrabble of claws or nails.

The street suddenly ended in a wall of compacted earth and debris forty feet high. A narrow tunnel penetrated the barrier. The light flickered within, though it was muted now. Horace started to enter but froze when he noticed the body lying facedown just inside the tunnel. It was a large man wearing mismatched armor and several weapons on his person. A bitter taste filled Horace's mouth as he knelt down and rolled the corpse over. It was Gurita.

Jin knelt down beside him to examine the body. Horace expected a strong reaction from the man—he and Gurita had been close—but Jin's expression was stony as he inspected his dead friend.

"He died fighting." Jin pointed out five wounds on Gurita's arms, torso, and one gaping tear on the side of his neck. "That bite is the one that killed him."

Horace's stomach dropped. He glanced over his shoulder. "We have to keep moving."

Stepping over the former captain of his guard, he entered the tunnel. It ran for about thirty paces between slanted stone walls before opening into a vast space. Horace paused at the threshold, struck by the sight before him. An ancient theater filled a space as large as the Grand Arena in Erugash. Tiers of stone benches rose in a graceful arc on either side of him. A raised stage stood on the far side, fifty yards away, backed by a row of thick pillars.

Torches burned in bronze cressets spaced along the low wall separating the bottommost seats from the open floor area. More torches burned on the stage. Horace squinted. Someone was chained between two pillars. It was a woman in a powder-blue gown. Her head was covered by a loose hood.

Horace was stricken by an icy paralysis as his gaze traced the woman's form, drinking in every line and curve. He knew her without seeing her face. She did not stir, and he was terrified what he would find if he lifted that hood. Yet he finally broke the paralysis that held him and approached the stage. He glanced around the theater, trying to pierce the darkness beyond the torchlight. This was clearly a trap, and this woman—whether or not she was Alyra—was clearly the bait. The calling sensation, the flickering lights, perhaps even Gurita's body—all had been designed to lead him here. *You want me to step in your web? Fine. Here I am.*

Motioning for Jin to stay back, Horace climbed onto the stage's riser. The stone was cool to the touch and clean, as if it had been recently scrubbed. Horace stepped closer to the bound woman. With a shaking hand, he pulled off the hood. His heart pounded as he looked upon the face of the woman he loved. She remained motionless. Horace lifted his hand to cup her cheek and let out a loud sigh as he felt her warm skin against his palm. She trembled as she opened her eyes.

"Don't move," he said. "I'll get you free."

The chains were heavy bronze, with links as thick as his thumb. Putting his arms around her, he used a burst from the Kishargal dominion to break the shackles and caught her as she fell. "I've got you."

Alyra shook her head. Slowly at first, as if she was coming out of a deep sleep, but with increasing vehemence. Her eyes were wide with panic.

Horace tried to calm her. "It's all right. I'm here."

A low moan came from her throat. Horace took her face in his hands. She was burning up. "Alyra, what's wrong? Tell me what's going on."

Tears ran from her eyes. Then her mouth sprang open and a black stream poured out. Horace leaned away as it splashed on the floor at their feet. Alyra's tiny frame heaved and shuddered as the stuff continued to bubble from her mouth. The stench was so bad he had to turn his head away.

Panicking, Horace used his power to See inside her. Flesh, sinew, and bone vanished in his mind's eye, replaced by a lattice of glowing nodes. The brightest points of light formed a straight line from the center of her forehead down to her pelvis. Yet, as he watched, a dark stain was building up inside her. It spread out to engulf those bright lights, one by one. Desperate, Horace opened a stream of pure Shinar and poured it directly into her. He didn't know what he was doing, but he acted on instinct, sending the void magic into the regions where the darkness was taking over. Alyra shuddered in his arms, and for a brief moment the dark tide slowed inside her. Then it rolled forward, swallowing the bright node at the base of her throat. He pushed harder, but he couldn't stop what was happening.

Alyra's shudders became less violent and eventually stilled. Her eyes narrowed to faded slits as the life drained from them. Horace shook her. "Alyra! Wake up! Alyra!"

But she did not respond, hanging loosely in his embrace. Horace set her down gently. He was too numb to cry, too shocked to do anything more than kneel at her side. She couldn't be gone.

His hands curled into fists. The power filled him, so fierce he thought it would spill from his pores. Through it he felt the stone under him, the stone holding up the ceiling, the stone above. He felt the pocket of air, so still in this place. He felt the nearness of the river moving in its channel outside the city. He felt the heat of the earth far below. And in between them all he felt the silence of the void.

Then a voice called from the wings of the stage. "I told you this would happen, Horace. I told you she would break your heart."

His rage found a focus as a slim lady clad in black emerged from the shadows at the end of the stage. Her face was shrouded behind a gauzy scarf, but he knew that voice, though it was hoarser than he remembered. Her hair was pulled back and coiled around her shoulders. She was thinner than before, and her sensual saunter had become more of a shuffle. He didn't know how it was possible, but here she was.

"Byleth," he said.

"I have missed you, Horace. It feels like a lifetime since I saw you."

Anger choked him. "You did this. You killed her."

"Poor Horace. You never understood. But she did. She played the big game. She played it well, but she lost. And this is what happens when you lose."

"I'll kill you."

She strolled closer like a specter, the tail of her gown trailing behind her. "How, dear Horace? I'm already dead."

Her throaty laughter rang out through the theater, mocking him from every direction. A great wind swirled around the chamber. With a guttural shout, Horace opened himself to the full measure of his power and let it go.

BLADE AND BONE

"Back! Get back!"

Jirom chopped at the fiend clutching his leg as he shouted. All around him, his men battled the living dead. They had been heading to meet up with Emanon's group when they ran into another group of undead. The creatures crawled out of windows and sprang from alleyways, leapt down from rooftops and crushed each other underfoot in their eagerness to taste human blood. The civilians had been hit the hardest. Jirom tried to protect them behind a ring of fighters, but as the rebels' numbers thinned, he had been forced to plug the holes with the lesser trained. The carnage was devastating.

"Back to the last block!" Jirom called out. Thunder rumbled overhead.

His nearest sergeants started herding their units backward. The fighters formed a rearguard, giving ground foot by foot. The action reduced the death toll, but they couldn't keep this up all night. Eventually, exhaustion and terror would catch up to them, and then it would be over.

Jirom pulled back from the front line and tried to come up with a new plan. If this part of the city was infested with undead, then they had to find another way around to Emanon. *He's probably facing the same problem. In which case, we'd better stop worrying about the Akeshians and focus on just staying alive.*

They came to a joining of three streets. The civilians were limping along. *Beysid* Giliam was with them, being supported by a pair of younger men. Grinding his teeth, Jirom looked for the best avenue of escape. Both the branching streets were empty at the moment, but there was no guarantee his group would get very far either way.

Jirom pointed out a tall, narrow building with lots of windows and a high front stoop. "Everyone inside there! Occupy the entrances!"

The fighters moved like a single-minded creature, instantly switching from retreat to assault as they charged at the building. The civilians followed quickly like a flock of ducklings.

Jirom was the first to the door. He kicked it open and jumped inside, finding himself in a wide room with two staircases. The air smelled of papyrus and old wax. After checking to make sure no enemies were in sight, he headed into the back. He found rooms with long desks and racks of scrolls but no people and no undead. Satisfied, he assigned half of his force to secure the ground floor. He put Sergeant Ralla in charge. "Barricade the outer doors. Put someone at every window. Shutter them if you can."

He went back to the stairs. One flight went up, the other down. He spotted Giliam in the front room with the rest of the civilians and grabbed him by the shoulder. Jirom dragged the *beysid* to the top of the descending staircase. "You stand right here and don't move."

"Now see here," Giliam started to blurt.

Jirom thrust a finger in his face. "Don't you fucking move! You hear me? Or there'll be hell to pay."

Giliam glared back, but he stayed in place.

A quick glance up the stairwell showed the building had four floors. Jirom stopped on the second for a quick look around. Hallways led off into several large rooms, all of them furnished with more desks but smaller ones low to the floor. The walls held racks and bins with clerical implements— pens, papyrus, jars, and such.

While he searched, Jirom kept his ears perked for signs of trouble below. So far, it was quiet except for the stamp of boots as his fighters got into position. It also sounded as if they were moving furniture to block the doors. He just hoped they could hold out. But for how long? Their situation was only going to get worse. As the undead killed the people of the city, their numbers would swell. His band might be able to fend off a hundred fiends but not thousands.

Sergeant Mamum caught up with him on the landing to the third floor. "There's something going on outside," Mamum said. "Lots of screams. Horses."

Jirom continued up the stairs at a run. "Let's see if we can get up on the roof. Take a look from there."

The stairwell accessed the roof through a trapdoor in the fourth-floor ceiling. After shoving open the trap, Jirom climbed out. The roof was flat and made of smooth clay, now slick with rainwater. A short wall ran around the perimeter.

Jirom and Mamum made their way to the southern edge. The street below was teeming with undead. Jirom's stomach clenched into knots at the sight. A few tried to enter this building, clawing at the front door, but so far it held fast. The rest scurried from street to street, breaking into other buildings. People were dragged from their homes, screaming with several undead latched onto them. The neighboring streets looked much the same. Where had all these creatures come from?

He looked west to the nearest city gate. It looked impossibly far away. *We'll never make it. Not if we had ten times as many fighters.*

"Commander!"

Pel, Mamum's corporal, emerged onto the roof. "We found some people hiding in a room on the top floor. They say they're students."

Jirom wiped his face with a forearm. "Give them weapons if they'll fight. If not, tell them to lock themselves in. We're heading out."

"Back out again?" Mamum asked. "We just got in here."

"It's just a breather. We're going to find Emanon's group."

"Maybe they're holed up in a place like this," the sergeant suggested.

"Then we'll all hole up together and make our stand. But we're not going to give up without knowing. Get your men ready to move."

They left the roof. Jirom spared a glance down the fourth-floor hallway as they passed. A few lean men in their late twenties stood at the far end, watching him with trepidation. Jirom kept going.

Down on the ground floor, his fighters had piled desks and benches against the front door. Faint thuds sounded from the other side, but the door held up. "Collect everyone," Jirom told Ralla. "We're going out the back."

She looked up the stairs. "What about the students?"

"They've made their choice. Where is Giliam?"

Ralla pointed toward a side room. "He says he's staying."

Jirom followed her finger to a large room that may have been a communal dining chamber. A long table was pushed against the far wall. The *beysid* and several civilian leaders were crowded together. They turned as Jirom entered.

"We're leaving," he growled.

Giliam stepped forward, limping slightly. "We have decided to stay here." He cleared his throat. "Until the fighting stops."

"The fighting isn't going to stop," Jirom shot back. "Haven't you learned anything yet? Those dead things don't stop to rest or shit or fucking parley. They just keep coming until you kill them or they kill you. Our only chance is to regroup with the others and try to escape this charnel house."

Giliam held his gaze. "We are staying. So unless you want to remove us by force, I suggest—"

Jirom walked out before he choked the *beysid* to death in front of his followers. Hands curled into fists, he found Ralla in the hallway. "Order the departure."

She raced to the rear of the building. Jirom heard the back door open and a clash of fighting. He waited by the front entrance until the last of his people had left, and then he followed. His fighters had cut a path through a small crowd of undead, trailed by a handful of civilians who had chosen to stay with them. Forcing his way through the press, Jirom got to the front just as the rebels broke free of containment. They were on a wide avenue running east-west through the neighborhood. From the roof, he had seen that this road led almost straight to the armory that had been Emanon's first target.

He took point, setting the pace at a slow jog. With each stride, he felt an invisible doom gathering over his head. All his plans to take the city were forgotten. Now it was all about finding Emanon and getting out. He thought of Horace and Alyra. What could he do about them? *Not a damned thing. But they'll be fine. Horace will find a way out.*

He was more worried about Silfar's unit, but he couldn't do anything for them right now either.

The downpour reduced visibility to a dozen yards. They had only advanced four blocks before sounds of fighting echoed down the street from somewhere ahead. He saw lights in that direction. Jirom lifted his sword and called for a full charge, not bothering to look back to see who was following. His heart thumped faster with the hope that Emanon was up ahead. Instead, the first thing he saw as he sprinted across a flooded intersection was an Akeshian uniform. A company of city militia was battling undead in the middle of the street. The Akeshians were being compressed into a tight knot as more undead poured into the melee. Then a flash of fire streaked through the hazy air, searing a knot of fiends who had been descending on the Akeshians' flank. Blinking past the sparkling afterimage, Jirom spotted two members of the Crimson brotherhood among the militia. Their bald heads with the bright tattoos glistened in the light of several torches as they wielded their sorcery, but Jirom could see at a glance that the Akeshians were losing this fight.

He halted and let his men catch up. The civilians had lagged dangerously far behind, possibly from exhaustion. More likely out of fear. If he pushed them too hard, they might break. *But what choice do any of us have? We're fighting for our lives.*

He was about to call for his units to go around the battle, but a tiny voice nagged at the back of his mind. *The Akeshians might be your enemies on another day, but right now you're both on the same side. The side of the living.*

Fuck it. We've come this far. Might as well finish it.

"Form up!" Jirom called, signaling for his best-armored fighters to take the front. "For the rebellion!"

Taking the point of the formation, Jirom led his fighters into the rear of the undead pack. The fiends, so focused on the Akeshians in their midst, didn't see it coming. Even as the rebels carved a path through them, they did not seem to care. It was ridiculously easy to cut them down.

Jirom chopped down what had once been an old man, and then he was suddenly face-to-face with a line of Akeshian soldiers. A sudden flash of light was the only warning he received before a bolt of red fire blasted him from inside the Akeshian formation. He raised his shield instinctively and closed his eyes, bracing for the onslaught of pain, but it never came. The shield grew warm in his grasp as the fire vanished. He was unhurt.

The Akeshian soldiers drew back. Jirom kept one eye on them as he directed his men to fan out and keep pushing back the undead. The militiamen continued to shrink away from him, their weapons raised as if he might charge them at any moment.

Jirom glanced down at the outer surface of the shield. Its black metal gleamed without a scratch or dent. Had it really just stopped a blast of magic from harming him? No wonder it had been locked up secure in the wrecked flying ship. *It must be made from* zoahadin, *maybe alloyed with iron. . . .*

"Holy hairy balls, sir," Sergeant Ralla said, stepping up beside him. "You sure got them spooked, eh?"

The last knots of fighting were wrapped up in short order. As the combat ended, the rebels pulled back, leaving a wide gap between them and the Akeshian force. Both sides studied each other, weapons in hand but not threatening.

Lowering his sword, but keeping his shield up, Jirom addressed the Akeshians. "Who commands here?"

An officer in a blood-drenched uniform pushed through the Akeshian ranks. He was young for a lieutenant, probably not even twenty. *Not much older than I was when I left home and became a freebooter. Too fucking young to live by the sword, that's for sure.*

"I'm Lesanep, acting commander of the Twelfth Company. We heard you were in Thuum," he said with an even tone. A cautious one, despite his years. "You attacked an armory in the *hekallum* district."

"And two others," Jirom replied. "But we've got a bigger problem." He kicked one of the fallen fiends, one wearing the uniform of a militia soldier. "We've fought these things before. They don't die easy. They'll swarm through your entire city, killing and turning people into monsters as they go. If that happens, we're all dead."

The two sorcerers approached. The soldiers parted before them as if terrified to even brush against the hems of their red robes. One was holding an arm across his middle. Blood soaked the sleeve. His face was pale. The other spoke up.

"You slaves! Drop your weapons or die where you stand!"

"The fuck we will," Ralla growled in a sharp whisper.

Lieutenant Lesanep interrupted. "Pardon, Honored Brother, but these . . . em, slaves just saved our lives."

The face of the sorcerer darkened, but his injured comrade nodded. "Aye, they did."

The first sorcerer frowned at Jirom. "Now you wish us to allow you to go on your way, rebel?"

"No," Jirom replied. "We should join forces."

BLADE AND BONE

Voices rose on both sides. Jirom ignored them. "The city is swarming with the risen dead. Separately, we'll get chewed up and slaughtered. But together, we stand a chance. We're going to the western armory."

The magic wielders put their heads together for a few seconds. Then the injured one said, "We are marching to the gatehouse. We'll escort you to the armory. But if your men attack any citizen or city militia . . ."

"We're on the same side," Jirom said. And added under his breath, "For now."

After a brief parley, it was decided that the rebels would form the front of the column with the Akeshians marching behind them. It wasn't ideal, and Jirom kept glancing back to make sure their new allies weren't up to anything, but he felt a little better having doubled the size of their force. However, he just imagined what Emanon would say. *He can cuss me out, dress me down, or even take back command. Just let him be alive.*

CHAPTER FIFTEEN

Bolts of white lightning shot from his fingertips to rake across the far end of the stage where she stood. Horace grimaced as burning pain ran through his hands and arms, but he kept up the electrical bombardment for several heartbeats before he released the power. Breathing hard, he squinted through the miasma of smoke. His rage kept him ready to deliver another blast if necessary to finish her off. Then he heard the laughter.

"Oh, Horace, you don't know how long I have waited for this moment."

Byleth sauntered out of the cloud of smoke and wafting dust. Her shroud was singed at the ends, but otherwise she appeared completely unharmed by his attack. Stunned, he could only shake his head. "How—?"

He dropped to his stomach as a hail of razor-sharp ice crystals flew through the space where he had been standing. His chin struck the ancient concrete floor, and he tasted blood as he started to rise. Then a great wind drove him down on his stomach and howled in his ears.

The *zoana* pulsed within him like a second, stronger heartbeat as he fought to regain his footing. A strange vibration hung in the air, something both odd and eerily familiar, but there was no time for contemplation. He cast a sheet of flames at Byleth. Her laughter continued as the bright fires wrapped around her, stopping several inches from touching her flesh. He followed up with a barrage of ice lances, each five feet long and tapered to a fine point. They shattered before reaching her. He summoned jagged pillars of stone from the ground, but they crumbled as they broke the surface of the stage.

Again and again he called forth the elements to destroy, and with each attack he saw Alyra's face. Those dull eyes that had been so full of life and love, her soft hands turning cold, her tender lips rotting and pulling back in a rictus. Each thought fueled his fury. The floor shook with the power as he traded blows with the woman—the thing—that had stolen Alyra from him forever.

Byleth deflected another burst of fire, and Horace felt the familiar sensation again. This time he took a moment to explore it, and a cold shiver ran through him. *She's using the void!*

BLADE AND BONE

And not just the minute increments that many *zoanii* could muster. She was pulling as much Shinar as he had ever managed. Maybe more. He found himself taking a step backward. A bolt of invisible energy sizzled toward him. Horace ducked aside and felt it pass over his head. A second bolt struck a pillar and gouged a deep furrow through its trunk.

Jin stole onto the stage behind Byleth. Horace saw him and started to launch a diversion, but it was too late. Byleth raised a finger, not even deigning to look back, and a gust of wind knocked the bodyguard backward with the force of a rampaging bull. Horace tried to catch him with his power, but another unseen bolt hissed in the air. He barely had time to throw up a shield of Shinar. The barrier rocked with the blow, but it bought him enough time to send back a counterattack. His answering bolt sailed wide and struck the stands abutting the stage. Horace was readying another attack when something hit his shield with the force of a runaway coach, shattering the protective barricade. The next bolt caught him square in the chest and hurled him off his feet. The shock of hitting the floor drove the wind from his lungs as he slid along the stage until he finally came to an abrupt stop at the foot of a pillar.

Byleth's voice resounded around him. "Don't fret, dear Horace. You'll be joining your lady love soon enough. You will both be my slaves for all eternity, so we need never part again. Aren't I a kind mistress?"

Growling in the back of his throat, Horace lashed out. He aimed not for Byleth but for the damaged column standing between them, hitting it with a combination of Shinar and Kishargal. The stone creaked as it shifted, and bits of masonry fell from the ceiling.

"Horace, what—?"

The former queen's words were drowned out as the support toppled over with a titanic crash. It fell sideways, colliding with the next pillar in line. They both fell, with the first pillar coming down where Byleth had been standing and the second smashing into the back wall. Bits of stone exploded across the stage. Horace covered himself with a shell of hardened air and lay still until the booming crashes ceased. When the dust settled, he stood up.

The stage was a disaster, with three of the four support columns lying in broken pieces. Horace stepped past their remains. His shield was the only thing that saved him as an inferno of wind and fiery ash surrounded him. A shadow moved to his right. He lashed out. Siphoning off the heat surrounding him, he redirected it toward the movement. After a few seconds, the fire was gone, leaving a sizable portion of the stage charred and smoking. Horace was moving to investigate the wreckage when a powerful force lifted him up and flung him toward the back wall. He barely had time to channel a thread of Kishargal before he hit.

The concussion pounded his entire body as he smashed through the weakened wall. He collapsed on the other side, with chunks of stone and mortar raining around him. Somehow his shield held, but he ended up half-buried under the avalanche of debris. Stifling a grunt, he called his power and flung the wreckage away.

The area behind the stage was pitch-dark. As he got back to his feet, Horace summoned a globe of light. He stood in a chamber that was much larger than he would have guessed, filled with the remains of ancient props—sagging furniture, piles of moldering cloth, and plaster statues. Dark archways exited to his left and right, but the right-hand opening was choked with the rubble.

Horace stalked toward the left-hand exit, which opened into another hallway running perpendicular. He took a couple of steps but then pulled back, his heart thumping hard, as his foot encountered nothing but open space. He sent out the glow-orb and confirmed it. The hallway's floor had fallen away, as had the far wall, all of it gone except for a narrow ledge. Cool air brushed Horace's face. He couldn't see very far over the ledge, but he got the feeling that the gap beyond was huge. And he had almost stumbled right over the edge.

Hugging the wall, he made his way down the hallway. After about fifty paces, he came to another dark archway to his right. The breeze was stronger now, whistling softly in his ear. Horace was about to step through the opening when the wall beside him exploded outward. The blast carried him over the ledge like a leaf caught in a river's grasp. With a howling wind screeching around him, Horace clutched at the floor even as he was dragged over the side. His nails scraped along the antique pavement until they caught on a projection of broken stone at the lip. Hanging on with both hands, he felt the vastness of the gulf below him. The gale continued to blast from the shattered wall until its invisible fingers managed to loosen his grip. With a shout, he fell.

Darkness swallowed him as he plummeted. He clawed for his power. A trickle of Imuvar leaked through his *qa*. He was fumbling with a weave when he struck the ground. His body folded up under the impact as the air became as thick as mud in his lungs. His grasp on consciousness shattered in a million slivers.

Three Moons sagged against the trunk of an azure tree. His legs were numb from running, his lungs burning as they struggled to keep up. The rest of the Bronze Blades sat down in formation, their attention on the surrounding woods. The silver stream ran by silently a few paces away.

They had been traveling for the better part of a day, as best as he could figure. The woods had grown denser the farther they ran. Looking up, he couldn't see a scrap of sky through the blue-green canopy forty feet over their heads. Only scattered rays of light penetrated down to the forest floor, barely enough to help them see where they were going.

Where were they going? Three Moons hadn't stopped thinking about that since the moment they landed in this altered world. If he was right, and this truly was the spirit realm, then legend suggested there should be ways back home. What disturbed him was that it could take a long time to find one, and what would they find when they returned? That decades had passed in the real world during their absence? *It looks like I failed you again, Jirom. I'm sorry. I truly am.*

Ino crawled over and offered him a strip of jerky. The big Isuranian's eyes glowed silver in the dim light. Three Moons accepted it with a tired nod. That was the other thing that was bothering him. All of them, himself included, had undergone the same transformation. Their skin, hair, teeth, and even their eyes had turned silver. He assumed it was because they had drunk and bathed in the quicksilver water. Was it permanent? There seemed to be no other ill effects, except for unusual vitality and stamina. He himself had run more miles this day than he had over the last ten years combined, and he still felt as if he could go on a little longer. But how long before this gift of endurance ran out?

He glanced back behind them. The woods were quiet. Not a single animal—not even a bird—disturbed the stillness. But he knew the blind fiends were out there, following them. They were virtually silent and damned hard to spot until they were right on you. The constant need to be alert was more draining than the running. Three Moons saw it on the faces of his brethren. Cracks were appearing in their composure. Discipline was strained. *It's just like the desert all over again. We're running ragged from an enemy that never stops. At some point we'll break, and then they win.*

Yet, he was beginning to understand some things. The spirit realm and the real world were more than just mirrors of each other. They were the same. He glanced around, imagining the woods as a desert plain. The creek bed would be long dead, just a natural depression winding through the wastes. He could also taste the dryness of the desert wind. It was so close to them.

Captain Paranas interrupted his thoughts by coming over. "How are you holding up, old man?"

"By my toenails. Where are we heading, Cap?"

The captain shook his canteen before taking a sip. "We're running blind. What can you tell us?"

"Besides that we're completely fucked?"

"Maybe something more productive. Like an idea how to get us out of this nightmare."

"Cap, I wish I had some clue, but—"

Three Moons shuddered as a ferocious roar pierced his skull. He clutched his ears, but it did no good. The roar sang on the air, as sharp as fine steel, penetrating straight into his mind. On one level, he wondered how the others weren't staggered from the onslaught, but on another he understood this call was purely psychic. And it had a direction. It called to him from back where they had come.

The captain caught him by the elbow before he fell over. "Moons, you all right?"

Before Three Moons could reply, a powerful gust of wind tore through the forest. He clung to the tree he leaned against. The soft bark crumbled under the force of his grip. Branches were torn away, leaves scattered, and the mercenaries hunkered down on the ground.

"What the fuck is going on?" Ino shouted.

"Higher ground," Three Moons whispered to himself.

"What's that?" Captain Paranas asked. The gusts had died down just enough that they could talk without needing to shout at the top of their lungs.

BLADE AND BONE

Three Moons swallowed. He looked his commander in the eyes, hoping the urgency he felt would be conveyed. "We need to get to higher ground."

Captain Paranas turned to the other mercs. "Everyone, up! We're heading upstream at double time! Niko, head out!"

The mercenaries climbed to their feet and resumed the hike with the wind at their backs. Three Moons hustled to keep up with them. Pie-Eye and Ivikson stayed close to him after the captain hurried ahead to the front of the column.

"You two playing nursemaid?" Three Moons asked with as much gruffness as he could muster.

Pie-Eye gave him a tired wink. "Just making sure our pet wizard doesn't drop dead before we can find a way out of here."

Right. A way out. Good one, kid.

They encountered a wide oxbow in the stream. Instead of navigating their way around it, Captain Paranas led the Blades across. Three Moons gasped as the cold silver water swallowed him to his waist. He risked a glance back and wished he hadn't. A great black cloud filled the sky behind them. That was what he first took it for, but then his vision sharpened and he saw the truth. It was no cloud but a beast. A vast leviathan flying over the forest. Long tentacles hung down from its black bulk, dragging through the trees, tearing them up like twigs and lifting them to the waiting maw at the beast's underside. The beast was devouring everything in its path as it headed toward them with terrifying speed. Three Moons stumbled and almost fell as another cacophonic roar shook the ground.

Pie-Eye caught him before he slipped deeper into the water. The young mercenary happened to glance back behind him. "Holy fuck! What is that?"

Clinging to the brawny arm holding him up, Three Moons wondered how this would look in their home realm, if the two worlds were truly matched. Then he understood. A vast, cyclonic force of nature tearing across the landscape . . . a chaos storm.

A powerful urge came over him, to fall down and wait for his doom. Their situation was hopeless. They were all going to die, so why keep fighting it? For a moment, Three Moons almost succumbed to the temptation. Pie-Eye must have felt it, too, because his knees started to bend, lowering them both into the stream. But Three Moons shook it off with a growl. "No! Get up!"

He had to half-drag Pie-Eye to the shore. Together they climbed onto the far bank where Ivikson and Meghan were setting up with their crossbows.

"Keep moving," Ivikson said, checking his bow's string. "We'll hold it off."

Pie-Eye released Three Moons's arm. "I'll stay, too."

Three Moons opened his mouth to protest. There was no way to hold off this thing. It would rip through them like a water buffalo tearing up shoots of bamboo. Yet, he kept the words to himself, giving them each a terse nod before he set off after the rest of the company.

Beyond the bend, the creek straightened, leading directly to the gap between the hills ahead. After a couple of hundred yards, the forest gave way to rocky slopes. The sky between the stony peaks was cobalt blue.

As he climbed the hill, Three Moons felt another sensation, starting at the base of his spine. An itching tingle like a swarm of bees pricking him with their stingers. *I'm going fucking mad in this place.*

Niko and Jauna had stopped at the top of the pass. Niko turned and waved back to the company.

"Move your asses!" Captain Paranas shouted as he ushered them up the slope.

But no one needed his cajoling. The Blades ran up the hillside as if their lives depended on it. As Three Moons approached the summit, he spared a glance behind him. The rearguard was just emerging from the tree line, walking backward up the foot of the hill slope while they fired their crossbows with practiced precision into the advancing monster. The soaring bolts were lost in the inky darkness that surrounded the thing. A tentacle reached down with lazy ease and plucked Ivikson from the ground. The mercenary fired one last bolt point-blank into the beast's underbelly before he was plunged into that voracious maw.

"What the fuck?" Ino swore. He had turned around and was now staring at the chaos creature.

Captain Paranas's face had turned a shade paler, but he kept urging the company to climb faster. "Eyes forward, soldier! Keep moving!"

Three Moons climbed the last few steps and almost swallowed his tongue as he looked over the top. Just over the pass, the land fell away in a steep cliff that dropped down without end as far as he could see. Beyond it was just empty space, a great sapphire-blue expanse studded with bright silver stars, except for a narrow path of stone that extended into the void. Supported by nothing, it stretched about a quarter mile over the starry abyss and ended in a bright blue-white oval. Three Moons knew what it was the moment he spotted it. The stinging sensation along his spine pulled him toward the portal like a siren's call.

He pointed. "That's our way out!"

Captain Paranas didn't waste any time, shoving Niko down the suspended pathway. "Form up in single file! Hurry but be careful. Moons, you go after Niko."

Eating the sharp retort that came to mind, Three Moons followed Niko onto the narrow path. The abyss yawned beneath them, but the suspended path was firm under his feet. *I'll be damned glad to get out of this insane place.*

He briefly considered that he had no idea where the portal went. For all he knew, it might carry them to somewhere worse than this. He packed up those thoughts and shoved them away. There was no use dithering. They couldn't stay here, so they had to roll the dice.

Three Moons stopped beside Niko at the foot of the portal. Sparks flashed within the radiant gateway, like tiny bursts of lightning. Their energy played across his skin. Holding his breath, he opened himself to the power. The air whistled through his teeth as a portion of his life force leapt out to make a connection with the portal. He hissed as sharp pains traveled through his body from crown to toes. He felt the etheric pathway open.

"Go on," he said between gritted teeth.

With a sideways glance, Niko stepped into the portal and vanished. The rest of the company tramped through after him. Each member hesitated for a moment at the threshold before going on. Three Moons understood. *We're in the hands of the gods now. All we can hope is that they don't bugger us too hard.*

Captain Paranas was the last in line. He looked back across the void to the mainland. "I wish I knew what this was all about. I just have this feeling . . ."

Three Moons felt it, too. But he was in too much pain to give it proper thought. "There ain't no sense in it, Cap. This place exists on the edge of chaos. It's a mess, and all we can do is get out before it eats us up. Now, if you don't mind, could you move your ass before I lose my grip on this?"

The captain gave him a short salute and stepped inside. Three Moons jumped in after him. Bright light blinded him for a moment. Then he was floating in the void, just like before. He was ready this time when the vertigo seized him, or he thought he was. But his courage failed as the great wall of nothingness rushed up to swallow him. He closed his eyes tightly and prayed to every god, goddess, and spirit he could name that it would end soon.

Rain rattled against their helmets and armor, and created deep puddles underfoot as they marched west along the main boulevard that bisected Thuum. The royal palace was behind them, its tall tiers lost in the darkness of the storm, save for when an emerald-green flash from the heavens illuminated everything in stark, eerie colors. The resulting thunder was instantaneous.

Jirom kept a gap of a couple of yards between his men and the Akeshians. Everyone was antsy, as testified by the hard glances exchanged between the two groups, but so far the alliance had held up under the strain of three skirmishes with the undead. There seemed to be no end to them. However, his people had limits. Some of them just trudged along, their weapons hanging loosely from their hands, not even able to summon the energy to fight when the undead came calling.

They had already found the first target of Emanon's unit—the western armory—smoldering steadily despite the heavy rain. So Jirom had led his fighters toward the secondary target, the slave pens near the city gate. With luck, they would reunite with Emanon's force there, and together they could gather the last of the civilians—the children and those too old to fight—and leave Thuum. That was the plan, at least.

Urlik ran up to Jirom. "We've got trouble, sir."

"The dead?"

"Yes, sir. A whole mess of them."

Jirom glanced down the nearest side street. It was too dark to make out anything. "Tell Sergeant Seng to stay put. I'm coming up."

After a sharp salute, the young scout hustled back to the point.

Jirom called over the rest of his squad leaders and handed out quick assignments. "We're going to push through, so move with a purpose," he told them. "No one falls behind. And if the man or woman beside you falls, by all the gods, do them a favor and make sure they stay dead."

His words were met with tired nods. They had already shared with the Akeshians how to kill the undead for good. Decapitation was the best method, although wounds that damaged the brain also tended to do the job. The worst part was putting down their own fallen, especially for Jirom. Years of military experience had instilled in him a reverence for his slain brothers and sisters. Cutting off their heads felt like desecration. Yet, allowing them to rise again was far worse.

Swallowing his fears, Jirom pushed to the front of the pack. The point squad was split up and positioned on either side of the street for cover. As he crept up to join them, Jirom saw why. A block away rose the circular walls of a grand stadium. A mob of undead seethed around the structure. Hundreds of them, all crawling over each other to get inside. Jirom looked up, and the curse strangled in his throat. Men stood on the stadium's tall ramparts, hurling objects down at the horde. He couldn't make them all out from this distance, but he recognized the man directing the defense. *There you are, you beautiful bastard. Right in the thick of a dilemma, like usual.*

Jirom waved for his fighters to advance. To his surprise, the Akeshians moved to the front line. Shields locked together in a wall of bronze that stretched across the street, they marched forward. Jirom joined them and took a place at the center. Their lieutenant gave him a grim nod as he raised his sword. "Double time!"

A few of the undead at the rear of the horde turned, snarling as they caught sight of the advancing soldiers, but most remained obsessed with Emanon's group up until the moment the Akeshian line crashed into them. Blades rose and fell, hacking into leathery tissue and bone. Sorcery tore through the air, flinging dark blood to tinge the falling rain.

Jirom kept his shield high as he cut his way through the crowd. He hacked through necks and tramped on skulls when they fell. He got so lost in the rhythm of the melee he almost didn't see the granite statue before it smashed on the pavement in front of him, crushing two undead beneath it. He looked up.

Emanon waved back.

Fighting the urge to flip off his love, Jirom gestured for him to come down. The undead were divided into small knots and cut down by the combined force. Jirom breathed easier. The losses to his people had been slight, mainly due to the Akeshians and to the undead not knowing they were under attack until it was too late. A living foe would have pivoted and met their assault before it ground them down. *Finally, something breaks in our favor. Now, Lords of the heavens, let us leave in one piece.*

A couple of minutes later, Emanon emerged from the stadium's arched gateway with his fighters. They were a ragged lot, and far fewer than the number that had started off this night. Jirom gave his lover a rueful glance. "Tough night?"

Emanon threw an arm around his shoulders. "I'm damned glad to see you." He pulled Jirom closer and said into his ear, "Found some new friends, eh?"

Jirom found Lieutenant Lesanep and made quick introductions. "We need to get out of the city," Jirom told them. "We can swing by the houses on the west end first and pick up the people we left there."

He didn't like the prospect of leading an army of civilians back out into the wilderness, but it would be far crueler to leave them behind.

Emanon kicked an undead corpse on the ground. "I never reached the slave pens. And there are more of these fuckers between us and the gates. We'll never make it unless you've got a lot more fighters waiting around the corner."

Jirom shook his head as he surveyed the mixed company. If they couldn't reach the gates, then they were well and truly fucked. He turned toward the center of the city. Its rooftops and towers were hidden in the storm's gloom, but the way was clear for as far as he could see. "We march for the palace. It's the most defensible position inside the city."

Emanon nodded wearily. Lesanep said nothing, though he glanced westward toward the gates. An Akeshian soldier ran up and spoke in the lieutenant's ear. They both left in a rush. With a look to Emanon, Jirom followed them. The soldier led them across the street from the stadium where one of the Crimson brothers knelt on the wet pavement, cradling the head of the other. The dead one had his throat torn out.

While Lesanep talked with the surviving sorcerer, Emanon pulled Jirom aside. "So what's going on? You've got the militia *and* a couple Order boys under your wing now?"

As Jirom explained how the temporary alliance had happened, Emanon listened with a doubtful expression.

"You think I made the wrong call?" Jirom asked.

"No. Everything changed when those dead things popped up. This entire plan has gone to shit."

"Regretting your decision to leave me in charge?"

Emanon gave a little laugh. "Not for a second. I haven't had this much fun since we were back in the training camp."

Jirom sighed. Those days seemed like forever ago. "I thought you were some kind of double agent at first. You looked too damned good to be a filthy rebel slave."

"Silver-tongued charmer." His smile dropped away. "Have you heard from Silfar?"

Jirom shook his head, his mood turning grim again.

"If they met the same resistance as us, they're probably holed up somewhere, trying to wait it out."

When Lieutenant Lesanep came over, Jirom asked, "Are you coming with us?"

"Yes. Brother Janzu agrees. We make for the palace. But we go to save His Majesty and the royal family. No harm can come to them."

Jirom held out his hand. "Agreed. We fight a common enemy. No need to spill the blood of the living this night."

The lieutenant clasped his hand, and then each of them saw to organizing their forces into a cohesive whole. After a few minutes, they were ready to march.

Jirom felt much better with Emanon by his side again. His fears had melted away, leaving only a burning desire to survive this night. He didn't know what the morning would bring, but he would worry about that later. "Ready?" he asked his lover.

Emanon wiped the rain from his face. "I was just thinking it would be damned nice to have Horace with us right about now."

Jirom agreed without saying anything. Lifting his sword and shield into place, he gave the order, and they marched.

CHAPTER SIXTEEN

Horace coughed and instantly regretted it as sharp pains stabbed into his sides. He rolled over, clutching his ribs, and hacked to clear the thick paste that coated his mouth and throat. When he opened his eyes, there was only darkness.

He was buried up to his waist in a powder that felt like sand. There was no sound around him. Taking a risk, he summoned a small ball of light. The *zoana* burned in his veins as he completed the sorcery.

The illumination revealed he had landed in a chamber with stone walls. The roof overhead was gone. Under him was a vast mound of something he took for brown dirt at first, but then he lifted a handful and saw the individual kernels. It was grain. He'd landed in an ancient granary.

Moving slowly, he extricated himself and slid down the mound to the tiled floor below. The air was thick with grain dust, presumably kicked up when he landed. Holding his sleeve over his mouth, Horace directed the glow-orb around the room until he found a stone door in one of the unadorned walls. He pushed the door to see if it would open. *Of course not. Why would anything be easy?*

Centering himself, he called for his power again. Pain shot through his system, but a trickle of Kishargal allowed him to see how the door had become settled into its frame. Horace lifted the heavy slab and slid it open with hardly a sound. Wiping the sweat from his face, he went through, into another room that was bisected by a long stone countertop at waist height. The wall to his right was coffered with a honeycomb of small cubbies. This room, too, had no roof, and its front door was gone, leaving only a frame leading out into more darkness.

Leaving the granary, Horace found himself on a wide street paved in stone. An eerie silence covered everything as his light played across the façades of homes, shops, and other buildings. Many of them were broken with missing walls and roofs, but a few appeared intact. Walking past them, he imagined the people who had once lived here, treading upon the same stones he now walked, trapped beneath the ground like a fairy realm out of a children's tale. He was passing between two tall buildings that leaned out over the street when her voice came to him.

"If you could only see the things I've seen, Horace. I have been reborn in the flames of pure chaos. And I've come to share that gift with you."

"You killed Alyra to serve your new master." He tried to pierce the shadows at the edge of his light, but there was no sign of her. "I know who he is. I defeated him before, and I can do it again."

Her laughter echoed all around him. "You know nothing, my dear. I never understood how narrow my perception was when I was mortal. But now I know what lies in store for the human race, and there is no stopping it, Horace. No one—not you, not I, not the entire empire—can stop it. The *Manalish* shall rule over all, forever and ever until the end of time."

Horace sensed something to his left in the space between two broken shop fronts. He pulled as much of the *zoana* as he could hold and released it in a wave of pure Shinar. The presence vanished.

"What's wrong, Your Excellency?" he called out. "Not willing to face me?"

This time her answer was silence. Horace gritted his teeth. He had been hoping that a little taunting would bring her out into the open. He turned down the alley between those shop fronts, keeping his *zoana* ready.

The alley led into a tunnel of sorts, formed by the walls of neighboring buildings and a low ceiling of rough stone. As the ceiling gradually declined, Horace started to feel trapped. After fifty or sixty paces, he was glad to see the tunnel opened into a small square fronted by more tall buildings, all of them missing their upper floors. A well was situated in the center of the square. Empty windows gaped all around him.

Horace turned in a slow circle. Byleth's presence lingered here, so strong he should have been able to see her. A brief itching down the back of his neck was the only warning he got before a sheet of black flame descended over him from the darkness above. He surrounded himself in a spray of cool mist as he tried to run. Pain engulfed his lower legs despite the mist, as the fire met his flesh and clung to him. Horace found the thread of void energy feeding the flames. Falling to the ground, he snipped the tether, and the fire vanished. The damage wasn't as bad as he had first thought, though his legs were weeping with open blisters.

Horace banished his glow-orb, plunging the undercity into absolute gloom. With slow movements, he crawled until he felt the short wall surrounding the well at the center of the square. He leaned back against the coarse bricks and held his breath, listening.

With his other Sight, he located the lines of power that ran all around him. Through the street, through the air, even inside him. He followed them outward, searching for a clue where his enemy hid. He frowned as the lines extended through the area, even out as far as the dense layers of bedrock surrounding the undercity, without finding anything. Had she left? Then her presence returned an instant before a wave of utter cold washed over him.

Horace wrapped himself in a cocoon of warmth as he traced the spell's energy back to its origin. Yet there was nothing there. Not even an echo of the power that had generated it. He was about to expand his search when a flicker of movement caught his Sight. A shadow slid between the lines of power, so subtle he hadn't noticed it before. *There you are.*

He grabbed hold of the buildings on either side of the lurking shadow with his power and brought them down. The ground shook as they fell in mountains of ancient masonry. A great cloud of dust filled the square. Stone creaked as the surrounding buildings swayed, some of them collapsing as well. After several minutes, the tremors ceased.

Horace breathed through his sleeve to filter out the particles hanging in the air. He'd lost track of the shadow in the tumult. He didn't see any movement under or around the great mound of debris he had created, but Byleth's presence still lingered like the echo of a nightmare. He was about to start sifting through the rubble when the attack came. A wave of pure Shinar hit him from the side. It ripped the *zoana* from his grasp and left him gasping. As he turned, a second blast grazed his head. Stunned, he fell to his knees and only barely managed to hold onto consciousness. Through a rush of pain-filled tears, he Saw her approach, hips moving in a jerky mockery of a saunter. He clawed at his *qa* but couldn't summon the power to erect a shield.

BLADE AND BONE

"Don't be afraid, Horace," she said. "You are going to know power like you've never felt. Death is only a transition between this pathetic existence and something much greater. Look what the *Manalish* has done with me. My power has never been greater, and I shall live forever. So, too, shall you relish the master's gifts." She stopped before him, a ghastly smile on her ruined lips. "It only hurts for a moment."

A black nimbus surrounded her hands. As she reached for him, Horace thought of Alyra, hanging in those chains. A lifeless shell of the woman he had loved. Every moment since he had seen her body, his heart had been crying out for vengeance, but now he understood. The only thing that mattered was that Byleth and her master be stopped, so their evil would not spread across the world like that dark ocean he had seen in the vision.

Fighting through the pain, he threw open his *qa*. Molten agony seared his insides as the *zoana* rushed into him. As Byleth's hands came down toward him, he caught her wrists. A vortex of coruscating energies surged at the juncture where the twin sides of the Shinar came into contact. In that instant, he unleashed everything he had. Not at her but above their heads. He penetrated the roof of the undercity with a spear of combined Kishargal and Shinar, drilling deep into the stone and bringing it all down. Byleth looked up, her ravaged features twisting in surprise as she strained in vain to break his grip. If he couldn't defeat her, then he would make damned sure she never hurt anyone else ever again. *For you, my love.*

A last-moment flicker of self-preservation made him conjure a quick shield of solid air around himself as the avalanche fell upon them. Byleth's hands were ripped from his grasp, and Horace lost sight of her. Then a massive weight drove him to the ground. His shield buckled and nearly failed even as he poured all his strength into maintaining its integrity. Then another, heavier weight smashed down. It felt as if a house had fallen on him. Suddenly, the street gave way. He scrambled for purchase, but there was nothing to hold onto as he fell through the pavement.

He dropped through an empty abyss for what felt like minutes, down into the dark. The jagged walls of a deep shaft rushed past him. Then the bottom appeared and leapt up to catch him. Clinging to consciousness, Horace reached out with the *zoana* to cushion his landing. Raw and painful, his *qa* was slow to obey. Pain spiked through his legs as he hit the ground, but he was alive. He took a deep breath. Then he looked up.

Fear left him as the mountain of falling stone and earth hurtled down at him. There was time for only one last thought before conscious fled. *I love you, Alyra. I hope I see you soon.*

Then his shield failed, and Horace was crushed under tons of rubble.

The earth shook beneath Jirom's sandaled feet as he led his men down the boulevard. His fighters stumbled and cursed as they fought to keep their balance for a brief moment before the tremor subsided.

What the fuck was that?

The storm still raged overhead, occasionally sending bolts of jagged green lightning down from the heavens. Through the driving rain, he could see the royal palace was only a couple of blocks ahead. After making sure his sergeants were okay, Jirom signaled the host forward. Lieutenant Lesanep's soldiers marched at the front, with the rebels strung out behind them.

Emanon came up from an inspection of the rear. His hair was plastered to his head. "Nothing's following us as far as I can tell. What the fuck was that jolt?"

Jirom shrugged. Something bad was happening, and he had the awful feeling things were about to get worse. Then a shout came from the front of the column. Jirom cursed aloud. "First platoon, forward!"

He and Emanon raced to the vanguard. The Akeshians had already met the enemy. A mass of undead clogged the avenue ahead. Beyond them stood the palace gates, hanging open. But where were the guards?

Pushing through the Akeshian lines, to many startled looks from the militiamen, Jirom and Emanon got to the fighting. Many of the undead wore Akeshian livery, including uniforms of the royal guard. One female was clad in a sheer silk gown, her breasts bared by the torn front, with a golden tiara askew in her hair.

BLADE AND BONE

Jirom looked for Lieutenant Lesanep, but he wasn't in sight. Nudging Emanon, he pointed to the center of the enemy mass. "We have to break them!"

They plunged into the melee together. To Jirom it felt like old times as they fought shoulder to shoulder, his sword and Emanon's spear matching the fury of the undead. Yet the tide of foes was unending. For every creature Jirom put down, three more arrived to take its place. The Akeshians had shifted into a box formation, but their lines were thinning. Soon there would be a breach, and then the entire unit would collapse.

"Get back to our men!" Jirom shouted as he pulled Emanon back behind the front line. "We have to break free of this encirclement before they crush us!"

Emanon looked through the press of soldiers. "There's nowhere to go, Jirom! We either get into the palace or die where we stand!"

Jirom ground his teeth together as he tried to come up with some plan to save his men, but Emanon was right. Undead were pouring into the avenue behind them, blocking their retreat. The plaza was clogged to the north and south, too. The only way out was straight ahead.

"All right! Get our wounded inside the formation."

Emanon shook his head. "But, Jirom—"

Jirom cut him off. "I don't care what the Akeshians say! Cut down anyone who tries to stop you. Get the wounded into the center and then lead the rest back up here."

"What about you?"

Jirom met the lunging tackle of a fiend in armor with a thrust through the shoulder and drove it to the ground. Then he chopped off the thing's head. "I'll be leading the way."

"Fuck that!" Emanon looked over at the first platoon's sergeant fighting alongside them. "Ralla! Over here!"

She left her men and hustled over to them. Several bleeding scratches showed on her arms and neck, but she seemed hale enough.

"Go back to our men," Emanon instructed. "Get them up here on the double time. Go right through the locals on the way and don't take any crap from them."

The sergeant glowered at them both. Giving a hasty half-salute, half-fuck-you gesture, she raced back through the lines.

Emanon winked at Jirom. "There. Now we finish this together."

The way he said it formed a cold lump in Jirom's stomach. "Yeah. I guess I'm stuck with you. So let's do this."

Leading the rest of the platoon, they charged back into the fray. They rushed to the weakest spot in the line, fighting to keep the undead at bay, but the fiends kept coming. Then a flash of light appeared in his peripheral vision. Jirom turned in time to see Brother Janzu collapse with a pair of undead latched to his throat and chest. Jirom speared each of the creatures through the skull, but it was too late to save the sorcerer. With a final thrust, Jirom made sure the Crimson brother stayed dead.

"Damn!" Emanon shouted, cutting down a foe that had gotten through the front line. "Now we're really fucked!"

Jirom had to agree. This battle was lost. He was searching for a way out for his men when a nearby explosion knocked him off his feet. Noise like a loud bell filled his head as he lay on the ground in three inches of water. Blinking away spectral afterimages, Jirom climbed to his knees. One of the tall shrines on the south side of the plaza had been demolished in a single stroke. A brilliant circle of white light shone within the newly made pile of blackened stone. Things emerged from the circle. People. About a dozen of them. Jirom braced himself to meet more undead, but then he saw the strange glimmer coming from these newcomers. They shone like statues of burnished silver. Jirom froze, remembering legends of gods and goddesses coming down from the sky to take part in the wars of old. Then hoarse battle cries rang from their mouths as the new arrivals charged into the mass of undead, and Jirom laughed as he recognized their faces.

"The gods-damned Bronze Blades," he murmured.

"About fucking time they got back," Emanon said. "But why are they painted up like that?"

Jirom shook his head as the Blades plunged into the fight. Their gleaming weapons cut through the undead mob with vicious efficacy. Every fiend they touched fell where it stood, no matter how slight the wound.

BLADE AND BONE

"Push ahead!" Jirom shouted as he joined them.

The rebels and militia fought with renewed ferocity, possibly enflamed by the arrival of the mercenaries. Sergeant Ralla returned with another platoon of fighters, adding their weight to the battle. In a handful of minutes, they pushed through the palace gates. Inside was a long walled courtyard. Rain drummed on the flagstones and rustled the leaves of decorative trees that formed an aisle up to the steps of the entrance. There were no people in sight. No guards or servants. Then Jirom spotted pools of blood mixed with the rainwater in several places, and a few weapons abandoned on the flagstones. There had been fighting, but no sign of the fallen. *They got up and joined their attackers.*

As their force squeezed into the plaza, the Akeshians plugged the gates with a shield wall. Jirom spotted Captain Paranas among the Blades and went to meet him. It was strange to walk among men he had known and see them so changed. Their skin gleamed like polished metal, even their eyes.

"You came just in time," Jirom said, offering his hand.

The mercenary captain took it. His grip was strong and warm to the touch. "We would have been back sooner, but we ran into some trouble."

"I only count thirteen," Jirom said.

Paranas looked up at the sky and seemed to relish the storm raging overhead. Or perhaps it was just the rain beating down on his face. "We're lucky this many survived."

"That story will have to wait. We're heading into the palace."

A gruff voice called from behind the captain. "Too busy for a report, Sergeant?"

Three Moons strode up to them. Jirom was even more shocked to see his old friend covered in the steely hue. It was like looking at a death mask. Yet the old wizard appeared taller than before, as if his gnarled spine had straightened since they last saw each other.

"Good to see you, old friend."

Three Moons grinned his old, half-crazy smile, revealing silver teeth. "Likewise. But I really think you'll want to hear about it."

"Damn!" Emanon said, joining them. "What the fuck happened to you bastards?"

"Later," Jirom growled. Though he couldn't place the source, he felt a vast danger pressing down on them all. "Em, we need to hold those gates, no matter what happens. Captain, I'll need your fighters to assault the palace with us."

Paranas gave a sharp nod. "Aye, sir. We'll take the point, if you don't mind."

The mercenary captain left, shouting orders. Three Moons started to follow, but Jirom stopped him with a touch on the arm. "I don't know how you got here, but it's good to have you back."

The old sorcerer made a face and spat on the slick ground. His spittle glistened in the rainwater. "That's the thing. I don't have the vaguest clue how we managed it."

There was a look in his eyes that spoke of trials faced. Jirom clasped him by the bony shoulder. "In any case, let's finish this together, eh?"

Three Moons glanced up at the boiling sky. "Finish? Son, this ain't barely started yet."

As they advanced on the palace entrance, Emanon asked, "What's the plan?"

Jirom studied the marble walls of the royal demesne, occasional flashes of lightning reflecting off its wet surfaces. "Won't know until we find out what's inside."

"Fair enough."

Lieutenant Lesanep approached with a score of militia soldiers. "We're going in with you. As agreed, no harm can come to the royal family."

"As agreed," Jirom said.

Together, they entered after the mercs. The grand atrium showed more signs of slaughter, including long streaks of dried blood on the pink marble walls, but no bodies. Up ahead, the Blades had forced their way into the main audience chamber, and the Akeshians were hustling to accompany them. Jirom stationed his fighters to guard the exits and staircases around the atrium before he and Emanon joined the mercenaries. Inside, the empty chamber reeked of death. Blood and other foul substances pooled all across the floor, and the throne atop a low stage was encrusted in dark ichor.

BLADE AND BONE

What in the gods name happened here? This was more than just a massacre. The place feels . . .

"Cold," Three Moons said. "Like a fresh grave."

Jirom hadn't noticed the sorcerer standing behind him. "What does it mean?"

"Bad magic happened here," the old man answered. "Whoever did this was playing for keeps."

"Fucking hell!" Emanon shouted. "Can't you do something to stop them, wizard?"

Three Moons gave him a long look.

Before Jirom had to step between them, Urlik came running into the chamber. "We've got movement upstairs."

Jirom ran with the scout back to the atrium. Lieutenant Lesanep and his soldiers came along. Sergeant Mamum's squad was positioned on the northern stairs, watching the floor above.

"What have you got?" Emanon asked.

Mamum gestured upward with the blade of his war-axe. "Heard someone moving around up there. It sounded like they were dragging something heavy."

"What's up there?" Jirom asked Lesanep.

"I'm not familiar with the palace layout," the lieutenant replied. "But there are several stories above us."

"You want to take point?"

As Lieutenant Lesanep ordered his men up the stairs, Emanon gave Jirom a sideways glance and gestured with his spear. Jirom shook his head. As long as the Akeshians acted in good faith, so would he.

"But stay ready," Jirom whispered. "Just in case."

"Always," Emanon mouthed back with a wink.

They followed the militiamen up to the next floor. They found their first body at the top of the steps. A bald man in a servant's robe, sprawled out on the mosaic-tiled floor. Blood covered his face from where his forehead had been caved in.

The stairs continued up, presumably to a third story. The Akeshians had fanned out to cover both directions of a long hallway, but Lesanep stood over the body. "This is Vanuka. He was the king's chamberlain."

Jirom knelt down to examine the wound. "He was hit with something blunt."

"Probably a club," Emanon offered. "Or the butt of a spear between the eyes."

"Possibly."

But even as he said that, Jirom noted the broad span of the wound and the narrow furrows radiating up the old man's forehead. It looked like a handprint had been pressed into his flesh.

Jirom gestured for his fighters to stay put. "Hold these stairs," he told Sergeant Mamum. "We're going to explore this level with the militia."

Ignoring Emanon's raised eyebrows, Jirom turned to Lesanep. "We'll search this level first. I'll—"

A sudden scream interrupted him. Jirom whirled to see one of his fighters drop to the floor beside the stairs, clutching at his throat. A thick green cloud billowed down the steps from above. The fallen rebel was caught in it. The rest of Mamum's squad backed away as the cloud spread toward them.

Without waiting, Jirom plunged into the cloud and up the stairs. He held his breath, hoping the green mist was not the kind of sorcery that killed on contact. His shield warmed instantly against his forearm as he raced up the steps. At the top stood a stooped man in a dingy gray robe, his face hidden inside the deep cowl. The venomous mists issued from his open hands. Jirom darted up the last steps separating them and cut the man down without stopping. Jumping over the falling figure, Jirom let go of the breath he had been holding.

The mists faded away the moment the robed man fell. He was dead, his neck half-severed. Jirom shoved back the cowl with the bloody tip of his sword. The face underneath was shriveled and malformed, with protruding cheekbones that seemed about to burst out of the flesh. His eyes were hidden within deep folds of dark skin. Jirom couldn't place it, but there was something familiar about this man.

Footsteps pounded on the stairs as Emanon ran up ahead of the Akeshians, coughing as he reached the landing. "More gods-damned sorcery." He peered closer at the fallen man. "Ugly son of a bitch. It don't look like he belongs here."

Lieutenant Lesanep arrived with his soldiers. "He's no palace servant. Not in those old robes. Perhaps these are the ones who reaped the slaughter in the throne room."

Then Jirom remembered where he'd seen such a man before. In the catacombs under Erugash when he and Alyra had rescued Horace. Men in the same robes and with similar features had tried to stop them.

"In that case," Emanon replied, hefting his spear, "let's go thank them for doing our work for us." He winked at the Akeshian lieutenant. "No offense, kid."

Lesanep looked to Jirom with his eyebrows raised. *I remember. No harm to the royals. But it doesn't look like we'll find any alive.*

A clatter of metal rang out from an archway to the south. Before Jirom could investigate, dull thuds echoed from the east hallway.

"Look out!" Emanon shouted.

Jirom turned as a pack of undead raced toward them. Most of the fiends were clad in finery and jewels, which stood in stark contrast to their pale, bestial faces. Jirom stood in their way, shield braced and sword held ready. The first fiends crashed into him like a herd of cattle. Their clawed hands yanked at his shield, weighing him down. He swung his sword like a thresher beating grain, chopping at any body part he could reach. Black gore sprayed over him and pooled on the floor.

Emanon and the Blades arrived to help him hold the hallway. "There's more coming from the other way!"

Jirom risked a glimpse over his shoulder where another wave of undead had appeared in the western corridor. The Akeshians had positioned themselves to repel them, but the odds were turning against them. Jirom was starting to regret the decision to come here. A feeling of unnamed dread came from the open archway to the south, a feeling that had little to do with the undead. Even as he cut down another fiend, he felt this danger pressing down on him.

"Close ranks!" he shouted as he backed away from the front line.

Emanon shot him a concerned glance but moved over to cover his retreat.

The mercenaries stood fast as the undead poured into the hall from the chambers beyond. Hating himself for leaving the fight, Jirom turned and ran. *This had better be worth it. Or Emanon will have my hide.*

The south archway opened into a large terrace overlooking the city. Rain pounded the far side, which stuck out beyond the overhanging roof. In the center of the wide platform, a dozen men in the same gray robes as the sorcerer he had killed on the stairs were constructing some kind of frame with bright metal beams. It almost resembled an inverted pyramid. Jirom couldn't tell what it was supposed to be, nor did he care. Whatever these strange ones were doing, he opposed it. He charged at them.

They reacted like a pack of scalded cats, wheeling toward him before he'd taken two steps. Knives appeared in their hands as Jirom raced into their midst, shield held high and sword sweeping out. He severed one knife-bearing hand from its wrist with a flick of his blade, but the owner kept lunging at him, wielding his bloody stump like a club.

Jirom blocked a low thrust aimed for his guts and speared the assailant through the lung. A knife sliced along his ribs, cutting through his leather cuirass and opening a gash from his shoulder to his hip. Biting back the pain, Jirom twisted and slashed open the face of another robed man, but there were too many of them. His pain turned to anger as the deformed men pressed him. The shield grew hot on his arm again.

One of the robed men recoiled away, and then another, making a space around Jirom. The rest hesitated, eyeing his shield. Jirom took the initiative and drove into their ranks. He cut down another foe with a slash across the stomach. Two others leapt at his offside, knives flashing. Just before they pounced, a great wind blew at Jirom's back. It picked up all of the robed men and cast them over the platform's edge. They didn't make a sound as they plummeted out of view.

Jirom was probing the cut along his ribs when Three Moons came up beside him. "That was well-timed," Jirom said. "Although I wouldn't have complained if you just did that from the start."

The old sorcerer smiled, showing his silver teeth. "At my age, it takes me a minute to get warmed up."

BLADE AND BONE

Jirom gestured to the strange contraption standing before them. "Have you ever seen such a thing before?"

"Can't say that I have. But I don't like the look of it. Reminds me of something out of a bad dream. Bad mojo, Sarge."

"So what should we—?"

A violent quake shook the palace. At the same instant, the sky exploded in a volley of brilliant lightning strikes. Jirom dropped his sword as Three Moons fell into him, and it was all he could do to keep them both on their feet. A thunderous roar like the opening of hell's maw reverberated throughout the city. After several minutes of continuous thunder and tremors, the tumult faded. The palace finally steadied itself. Jirom let go of Three Moons.

"I'm getting," the old man murmured, "too fucking old for this shit. Consider me retired, Sarge."

"Oh, no." Jirom helped his friend stand up straight. "We've got too much work for a valuable resource like you."

Three Moons worked his mouth as if trying to summon the saliva to spit but gave up. "I knew being useful would end up biting me in the ass."

Pounding boots from the archway announced the arrival of Emanon and the Bronze Blades. Jirom went to his man and grabbed him in a fierce hug. "Glad to see you, Em. The dead?"

"They broke and ran when the place started shaking. I damn near shat myself with relief. Did you see the fireworks outside?"

Jirom turned to the open sky. A bitter wind blew in from over the city, carrying bits of ash. "Aye. And I don't like the look of it."

"Something's happened, Jirom," Emanon said. "I feel it in my bones."

Jirom lowered his gaze to the silvery construction before them. "Me too. It feels like we're waiting for the executioner's axe to fall."

"So what do we do?"

"We survive until tomorrow, and then we do it all over again."

CHAPTER SEVENTEEN

Pumash leaned hard on Deemu's shoulder as they climbed the steep hill. Behind them, Thuum lay under a pall of dark clouds, but out here beyond its walls the rain was only a stinging mist. Reaching the hill's top, they paused to rest. Pumash sighed with relief.

"Rest, Master," Deemu said. "The worst is over."

The worst? Pumash doubted that very much. They had left the palace at the height of the storm, with the thunder ringing in their ears, only to find the royal grounds abandoned. The dead had risen. More soldiers for the *Manalish's* legions. It was the same tale outside the royal compound. Quiet streets that stank of death but blessed few souls left. They had passed many homes shuttered tight and sensed people hiding within, but it was only a matter of time before the undead found them. With every step, the knowledge of what he had done sank deeper into Pumash's bones. He had destroyed Thuum. Sentenced thousands to their deaths. No, worse than death. *So much for my grand scheme to save them all. I merely hastened their doom.*

They found the southern gates open and unguarded. Passing through them had felt like crawling out of his own grave. Stricken by sudden weakness, Pumash would have fallen to the ground, perhaps never to rise, if not for Deemu's support. The old man had half-carried him out the gates and across the long stone bridge spanning the swollen river, over to the rocky hills south of the city. Despite his feebleness, Pumash had insisted they climb the first tor. He needed to look upon his handiwork one last time. He wanted to sear its lesson into his mind so he never forgot. As he gazed upon the dark walls and the smoke rising from within, a great sigh wracked his body.

"I can't do this anymore," he said, not meaning to speak his blasphemy out loud.

"You're not to blame," Deemu replied, patting his sodden back. "You did what you thought was best."

Pumash looked hard at his servant. He had never paid much attention to those who served before. They had been merely his property, an extension of his wealth and power. So much had changed since then. Now he, too, was a servant. *No, I am a slave. The* Manalish *holds my leash.*

"I am to blame," he said, gaining strength from the words. If only here, if only now, he would speak the truth. "I did this. In my arrogance, I thought I could deliver this city without bloodshed. Instead, I killed them all. We must leave."

"Of course, Master. We'll leave, if that's what you want."

Yes. They had to flee far away. But where could they go that the *Manalish* would not find them?

Without warning, the sky exploded in a cacophony of thunder. Pumash fell to the ground as vivid green bolts of lightning—dozens of them—struck inside the city. Deemu tried to help him up, but he pushed the old man away. Below, a horde of undead poured out of the city gates. They crossed the river, surging toward them. Then the master's voice echoed in his mind.

YOUR TASK HERE IS FINISHED. NOW THE TRUE BATTLE LIES AHEAD. ALL SHALL FALL BEFORE US AND BE REMADE.

"Forgive me, Great Lord," Pumash whispered, tears spilling down his face.

Images raced through his mind, of great cities deluged in flames. Undead prowled their soot-stained streets, hunting down panicking citizens. Pumash squeezed his eyes shut and pressed his forehead to the wet earth.

Deemu whimpered as a shadow fell over them. A great wind surrounded the hilltop, wrapping them in its stench of ancient death. Then the ground fell away, and they were carried off at a terrific speed. Up into the sky amid the roiling clouds, where they were buffeted by fierce gales and crackling jolts of lightning. Deemu clutched his arm, but they remained safe in the cocoon of darkness as they sailed toward the southern horizon.

Yet, despite the grand vista spread out below, Pumash still felt yoked to the ground by the heaviness of his guilt.

The bedrock beneath Thuum shuddered. Power grew from deep below, building upon itself.

Horace gasped as he awoke. Pain split his skull like a red-hot spike through the brain, driving away the fog of unconsciousness. He could not move. He could not see. Sensations crowded inside his mind. He tasted blood in his mouth. He felt the massive weight of earth and stone pressing down on him from above. He felt the pain of his crushed and broken body reknitting itself. Lines of power flowed around him and through him, pulsing with energy. He reached out with his mind, and the lines of *zoana* flared brighter.

He recalled the battle now, and remembrance brought its own agony. The exchange of magical blows with Byleth. His fall. The bones of the undercity piling on top of him. The rush of darkness sweeping over him. Somehow, he still lived. A voice whispered in his head.

You are not finished yet, Horace Delrosa. The final confrontation awaits. Which aspect shall prevail? We must know.

Horace swallowed as moisture crept into his dry mouth. Had he gone insane? Or was he dead, and this was some cruel afterlife?

Life returns. The cycle must be completed.

As crazy as it sounded, he understood. The woman of the ruins had shown him the way, but it had taken until this moment before he realized it. He had to become what he was supposed to be. If Astaptah was the all-devouring, destructive side of the Shinar, then he needed to embody the creative force. Looking within himself, he found the current of the void, pulsing like a stronger heartbeat. Throwing away his last reservations, he grasped it, and the power filled him.

Horace moved, and the earth parted for him. Pushing upward like a swimmer kicking for the surface, he climbed up and out of his rocky tomb, shoving aside boulders the size of houses as if they were soap bubbles. The *zoana* shrieked in his ears as his lungs burned for fresh air. Finally, with a ragged cry, he crawled free of the debris.

He took a deep breath and choked as a surge of blood exploded from his lungs. After coughing out the last of it, he tried shorter, shallower breaths. Each one was a separate agony for the first few minutes. A soft caress ran across his face, around his neck, and down his chest. Everywhere it touched, the pain vanished.

It took him some time to find his way back to the underground amphitheater. Jin's body lay at the base of the stage, bent in a horrible angle that suggested his spine had been snapped in half.

Sifting through the rubble left behind by the battle, Horace cleared a path until he found her. She was trying to crawl, but her legs were pinned under a section of a fallen column. Her head turned as the light from his glow-orb touched her. Deep scratches marred her lovely features. Her left arm was bent at an awkward angle, with a piece of bone protruding through the skin near the elbow. Yet, only darkness reflected in her eyes.

Horace watched her for a while. Her mouth opened and closed as she tried to reach him, but no sounds came out. Black spittle dribbled from the lips he had loved to kiss. He could See that the black tide within had taken over her entire being. Tears streamed down his face as he wove a narrow stream of Kishargal. He drove the stone spike down through the top of her skull, piercing her brain. Alyra shuddered, and then dropped still to the floor. Her outstretched fingers pointed to him.

After shoving aside the stones crushing her legs, Horace knelt down and gathered her into his arms. She felt so light as he lifted her, as if she were a child. Her head lolled against his chest. Horace took a deep breath and summoned a tightly controlled cyclone of air. It picked them both up and carried them up off the stage. The ceiling overhead parted as they rose, straight up through the layers of rock. A minute later, they were free of the earth and soaring into the open air.

The storm had passed. The first rays of red-orange light were breaking above the horizon, pushing back the banks of leaden clouds. Columns of smoke rose in several places about the city, but he saw no fires raging.

Horace looked around until he found the right spot, near the eastern edge of the Stone Gardens. Then he and Alyra floated down to meet the ground.

"I have no damned idea how the portal brought us here to Thuum, Jirom. But then again, I've got no real clue how they work in the first place. Maybe the magic knew you needed us, if that makes any sense."

Jirom only half-listened as Three Moons concluded his tale of the Bronze Blades' flight from the dead city of Omikur, across the desert, and through some alternate reality with monsters and killer plants. It sounded like an epic journey, but his mind was elsewhere.

The battle was over. They stood on the elevated terrace of the royal palace, watching as Sergeant Mamum's squad wrestled the metallic construct to the ledge. With one last heave, they toppled it over the side. It fell to the plaza below and shattered into a thousand pieces. *If only all the damage dealt this night could be undone so easily.*

The storm had lifted, leaving behind a hazy mist that clung to the city like an old cloak. His rebels had suffered heavy casualties. Almost half of their original force was dead, and that figure would likely go up in the next couple of days as some of the seriously injured succumbed to their wounds. A squad sent to the scribe school reported back that the building was empty with no sign of the students or civilians who had stayed behind.

Yet, not all the news was bad. Silfar's unit had survived, holed up in a textile warehouse. Also, witnesses said the undead had left the city. To whom or what Jirom owed that debt of gratitude, he had no idea. He was almost inspired to offer a prayer of thanks. Almost.

"Thank you, Moons," Jirom said. The old sorcerer appeared to have recovered from his labors. Still, it was shocking to see him so hale and bright-eyed, not to mention the reflective hue of his skin. "You and your men should grab some rest. The war's not over."

Three Moons played with the shimmering hair of his beard. "I suppose not. You got any idea what our next move will be?"

"Did Paranas tell you to ask me that?"

"The captain is career military. He'll follow orders to the end. But the rest of us would like to know where we'll be heading."

Jirom remembered how it had felt to live under another's commands, to have someone else do all the thinking. He longed for those days. "I sent the

BLADE AND BONE

scouts south to find out what's happening in the rest of the empire. I won't have a solid idea until we hear back from them."

Three Moons nodded and started to turn away.

"Moons, tell the Blades . . . tell them they have our thanks. You saved our asses."

Three Moons winked over his shoulder. "That's what we do, Sarge. We're gods-damned heroes."

As the old man left, Emanon came over, limping slightly. "So we won?"

"I suppose we did."

"I just talked to Lesanep. He told me about the deal."

Jirom nodded, still looking out over the city. He and the Akeshian commander had come to an agreement. The rebels and locals would coexist in peace as they rebuilt the city. It sounded good, but he knew it was only a temporary truce. His demand that all the slaves in Thuum be freed had been a bitter pill for the young lieutenant to swallow, but he had agreed, to his credit. Jirom wondered what the surviving nobles would think of the new arrangement, but then decided he really didn't care.

His fighters controlled the palace, the armories—or what was left of them—and two of the three main gates. The bulk of the city militia was dead. He had no idea how many civilians had survived. Most of them were still locked up in their homes. The streets were empty, except for the leftover dead. The caretakers of the Stone Gardens would have their hands full for days to come.

"How long can we trust them?" Emanon asked.

"For as long as it's in their best interest. With the *Manalish* on the march, the people of Thuum might be willing to accept our presence as added protection. For a while, at least."

"Right up until they make a deal with the usurper," Emanon said.

"I don't think he's the type to make deals, Em. How go the preparations for the funeral?"

Emanon had taken charge of recovering the rebel dead and arranging for their burial. "We'll hold games after sundown. Will you speak to the men?"

Jirom nodded. He had no idea what he would say. There were no words to express the feelings he had over leading so many to their deaths. And for what? A piece of temporary safety? It all seemed pointless now. But he would speak at the burial. He owed the dead that much. "Have you taken a head count? How bad is it?"

"Bad, but we'll survive. A lot of the freed slaves have formally joined up. More than three thousand of them. We've got weapons, armor, and a steady food supply. Fuck, give us a year and we'll be ready to tangle with the legions."

"We don't have a year."

Emanon rubbed the back of his neck. "Yeah, well. Lesanep told me a rumor. Those undead are heading southeast. It looks like the heart of the empire is going to feel the brunt of it."

That was Jirom's fear, too. For all they had suffered here in Thuum, all the people they had lost, this felt like a distraction from the main event.

Thinking of the fallen, he couldn't help but worry about Alyra and Horace. He hadn't seen either of them since the battle began. *Are you out there among the dead? Will you be buried with the others, destined to be forgotten?*

Jirom released a deep breath. He was too tired to talk anymore. Not just his body, though most of him felt as if he had been tied up in a sack and beaten with clubs. His mind wandered down dour avenues to the murky thoughts he hadn't taken the time to consider before.

Emanon put a hand on his shoulder and gave a gentle squeeze. "Hey, we just took one of the ten cities of the Akeshian Empire. Did you ever imagine?"

Jirom clasped Emanon's hand and had to laugh. "No. Not really. I thought we'd all end up back in chains or dead before now. I don't know where to go from here."

"Yes, you do. You're just afraid to admit it. We could stay here, holed up behind these walls, and let the empire slug it out with those dead things, but that's not what you've got in mind, is it?"

Jirom felt a stinging behind his eyes. How much more could he ask of these people who had entrusted him with their lives?

He was starting to turn away when a tremor ran through the terrace. He looked up, half-expecting to see another storm front moving in, but the sky remained dull gray with no signs of thunderheads reappearing. A distant sound like cracking stone rose from the north. Then a ball of smoke billowed from the Stone Gardens. Jirom shifted, waiting. Something in his gut told him this wasn't the enemy. *What if it's . . . ? No, it couldn't be. . . .*

Following a hunch, Jirom turned and ran to the stairs.

"Where are you going?" Emanon called after him.

"They're alive!" Jirom shouted back.

On his way to the exit, he almost ran over Horace's secretary.

"Sir?" Mczim said. His right arm hung in a sling, and a bandage was wrapped around his neck.

"Come with me!" Jirom told him.

They raced down the steps, with a growing crowd of people behind them.

Ten minutes later, Jirom jogged up the paved pathway climbing the ridge at the north end of the city. Above him, the iron gates yawned open. As he passed into the Gardens, he peered through the forest of trees and stone monuments, trying to get his bearings. The smoke had risen from the eastern side of the ridge. Following a trail of crushed stone past a stand of cedar trees, he saw a pillar of flame rising ten feet from the top of a grassy mound at the edge of the graveyard.

Horace stood before the conflagration. As Jirom got closer, he saw the pyre set atop a low block of stone. Motioning for Mezim and the others who had followed him to stay back, Jirom approached. He climbed the mound to stand beside his friend. As he did, he saw the body lying at the heart of the pyre. By some twist of magic, it remained untouched by the flames.

"What happened?" he asked.

"Byleth was waiting for us," Horace replied. His eyes were bloodshot as he had been crying, but his face was calm. His clothes were ripped and burnt. Dried blood streaked down his face and neck. "By the time I got there, it was too late."

"I'm sorry," Jirom said. "I know you loved her."

"She died doing what she was born to do. Helping others. She was a hero."

"And the queen now?"

"Dead again. Gone forever, we can hope." Horace let out a deep breath. "Jirom, our fight is not with the empire."

"We know. After you left, we fought our way into the palace." Jirom related how he had forged a peace with the locals during the battle, and what they had found inside the palace. "It was a machine just as you described from the catacombs under Erugash. It seemed to be calling the storm."

"Astaptah's contraption. I think it's what creates the undead."

They exchanged a long glance, and Jirom saw something new in Horace, something he had never seen before. It was more than just confidence or power. *Resolve. He is committed now. And may the gods help our enemies.*

"I told you before," Horace said. "I wasn't sure if I was ready for this."

"I remember."

"I'm ready now. The war isn't over. It's just beginning."

"I know," Jirom answered. His heart beat faster.

As they stood before the pyre, both of them lost in their own thoughts, the first rays of sun broke above the battlements, spreading quickly across the city. Thuum would awaken soon. Its sons and daughters, slave and free alike.

Jirom felt a stirring in his blood, pulsing to the rhythm of an old, familiar battle hymn.

HERE ENDS THE THIRD PART OF THE BOOK OF THE BLACK EARTH.

GLOSSARY

aburami: a term for people who do not possess a gift for using magic.

assurana: a two-handed sword with a curved, single-edged blade; true *assurana* swords are made from an alloy of red gold and *zoahadin*.

beysid: a term meaning "wise one."

dominion: one of the five aspects of Akeshian sorcery, each corresponding to a primordial element of the cosmos; they are Girru, Imuvar, Kishargal, Mordab, and Shinar.

Girru: the dominion of fire, which represents aggression and industry.

hekallum: the district in many Akeshian cities where the military garrison and support components are housed.

hekatatum: the warrior caste.

Imuvar: the dominion of air, embodying the principles of harmony and serenity.

kafir: a hallucinogenic herb that is typically smoked but sometimes eaten.

khalata: the caste of freed slaves; they may own property, but they cannot marry into a higher caste.

Kishargal: the dominion of earth, which is tied to stability and strength.

kunukatum: the scribe caste.

Mordab: the dominion of water, signifying flexibility and adaptability.

qa: the location where a person's spiritual energy originates, thought to be in the lower stomach.

Shinar: the dominion of the void, the power that binds the elements together.

zoana: the Akeshian name for magic, a spiritual energy that allows its user to affect change in the physical world.

zoanii (or Ascendents): a term for persons who possess the ability to manipulate magical power and who make up the highest caste of Akeshian society; as a caste, *zoanii* are divided into ten ranks.

zoahadin: a metal rarely found in meteorites that is antithetical to sorcery; the word means "star metal."

ABOUT THE AUTHOR

Jon lives in central Pennsylvania with his wife, Jenny, and their son, Logan. His first book, *Shadow's Son*, was a finalist for the Compton Crook Award, as well as a nominee for the David Gemmell Award in the categories for Best Debut Novel and Best Fantasy Novel. For more on Jon's life and works, visit www.jonsprunk.com.

Author photo by Jenny Sprunk